THE UNICORN AND THE CLOCKWORK QUEST

LOU WILHAM

Midnight Tide
PUBLISHING

*To Mom & Dad
who nurtured the story teller, the artist,
and the dream inside of me.*

The Unicorn and the Clockwork Quest

A Steampunk Unicorn Story

Lou Wilham

Daiwynn
Provence Four
Provence Two
Provence Three
Provence One
Provence Seven
The Capital
Provence Five
Provence Six
The Wilds
N
NW
NE
W
E
SW
SE
S

The water ran scalding hot, turning Agnes's pale hands pink as he scrubbed them near raw. He stared down, unseeing, at the furious motion of his hand as his mind drifted back. So far back . . . How long had it been? A hundred? A hundred and twenty years ago?

"Agnes, Agnes, we all fall down." The sing-song voices of children echoed through the recesses of his memory, growing louder as he squeezed his eyes shut.

"No," he said, no more than a whisper. Not nearly loud enough to drown out the racing footsteps of the children.

"Agnes, Agnes, we all fall down," they chorused again as they drew nearer.

"Leave me alone." This time when the words left his throat, they were small, so small. A little baby unicorn, not more than three. The first Enchanted child ever raised in the heart of MOTHER headquarters—amidst the utter hatred of all things magical.

"What's wrong, Agnes, don't you want to play with us?" the boy had jeered as he loomed over Agnes.

Agnes hardly remembered their faces anymore—just the jeering and the pain.

"No, thank you," the little rainbow-haired boy had

replied, pulling himself up a little taller to make himself seem larger than he was. Maybe this time it would work.

The group of faceless children stared at him silently, blinking, before they all burst into laughter. Agnes could have run and hid while they cackled, holding their bellies, but he stood his ground. An act he lived to regret as the group of children circled him slowly, leaving him no way out.

"Agnes, Agnes, we all fall down," they began to chant over and over.

There was no yelped surprise when the first blow came —not this time. One by one, each of the children took turns shoving the smaller boy until he fell to the ground. Then they spun in a circle around Agnes until he pulled himself to his feet and it all started anew.

"Agnes, Agnes, we all fall down."

The cycle continued until Agnes's hands were bloody and raw from the rough floor; then the children ran off, laughter echoing behind them. Agnes took a deep breath, pulling himself to his feet.

The water had run scalding hot that day, too, when he washed away the blood and the grime from the floor. Tried to wash away what he *was*, as if he could. Little, chubby, pale hands scrubbed angrily against one another over and over again until he'd emptied all of the soap from the dispenser.

Agnes remembered that feeling, that hopelessly lost mania that had almost eaten him up inside while he tried to scrub away dirt and germs and bacteria he couldn't see. That same feeling threatened to engulf him twofold now as the panic of the past few days settled into his chest.

"Stupid kelpie," he muttered to himself, reaching over to pump more soap onto his hands before lathering up once more. "Stupid kelpie and his stupid ideas."

Agnes stared down at his hands, trying to see if he'd finally washed the invisible grime of the corridor away, but they still held that phantom cling of germs.

He rinsed away the soap, and looked at himself in the mirror.

How long had it been since he'd last seen Sully?

Twenty-one years, three months, and twelve days.

Had Sully aged? Did he look as old and haggard as Agnes felt? A twinge tugged at Agnes's chest, and he shook his head, reaching down to fill his hands with water and scrub at his face next. It had been so many years now; he'd almost forgotten what Sully looked like, all except that too-wide, toothy smile, and those black eyes that stared down into his soul.

A knock ripped Agnes from his thoughts.

"What is it?" he growled, gaze narrowing on the door behind him in the mirror.

"Agent Kore is waiting for you, 95," a stiff, robotic voice called through the door.

Pale hands balled into fists beneath the water as Agnes inhaled deeply through his nose to control his rage. Five minutes. All he'd wanted was five minutes. He couldn't even get that with the undercurrent of tension in headquarters since Persinette's escape.

"You can tell Agent Kore that I will be out shortly." He kept his voice calm, but a scream itched at his throat, begging to be released.

A *tsk* left the robot—a sound that was strangely human for a MOTHER droid. Kore must have programmed that into it after she'd inherited it from her father. "You don't want to keep your handler waiting, 95."

"Don't I?" Agnes mumbled, shutting off the water and reaching for a hand towel.

"What was that, 95?"

Agnes was sure it had heard him just fine. Throwing his long rainbow braid over his shoulder, Agnes took a deep breath and flung the door open, so forcefully it caused the bucket of bolts on the other side to wobble.

"Well? Where the hell is she, then?"

The clockwork machine puffed and stuttered and ticked as it tried to process the sudden change and return to its mandate.

Agnes's lips twitched as he watched with a morbid fascination, half-wondering if, perhaps, the blasted machine would overheat and die on the spot. That would serve Kore right for sending it to pester him.

Unfortunately—after a few more moments of sputtering and spewing steam from its 'ears'—it seemed to regain itself and return to normal functionality.

"This way," it replied briskly before spinning around on its base and then wheeling across the plush rug—leaving a deep trail in it—to the door that led from Agnes's quarters out into the hall.

"Damn it," he grumbled to himself as he followed behind the ticking machine.

The robot led him through the cold, tiled halls of the Tower to the elevator, which groaned and ticked irritably all the way down to the holding cells in the basement of MOTHER headquarters that they'd set up for Sullivan— just in case.

No people bustled through the corridor. A few guards resided on each end of a long hall. They'd pulled the bulbs from half of the lights, likely to keep Sully disoriented.

As they drew closer to the cell, an unfamiliar and unwelcome emotion welled up in Agnes's throat. He struggled to breathe around it.

Agnes had spent a lifetime amongst MOTHER, keeping himself safe by carefully hiding away anything he felt. Now, with Sully under MOTHER's control, Agnes could feel it all bubbling up to the surface. All the fear, the anguish, the anxiety. It was all there, a wad of sickening emotion unable to be swallowed down. This game of chicken he was playing with MOTHER was dangerous, and it was about to come to a head.

Agnes recognized too, a sense of loss. There had been some foolish, boyish, innocent part of himself that had dreamed of meeting Sully again after all these years. In those dreams, they had both been free, safe, and happy for the first time in their long lives. Even if he had had to wait hundreds of years to see Sully again, he had hoped that, by then, they would both be done with this infernal war. He could go hundreds of years if it meant Sully was safe.

What awaited Agnes in that cell sliced those hopes to ribbons. His heart sank to his feet. The sight of the battered and bloodied kelpie . . . Bile rose in his throat, burning on the back of his tongue. Agnes ripped his eyes away and focused on the slight brunette girl leaning against the wall outside the cell.

Agent Katherine Kore's weight rested on one foot, her arms crossed tightly over her chest. A perturbed look had mashed her youthful features into an appearance that Agnes could only describe as *constipated pug*. Agnes's lip curled; he hoped it would give her wrinkles.

"Took you long enough!" Kore snapped as she stood to her full height—not much more than five foot five, still plenty short enough for Agnes to look down his nose at her. She tilted her chin back, as if she could look down on him instead.

Agnes wondered if she was aware of how utterly ridiculous she looked when she did things like that—like a little girl sitting behind daddy's desk.

"Perhaps if you hadn't sent that useless bucket of bolts

and had instead dragged your lazy ass to my room in the Tower to let me know you needed me, I'd have been here sooner."

A snort left Kore, the corners of her lips tugging further downward. *Definitely an overweight pug.* "And defile my new corset with the stench of Enchanted filth? I think not."

Worrying over Sully for the last few days must have worn down some of Agnes's barriers, because her words registered like a slap. The slip was so minor, he thought perhaps she wouldn't catch it. She did. He pursed his lips. And Agent Kore reveled in it, her face shifting from annoyance to smug satisfaction.

"Let us begin then, shall we?" Her tone had dipped into something sickly sweet and cooing as she turned to open the cell door.

On the other side of the heavy steel door, cuffed to a metal chair, sat Sullivan Hunter.

The brief glance Agnes had gotten inside had done nothing to prepare him for the throat-clenching despair at the sight of Sully. Sully, *his* brash, overconfident, always-smiling kelpie, strapped to that chair. Agnes's gaze flicked first from the cuffs which were so tight around Sully's large wrists that they cut into his dark skin, to the bare chest striped with what looked to be still-healing lashes, and then up-up-up to Sullivan's heavily lidded eyes. He looked so tired . . .

"Something wrong, 95?" Kore asked, jerking Agnes from his thoughts.

A rough swallow burned a trail of bile down Agnes's throat as he tried to find the words to say that he was 'just fine, thank you' and move on with things. But they seemed to get stuck somewhere in his chest as he fixated on the beaten and bloodied kelpie before him. His mind tried to reconcile the scene with the memory of the very same kelpie much earlier in life: a bundle of too-big eyes and squirming limbs.

Even still, sixty years later, Agnes remembered those deep, dark eyes blinking up at him with all the innocence in the world.

"Asset 95." Agent Kore brought him back to the tiny, dank cell where Sully was strapped to the chair.

It took Agnes a moment to regain himself, to register those black eyes staring back at him, and the situation around him. Too long, it would seem, as a sharp smack stung his cheek, the sound reverberating off the stone walls.

Agnes hissed, lifting his hand to hold the quickly reddening cheek.

"Keep your hands to yourself, *child*," he spat at Agent Kore.

One brow lifted on the girl's face in a challenge. Kore wanted him to retaliate. *Do something*, she said without words.

Agnes balled his hands into fists at his sides, doing everything in his power to keep his rage in check and his face as impassive as possible. It would be easy—effortless—to snap her skinny little neck. He outweighed the teenager by at least twenty pounds and had over a century of training more than she did. He could have Agent Katherine Kore lifeless on the floor, in seconds, and be on his merry way with Sully in tow before anyone suspected something was amiss.

A hoarse laugh pulled Agnes and Agent Kore's attention away from each other. Sully chuckled darkly, his teeth stained with blood as they flashed in the dark room.

"Now, now, ladies, no need to quibble. There's plenty of me to go around." Sully's usually smooth, deep voice was raspy, either from screaming or disuse. Agnes's stomach turned.

"Be silent, you pathetic creature," Kore spat. Her hand flew then to strike Sully's strong jaw. Agnes found himself biting down hard on the inside of his cheek to keep quiet as blood dripped down from the corner of Sully's lips.

Agent Kore turned quickly to exit the cell, leaving Agnes staring down at the man before him.

"You fool," Agnes whispered almost brokenly, shaking his head. His chest heaved with a stuttering breath, fighting to find calm.

"Aren't you happy to see me, Aggy?" Sully asked, lifting his head so that those dark eyes could peer up at Agnes as they always had—like they could see into his very soul.

Agnes narrowed his gaze on Sully and frowned deeply. "No, I most certainly am not happy to see you."

Sullivan laughed softly. In spite of his battered face and body, his rough voice, he looked up at Agnes with a glimmer of hope in his eyes.

"Oh, Aggy, let's not lie to one another. When will we ever stop dancing this waltz, huh?" A mischievous, boyish smile tugged at his dark lips.

"95!" Kore barked from the corridor beyond the cell, and Agnes stood up straighter, realizing belatedly that he'd let his emotions slip again. What if Kore saw? What if she realized? He shook himself, forced a cool, impassive expression and headed back out into the hall without a second glance at the prisoner. *It's better for both of us*, he told himself.

"Agent Kore?" he asked with some mild annoyance, examining his perfectly manicured nails to be sure they hadn't been dirtied or scuffed in the cell.

Kore watched him with those insipid, puppy-dog eyes of hers. Suspicion lingered just below the surface, and Agnes made a note of it. *Best be careful.* She'd propped herself up against the wall again, looking for all the world like she didn't care one way or the other if Agnes and Sully burned.

"The order from higher up is that you're in charge of questioning the kelpie from here on out. There will be someone on guard at all times, and you're free to use any tactics you deem necessary to get it to talk. That includes magical torture"—a twisted little grin tugged at the corners of her lips—"if you so desire."

Agnes lifted one dark brow. It wasn't unheard of for an asset to be used to question another Enchanted; their magic had ways of making people talk that humans didn't. But it was also a dangerous game to play, as more than once an asset had broken beneath the weight of being forced to hurt one of their own kind and turned against MOTHER. Agnes supposed Kore thought this would be killing two birds with one stone, she would get the information MOTHER wanted, or she could make a case that Agnes was a traitor.

"Is that all?" Agnes asked, refusing to let her ruffle him.

"Yes, but be aware that the guards will be reporting directly to me. No funny business." She wagged her finger almost playfully at him before adding, "Oh, and you are expected to meet with me regularly to keep me apprised of what you find out. I know how you love that. Maybe it'll entice you to work more quickly."

"Of course, Agent Kore," he murmured, ducking his head in a bow low enough that his rainbow braid fell over his shoulder to hang before him. He refused to straighten until he could no longer hear her retreating footsteps.

With a deep breath, Agnes allowed himself one more glance at the battered Sullivan on the other side of the barred window. He fought to swallow down any lingering feelings before he turned to the guard posted outside the door.

"See to it that he's fed and has water," Agnes ordered curtly, before heading down the corridor himself. "And for god's sake, get him cleaned up. I want to start fresh in the morning," he shouted over his shoulder then turned back toward the Tower to try to sort this mess out somehow.

One, two, three. One, two, three. One, two, three.

Agnes counted the steps like a waltz, trying to keep his pace calm. His ears rang. His vision narrowed to just a pinprick. He breathed through the panic.

One, two, three. One, two, three. One, two, three.

By the time the door to his rooms shut behind him, Agnes's heart was beating so loudly he was sure everyone on his floor could hear it. His chest heaved with panting breaths before he lifted one long-fingered hand to scrub at his face. He needed to calm down.

"You aren't going to do Sully any good in this state," he scolded himself.

His legs trembled beneath him, threatening to give out at the knees and bring him down to the plush rug. Agnes closed his eyes, forcing away the image of Sully strapped to that chair, hunting for a happy memory instead. He needed to see that smile, the one he'd seen so many times before, and there it was—all crinkled eyes, a dimple in his right cheek.

"Like the sun," Agnes breathed in relief.

After a few long moments of deep breaths with Sully's smile swimming in his memories, Agnes finally felt that he had a handle on himself once more. He pulled himself up a little straighter, tugged the carefully tailored waistcoat back down into place, and made his way into his small bedroom. Tucked into the corner between the bed and a barred window was a small vanity with a mirror attached to it. Nothing too extravagant, but enough to suit Agnes's needs.

He took a minute to arrange himself, hiding any signs that he had been frazzled moments before. Then he pressed his hand to the smooth surface of the glass, not even feeling the bite as it took its pound of flesh: a thin trail of blood slid down the surface as he waited. The glass shimmered and flickered for a few brief seconds before Agnes found himself blinking at a tiny creature with a pair of oversized goggles that magnified its eyes to bug-like proportions.

"Eddi," he muttered, dipping his head and pulling his hand away.

"Agnes," the Uprising leader responded in a tone devoid of any surprise. Agnes supposed he should have found that unsettling, but now was not the time to be bothered by such things. "What can I do for you?"

"The agent you sent in to help Persinette. I need him out," Agnes said calmly, but with a tone of urgency he didn't usually use with Eddi. Maybe it sounded a little like he was ordering the Uprising leader to do something, but he didn't much care.

Eddi blinked at him from beneath their too-big goggles once more, their brows disappearing into that truly disastrous fringe. "What?"

"MOTHER plans to torture information out of him about the mole. We can't have that."

"Why not?"

"Because *I'm* the mole," Agnes said, exasperated.

A part of Agnes hoped that Eddi would just assume he was worried about saving his own skin. But then another part worried that if that were the case, the Uprising leader would choose Agnes's life over Sully's, and that was something he couldn't live with, no matter how selfish he was.

"I need him out of here, and safe," he murmured—not really sure where the word 'need' had come from but feeling it to his core. He *needed* Sullivan to be safe. He *needed* it like he needed his next breath.

Eddi stared at him as if he'd sprouted a second head, the

silence between them growing uncomfortable until Agnes was almost shifting on the lush, velvet cushion of his chair.

"Agent Sullivan knew the risks when he accepted that mission. He volunteered." Eddi's tone was brisk, and matter of fact.

Agnes swallowed roughly; his sweaty palms moved to rub against the fabric on his thighs. The trousers would need to be washed right away or it'd stain. Sully had volunteered. He had wanted this. Somehow that didn't get rid of the shaky feeling that had settled into Agnes's muscles.

"I don't care!" Agnes burst suddenly, his cheeks heating with agitation. Gods, he was going all blotchy and ugly; what a sight he must have been.

Eddi remained infuriatingly calm, their bug eyes watching Agnes as if he were something strange and fascinating. One quirked eyebrow was the only sign that the Uprising leader was even mildly interested in what was going on. "Why?"

Agnes jerked, taken aback by the question. He hadn't expected to be asked *why* he needed Sully safe. Did there have to be a reason? If there were one, he'd never given words to it. In fact, in the sixty years he had known Sullivan, Agnes had never once told Sully how he felt. There had been a time—or two, perhaps—when he had tried to tell him, but the words never came.

"He's in danger." It sounded weak even to his ears. It was a stupid, childish argument. They were *all* in danger.

"And as I said, Sullivan knew what he was signing up for when he volunteered." Their voice remained even and dispassionate. "He knew that his life might be forfeit for his decision, and yet he volunteered anyway." Eddi had made up their mind about this, and Agnes could do nothing but sit dumbfounded with his mouth hanging open.

"I will not be sending a team to extract Agent Sullivan.

We will let this play out and see what happens. Now if that is all Agnes, I have work to do, and I'm sure you do as well." Nothing more was said; the old creature reached forward and closed the link between them, leaving Agnes to stare blankly at his disgustingly pale reflection, made paler and sicklier still next to the smear of blood trailing down the mirror.

The longer Agnes stared at the face in the mirror, the more the hatred welled up inside of him. This was his fault. Sullivan was going to die, and it was all *his* fault.

"Come on. It'll be fun. We'll change the world!" he heard himself telling Sullivan as they lay in tall grass atop the hill overlooking the Hunter farm.

Sloan and Dalton and their little farm had been the safest place Agnes could think of as he held the baby kelpie in his arms. Out in the country, far away from MOTHER, no one would bother to look for him there. Sullivan had had a good life on that farm. A simple life, but a good one. It was secluded, and Sullivan had been happy, or at least he had always seemed so to Agnes.

Sully let out a snort, his dark eyes rolling up to watch the clouds drift through the blue sky. It had been so peaceful out there where the steam from the cities couldn't obscure the clouds—peaceful and beautiful.

"Is this the speech you give all the recruits? Did Eddi write this up for you? Do you have the script written on your arm?" Sully had reached over to grasp Agnes's wrist and tug the sleeve up as if he were looking for words scrawled on the smooth skin beneath.

Agnes snatched his wrist away, scoffing. "What? Are you scared?" He rolled onto his side to offer Sully a little smirk.

Those words should have left him feeling guilty at the time, but only years later did Agnes realize how dangerous they had been. He'd been goading Sully, that much had been clear, and now he felt his stomach twist as he thought about it. It hadn't been the fairest tactic, but at the time, Agnes wasn't the sort to play fair, and all he'd been thinking of was how amazing it would be to be working alongside Sully finally.

Sullivan's laughter had filled the air as he shouted his response to the hills and the sky and the grazing goats, letting it echo back to them: "Never!"

Agnes shook himself, trying to shake away the memory, and scrubbed at his face again. Now was not the time to stroll down memory lane; he needed a plan. He stood abruptly, nearly toppling the vanity in the process, and all but ran from the room. He prayed that no one would notice his hurried steps through the Tower, down the stairs, and to the evidence lock-up.

There, behind a desk, sat an old woman with a pair of metal spectacles atop her head as she read through what looked to be a trashy human romance novel.

"Ah, Gladys, just the girl was I was looking for." Agnes smiled, leaning over the desk to hit her with the full force of his charm.

The old woman looked up from her book, blinking eyes that looked oddly big for her face in a mint-green color that wasn't quite human. Then a smile twitched the pixie's lips, and she laughed.

"Agnes! What brings you down to see the dregs of MOTHER?"

"Oh pish, Gladys, you aren't the dregs." He shook his head, laughing. First one, then the other elbow rested on the desk, and he leaned over more so that he could meet her strange gaze.

"Oh, Agnes, you always know just what to say," she snorted. "What do you want?"

The charming grin fell from his lips, settling instead into something altogether more serious. "I need you to call a meeting."

Before the words had even fully left his lips, her wrinkled hands had pulled a bit of paper from under his elbow and grabbed a pen. "When and where?"

Agnes silently thanked the heavens for assets like Gladys. She had been a part of MOTHER almost as long as he had, and she did everything in her power to help the Uprising along. Gladys's specialty was getting messages around the compound without MOTHER being the wiser, and she'd been essential to his recruitment process as he'd built up his small army of assets inside the heart of the enemy's Headquarters.

"Three a.m. In the Enchanted cafeteria. Two days from now." To the point. There was to be no confusion.

"Aye, aye, sir," Gladys murmured, the pen scratching across the parchment. Then she offered Agnes a crooked-toothed smile. "Any particular reason behind the urgency?"

Agnes sighed, letting more of his weight rest against the desk, his head hanging down so his hair brushed the papers below. "I want to save an asset MOTHER has locked up in the holding cells and Eddi refuses to help."

Gladys was silent for perhaps a beat too long and then she huffed.

"Of course they do." She set down her book, the pages splayed open to mark her page. "Eddi only cares about what's in it for Eddi," Gladys said, voice hushed. "The Uprising isn't in this to be fair, or equal. They're in it to dominate Daiwynn. What's one dead kelpie?"

"I didn't say—"

Gladys leveled him with a pointed look.

"Right." He cleared his throat awkwardly. "Well, you're

a gem, Gladys," Agnes said with a nervous laugh and shot her a playful wink.

The old pixie flushed lightly, her wings fluttering in delight as she ducked back behind her book. When he turned, heading back to the Tower, his mind raced with everything there was to handle before the meeting.

$\mathcal{E}$ver since Sullivan was a child, he'd known somewhere deep within himself that he was going to save Agnes. He was twenty-one when he finally said it out loud. The realization had happened in a second, he remembered very vividly.

In the damp darkness of his cell, Sullivan let his mind wander to that day on the hill with Agnes.

He felt the light breeze tickling the skin of his face, carrying the smell of fresh sea air as it blew through the tall grass. Agnes had come to convince him that it was time to join the Uprising. Sully wasn't sure why Agnes thought there needed to be a formal discussion about the topic. They both knew that Sullivan had decided to join the Uprising when he was five years old, and he was unlikely ever to change his mind. So convincing was utterly unnecessary.

Still, as Sully's dark fingers brushed the warm, pale skin of Agnes's wrist—gods, he was beautiful—he knew it then. He would move mountains to save this man.

"What? Are you scared?" Agnes had asked as he grinned at Sully, long dark lashes fluttering over blue eyes.

Sullivan released a laugh and shouted, "Never!" to the

treetops in the distance, and the sea hidden behind them. Then he shoved Agnes playfully.

Sully had hidden behind his bravado that day, but the truth of it was that even then, he was terrified. Not for himself, never for himself, but he had seen the way working in the heart of MOTHER had hardened Agnes over the years. Sully knew without a doubt that one day it would destroy the beautiful unicorn.

If there had ever been even a sliver of a doubt that what he was doing was right, it had disappeared when Agnes leaned in to press a quick kiss to the tip of Sully's nose. That single kiss, as innocent as it was, it had sealed Sullivan Hunter's fate. He would die for his unicorn if he had to.

Sullivan was torn from the warm happiness of the hill back to the present of the cold cell by the door opening. He looked up on a stout guard who had come into the room on tiptoes. A little sneer pulled Sully's full mouth up at the corners, reopening the split in his lip that bled anew.

"What's wrong, little man? Scared of the big bad kelpie?" As much as he tried to fight it, it was in Sullivan's nature to thrive on fear. Kelpies were vicious creatures hell-bent on drowning anyone who upset them, and there was a deep hatred of all human MOTHER agents that Sully couldn't seem to quell.

The young guard cleared his throat and straightened himself back up to his full height—which admittedly wasn't much taller than Sully's chest if he were standing. Perhaps the little creature wasn't entirely human at all. Maybe he was some kind of halfling, mixed with troll somewhere in his lineage? As much as the humans tried to pretend it didn't happen, the truth of it was, most of them weren't entirely human at all.

"Agnes ordered you to be cleaned up before he returns to question you." The guard's voice came out more like a squawk than the firm, authoritative tone he seemed to be aiming for.

Sully's lips stretched further upward at the corners. *Gods, it's so easy to make these creatures nervous.*

"Is that so? Agnes wants me all prettied up for him?" Thoughts of Agnes shifted the sinister leer into something more fond, more akin to a smile. Agnes would be coming to him soon. "And when, pray tell, will Agnes be joining us?"

The guard shrugged and moved toward him before stopping just out of reach. Sully tilted his head in amusement, watching the man shift from foot to foot.

"Are you going to give me any trouble?"

"What's your name, little man?" He allowed the words to be laced with some of the magic he would use to lure people to their watery graves.

"Ro-Roy." Roy's eyes widened as if he'd said the words completely unbidden, his hands clapping over his lips, taking two quick steps backward to make a hasty retreat to the exit.

"Well, Roy, let me ask you this. Who are you more afraid of? Me? Or Agnes?" Sully had a feeling he knew the answer. Agnes could be a fearful thing to behold when angry, all blazing, white-hot eyes, and rainbow hair that seemed to take on a life of its own. Sully would never want to be the one Agnes turned his wrath on.

Without another word, Roy took several quick steps forward and unstrapped Sully from the chair. Steel still attached one wrist to the other. It clanked when he stood at the end of what felt like a leash of chains around his waist that Roy used to tug him down the hall.

Sullivan took note that although there were other cells on the corridor, none of them were occupied. They rounded the corner to a big open shower room with tiled walls and floors, and shower heads spaced neatly apart to allow multiple users.

"Get cleaned up," Roy said gruffly, shackling Sully's chains to a hook on the wall before turning on one of the showers.

It was easy to tune Roy out after that. Sully leaned into the water and allowed the beast within him to relish in his natural element. He closed his dark eyes, letting it rinse away the blood and grime. He'd have to thank Agnes for this later. Although the water wasn't warm, it did wonders for his aching body.

No soap was provided, nor any washing things, so all that was left was for Sully to stand there and wait until the water ran clean. By that point, his fingers had grown wrinkled, but he didn't mind. Then Roy shut off the water and thrust a clean, dry uniform into his hands, unchained his wrists, and turned to stand some feet away at the door with his back turned.

With an amused smile, much clanking, and some struggles, Sullivan changed from his dirty clothes into the scratchy uniform. He recognized it immediately as one that MOTHER would put an Enchanted in at the camps. Sully's skin prickled at the coarse fabric and the label it came with, but he shook it away. He had known that was very likely where he would end up by coming here, he'd accepted that —it was much too late to be getting cold feet now.

With a quick glance at the guard's back, Sully reached into his soaked pocket to pull a small, gold pocket watch from it. He pushed the button to open the watch with a *tink* and waited with bated breath for the little hand to move. When it finally did, Sully's shoulders relaxed and he tucked it into the pocket of the dry pants.

"Well, all set to head back to the dungeon, Sir Roy," Sully announced teasingly.

All he earned for his trouble was a blank look, and a tug on the chains around his wrist as Roy took him back to his cell.

Once there, he was deposited into the chair, the shackles locked over his wrists once more. A scoff left Sullivan as he realized that some time in his absence, someone had replaced the steel cuffs with iron ones that now burned into his skin at the wrists. He wondered idly why they had suddenly decided his magic was a threat, but, in the end, it didn't matter.

Nothing mattered other than the fact that soon he'd get to see Aggy again.

TIME MOVED STRANGELY when one was chained up and forced to sit watching a mostly empty hallway for hours on end. Even though the seconds seemed to tick by slowly, it also felt as though all at once, hours had passed him by.

The changing of the guard was done in silence. Roy gave the large goon a nod before he trotted off to only gods knew where.

The minutes slipped past him again, and Sully tried to find ways to amuse himself, but there was nothing. MOTHER had placed him on an empty hall, and he didn't even see any guards other than the one standing outside his door. Was it hours or minutes later when the goon was replaced with a stony-faced woman? He wasn't sure. Perhaps Sully had dozed off somewhere in between; he couldn't tell anymore.

All he knew for certain was that the harsh tone of the guard seemed to rouse him when she growled, "You are not scheduled to see the prisoner until tomorrow, 95."

95? Sully's nose wrinkled. He'd never get used to the way MOTHER referred to Enchanted by numbers and not names.

A sharp bark of laughter brought Sully's mind into focus. *Agnes*. 95 was Agnes.

"I'm supposed to be extracting information from it. If that is to be done, there can be no set schedule, Graham. I would have thought you'd know that. Seeing as you're *so* experienced in these matters." Agnes's voice was smooth and cutting like the edge of a knife. Sully could imagine the superior twist of his lips as he looked down on the woman. "Now, if you'll excuse me, I have a suspect to question."

Scuffling echoed through the empty corridor; Sully could see the shape of the woman move to block Agnes's access to the door.

"That's a mistake," Sully said to himself, shaking his head. A little smile crept onto this face as he heard the all-too-familiar sound of Agnes growling threateningly at the woman.

"I will not be cowed into taking orders from an *Enchanted*," the woman—who Sully supposed was Agent Graham—spat. "You may be able to boss around that gummy bear, Roy, but you won't boss me."

Agnes chuckled, the sound so quiet and cold it made the hairs on the back of Sully's neck stand on end. "I think you'll find, my dear darling Graham, that as I am fulfilling orders handed down from superiors so high up you've never met them, that I can and will boss you around. Now get out of my way before I inform them of your insubordination." With that, the shape of Graham was shoved away, and a beep marked the opening of the cell door.

"Why don't you make yourself useful?" Agnes threw over his shoulder as he stepped into the room. "Go get me a coffee."

"I'll have to lock you in with it," she responded with a smug smile. "Wouldn't want it escaping past you."

Agnes shrugged. "Like you care. Coffee."

Graham slammed the door shut, and walked off, leaving Agnes to turn his full attention to Sully at last. It had been years since Sully had really gotten to look at Agnes, and the sight of him made it hard to breathe. During that time, Agnes had grown a well-groomed dark beard and his beautiful rainbow hair—which had for so long been just shoulder length—was now halfway down his back. There was something breathtaking and terrifying about him all at once. As if at any moment Agnes could bring Sully to his knees with words as sharp as a blade, or kisses as sweet as summer rain.

Sully must have been staring with his mouth wide open, Agnes tilted his head in curiosity, and Sully felt his jaw clamp shut quickly.

"You just wanted to be alone with me," he teased to cover his obvious gawking, licking dry lips as they spread into a wide smile.

Agnes's eyes narrowed on him, lips pressed into a thin line beneath the dark beard, and Sully thought perhaps he'd lost Agnes for good. Sully didn't breathe as he watched Agnes's face. Had Agnes finally cracked under the pressures of hiding himself beneath the mask of the MOTHER asset, and *become* the MOTHER asset? Maybe the Agnes he'd loved all his life was no longer there, replaced with an angry, bitter creature who would sooner see his own people burn than give up his favorite cravat to save them. They stared at each other for what seemed a lifetime and Sully's heart stopped altogether.

Then in one swift motion, Agnes lunged forward and smacked Sully as hard as he could muster across the cheek, knocking Sully's head to one side and leaving a dark red mark in his wake.

"You fool," Agnes hissed, typically dark blue eyes burning brighter with his fury. "You complete and utter moron. What in the hell were you thinking coming here?"

If Sully didn't know better, he'd say there were tears sparkling in Agnes's eyes as he whisper-shouted in his face. Good thing he did know better.

"I thought I'd come and save my damsel in distress and we could live happily ever after." Sully righted himself with a hoarse laugh.

"Eddi won't send in an extraction team," Agnes said in a broken tone as he paced the length of the cell. His hands went to tug at the length of hair twisted into a neat braid, petting it as though to soothe himself. "Until your mission is complete, we can't expect any assistance from the Uprising."

His well-shined boots took him from one wall of the cell to the next. Giving the braid a harsh tug, Agnes released a hushed noise of upset. "I can't believe you volunteered for this."

"Aggy," Sully called gently, trying to draw Agnes's attention back to him. "Aggy," he said a little louder this time, but Agnes continued to pace and mutter to himself.

"Agnes!" He growled the word this time, and Agnes stopped mid-step, looking at him with wide eyes.

"What?!" Agnes spat, seemingly annoyed that he'd been stopped on his tirade.

"Would you be a darling and unchain me from this blasted chair so I can stretch my legs?" Sully offered Agnes his most winning smile, hoping if not to be released, then at least to draw something besides worry and agitation from Agnes.

No such luck. Agnes grumbled, dragged a hand down

his face, and moved to unstrap the shackles without any such reaction. "There. Stretch."

Releasing a deep sigh, Sully stood to straighten his legs for the first time in hours. Both knees popped from disuse, but it felt good to move them.

"Much better." He stretched his arms above his head so that his shoulders popped as well, drawing a groan from his lips. Then he turned a playful, assessing look to Agnes. "My dear Aggy, I think you've gotten shorter."

Agnes—who by then was pacing and muttering to himself again—stopped and turned slowly to glare at Sully. "Excuse me?"

A low, deep laugh built up in Sully's throat, threatening to burble out, but he swallowed it down, offering Agnes a bright flash of teeth.

"I said, I think you've shrunk, darling."

"I have not *shrunk*!" Agnes shouted indignantly, standing up straighter as if to prove his point. "You've just gotten taller. *Again*. Do you ever stop growing?" Agnes's eyes shone with wry amusement.

It was working.

The laugh Sully had managed to swallow down before now bubbled up and out of him. His eyes glittered with happiness as he drank in the amused glint in Agnes's gaze. It had been too long, far too long.

"No, it would seem I do not. Must be what they feed us in the Uprising."

"Must be," Agnes agreed, his lips twitching up into a small smile.

"What about this?" Sully asked suddenly, the shackles clanking as he lifted one large hand to brush his fingertips over Agnes's beard. It was soft, just as he'd remembered Agnes's hair being when he'd run his fingers through it.

Agnes leaned into the touch for a heartbeat, his lids fluttering over dark eyes before he seemed to regain himself and brush the hand away abruptly. "What about it?"

"It's brown." Sully responded plainly, his brows knitting in confusion. He'd always assumed that if Agnes were to grow facial hair, it would be the same beautiful spectrum of colors as the tresses growing from his crown. But this hair, though well-groomed as Agnes's hair always was, was strangely muted.

It seemed it was Agnes's turn to laugh. He snickered, shaking his head.

"The carpet doesn't match the drapes, or have you forgotten?" His eyes crinkled at the edges, finally meeting Sully's gaze head-on.

A flush settled into Sully's cheeks at the memory of the years when they'd had that privacy. Two, to be precise, in a little cottage on the . . . No. It wouldn't do to dwell on those memories now. Not when Agnes was right in front of him.

"Well," Sully started with much bravado, and ended it with, "that's weird."

The shorter man's slim shoulders shrugged, a grin still on his lips. "I don't make the rules, darling."

"Right," Sullivan cleared his throat, but it didn't seem to do anything. Now all he could think of was . . . *well.*

"Now, why in gods' name are you here anyway?" Agnes asked. He moved to flop casually into the chair Sully had been strapped to, one leg flinging over the armrest, entirely relaxed. "I know it's not just to see me."

It was even harder to focus with Agnes slouching there, all lackadaisical; it brought back too many memories. Sully shook himself internally and forced a shrug.

"Who says that's not the reason? Am I not allowed to get myself captured just so that I can visit with you?"

Dark blue eyes looked up from where they'd been

examining perfectly manicured fingernails to fix Sully with a sharp glare.

"No. You are not." Agnes's Cupid's bow lips drew into an angry line once more, his eyes narrowing in an expression that would have stopped the blood of just about anyone else.

"Well then, what would you have me say, Aggy?" Sullivan asked with a heavy sigh, his lumbering form slouching against the cold stone wall. Sinking to a squat, he let his shoulders curl in on themselves. "Would you have me say that I did it for the betterment of Enchanted everywhere? Would you have me say I volunteered so we could finally put an end to this whole thing?"

Agnes's dark eyes had followed him to the wall, that cold look still threatening to freeze Sully to his spot.

"I would have you be honest with me. This isn't about that stupid girl, is it?" A scowl twisted his mouth into something terrifying. "I knew she'd be nothing but trouble from the moment Eddi thought to bring her into the fold."

With a hollow laugh, Sully lifted his head to fix Agnes with an incredulous stare. Didn't he know? How could he not know? After all these years?

"Oh, Aggy, are you jealous?" Sully asked, almost hoping that he'd say yes. No such luck, Agnes just stared at him expectantly, waiting for an answer. "No, this isn't about Persinette."

There was a long silence during which Sully debated what exactly to tell Agnes. If he didn't know at this point what Sully's feelings were, Sully wasn't sure they would be welcome. And besides that, Agnes had never been very good with emotion, so Sully wasn't sure he was ready to lay himself bare at Agnes's feet and wait for a kicking. In the end, he decided his heart might not be able to take such punishment and shook it off.

"Eddi wants a camp cleared out, entirely. To prove a point to MOTHER that we can get to them anytime, anywhere, and it's just a matter of time before we finish them."

"And to incite a war!" Agnes near-shouted at Sully in panic, his dark eyes going wide and wild. He sat up abruptly from his lazy posture, body and mind now seemingly alert. "That's what the goal is, isn't it? Start a war. Get us all killed. This whole place will go up in smoke."

"Either way, that is what I was sent in here to do." He didn't see why Agnes was so bothered anyway; they had always known this was how it would end. The two sides would duke it out, and they would both die.

"And how in the hell does Eddi plan to clear out a camp? No one has ever done it before!"

"From the inside, obviously," Sully said simply.

Agnes's back stiffened, and his eyes narrowed dangerously on Sully. "They'll kill you."

Sully thought to be glib about it. He thought to say something like 'but what a way to go, am I right?' Instead, all he could muster was a disinterested lift of his shoulders. "Then I'll die."

"No." Agnes's tone was no longer surprised, upset, or angry. It was resolute. He stood and paced again. A strand of brilliant blue hair wriggled its way free from the braid, calling to Sully to brush it back behind his ear, but Sully stayed still. "No, I won't allow it."

His words pulled a startled laugh from Sully. "Allow it? Oh, Aggy, who said you had any say in this?"

Agnes turned on him, eyes blazing with fury once more and narrowing on Sully still sitting on the floor.

"You will not leave this cell until I convince you to give up this ludicrous idea," Agnes growled. Then, with one swift step, he grabbed the chain around Sully's wrist and forced him back into the chair. "I'd suggest you get bloody comfortable, *Sullivan*. You won't be going anywhere for a while." He clapped the iron restraints back into place over Sully's wrists with a definitive clank.

"Come now, Aggy, let's not play games." Sully let the words out on a breath of exasperation, following Agnes's retreating form with his eyes.

"This is not a game," Agnes said, baring his teeth at Sully from the doorway. Then he slammed it shut, and Sully could hear his angry footsteps retreating down the corridor.

Sully blinked once before shaking his head.

"Well, best get comfy," he said, leaning his broad shoulders back into the chair to relax as best he could.

Agnes slammed the bathroom door so hard, he was sure the sound echoed all through the Tower. It didn't matter. He couldn't bring himself to think of or care about anything except the burning rage that filled him right down to his toes. Anger was not a new emotion for Agnes, but this searing-hot rage that scorched him all the way through left him near breathless.

When he turned to meet his reflection in the mirror, he found a glowing pair of electric blue eyes staring back at him. The crazed-looking man in the mirror panted roughly, his chest heaving with each breath, and the rainbow mane of hair on his head seemed to have taken on a life of its own. Agnes inhaled to try to calm himself a little.

"All right, Agnes, what's the plan?"

To Agnes's terror, his reflection stared back at him just as lost for an answer. For over a hundred years, Agnes had always had a plan. They needed to help Persinette escape? He had a plan for that. There was a group of trolls that needed to hide from a MOTHER Collection? He had a plan for that too. For years upon years, he'd come up with so many plans he had lost count.

Now, when he really needed it? When it was someone he *cared* about . . . nothing.

Sullivan was in danger as long as he was under MOTHER's roof. His very life depended on Agnes being clever enough to get him out, and Agnes was a miserable failure of a man.

A memory—or perhaps it was his wild imagination torturing him—of Sully slumped in a chair, bleeding, drawing in one last wheezing breath, burned itself into Agnes's mind.

Useless. He was *useless*! What good was he to Sully if after rescuing that stupid girl, he couldn't think of a way to save the person he actually cared about?

"Pathetic," Agnes muttered, reaching to turn on the water as hot as it would go.

He grabbed the soap dispenser, giving it one then two then five pumps in quick succession.

Empty.

"AGH!" A shout of frustration left Agnes as he drew back his fist and slammed it into the mirror, shattering his reflection into a million tiny pieces.

Then it came. Momentary relief from the feeling of helplessness as his brain was distracted by the pain of broken glass cutting into his knuckles.

His eyes flicked down to the bloody knuckles, watching the way a single shard of glass stuck from them enough to reflect his nose back to him. Agnes's attention was drawn away from the blood by a knock on the door behind him.

"What is it?" he hissed.

"Are you all right in there, Agnes?" a distinctly feminine voice asked from the other side of the door. "The meeting will be starting soon, and we need to make our way down to the cafeteria."

The meeting? Agnes's brows furrowed. How long had

he been in with Sully? How long had he been cowering in the bathroom, trying to get control of himself? What time was it!

"Right, thank you, Sabina," he muttered distractedly. "I'll be right out." He dipped forward to run his hand beneath the hot water, letting the pressure clean the glass from his skin. Pieces pinged against the copper sink.

"Are you sure you're all right?" Sabina pressed, but despite the apparent worry lacing her tone, she didn't attempt to open the door and intrude upon his solitude.

"I'm fine, Sabina. We shouldn't all be wandering the corridors at the same time anyway. You head down without me." As much as he wanted to be alone right then, he wasn't lying. They shouldn't all be wandering around together; it would be best if they arrived at the cafeteria in a slow trickle rather than a steady stream. His people knew that.

"Right." Agnes heard the faint click of her boots retreating from the door.

Once the door to his room had slid shut, Agnes inhaled a shaky breath. Shame washed over him suddenly as his eyes drank in the bloodied hand again.

He'd lost control. He never lost control—not like this.

Dropping to his knees, Agnes dug through the cupboard beneath the sink until he found some gauze. He took his time ensuring all the glass was removed and the wounds were clean and dry, then wrapped it tightly. The wound dressed, Agnes made his way into his sparse bedroom, and grabbed a pair of soft leather gloves from the vanity. This was for them, he reasoned; it wouldn't do to let the others see the injury and have them jumping to conclusions.

Then he was off.

The padding sound of well-polished boots echoed off the walls of the sleeping corridors in MOTHER. At three in the morning, most of the agents were asleep—preparing for another day of slaughter—leaving the path to his meeting unhindered. But the quiet didn't fool Agnes. He knew that so long as he was in MOTHER headquarters, he was being watched, and he was not safe. He played the obedient and cruel asset—often going out of his way to make other Enchanted miserable. Because he was not safe here. Because he knew what would become of him if anyone were to suspect.

"You'll just have to make sure they never do," he reminded himself.

As he approached, the door to the cafeteria slid open with a hiss. Agnes flicked his gaze over the ragtag group of Uprising assets that he had amassed during his time with MOTHER. In the old wooden chairs sat every type of Enchanted, from a short goblin with pointed ears and glowing green eyes to a gray-skinned nixie with ever-changing features. A few humans, even. He had convinced each of them to dedicate themselves to his cause, and Agnes prayed all of them were ready to die for it as it may come to that very soon.

"What's going on, Agnes?" Roy asked, shifting anxiously from foot to foot. "Is this about the kelpie?"

The green-skinned pixie beside Roy pulled him in a little closer, presumably to comfort him. Her name was Penny, and she was the sole reason Roy had joined them—love was a stupid reason to join a rebellion, in Agnes's opinion, but he wasn't about to look a gift horse in the mouth. They needed every extra set of hands they could get, especially the human ones who could get away with more.

An amused chuckle left Agnes. "Yes, I suppose it is."

A rumble of dissent rippled through the group. They looked to one another, muttering their displeasure. Agnes couldn't make out all of the words, but he could hear some of them.

"The kelpie has just made thing worse for us."

"MOTHER has been so much crueler since . . ."

"They're all more on edge than ever . . ."

"Why should we even bother with . . . ?"

Agnes allowed them to mutter and grumble until one of the trolls in the back said over the others, "What's that got to do with us?"

All chatter stopped, and again every eye was on him. Worry, curiosity, and fear played on their faces.

"Yeah, are we in danger now?" someone else asked—one of the witches.

With things rapidly escalating, his ranks could dwindle. That had been Agnes's fear all along. He had hoped that with the raid of the holding cells to break out Persinette, he had weeded out those who weren't dedicated to their cause. But it would seem there were still some amongst them. Agnes's stomach twisted as he looked around at the group. How many of them would he lose because they were too scared to do what needed to be done?

"Isn't that what we signed on for?" Roy asked suddenly, his hand gripping Penny's more tightly. "Didn't we know the risks when we joined?" There was a determination in his watery blue eyes the likes of which Agnes hadn't seen in a long time. And for that, Agnes thanked Penny.

"Who asked you, *human*?" a faceless voice shouted from amongst them, spitting the word 'human' like an obscenity.

What followed was chaos. Everyone shouted over one another. Agnes couldn't even follow who was saying what, or who was on which side anymore. Their voices quickly grew to a din that Agnes feared would bring the MOTHER agents down upon them.

"Everyone be quiet," Agnes tried to say above the noise without raising his voice too high.

"Quiet it down. Shut up!" he continued, gradually getting louder, but they kept shouting, and the longer they went on, the angrier everyone seemed to get.

Taking a deep breath, Agnes closed his eyes to draw on his power. When he opened his eyes again, they glowed that same electric-blue color, and his rainbow mane of hair seemed to be floating in water around him.

"I said, be silent!" His roar reverberated not just through the air around them but through everyone's minds as well, as though the words had been thought, not heard.

The entire group fell silent all at once. Their eyes turned from one another to Agnes—who drew a steady inhale to release the magic and let his hair settle back to his shoulders.

"Everyone, sit," Agnes ordered.

Nothing could be heard outside the scraping of chair legs across the lacquered floor. Once they were all seated, Agnes paced between the tables. He took a deep breath to prepare himself for the conversation ahead and then waded in.

"We need a plan to get the kelpie out of here, and we need it soon." He took another lap between the tables, keeping his steps careful and measured. "Once he is sent to the camps, he has been ordered to stage an attack. I have very little doubt that the Uprising leader does not mean for anyone to survive, even our own people. This—"

"An attack?"

"At the camps!"

"Why would they do that?"

"What is the Uprising thinking?"

"They can't be serious!"

Since the Uprising's inception, the threat of war had

always been there, lurking on the periphery. All of them had known that one day these isolated attacks from both sides would escalate into something more dangerous, something world-ending. They, like Agnes, had always thought of it as a day that would never come. And now it had.

He stood waiting as they talked, panicked, shouted, worried, and argued at one another. He let them get their fear out if they could. Agnes's eyes flicked up to the clock, giving them precisely a minute to calm themselves down.

When that didn't happen, he raised his voice again: "Silence!"

This time it didn't take the power of a unicorn to quiet them. When they all turned their worried, terrified eyes to him, he knew why. They were looking to their leader. They wanted answers. They needed direction. Agnes would have to step up and provide that if he could.

"What do we do now?" Penny asked, her orange eyes wide, reflecting the fear and uncertainty he saw all over the room.

"We do the only thing we can do: we try to get Sullivan out without starting a war. And if the time should arise that we haven't any other options, we fight with everything that we have and pray that it will be enough." Agnes's words were quiet, but they carried. It wasn't the most uplifting of battle speeches, but it was all he had to give them.

The faces around him were grave, but no one argued. It looked as if they had all come to the same realization Agnes had: they didn't have a choice.

Gladys was the first one to speak. "What do you need us to do, Agnes dear?"

Agnes looked over at her, a smile lifting the corners of his lips. There she sat, in her oversized potato sack of a nightgown and fuzzy pink slippers, with thick glasses perched on her nose. She looked for all the world like the grandmother from that Red Riding Hood story he had read when he was a child—before MOTHER had confiscated most of the books.

She lifted one gray brow at him expectantly, and Agnes felt his own face pinch in frustration. He hadn't gotten that far yet. Between the anger, the despair, and facing Sully for the first time in decades, Agnes hadn't been able to think of any kind of plan. Now, he was asking them to prepare for a mission, but he had no tasks to give them. What an idiot.

"Are you quite all right, dear?" Gladys pushed her glasses further up her nose.

"That's why I called this meeting. So we could weigh our options." *Nice save, Agnes.* "Roy, is there any way we could smuggle him out of here before he gets to the camp? Maybe on a supply shipment?"

Roy shook his head, frowning deeply. "No. After the last escape, security has been doubled. And even if it hadn't been, they're keeping him under special watch. It'd be impossible."

"What about in transit?" Agnes asked, turning to another human guard, Thelma.

The steel-haired woman shook her head. "If you did that, you'd have to shoot the zeppelin out of the sky. You'd probably kill everyone inside in the attempt, and then we'd still have an act of war on our hands. Besides, who would you get to stage the attack?"

Who *would* he get to stage the attack? If there was no way to get Sully out while in MOTHER Headquarters, then someone on the outside would have to rescue him.

That left only one person who he could think to help . . .

"Damn it all to hell." he grumbled, fists clenching so tightly behind his back that he felt the skin on his knuckles split further.

"What?" Roy asked, his eyes wide. "What is it? What's wrong?"

"I need that damnable captain," Agnes growled darkly.

There was a collective blink of confusion.

"What . . . what captain?" Penny asked.

"Kelii. I need Captain Kelii," Agnes muttered, moving to a chair to slump into it in defeat.

He had hoped never to see Manu and Persinette again, but now he needed them. The captain and his pretty lavender-haired sidekick—or maybe it was Persinette and her pretty captain sidekick—were the only people in the entire kingdom of Daiwynn who had dared to defy Eddi's orders and attempt a raid on MOTHER directly. Not just that, but they had been successful (partly thanks to him). If it was an attack on one of MOTHER's labor camps he was after, it was Manu and Persinette he would need.

"I'm never going to live this down," he mumbled, pressing his forehead to the rough wood of the table.

"Never going to live what down, dear?" Gladys asked.

Sucking in a breath, Agnes looked up to meet her eyes. "The mirror they confiscated from Persinette when they raided her room. It hasn't been destroyed yet, has it?"

"I don't think so. I think the agents hoped to get it working so they could track her. Not that they could."

A manic laugh left Agnes of its own accord as hope seized him. This just might work. "No, I'll bet they couldn't. It was sealed with blood magic. Do you know where it is?"

"Well, of course, I do!" Gladys sounded affronted as she sat up straighter. "I may not be allowed into the cage, but I keep track of everything just like I was ordered to do."

"I want it."

Gladys blinked at him for a moment as if she didn't understand what he was on about. Then she nodded quickly. "All right, when do you want me to get it to you?"

"Right now. I want to go and get it right now." At that point Agnes wasn't even wondering how he would get into the evidence cage to get to the mirror—he just knew he needed it. The sooner he got his hands on the mirror, the sooner he could put his plan into motion. Sully would be safe at last.

Without a word, Agnes rose from his chair and headed toward the door.

"Agnes," someone said, pulling him up short.

He turned to blink in confusion at the voice, only to remember that there was a room full of people awaiting his orders.

"Right," Agnes shifted awkwardly on his feet to face them again. "You are all dismissed. Head back to your quarters and do try to go separately."

A collective nod went through the group, and they all rose from their seats in a cacophony of chairs scraping floor. Agnes watched for a moment as one by one, they slipped through the many doors out into the hallway beyond, each slipping off a different direction.

"We'll head through the kitchens," Gladys said as she rose from her own chair.

Agnes's eyes flicked from the group to her, and he nodded.

They both slipped into the kitchens—past a row of sleeping cafeteria automatons—and out into the less-traveled corridor behind the cafeteria. He followed the old pixie who led him on shuffling feet through the dark halls as if she'd done this a million times and more. Perhaps she had; Gladys seemed the type to sneak to the kitchens late at night for a snack.

"I hope you know what you're doing, dear," Gladys said as the elevator carried them down into the depths of MOTHER.

"It'll be all right, Gladys. Don't you trust me?" Agnes asked, trying to force some of that bravado he always showed to his recruits. It wouldn't do for them to see him falter.

She turned, peering at him through thick spectacles with her gray head tilted. She didn't believe him, that much was clear. Gladys had known him far too long not to be able to see through his mask. She'd practically raised him. Of course, she'd know better than to be fooled.

"Right then." He cleared his throat self-consciously, and headed toward the lock-up. To change the subject, and so she'd stop looking at him with those knowing eyes, he asked, "How did you manage to get a key card to the evidence lock-up anyways?"

It worked: she looked away to pull the key card from her nightgown pocket with a scoff.

"I have my ways, little unicorn. Don't underestimate me just because I've been around since before the queen herself was born." With that, the pixie winked at him, and scanned the card. The heavy copper gate opened with a hiss of steam.

"Wouldn't dream of it, Gladys." Agnes chuckled dryly, bending down to kiss her cheek.

"Quit your flirting, you fool," Gladys cackled and shook her head.

Her feet scuffed across the floor as her steps took her down an aisle. She came to a spot marked with the number '112410' on the shelf. Gladys's wings fluttered, lifting her from the ground so that she could grab the box that was just out of reach. It *thunked* when she set it down and dug through it with a whistle on her lips.

After a few moments, Gladys held out the silver mirror they had confiscated from Persinette. "There now. Go and call your captain. And let an old lady get her sleep."

Agnes dipped his head to kiss her cheek once more. "You're the best, Gladys!"

"Of course I am. Now shoo." Gladys flicked her hands and returned the box to its shelf.

Agnes nodded quickly and made a beeline for the elevators up to the Tower. The mirror seemed to burn against his skin where it was hidden away in his pocket.

When he finally reached his room, Agnes leaned against the door, looking at the small sitting room. It was just him, the two wrought iron chairs, and the little table before the fire. He turned for his bedroom. His fingers trembled as he pulled a waxy envelope from the vanity drawer. He slid one long finger under the seal, which broke easily. Then he dumped the contents onto the vanity top.

One chunk of lavender hair glistened in the warm light of his room, bringing a tired smile to his lips.

"I knew you would come in handy."

Agnes took a deep breath and retrieved the dagger from one of the other drawers. Calling upon his magic, he murmured the spell Eddi had taught him just in case he needed to do something like this. Then he cut open his hand and poured a few droplets onto the chunk of hair and mirror. Both glowed faintly, and he could only hope that that meant it had worked.

But there was only one way to find out.

"Do not call Hiccup a bucket of bolts!" Persinette growled as she rushed across the room—boots smacking against the uneven floorboards—to keep the teetering robot from falling over. "He's just trying to help you! You . . . you . . . you ungrateful, cranky ass!"

She patted the robot on the head with one freckled hand, and Hiccup responded with a gratified whistle.

"Don't worry Hiccup. The captain doesn't mean to be so rude."

The copper and rose-colored robot twittered happily, letting out a delighted *whirr* at the attention. The glowing light bulb atop its head burned brighter.

"I don't need a seeing-eye robot to be able to get around my ship, Persinette." Manu sulked, leaning more heavily back into the plush velvet chair by the fire. "I am perfectly capable of making it around this place on my own. I know my ship like the back of my hand."

He rose and walked across his office with some swagger, as if to illustrate this point. The walk ended promptly, however, when Manu stubbed his toe on the large desk by the window. He glowered, shouting obscenities at the piece of furniture as if the injury were its fault.

Hiccup released two short puffs of steam that sounded strangely like a snicker.

Persi's lips spread into a smug smile that she fought to keep from her voice. "I'm sorry, what was that, Captain?"

"It's laughing at me, Pers! That bucket of bolts is laughing at me!" Manu whined loudly, pointing in the vague direction of where he thought Hiccup was and wagging his finger threateningly.

Persi wondered how long it would take before he learned to get around on his own—all the while silently praying that they would find a way to break the curse before then.

"You mark my words, little robot: I'll have you disassembled and used as spare parts!"

Hiccup whirred in panic, rushing as best he could to hide behind Persi, wrapping short metal arms around her legs rather like a child.

"Don't worry, Hiccup. He's just blustering. The captain wouldn't dare hurt you. Not if he ever wanted to hear the end of it from Felicity."

Manu seemed to deflate. His shoulders drooped in defeat.

"I just—" He broke off with a long, pained sigh.

"I know you don't like it," Persinette murmured. A few quick steps found her taking his hand and pulling him into a tight hug. "But Benard and I are doing the best we can to find a counter-spell for you. For now, let Hiccup help you, all right? And try not to be too mean to him. He likes you."

The captain nodded his dark head, shaggy hair falling into his strange silver eyes before he turned to look in the direction where Hiccup had been. "I'm sorry I took it out on you, Hiccup. Can you forgive me?"

Hiccup released a *whirr* of approval, then wrapped his arms around Manu and Persi's legs in a tight hug.

"See? I told you he likes you." Persinette giggled.

Manu grumbled but pulled her into the hug more tightly before pressing a kiss to the top of her head. They stood there, soaking up the comfort that the other provided until a jingling sound from the desk pulled their attention away from each other. On the desktop, an old iron-handled makeup mirror rattled—presumably trying to get their attention.

"I thought that thing was disconnected," Manu muttered, recognizing the sound. He leaned over the desk to run his hands along the top of it until he reached the mirror.

"Is there any way MOTHER could have figured out how to open it?" Persinette worried her bottom lip, watching the mirror.

"Not a chance. It was blood magic. They've never been able to figure out blood magic." Once he'd pulled the mirror close enough, he tilted it upward and waved his hand over the smooth surface.

The glass rippled like water for a time before it settled to reveal a face.

"Agnes?" Persinette asked, pursing her lips.

"Agnes? You mean the unicorn? Like the one who helped you escape?"

"Yes, that Agnes." Agnes confirmed in a drawl.

The captain grumbled and rolled his eyes. "What's he want?"

"Well, if you'd shut up for two seconds, you could find out," Agnes snapped, his dark eyes narrowing to a glare.

"You don't give me orders, unicorn. This is my ship and I'm—"

"Manu. Stop. Let's hear him out," Persinette said, her hand moving to grab his from where it had been thrown up in the air and squeeze it. "Please."

Manu nodded, falling silent, and returned the squeeze with one of his own.

"Don't you worry, Kelii. You weren't my first or even second choice." Agnes huffed, then narrowed his eyes at something. "What's wrong with him? Why are his eyes a different color? Why isn't he looking at me? Did something happen?" He shook himself and waved a hand. "Doesn't matter. I need to set up a meet."

"No. Absolutely, not." With that, Manu went to close the connection between the two mirrors.

"Let him talk, Manu." Persi reached to stop him. "What for?"

She tugged Manu's hand away to prevent him from trying again.

The unicorn let out a deep sigh, clearly struggling to find the words to ask for what he needed. Persinette knew him well enough to know that he'd likely never asked for help before. Now, having to ask someone who he had shown very little respect . . . well, it couldn't have been easy for him. But he would need to ask; Persinette was not going to provide help to someone who was too proud to ask for it.

"I . . ." He drifted off for a moment, seeming to ponder his words to choose just the right ones. "Eddi wants to stage a raid on one of the labor camps."

Persinette gasped sharply. That kind of attack could only mean one thing. It meant . . . it meant the Uprising intended to take the fight to MOTHER.

"What of it?" Manu asked. This had been a long time coming, in his mind. It also mattered little to him. His crew had been cut nearly in half during the raid on MOTHER HQ, and those who were still alive were healing. He had no desire to drag them into another fight with MOTHER that would end in even more bloodshed.

A long silence stretched between them while Agnes

searched for the words he needed to say, rubbing the bridge of his nose.

"I want you two to launch a preemptive strike on MOTHER. Get Sullivan out before Eddi can make their move. I can't trust the Uprising to try to minimize the bloodshed. If their people are sent in, it'll be a slaughter. None of us want that."

Manu snorted, still skeptical.

But Persinette was already nodding. "We'll need to time it right, and train some of the new crew to help. I don't want anyone going in there who isn't completely capable of defending themselves."

"I'll be back in touch soon, and we can set up the meet for when I'm on mission." With one final nod, Agnes closed the connection between them.

Tension had tightened Manu's grip on the desk in front of him. Persinette took a deep breath, squaring her shoulders. Then she turned to the flabbergasted captain still blinking blankly in the direction of the mirror.

"I'm sorry, we need to what now?" Manu asked.

"We have to help them, Manu." Persinette's tone was firm; she had made up her mind about this, and he'd best get on board.

"No, we don't. Eddi wanted to leave you there to die! You don't owe them or the Uprising anything!"

"No, but I owe Agnes and Sully my life, and I can't leave a camp full of innocents to the hands of Uprising agents. We are going to help." Persinette stood firm, her arms crossed over her chest. She would not, and could not, back down from this fight.

Manu opened his mouth to argue further.

"Agnes is right," she continued. "If the Uprising agents go in there, they won't care who they kill. It'll be a massacre. At least this way we have some small chance of getting most of them out."

"This won't stop the inevitable, Persinette."

"No, it won't." She nodded. "There will still be a war. This will be enough of an open attack on MOTHER to incite it, no matter what we do. We'll have to talk to Agnes about getting his people out of Headquarters in the meantime." Persinette muttered this last part to herself, as if making up a list of things to pick up at the market. "At least this way, we can save lives."

Manu sighed, shaking his head. "Pers . . . it'll be impossible."

A little smile stretched her lips, and she laughed. "Come now, Captain, when was the last time you let that stop you?"

gnes was up with the sun. A bone-deep weariness had settled into him the previous night, but still he was up with the sun. Not that he had a choice in the matter. Agent Kore had scheduled an early morning meeting that, were he to miss—well, things could get very ugly very quickly for him.

He couldn't let anything stand in his way now, not even Agent Kore's perpetual displeasure. He was too close. Sullivan's freedom hung in the balance. And Agnes was too close.

After being yelled at the first time for his tardiness, Agnes had taken to arriving to all meetings with Agent Kore at least ten minutes early. That was how he found himself dressed, tugging on a pair of leather gloves, and padding quickly across the sickly blue tiles of MOTHER's halls as the sun peaked over the horizon. Even this early, the hallways bustled with people. Assets, agents, and automatons alike made their way up and down the corridors. Each moved at an unhurried pace as though they were precisely on time.

As Agnes turned the corner toward the hall that housed the bulk of MOTHER's agent offices, a robot came whizzing around the corner. Yelping, he lurched out of the way, thanking MOTHER for centuries of footwork training.

"Watch it, you useless rust bucket!" he shouted, landing a kick to the automaton's metal back.

It lurched forward and nearly toppled over before emitting a whine.

"Oh, don't act like I hurt you. Go on, get."

A panicked whistle left it, like a gasp, and it was off down the hall again in a rush.

Agnes turned toward Kore's office, knocking loudly. The previous Agents Kore—Katherine Kore's parents—had been happy enough to meet in one of the many conference rooms for their briefings, but it would seem their offspring had a chip on her shoulder. In Agnes's opinion, the little girl wanted to be seen sitting behind the big desk with the name placard so she could feel more grown up.

"Enter," a voice came from within, and the doors opened.

It didn't work. Every time Agnes saw her behind the desk he was reminded that the current Agent Kore was just a spoiled child playing at being an adult. At sixteen, she did not now, nor would she likely ever, fill the shoes of her parents.

"You called for me," Agnes said, sprawling his lean form into one of the chairs in front of the desk.

This gesture of ease earned him that same pug-like expression of disgust Kore had worn but a few days prior outside Sully's cell. He paid it no heed, and even propped his well-shined boots up on the other chair. Was he pushing it? Yes. Did he care? No.

Kore's insipid brown eyes fixated on his boots as if she could force him to remove them with just her mind. She couldn't, and he didn't—a fact that sent a tingle of satisfaction up Agnes's spine, causing the corners of his lips to twitch up.

After what seemed like far too long for any mature adult to do so, Agent Kore stopped staring at his boots and fixed him with an irritated glare.

"Yes, we have a mission."

"You don't just want to have tea and crumpets then?"

"No," she said flatly—like the boring little girl she was from head to toe, she was not taking the bait. "We are headed to Maximus to retrieve a small group of trolls. You have dealt with trolls before, haven't you, 95?"

He shrugged. "Once or twice. When do we leave?"

"In a week. I assume you can have yourself adequately prepared by then?" *Not that I care*, her bored tone said. If he died while they were out on mission, she'd be just fine with it. After all, that's what happened to her parents.

"Yes, I can be. How many men will we have?"

"Five outside of ourselves, so a whole party of seven. That should be plenty to bring in one full-grown female and its two offspring."

A 'mother and her children' were the words Kore didn't use—gods forbid she use language that might liken their targets to people. She wasn't the only one; every time Agnes had ever heard about a Collection, those 'Collected' were always spoken of as creatures or things. He assumed this dehumanization was considered proper, as they were not, in fact, human at all.

"I heard you've had a session with the kelpie already," she continued.

"I wouldn't call it a session so much as an introduction," he said, relaxing himself even further into the chair. "What of it?"

"I see." She tidied the papers on her desk and sat up a little straighter in her chair to meet his gaze more easily.

Oh no, I'm in for it now. Kore's gone all business, he thought snidely.

"And you learned what from it?"

The lie came more easily to his tongue than the truth might have. After all, Agnes had been lying to MOTHER agents for decades at this point. What was one more?

"Nothing as of yet. I'm not even sure how much it actually knows." *Cool and casual, that's the way to do it.* "For all, we know, it could be one of their lower-ranking peons."

His tongue burned, turning to sandpaper against the roof of his mouth, at calling Sully an 'it' instead of a 'him' but it was necessary. Agnes needed to keep his distance from Sully in Kore's eyes, even verbally.

Agnes met her gaze dead-on, and a reckless part of him thought that perhaps with enough smooth talk, he could convince Agent Kore that Sully wasn't important at all. He calculated each word in that hope. It was Sully's best chance of survival. If MOTHER ever realized just how high up Sullivan was in the Uprising, Agnes was sure they'd kill him on the spot versus send him to the camp—which made sense. A high-ranking Uprising agent would only stir the pot in the camps. But if Agnes could convince them that Sully was just a grunt, maybe—just maybe—he'd be able to save Sully.

"Well, that's a disappointment." Agent Kore sighed, slumping back into her chair. Her expression fell into what Agnes could only describe as a sulk. "I hope it proves to be more useful than all that—for your sake."

He'd been so focused on lying to her convincingly and choosing the right words, that he'd almost missed that little add on at the end. "Excuse me?"

"There's been talk," she said simply.

"What kind of talk? I have been nothing but obedient and loyal to this organization for the last hundred-odd years." His tone was perhaps a little more defensive than he intended—*naughty Agnes*. But his heart was so loud in his ears all of the sudden, it was hard to regulate his tone. It may have just been an idle threat—something Kore was saying to send him over the edge and make him falter—but in Agnes's position, he couldn't take that chance.

"Perhaps that's the problem. You've been around so long, and then with what happened to my parents . . ." She let her words drift off, presumably for his imagination do the rest. And it did.

"That was ruled an accident by the Council," Agnes growled. But of course, he knew better. An official ruling wouldn't be enough to stop Kore from exacting what she saw as justice for what happened to her parents.

Kore shrugged daintily, a twisted sneer creeping onto her lips. She could see she was getting to him, damn it.

"Yes, well, it was awfully convenient, wasn't it? You just happened to be outnumbered like that, when all of our intel had indicated that the target would be alone in that warehouse. And should new evidence come to light? I wouldn't be surprised if the Council reconvened and came back with a new ruling."

"I will not sit here and allow you to hurl around false accusations. This meeting is over." He stood abruptly from his seat—nearly toppling the chair in his anger—and made his way to the door, giving her no chance to respond.

He didn't stop, not when he reached the door, not when he was in the hallway. He didn't stop until he was three corridors down, surrounded by the bustling of MOTHER headquarters. Then he let his mind wander back to the day when he'd inadvertently drawn too much attention to himself.

It had been six months ago.

Agnes's most recent handlers in the Kore line were

Elinor and Emmett Kore. They were decent people, as far as MOTHER agents went. They had never called him by his number, always by his name, and they genuinely seemed to care what might happen to him when they were on a mission. Agnes liked them well enough—better than some of their predecessors anyway—even if they were working for an agency that enslaved his people.

MOTHER instructed them to collect a vampire that had been draining people in the area. In Agnes's mind, this was the kind of Enchanted MOTHER *should* be taking care of. Vampires should have to ask permission before feeding on anyone. But this delightful chap had taken to luring young women in and draining them dry, overall making an ass of himself.

Even with the target being a vampire, the mission should have been a reasonably simple Collection. One vampire versus three highly trained MOTHER agents. Easy.

The trio snuck around the outside of the building—hoping not to give away their location with noise. It was slow progress, but the group reached the door unmolested.

Emmett motioned for them to fall into formation—Elinor brought up the rear and moved with her back to Agnes in case they were attacked from behind. Agnes drew on his magic, using it to cloak them as they walked silently through the abandoned building.

The smell of blood hanging heavy in the air made him nauseous and Agnes tried to breathe as shallowly as possible.

Emmett held up a hand, and the two behind him stopped mid-step, waiting motionless for the signal. Emmett peeked his blonde head around the corner, and with another motion they were moving again.

One of the hanging lights flickered overhead. On. Off.

On. Off. Making everything feel like it was moving faster than it was.

One moment, a single vampire was standing in the middle of the open room.

Off. On.

Then there were five.

Off. On.

Then ten. All of them young women, each with the same ravenous look in her eyes.

Panic settled in quickly, making Agnes's heart thump so loudly, it nearly ripped from his chest. He tried to tell the others to make a hasty retreat, he tried to get them to see the danger. They could come back when they had more men. But just as he opened his mouth to speak, there was a pop.

Off.

In the pitch-black, sight was unnecessary, for the screams of Emmett and Elinor Kore revealed all.

In a few seconds, the two MOTHER agents were drained and discarded by the horde. Leaving Agnes standing alone, and mostly unarmed in the black.

Agnes pressed his hands to the wall, trying to feel his way back out. He stumbled over something in the dark and forced himself not to think of *who* it might have been.

"Not so fast, little unicorn," a voice cooed soft and close —too close. The hairs on the back of Agnes's neck stood on end, alerting him to the danger he was in. "I have a message for your masters—*both* of them. You tell them to leave me be, or I'll burn this entire kingdom to the ground."

There should have been fear niggling at the back of his mind. He should have pulled away from the creature whose breath stank of rotting flesh and ran away as far and as fast as he could. But there had been a plan B—there was always a plan B.

Without a word, he pulled the small bomb from the belt at his waist and said, "Hold this for me, would you?"

The weapon ticked faintly as soon as it was in the cold fingers of the vampire. Then Agnes pulled a second item from his belt, murmuring a spell that opened a portal beneath them. Just before falling through, he could see the shocked look on the vampire's face in the light from the portal.

The explosion destroyed several city blocks—a small price to pay for stopping a vampire army in Agnes's mind. Neither MOTHER nor the Uprising wanted an undead outbreak.

He'd done the right thing.

THAT EVENING, as Agnes made his way toward Sully's cell, he fiddled with his collar. His polished boots halted for a moment, and he turned into one of the designated Enchanted bathrooms. He headed for the mirror to eye himself. Then, after a deep breath, he reached up to untie his long hair, and let the multi-colored tresses fall free over his shoulders. He ran his long, fair-skinned fingers through the strands.

"I like it this way," Sully had always said. "You usually have it back in one of those pompous-ass braids."

Those had been Sully's words the first time Agnes had let him touch his hair. He remembered it like it was yesterday—back on that hill overlooking the Hunter's small farm.

Forty-two years, seven months, and three weeks ago.

The years without Sully had blended into naught but a

bland and colorless wash of memories, only broken up by the harsh red of bloodshed. Still, Agnes kept count.

That had been long before everything had become complicated. Before Agnes had goaded Sully into joining the Uprising.

"And look at you now." Agnes sneered at his reflection. "Look at the hell you've brought him into."

Disgusting.

Without thinking, he turned on the water as hot as it would go, removed the gloves and the bandage, and began to wash his hands. He wasn't sure how long he stood there, or how much soap he had used. But after what felt like hours, the water running cold, he was sure they were clean —or as clean as they were going to get, anyway—and that somehow calmed him enough to turn off the water.

Agnes's injured hand was bleeding again, but he rewrapped it, replaced the gloves, and went on his way.

"Disgusting," he repeated to himself as he continued his trek to Sully's cell.

*S*leeping sitting up for days at a time had left Sully with a stiff neck and a sore lower back, but at some point in his long life, Sully had grown used to it. The exact moment escaped him. Between stakeouts with the Uprising and being captured more than once by rogue MOTHER agents—always on purpose, mind you. He never got caught by accident—he'd learned to manage it. If Sully tilted his head just so, he could almost use his shoulder as a pillow. Almost.

The door sprang open, pulling Sully from what little sleep he'd been getting. Standing there, silhouetted by the dim lights outside, was what Sully could only call an avenging angel in the form of Agnes. Agnes's face was cut into a hard but breath-taking expression of anger and self-righteousness. His long, vibrant hair streamed around his face, free of its usual braid. The light shone just so on his features to make him look both stunningly beautiful and terrifying all at once. And those piercing dark blue eyes had begun to glow a strange aqua color. Sully's fingers shifted on the wood of the arm rests, yearning to reach out to his Aggy.

Sullivan couldn't help the broad smile that took over his

face, splitting his still-healing lip and showing every one of his teeth—even if he'd wanted to. Aggy had always been stunning, but he was never quite so lovely as when he was like this. Furious.

"Ah, Aggy, how nice of you to join me."

Agnes's eyes remained trained on him, blazing with rage. Sully's own gaze flicked past him to see which guard was standing outside of the cell. It didn't look to be the stout Roy, who'd so helpfully taken him to the showers the previous day. Nor the easily disgruntled woman who had stormed off for a coffee before. Which meant, this time, the torture may be real.

"Cut the sass, kelpie," Agnes growled, stepping closer to the chair Sully was strapped to. "You know what I'm here for."

Agnes's thin, pale hands took hold of each armrest so that he could lean his face in close enough that, if Sully got it into his head, he could have kissed him. Sully recognized this thought as both appealing and unwise.

"Haven't the foggiest, unicorn." Sully winked arrogantly in return.

If they were going to play this game, he supposed he should get into the part. He had played this role more than once, just never with Agnes. There was a part of Sully that might have found it sexy to have Agnes in control like this—if it weren't for the other, much larger part that didn't like the idea of his Aggy torturing him. Swallowing roughly, Sullivan prepared himself for what would be a long hour, at the very least.

The first harsh sound of skin-on-skin left Sully stunned, not quite registering that Agnes had slapped him until his cheek began to sting. Flexing his jaw, and his neck, Sully listened to them both pop in protest before returning his eyes to Agnes with a quirked brow.

"Don't be an idiot," Agnes whispered—his eyes almost pleading with Sully, *Please don't do this. Please don't make me do this.*

"That all you've got, unicorn?" Sully challenged. He held Agnes's gaze, hoping to tell him without words, *I have no choice* and, *Don't worry about me. I can take it.*

Just a single moment of hesitation—that was all it took for Agnes to decide. No one else would have even noticed it, but Sully knew Agnes well, and he knew that when Agnes meant to act, he did so with brutal efficiency. Sully nodded his head, just enough to acknowledge what was about to happen, and then steeled himself for the next blow.

Another open-handed smack left his cheek red and ears ringing.

"What is the Uprising planning?" Agnes shouted loud enough for the guard outside the door to hear.

Sully chuckled, pulling himself upright in the chair again. This was how the game would have to go. It had to look as if Agnes needed to break him. If not, this whole lie would never be believable, and Agnes would be in danger.

"Tell me!" The shout reverberated off the stone walls, and in Sully's mind as Agnes's magic compelled him to answer. It would have been easy to tell him, to let the compulsion take over and spill it all out, but then they'd both be dead. Instead, Sully grit his teeth against the following smack that brought the taste of metal to his tongue.

"Where will they strike next? Where are their safe houses? Who's in charge?" The questions came now in rapid-fire succession, a tactic Sully was familiar with. He had endured this enough to know that, eventually, the one questioning him would get tired. He'd be given a break, however brief. "What are they planning?"

Another blow landed on Sully's jaw. Agnes's hand had

curled into a fist before swinging this time, causing him to flex and hold in a groan.

It went on that way for a while. Agnes would ask a series of questions, not get an answer, and punch Sully with all of his might — then it would start over. Over the next two hours — or at least Sully thought it must have been that long — Agnes's appearance grew steadily more haggard. If Sully didn't know any better, he'd say that Agnes was on the verge of tears by the end of it.

Sully's jaw ached, and he could feel his battered face bleeding — one eye swelling shut. But to him, it was Agnes who was in pain, chest heaving with sharp pants, and his normally neatly pressed clothes in utter disarray.

"We will pick this back up tomorrow." Agnes straightened his spine to stand tall, tugged his clothes back into place, and tried to tidy his hair with one hand.

"Sweet dreams, Aggy," Sully croaked, being sure the guard couldn't hear him. He offered the other man a toothy smile that he was sure was full of blood.

"Goodnight, Sully," Agnes whispered back, just loud enough for him to hear. Then Agnes turned on his heel and left Sully alone in his cell.

Sully's head rang with the sound of the door slamming shut behind Agnes. He leaned forward and let out a muted moan of pain, squeezing his eyes closed. Without Agnes before him, Sully assessed the damage. He'd known that Agnes would have to make it look good, but damn if it didn't hurt. His wounds seemed superficial, but that didn't stop his aching neck and ringing ears.

The door opened once more, and in came the guard. Sully looked up at the young man in confusion. Agnes had just finished questioning him; there shouldn't be any more. He didn't think this was a game of bad cop, worse cop.

"I'm under orders," was all the young man said.

Another came in after him, dragging a dirty looking cot and the first moved to unshackle Sully from the chair. While the iron was no longer pressed tight enough to burn his skin, the extended length of chain attached to the stone wall, left him no means of escape. They flopped the cot down with a *thunk*, and then the two guards left.

"Get some sleep," the first called through the door.

Then he was alone in the dark, damp cell again. Taking a deep breath, Sully stood—the chains jingling—and moved to the back corner to drop down onto the cot. Sleep might not come, but at least he could rest. He closed his eyes and let his mind drift, escaping the pain if only for a moment.

A MUCH YOUNGER, much happier, Sullivan Hunter opened his black eyes to glare at the city in the distance. The faint breeze rustled the tall grass around him and the bleating of goats in the distance was the only sound for miles. The Hunter farm had provided him with a peaceful childhood. It was far enough from the cities of Daiwynn that it felt to Sully as if the war between MOTHER and the Uprising were a world away. Sloane and Dalton Hunter were good, kind people, who helped to smuggle many an Enchanted across the Great Wall and into the wild, untamed of the Wastes on the other side.

"You can't go there," Dalton had told him once when Sully had begged to head over the wall with him.

"But why?" He'd blinked big dark eyes at his father.

"The Wastes has no laws, and magic roams free completely unchecked. It's like the Wild West out there, Sul. You'd be in too much danger." Dalton reached down to pat Sully's shoulder gently and said no more on the topic.

Sully had always supposed that there were worse things than a lawless land.

The refugees looking for an escape continued to come steadily over the years. By the time Sully was eight, he had met all manner of Enchanted from fae to werewolf and everything between.

"It's an excellent way for you to learn about others of your kind," Sloane had told him once when he'd asked why they always had dinner with the refugees.

"And they're usually hungry," Dalton added.

This seemed reasonable enough.

But none of the refugees—neither pixie nor siren—were more exciting or beautiful than the unicorn. Agnes's visits were by no means regular, and he never spoke to Sully when he came. Instead, remaining at the edge of the property to hand off the refugees he'd saved to Dalton, where Sully had to watch him from a window.

In the beginning, the excitement was because Agnes always came with someone new. Someone that Sully could learn from. A new friend to expand his view of the world that did not extend much beyond the cottage, and the tiny village at the bottom of the hill.

Things changed as Sully grew. His fondness for the man who had saved his life grew from idolized heroism to something more like a boyish crush.

Sully was thirteen when he first realized that every time Agnes would walk up the long drive to the farmhouse, he could feel his heart skipping along in his chest. His parents told him often that it was just gratitude because Agnes had saved him. Nothing more, nothing less. Sully knew differently; he could feel it.

Nothing changed, though. Agnes continued to keep his distance, remaining on the periphery of their operation, and Sully continued to watch from the window.

At least until the twentieth anniversary of Sully's adoption. It had been months since Agnes was able to bring any refugees by, MOTHER having tightened their control of his movements. And in those months, Sully found himself feeling different. Strangely, he felt more adult, less like a hero-worshipping child, and more like Agnes's equal. Part of this had been due to beginning Uprising training, and part may have been because the young man had grown nearly a foot in the time they had been apart. By the time Sully's dark eyes finally drank in Agnes again, he found himself easily a head taller than his childhood hero.

"Sully, you've grown," Agnes said with a little smirk as he approached. The first words he had said to Sully likely since the day he had handed him off to the Daltons. Sully had decided to wait for him at the end of the long drive so he could have some time alone with Agnes.

"Just a little." Sully shrugged his broad, skinny shoulders, his cheeks reddening. It wasn't possible, but it felt that Agnes had grown more beautiful. His mane of rainbow hair, that he'd stopped cutting, had finally reached his shoulders and Sully's fingers ached with the desire to touch those silken strands. He didn't dare. There was still so much time between them. There would always be so much time between them, however immortal they may be.

"Are you going to invite me in? Or are we going to stand out in the sun all day?" Agnes asked, a teasing glint sparkling in his eyes.

"Oh! Right!" Sully's flush deepened. Agnes had never come in before, but then, he'd also never shown up without a refugee in tow before. "Mum made sandwiches," he muttered, turning on his heel to head back into the small farmhouse. Lunch was waiting for them on the rough-hewn table in the big open space that served as kitchen, dining room, and sitting room all in one. The Hunters were myste-riously absent.

Agnes settled elegantly into one of the tall-backed chairs, and Sully flopped awkwardly into the one across from him. Silence spread between them as the pair began to eat.

Sully did his best impression of eating like a normal person. A feat he was finding himself completely incapable of performing. Self-consciously, he took a bite that wound up being a bit too large, and winced as the contents of his sandwich squished out and down onto his shirt.

His stomach sank to his feet, his mortification complete when he heard Agnes snickering. Sully's eyes flicked from the mustard staining his shirt to the chortling man on the other side of the table and felt his face heat to the color of an overripe tomato. Without another word and still laugh-ing, Agnes grabbed his napkin and reached over to wipe a bit of mustard from the corner of Sully's mouth.

"All better," Agnes murmured, still biting back a smile.

Surprise replaced mortification. Sully sat for what felt like hours blinking at Agnes, allowing the contents of his sandwich to soak further into his shirt.

"All better," Sully repeated, the words leaving his lips without thought. "I should . . . I should go—go and umm . . . and um . . . change."

Sully rose to his feet abruptly—nearly toppling the table in his rush—and made a hasty retreat. His heart pounded wildly in his chest as he ran up the steps. Then, away from Agnes, he tried to get a hold of himself. Breathing deeply, he moved to his dresser to pull out a new shirt and change, taking his time in the hopes that he could go back down to the kitchen with some composure.

When it didn't come, Sully returned without it to find a small velvet box perched neatly beside his plate. The sight brought him up short, and his heart raced once more. Tall and suddenly very awkward, Sully shifted from foot to foot behind his chair just staring at the box.

"I missed Christmas," Agnes said by way of explanation, shrugging. "Besides, you're a man now. Seems well past time people stop getting you cheap toys."

All Sully could manage in response was a dumbfounded nod. He sank into the chair, gaze still fixed on the little box. What came in such a box? He had no idea. What did it mean? He wasn't sure. Should he even accept such a gift? Maybe not. The only thing he was confident of was whatever was in the box had been expensive.

"Oh, for crying out loud, Sullivan." Agnes huffed. "It's not going to bite you! Just open it!"

Sully wasn't so sure that that was true. The air between the two of them seemed to shift as if it were alive when he reached for the box. Under his fingertips, the velvet was smooth, but it did little to soothe the feeling of tension. His dark eyes flicked over to Agnes once more, to find him watching with an expression of mild annoyance.

He hadn't known what to expect beneath the velvet lid, but what Sully found was a gold pocket watch. It was on the small side—as far as men's pocket watches went—but it shone beautifully in the dim kitchen lights. Etched on the casing outside was a delicate unicorn, eyes blazing and chin tilted up proudly. Its horn seemed to gleam more brightly than the rest of the watch.

A breath left Sully. He reached for it, fingers twitching nervously, as he brushed the cool metal of the watch case.

"Agnes," he gasped. He was going to tell Agnes he couldn't accept it. He was going to say, 'thank you, it's beautiful, but I can't' before sliding it back. It was too expensive.

Agnes snorted and rolled his eyes. Sully's protests died in his throat.

"Twenty is a big birthday. Just don't break the damn thing. Okay?"

"I won't," Sully swore. Then he pulled the watch from the box to run his fingers reverently over the etched unicorn.

NOW—SOME forty years later—Sully pulled the watch from his pocket again. It had been a long time, but he'd kept his promise, for the most part. There had been one mishap during a chase in Kristoff, but he'd replaced the crystal promptly. Otherwise, the watch was intact though much aged and worn from being pulled out of his pocket so frequently.

The etched unicorn on the front had almost been rubbed smooth—a shadow of what it had once been. Still, Sully could feel the proud creature's face as he rubbed his thumb across the surface in the dark. He allowed it to bring him comfort and memories of happier times. Aggy was with him now. Aggy would get him out. Sully had faith.

Sleep did not find Agnes that evening, nor any evening in the coming week. Between the brutal torture he continually inflicted on Sully, and Agent Kore's threats, he found himself hardly able to eat much less sleep.

He sat up in the plush, velvety chair next to the fireplace all evening—the flames reflecting harshly against the glassy film of his eyes made his head throb.

There was only one option. Only one way out.

Agnes had secretly hoped he could get Manu and Persinette to stage a rescue from MOTHER headquarters —they had done it once before—but he knew better. MOTHER had upped their security of the compound since the last break. Even with the full force of Agnes's Uprising insiders on their side, it would be difficult. And if they did succeed, then what? The attack would expose Agnes and the others. Meaning they would have to escape as well. No, it was too risky for all parties involved, just as Roy had said.

The camps, however . . . the camps were a different story. MOTHER agents there were trained to deal with internal attacks, not external ones. There had never been a thought that someone might stage a prison break, only that those inside it might try to escape. And even if they did, it was widely assumed that it wouldn't be a large-scale thing. Just a couple of inmates trying to dig under the wire or something. Easy enough to dispatch by a few minimally trained men.

The camps would be the perfect target. Agnes could see why Eddi had decided to stage the attack there.

The trouble was that there were so many people to rescue. Even with an airship, there would be causalities. Those escaping would make for easy targets, especially the children and elderly.

The thought pulled a tired sigh from his lungs. He scrubbed at his face, the weariness settling into his bones. Although Agnes believed that Persinette's heart was in the right place, he didn't know if he could trust Manu. The captain had looked entirely unenthused about the idea. Agnes supposed all he could do was pray that they held up their end of the bargain once the plan was set.

Agnes stifled a yawn and glared at the rising sun casting its light through the barred windows of his quarters. He rose from his chair and tugged his clothes down into place, using a little magic to press them into unwrinkled perfection.

A brisk knock, and the voice that followed made him clench his teeth.

"Time to get a move on, 95." *Graham.*

"I'll be ready in a moment," he called.

Agnes spun to look about the room, making sure he was leaving nothing behind. The little brass table and wrought iron chairs beside the fire were clear of anything important, and the rest of the space was completely empty. Satisfied, he nodded and moved to open the door, using the keypad beside it.

Graham gave him an irritated look, her arms crossed over her chest.

"Good morning, Graham," he chirped pleasantly, offering her a little bow of his head.

All he received for his trouble was a grunt. Then the woman spun, and they both headed down the corridor. With a three-day mission ahead of them, there were supplies to pack, weapons to gather, and agents to assemble.

The supply room was cramped with agents and assets alike, all fighting to grab what they needed and get out of there as quickly as possible. Agnes lifted his chin to peer over the heads of the crowd, and spotted Agent Kore's mousy brunette head. The girl shoved one of the other agents aside to grab the last of the ammunition they needed, then elbowed her way to the exit.

"Well?" Kore growled. "Why are you two standing there gawking? Let's go! We have a 6:30 portal time." She brushed past them—slamming into Agnes's shoulder—to storm down the hall toward the portal room.

MOTHER's portal room was a wide-open space featuring portals of all shapes and sizes the humans had stolen from around the world. There were magic mirrors and fairy rings and doorways without doors. All of which were made ages ago by Enchanted looking to escape from the realm of the "real". When the two worlds merged, MOTHER had scoured the land for gateways that hadn't been destroyed or lost in the ocean. It had taken time, but eventually, MOTHER found a way to change the magic of the portals so they could use them to travel around Daiwynn.

Light flashed through the room as another Collection party came through with their bounty—a fairy with a bent wing and a bloodied face.

Someone smacked Agnes lightly with a pistol to grab his

attention. He mindlessly took the weapon and strapped it around his waist. Then the group lined up while an Enchanted got the doorway running. A washed out reflection of Maximus appeared in the shimmering surface. The sound of rushing water accompanied the open portal.

"Today is just recon?" Agnes asked, pulling a golden pocket watch from his waistcoat. His lean fingers rubbed over the kelpie-etched front for a moment. At the press of a button, the small watch popped open with a *tink* to reveal the time.

"Right," someone agreed from behind him.

With a nod, he tucked the watch safely back into his pocket. He was jostled as they huddled closer to the wet sound of the open path. Agnes closed his eyes, and stepped through the rippling surface, frowning at the strange feeling of his clothes heavy and clinging with water, before coming out on the other side bone dry. The group fumbled as they stepped into an abandoned office building in Maximus.

With all of them through, the light of the portal faded, leaving them in pitch blackness. There was a loud curse as one of the other agents fumbled with a flashlight. Grinding filled the air; the clockwork motor protesting at being forced on.

It finally flickered to life, and Agent Kore snapped, "Jesus, Samuel, did you grab the oldest flashlight in the supply closet?"

Harold—who was maybe a handful of years older than Kore—shrugged before saying, "I think it's this way." He padded across the linoleum, his light shining on rusted desks and floors covered in half-disintegrated paper.

Gods, the humans of old used so much paper, Agnes thought as his feet crunched on another brittle piece. A few fumbling minutes through the dark building—during which one of the agents ran headfirst into a desk—found the group outside again. Agnes let his eyes adjust, inhaling the scents of the city around them. The air in Daiwynn's seven cities always smelled more interesting—though not necessarily more *pleasant*, due to all the sulfur and unwashed people—than the processed, filtered air of MOTHER.

"What's the address?" Agnes asked, turning to Kore.

Uninspiringly dull eyes blinked up at him suspiciously for an uncomfortably long time—long enough that anyone who didn't know Kore would think she hadn't heard or understood the question—searching his face, perhaps for some sign that he was up to something.

Agnes held her gaze, unblinking. He'd never tried to break off from the pack with Katherine Kore before; perhaps she wouldn't let it happen. Maybe she wouldn't trust him enough to come back. All he could hope was that she'd realize if he didn't come back that *she* could lead the manhunt. A hunt Agnes had little doubt that would end in his death.

"Why?" Kore asked, narrowing her eyes on him more.

A lie readied itself on the tip of his tongue, and Agnes opened his lips to answer. "I—"

"Ah, come on, Kore, let him go and blow off some steam." The eldest of their group—Malcolm, Agnes thought, was his name—moved up to clap Agnes on the back with a substantial hand and a jovial laugh. "We can't all be saints like you. Right, Agnes? Besides, he's got a tracker on him, it's not like he can get too far."

Agnes had never much cared for Malcolm. The man was a buffoon. He was regularly found drunk or sleeping it off at some bar when they went out on a mission. Yet, at that moment, Agnes could have kissed him.

"Fine. Whatever. Go! Have fun while the rest of us set up for recon. But I'll expect you back before sundown, you've got the red-eye shift, 95."

With a curt nod, Agnes turned and nearly speed-walked away before anyone could stop him. He even outpaced Malcolm, who was making an apparent beeline for the nearest pub.

It took at least ten blocks before Agnes felt that he was a safe distance from the rest of the group. He took a breath and slowed his pace to something more reasonable.

Manu and Persinette were to meet him at a pub well away from where Agent Kore and the others would be set up for the Collection. It would be a safe distance from the others, or at least Agnes hoped so. He didn't need any MOTHER operatives wandering by his secret meeting with two pirates. Nor did he need any Uprising agents stumbling upon them in case it got back to Eddi. They had all agreed that it was best to keep this meeting to themselves for the time being. He'd even instructed Manu and Persinette to keep it from their crew.

Ducking into the tavern, he found Manu and Persinette already seated at a table in the back. Agnes's eyes swept the mostly empty room before he took measured steps toward them.

"You're late," Manu groused in greeting, looking vaguely in Agnes's direction. The captain's irises—which had once been nearly as dark as Sully's—were now washed of all color, and left Agnes feeling as if Manu were looking through him instead of at him.

The slight, lavender-haired woman beside him nudged him with her elbow, shaking her head.

"Manu, stop being grumpy," Persinette chastised.

"What? We could have slept in," Manu complained, lifting one brown hand to his face to yawn dramatically behind it.

Persinette rolled her cheerful green eyes and turned

back to Agnes to offer him a welcoming smile. "You didn't have too much trouble getting away, did you?"

"No," Agnes said shortly, settling into the booth across from them. "Let's skip the pleasantries. We're not here for that."

Persinette's freckled features fell a little—clearly, she'd thought they were friends, now that he'd saved her. She had been wrong. He needed something from her, nothing more, nothing less. He didn't have *friends*.

"Right." Manu nodded in agreement. "What's your plan? I'm sure MOTHER has upped their security since our last break-in, so I hope it's good." In spite of the lack of faith the words inspired, Manu's tone was full of excitement.

Agnes inhaled deeply, preparing himself for what he was sure would be a bothersome battle of wills from the word *go*. Then he spoke in a low tone so as not to be overheard. "It would seem that the only clear line of attack is to hit the camps. MOTHER will be ready for another attempted break-in on their headquarters, and I can't put my own people in danger of being found out again. But, in my experience, the security at the camps has always been lax at best. They're more worried about prisoners scaling the walls than anyone coming to save them."

Both nodded as they listened, but at some point, Persinette's bright eyes had gone from cheerful and welcoming to full of sadness.

"You're going to let them send him there?" she asked when he got to the end. The corners of her full lips tugged down, and Agnes could swear she'd gotten paler.

Agnes scowled, letting out a harsh sigh, but he nodded in confirmation. He had thought over this long and hard. This was their only real chance to save Sully.

"We're backed into a corner. This is the only viable option. We can't attack MOTHER Headquarters again without completely exposing all of my people inside, and an in-transit attack would risk the lives of everyone in the zeppelin. The only way to save Sully is from the camp directly."

She shook her head, eyes glassy with unshed tears. Good lords, he hoped she didn't cry. That would be annoying.

"We'll help you, but there is a condition," Manu said.

Agnes blinked at him in surprise. He had been well and truly prepared to play on Persinette's emotions to get what he needed, but it seemed that wouldn't be necessary.

"Conditions? No, there are no *conditions*. We follow my plan." There was no time for negotiating with Manu. Things needed to be set into motion now, or they would miss their window.

"Yes, there will be some conditions." Persinette met Agnes's eyes bravely for the first time since he'd known her.

He held her gaze, unsettled by the terrified little mouse suddenly looking at him so brazenly. Where had the girl gone who he had bullied and pushed around? When had this woman taken her place? Agnes arrogantly wondered if he himself could take any credit for the transformation, but decided not to ask.

"Fine. What are these *conditions*?"

"You will give yourself up and be sent to the camps alongside Sully. There, we will rescue everyone in the camp, and you'll come with us." Though the words left Persinette's lips steadily, Agnes had a sinking feeling they weren't hers at all. Someone else had planned this out and told them both what to say. The question was, who? Eddi? Maybe.

Agnes's eye twinged. They didn't have time for this. He didn't have time to be caught up in the trial that would ensue should MOTHER realize he was a double agent.

"That's ludicrous!" Too loud, his words were much too loud. "I most certainly will not give up my position as the head of the Uprising faction inside MOTHER just so that you two idiots can play hero."

He looked around quickly to make sure no one was looking at them, but the only other patron—a man passed out at the bar—hadn't even lifted his head. He watched the man for a moment, waiting for some sign that he wasn't really asleep, but he continued to breathe deeply and murmur drunkenly in his sleep.

Then Agnes leaned onto his palms, crowding into their side of the table. "I will not be giving myself up for this."

"Then we can't help you," Manu said simply, leaning back in his seat as if washing his hands of the whole thing. "Those are our terms. Take them or leave them."

Agnes's scowl deepened. "Where is this—" He stopped mid-sentence when he realized exactly who this all sounded like. "Sullivan."

Persinette's lips fluttered a little as Sully's name left Agnes's tongue, leaving no room for guessing.

"He said he wouldn't leave without *you*." Her smile grew, making it clear she thought the notion romantic, or some such rubbish.

Agnes was having none of it. "That's insane. He can't really expect me to do that. I've worked too long to entrench myself into MOTHER's machinery to give it up now."

Manu shrugged his shoulders, disinterested now that Agnes seemed like he wasn't willing to play along. Persinette, on the other hand, leaned in closer. An almost manic smile had spread her lips, making her look a little unhinged.

"He wants to make sure you're safe, Agnes. He cares about you." Her voice held an urgency he didn't quite understand.

Agnes merely shook his head, a brightly colored strand of green hair falling into his face. He couldn't possibly agree to this. MOTHER was all Agnes had ever known; he didn't think that he could live in a world where he wasn't under their control. He'd been born there, raised there, he didn't know anyone outside of Headquarters—apart from Sully and these two morons. What would become of him without the strictly regimented routine of MOTHER? His life would be sheer chaos. Fear settled into Agnes's bones at the mere thought, making him swallow against a slowly closing throat.

A small hand grasped Agnes's, yanking him from his terror. He jerked away from Persinette's hold, not wanting to be touched or comforted by her. She seemed unfazed by the action and pressed on.

"Maybe it's time you let someone else do that, Agnes. Give yourself leave to be happy, finally."

Agnes barked out a laugh at the foolishness of that statement. Persinette was naive and stupid, that was clear. She didn't know any better. "That's crazy. This all is just . . . crazy. He can't really expect me to just . . . just . . . abandon my position and run away with him."

Can he?

Persinette's freckled chin lifted, and she nodded before sitting back next to Manu again. "Those were Sully's terms, not ours. He told Manu that either we got both of you out of there, or we shouldn't bother to come at all."

"He won't leave you behind," Manu added to further her point.

Agnes felt his Adam's apple bob around another strange well of emotion threatening to choke off his air supply.

Gods, when had he gotten so damn sentimental? Probably when Sully had volunteered to be savagely tortured all in the name of, apparently, rescuing him. No one had ever done anything like that for Agnes before.

"I can't," he choked out.

"I don't see where you have much of a choice," Manu responded—saying the words Agnes was thinking. Sully hadn't left him any choice. This was the only way.

"You have to," Persinette said. "If you love him, you have to."

Love. That single word ripped Agnes from his thoughts. They had never once said the word between them, he and Sully. But the truth was that Agnes had loved him since the very first day. Admittedly, in the beginning, it had been a different kind of love. There had been nothing romantic about it; Agnes had simply felt protective toward the little kelpie. Agnes wasn't sure he'd call it love in the sense Persinette meant. It was so much more than that.

Taking a deep breath, Agnes closed his eyes to think. He had to save Sully, he had to protect him, there had never been any discussion of that. Now he saw that the only choice was to save himself as well.

He nodded. "All right, here's the plan."

For two hours, the trio sat together and went over everything. From back up plans to the agreement that they would need to bring in another ship, they covered it all.

By the time Agnes went to leave, he felt reasonably satisfied that this plan would save as many lives as possible. He stood, nodded to each in turn, and took his leave to head back to Kore and the other agents while Manu and Persinette presumably headed back to their ship.

IT WAS STILL EARLY when Agnes returned to the apartment that Kore and the others had set up.

He allowed himself the leisure of zoning out in a corner. Not quite sleeping, but not quite awake either. He pondered how his life would change now that he had agreed to give up the only part of it that had ever made sense. Terror—his throat closed, and heart raced.

He forced himself to focus on the mission at hand. Surely, there would be lots to do while they waited for the perfect moment to strike.

The little troll family seemed to live a quiet existence in their small one-bedroom apartment. While the single mother cooked, the two children sat at the table, coloring and chattering.

After six months of working with her, Agnes knew Kore's routine by now. She would attack when the group seemed to be at their least vulnerable. Her preference— Agnes was sure—came from the need for a fight. If there was a fight, there was a higher chance of bloodshed. And above all things, Kore seemed to have an insatiable blood-lust. She wanted to hurt Enchanted any way that she could, but forced herself to stick to MOTHER's rules.

"What's the word on where these things will be sent once Collected?" one of the other agents asked Kore.

Kore shrugged, her eyes fixed on the window where she could see into the little family's yellow-tiled kitchen. There was something predatory about how her gaze followed the mother's movements around the room. Like a wolf waiting for the best opportunity to attack. The family's fate beyond Collection seemed to hold no interest for her.

"What condition do they need to be brought back in?"

Curious little thing. Even as those thoughts crossed Agnes's mind, he saw the subtle tug of a knowing grin on the boy's face.

"Dead or alive," Kore responded with an equally cruel smile stretching her lips. They both let out a brief, cold laugh that sounded too cliché to be real. Agnes swallowed roughly to keep the stale toast he'd had for lunch from making a reappearance. "They'll be getting ready to sit down to eat dinner soon. We should strike then."

"But wouldn't it be better to wait until the children have gone to bed?" Agnes asked quietly. He knew it was stupid, but there was a small voice inside of him that dared to hope. That little voice sent up a silent prayer that Agnes could convince Kore to spare their lives. Even if the only ones he saved were the children. That voice was a moron.

Kore snorted, rolling her eyes at him. "Have you gone soft on me, 95? Of *course* we won't wait till they're in bed!"

Taking a deep breath, Agnes willed that voice to shut up. But it wouldn't.

"It's just that—well, then the mother would come quietly to protect them," he continued, still wishing he could stop himself.

Another snort—which made her sound like an overweight truffle pig—came from Kore.

"No," was all she said in response before turning once more to watch the family through the window.

With dinner finally ready, the children cleared the table, washed their hands, and settled at their spots to prepare to eat. Agnes's heart hammered in his ears as his eyes followed the mother. She scooped what looked to be pasta into each of their bowls, then settled at the table herself. He watched the little family tuck into their food, the children eating hungrily. This was probably the first meal they'd had all day, and here he was with these people about to rip it away from them.

"Now," Kore announced, standing from where she was crouched on the balcony.

She led her team downstairs, across the street, and up through the other building toward the home of the unsuspecting—and innocent—troll family. Agnes hadn't time to breathe, much less argue with what was about to happen before they were in front of the wooden door.

A loud boom shook the building, and the door clattered to the living room floor. Malcolm stood in the settling dust, grinning like a maniac. Then the group filed in, fanned out, and headed for the kitchen.

Agnes's ears rang from the blast, but he could still hear the whimpering of the children as they all approached the room. There, backed against one of the yellowed countertops, was the mother. Her two children tucked behind her legs, sobbing with tears streaming down their faces. The little girl looked at Agnes. Met his eyes. Agnes felt his heart clench in sympathy. He knew the look on her face better than he knew his own reflection at this point.

He was so distracted that the resounding pop of the pistol made him jump. Agnes's eyes jerked around to see who had fired first, but he couldn't find the smoking gun. His ears were ringing again; the children were screaming. He swiveled to see the mother on the ground now, bleeding from a head wound that left her eyes frozen open.

Her little girl tried to shake her, screaming, "Mommy!" at the top of her lungs, but there was no answer.

They were still screaming and crying for their mother as Malcolm and Graham moved to scoop up one of the squirming children each. With little care, they were slapped into a pair of iron manacles as if they were no better than criminals and dragged from the apartment. The whole operation lasted maybe a minute, tops.

"It burns," the little girl whined, scratching at the manacle on her wrist. Agnes wanted to tell her he knew, and he was sorry for it. But the words lodged in his throat.

Soon enough, the children's pleas faded into the background as his mind took him away. Away from the pain they had just inflicted on an innocent family. To a Collection operation eerily similar to this one. That mission had thankfully ended a little happier.

It had been sixty years ago now—almost to the day—when Agnes was given an assignment that would change his life forever. Their job was to destroy an Uprising safe house. Agent Percival Kore was excited about the mission. Percival—the current Agent Kore's grandfather—was just as cruel as his granddaughter, if not worse.

The safe house in the briefing had rested on the outskirts of Maximus and had a reputation of being one of the big stops along the Uprising's Freedom Trail. Agnes was sure MOTHER didn't know what the safe house did as there was never any talk of stemming the flow of Enchanted escaping to the Waste. He supposed they thought that these safe houses were set up merely to hide Enchanted who were on the run. MOTHER's primary intent was to disband these houses so those 'running from the law' had nowhere to hide.

"I don't know why they bother," Percival muttered to himself. He'd been grumpy since they'd been given the order, but Agnes wasn't sure how much of it was real and how much was an act. After all, he was grumbling while loading a pistol. "It's not like the houses are accomplishing anything. Stupid Enchanted don't know their ass from a hole in the ground."

Agnes shook his head. The prevailing notion at the time had been that the Enchanted couldn't organize. They were too simple-minded, and thus any attempt to stop them from doing so was a waste of time and resources. Agent Percival Kore held fast to this idea with everything he had. Agnes sometimes wondered if it was to vindicate Percival's bloodlust.

"None of your bullshit this time, 95," Percival growled with a deadly glint in his eyes. "I won't have you getting in the way. We're going to go in there and plow them all down. No survivors."

Agnes's gut twisted. It wasn't that Agnes hadn't killed before—he had. After some forty years with MOTHER, he had killed more of his kind than he ever cared to count. His hands dripped with the blood of the folk. But he'd never shot so many at one time, not an entire safe house.

"I don't think that's necessary, Agent Kore," he murmured.

Percival looked up from the pistol in his hands, then without a word, smacked Agnes across the cheek with it. The blow left a deep gash, already weeping with blood, but he refused to lift a hand to touch it.

"I said none of your bullshit, 95," the old man growled again.

Agnes ducked his head in obedience. "Yes, sir."

An hour later found Agnes and Percival Kore standing before a rushing portal. Agnes was doing his best to hide the red welt on his cheek, and Percival was looking angrier than usual. They stepped through the portal, and out in front of a small townhouse on the outskirts of the city.

Their boots hit the ground, and Percival didn't wait a beat before he had kicked the door in. Agnes was left to either follow or get left behind.

He followed.

Inside the small house, the floor was already slick with blood, and the sounds of screaming set Agnes's ears to ringing. He nearly lost his balance as he stepped over one of the prone bodies, keen eyes searching out the gray-haired MOTHER agent.

Percival stood still, with one foot in the air, mid-step in the middle of the hall.

"Shhh," he hissed at Agnes, who had stepped onto a creaky floorboard.

Everything fell still and silent, and in the silence, Agnes could hear the cry of a baby. Percival looked at him for a moment, and slowly, the older man's face morphed into a terrifying rictus of malice. Then he turned that smile on the hallway wall. Somewhere behind the wall, a child cried.

Agnes recognized the newer wood, painted to look as aged as the rest of the hall—a false wall. Perfect for concealing illegal Enchanted. In what felt like slow motion, Percival lifted his foot to kick down the flimsy plywood. As the dust settled, Agnes saw the form of a woman, cuddling something tightly to her chest. The babe wept on, and she desperately tried to hush it.

She was frozen and trembling, not even trying to scramble to her feet to run away. All she seemed to be able to do was curl more tightly around the baby to try to protect it.

Percival didn't give her time to break from the fear and fight. He lifted his pistol, there was a pop, and her arms fell limp. The wailing babe, still nestled against her chest, was now splattered with blood.

Percival moved closer to the screaming bundle of blankets, his pistol raised and ready to fire again. Agnes didn't think, he just acted. He grabbed the nearest blunt object and swung. A second later, Percival crumpled to the bloody ground in a heap with a deep gash in his head.

Panting roughly, Agnes watched to see if the agent would move again, and when he didn't, Agnes crouched beside the mother. He took his time extracting the baby from her arms.

There was a moment where Agnes thought to himself

that the kindest thing he could do for the child was to kill it. Quick, painless, and then the baby would never have to know a world that despised it. A quick death would surely have been better than the slow one ahead of it, Agnes knew that better than anyone. It would have been easy to smother the child or snap its little neck—to put it out of its misery before it began.

Except just as he was about to, the child stopped screaming and peered up at him with an enormous pair of black eyes. Agnes couldn't explain it; he felt like the child was peering down into his soul, and his heart gave a tug.

"Well, damn it," he huffed.

What had followed was a mad scramble that all seemed to blur together, even now. Agnes still wasn't sure how he had managed all of it, but in the end, he'd given the babe to an Uprising agent nearby with explicit instructions to get it to the Hunters. Then Agnes stayed in that blood-soaked house and waited. It took hours for the MOTHER agents to realize something was amiss and find him.

When they finally reached him, he had worked himself into a frenzy. With several self-inflicted wounds, he spun a half-conscious tale of how the Uprising had been waiting for them there. That they had killed Agent Percival Kore and only left him because they thought he was dead. The agents believed it, every slurred word of it. After all, there was no one left to say otherwise.

Agnes wished he could have done that for the troll family. He wanted to save those children from the slow death they would face in the labor camps, just as he had Sully. Even if Agnes couldn't find them a home as he had with Sully, maybe he should have snapped their necks as he had thought to all those years ago. But he couldn't, and he didn't.

He sat in his chair that evening, staring unblinkingly

into the fire, sleep evading him once more. In the hundred-plus years he had served MOTHER, Agnes had saved one child, and that had been Sully. Just one out of the countless others. And now he was being given a chance at happiness. To escape this life and live a one free of MOTHER and the Uprising and the blood. But how could Agnes ever let himself be happy when there were so many he'd been unable to save?

It was almost too easy to lose himself to the memories with the dark pressing in around him. With no light or sound but the muffled noise of guards in the hall, there was nothing to distract Sully from the memory of a sleep-tousled Agnes smiling up at him after a long mid-afternoon nap. No noise to drown out the gentle laughter that left Agnes after they'd raced up the hill and Sully had beaten him. The memories flooded Sullivan's mind, chasing away the pain and cold he felt from the damp cell and lengthy beatings, leaving in their wake warmth and a smile.

After twenty long years apart, it had been heaven and hell to see Agnes again. A part of Sully thrilled at being able to be close enough to touch Agnes, and that same part despaired at not being able to. Agnes was so near now, in the same building even, and still, they were apart. Despite that, Sully felt closer than he'd been in a very long time.

"Soon," he told himself. Soon. Agnes would see reason, and they both would escape this hateful place. A slight smile split his face, growing wider when he heard the door open with a groan. Aggy.

"Well," Agnes started with a derisive sniff. "Don't you look cozy."

The words pulled Sully away from their future and back to the present. He peeked one bruised and swollen eye open to peer at the irritable unicorn.

"I was just having the most delightful dream. You woke me," Sully said flatly before pulling himself up to sit with a groan of pain. "What do you want, Aggy?" The last word left him on a breath, knowing not to say the name too loud for fear the guards would hear.

Agnes took one look at the guard behind him, seeming to weigh up his options, and then turned back to Sully. He moved closer, crouching beside the dirty cot where Sully laid.

"I have a plan," he mumbled.

Sully's dark brows lifted as he searched Agnes's face. A plan. Agnes had come to admit he had finally seen sense, and now they could escape? So soon? It didn't make sense but hope swelled sharp and hot in Sully's chest.

"What kind of plan?" Sully asked.

Agnes shifted on his feet as if perhaps he'd sit on the cot beside Sully, and then with a wrinkled nose seemed to think better of it. "Manu and Persinette have agreed to help."

Sully's full lips tugged down into a frown, his eyes narrowing to watch for any sign of deception. He had been perfectly clear with the captain—he would not leave MOTHER alive without Agnes. Period.

Agnes seemed to notice and sighed deeply, running a hand through his long hair. "They told me that there were some conditions for your release."

"There are."

Agnes shifted his weight on his heels again, seeming to struggle with whatever he was trying to say. Sully smiled. He'd never seen Agnes look so unsure before. Over the last several decades, Agnes had always seemed so confident. Agnes knew where he was going and what he was doing. But now, as he shifted before Sully, he looked — for lack of a better word — lost.

When he finally found the words, Agnes looked at Sully with an expression of hope and pleading.

"I can get you out. You'll have to be sent to one of the camps first, but then we can get you out from there. Manu and Persinette will stage a coup and rescue you. Then you guys can fight this war in style." Agnes's lips lifted at the corners as if he were teasing.

But if Agnes thought those words would change Sully's mind — he was sorely mistaken. For as stubborn as the old unicorn could be, Sully was doubly so. After all, he had learned from the best. Agnes should not have been surprised when Sully clenched his jaw and met his eyes without a trace of a smile.

"I won't be leaving without you. We either escape together or not at all."

Agnes's lips settled into a firm line. "Sullivan, be reasonable," he said sternly, like he was speaking to an errant child. "I still have work to do here. There is no sense in sacrificing yourself for me. Besides, Eddi needs me here."

A tired sigh left Sully. He scrubbed at his eyes. He'd known there would be a fight over this, but he had never much cared for fighting with Agnes. "Aggy, you've been doing this for over a century now. Don't you think it's time Eddi found someone else?"

"That's even more reason for me to stay! They trust me here. I've established a relationship with the agents and assets here. *I can't go.*" The last three words left Agnes as more of a plea than an argument.

Sully breathed past the tugging in his chest.

"I will not leave you here to die, Aggy. And you know

that's what will happen when MOTHER realizes that war is imminent. Every Enchanted in this place will be exterminated out of fear. We need to get you and all of others out while we still can." Pain settled into Sully's chest as he watched Agnes's eyes flicker from determined to nearly hopeless. "Please, Aggy, please come with me."

Agnes's well-tailored form puffed with a deep breath before he exhaled long and low. "Sullivan."

"Agnes."

He held Agnes's gaze, not giving any ground or showing any inclination of giving up. He didn't even blink. Sully would not back down. Either Agnes came with him, or they both died here. Sully would not continue to live his life without Agnes in it. That was the end of it.

Another deep sigh left Agnes before he nodded as if, perhaps, he'd always known this was how it would end. "Very well, then."

A part of Sully had clenched itself so tight that he hardly knew it existed anymore until it finally relaxed. He'd been so sure that this would be the end of both of them, and he'd been ready for it. Sully was more than happy to die alongside his Aggy, or in the pursuit of his Aggy, whatever was required of him. So long as Sully was just a little closer to him.

"Really?"

Agnes stared at him for a long moment before nodding. "I don't see where you've left me much choice in the matter. If I want to keep you safe, this is what I have to do."

But Sully felt lighter, brighter, happier than he'd felt in decades. A broad, toothy smile split his face, and he gave Agnes's hands an affectionate squeeze, then laughed.

"Well then, what's the plan, my darling?" He fought the urge to reach forward and stroke Agnes's cheek with his bloody fingers, afraid of tarnishing Agnes's beauty.

Agnes finally gave up and slumped onto the cot beside him. His rainbow head rested on Sully's broad shoulder, seeming to relax at last. "I suppose you're going to have to expose me as the mole."

It took a moment for the words to sink in, but when they finally did, Sully pulled back, grabbing Agnes by the shoulders so he could look at him closely.

"No." Sully shook his head, horrified at the thought. "They'll kill you." His stomach jerked. What little food he'd eaten since coming to MOTHER crawled up his throat thickly.

"Maybe. Maybe not." Agnes shrugged. His tone was calm, disinterested, rational. "Seems the only way, though. Then they'll get what they want out of you, and I'll stand trial for my crimes as a traitor."

That was Agnes: logical. He saw every option for what it was, and he proposed the most reasonable solution. That's what made him such an accomplished Uprising agent in many of the others' eyes. But for Sully, it had always been Agnes's heart. Agnes cared, even if he didn't always show it. And Sully would do everything in his power to protect that.

"But . . . what if they do?" Sully's heart stuttered in fear.

Agnes's eyes went gentle, one long-fingered hand lifted to brush against Sully's cheek. "They'll be able to punish me far better by sending me to a labor camp than executing me. A long slow death will satisfy them. Don't worry."

Sully nodded, his hand lifting to brush through Agnes's hair, searching for the comfort the silken strands had always provided him before. The rainbow tresses calmed him a little, and he nodded again allowing his heart to beat normally once more.

"What does this mean?"

"I have to convince Kore I'm inept so she can question

you herself. Shouldn't be too hard." Agnes chuckled, but the laugh died suddenly, and he frowned.

"I'm afraid she's going to be much worse on you than I could ever be," Agnes whispered, tone suddenly tight with pain.

"I can take it."

irst things first: Agnes had to call another meeting with his inner circle. Sully had been right—not that he hadn't known already. When it came time for the attack on the labor camp, it would be an act of war that MOTHER could no longer ignore. And once the war began, MOTHER would exterminate every Enchanted within their walls for fear of retaliation. It would be the end of all those assets Agnes had carefully accumulated over the years. And although he wouldn't be there to see the slaughter, he felt responsible for them. They would need an escape as well.

Two meetings in as many weeks brought panic to the small group. When Agnes entered the cramped supply closet they had chosen as this week's meeting place, the room went from chattering to silent in seconds. Every pair of eyes looked at him wide with worry. The tall shelves stacked with cleaning supplies seemed to bear down on him. Agnes forced himself to remain calm.

"Agnes?" Roy asked, struggling forward through the group. "What's going on?"

Agnes took a deep breath to ready himself for the

barrage of questions that were sure to follow his words. "I will be leaving MOTHER very soon."

Panic erupted.

"Soon?"

"How soon?"

"What does soon mean?"

"Why?"

"What will we do?"

"Who will lead us?"

The questions tumbled through the air, one over top of the other, like snowflakes in a blizzard. To Agnes's surprise, it was Roy who held up a hand to silence them.

"Then we will need a new leader," Roy said.

"You will." Agnes didn't take his eyes off Roy.

"But who?" someone asked, too short and too far back for Agnes to see who it was.

The room was chaos again, everyone seeming to argue for this or that person or even for themselves. Agnes let them bicker for but a moment before he opened his mouth.

"Your new leader will be Roy."

Silence fell. They all blinked in confusion at Roy, who in turn blinked in confusion at Agnes.

"But . . . I'm human." Roy said in a whisper as if the others didn't know.

"You are."

"Wouldn't it be better if you chose another Enchanted?" Roy's eyes widened with increasing panic, but Agnes shook his head.

"No. It is long past time that we stop seeing the division of human and Enchanted and start fighting this thing on a united front." Agnes's voice was quiet, but his words carried in the silence. "We will have no peace so long as we continue to see each other as *other*. This fight will be about treating everyone as people, and nothing else."

Roy lifted his chin. "Then I'll do my best."

"Good," Agnes replied. "Now, my other order of business is . . . I have been in touch with the captain of the *Defiant Duchess*. He and Persinette have agreed to help us free the kelpie once we are sent to a labor camp."

Visible relief washed through the group. Everyone seemed happy to know that they would not be responsible for that.

"But?" Gladys prompted from where she sat on an overturned bucket. Her knowing eyes bore down on Agnes—if he were a lesser man, he might have gulped in discomfort.

Taking the cue, Agnes continued. "Unfortunately, I don't see any way around it being a declaration of war. Even if MOTHER realizes it isn't an attack from the Uprising, I have little doubt they will portray it as such to their own."

What Agnes had been expecting was an uproar, but the whole room remained silent, all present looking at him with fear and realization.

"Roy"—he turned to address the new leader—"I'll set up a meet with Manu and Persinette, and they will help you coordinate what's to come."

"And what's that?" one of the trolls asked, fury etched his face. "Are you just going to leave us here to die? That's what'll happen, isn't it? We'll die. MOTHER won't let us live once a war breaks out."

A murmur of agreement went through the group. If it weren't for how determined Agnes was to keep the meeting under control, he might have snarled at the insinuation that they all thought he had such disregard for their lives.

"No," he said, quieting them again. "I expect they'll put me on trial for my crimes, which will give Roy time to smuggle out all of you who wish to leave before MOTHER decides to cull their Enchanted assets." These people were his responsibility, and he couldn't leave them without a plan.

Roy nodded in agreement. Relief washed over Agnes knowing Roy was taking this seriously. For the first time in over a century, this group was not just his responsibility anymore. They were Roy's too.

ANOTHER WEEK OF SLEEPLESS NIGHTS—AND torture that left Sully sore and Agnes exhausted—passed. Agnes did all he could to try to lessen Sully's suffering. Sully was seen by a medic, given ample food, and taken to bathe daily, despite Kore's complaints that this was a prison, not a day spa.

Then the day finally came that Agnes was called to Agent Kore's office once more, and they discussed another Collection.

"In a week, we'll be headed to Kristoff," she said sliding a folder across the table to him.

He picked up the folder to open it and survey the images inside—another family. This time a father, mother, an elder, and an infant. Agnes's stomach lurched.

"All right." Agnes nodded, shutting the folder, and sliding it back to her. He stood to head out the door, and then as if the thought had just struck him, he turned back to look at her again. "I had heard that Agent Buckingham was looking for more field experience."

"Roy?" Kore asked, forehead wrinkling in confusion—and nose in distaste. "What would he want field experience for?"

Agnes shrugged. He wondered if it were wise to try to con Agent Kore into doing his bidding this way, but she was his best shot.

"Don't know. Maybe he's suicidal," he responded with a mean grin.

Kore let out a laugh so cold Agnes could feel a shiver run down his spine. "Well, let us oblige him, shall we? I'll put him on the paperwork."

He nodded and left the room, exhaling deeply to get his skin to stop crawling once he was away from her, but no luck. How could she have such utter disregard for the lives of others? Even her own people? His fingers smoothed over the neatly pressed dress shirt, and he shook himself, vowing not to think further on it. He'd gotten what he wanted.

That was all that mattered.

By the time the Collection arrived, Agnes felt like he was teetering on the edge of something—consciousness, perhaps. Or maybe he was just about to lose his mind. Nearly a month without sleep could do that to a person, even if that person were immortal. He was given a small respite when it was Roy's turn to guard Sully, and he allowed himself to curl up alongside Sully on the dirty cot. There was a comfort to be found in his strong arms. Agnes let himself relish in it, for he knew that one day, very soon, he might never feel anything again.

"You look absolutely awful," Agent Kore broke his thoughts with a nasty sneer in her words.

"Yes, well, questioning the kelpie is harder than I'd originally anticipated," he muttered, scrubbing at his eyes. There it was—the first seed of doubt. Agnes knew he needed to plant them, but he wasn't happy with having to convince someone of his incompetence. He resisted the urge to scowl at the words.

"Too much for you?" she asked, the sneer changing into something more self-satisfied.

"Yeah, maybe," he said. He was grateful when Roy joined them on the small balcony overlooking Kristoff.

"What is it, Buckingham?" Kore turned to the young man, her eye twitching in irritation. "Didn't I tell you to stay inside and set up the surveillance equipment?"

"Yes, ma'am, you did," Roy confirmed with a nod. "I've finished. Graham asked if I could go out and pick up some food for the evening. She's hungry."

Agnes wondered what kind of manipulations Roy had to do to convince Graham she was hungry, but he decided it was better not to ask.

Agent Kore let out a disgusted sound of annoyance before muttering, "You can't go alone."

"I'll go with him," Agnes volunteered, perhaps a little too quickly. Kore's mousy brows raised, but he merely shrugged. "Getting out might wake me up some."

Kore's eyes narrowed on them suspiciously before she nodded. "You have two hours. Not a minute more."

He'd hoped for more, but it would have to be enough. Agnes nodded, and he headed back into the empty apartment they were using as their base. He and Roy didn't pause to check with anyone else and left. There was no time to be bothered with requests or questions.

It took them fifteen minutes to wind their way through the alleys of Kristoff. Fifteen minutes out of the two hours they had been given wasted because Agnes didn't want to be seen. Was he paranoid? Maybe. But he'd learned a long time ago that it was better to be paranoid than be sorry.

That day's meeting place was a stationery store, a front for a musty bookshop, packed to the brim with dusty tomes.

Roy whistled as his head swiveled to look at all of the

books. "I thought MOTHER had confiscated most of these things."

"They tried," Agnes responded with a shrug.

"But, as with so many other things," a smooth-looking young man offered with a wide wolfish smile as he slipped through the stacks, "MOTHER underestimated the ingenuity of those they sought to suppress. It's a tale as old as time really."

"Uh . . . right," Roy muttered, shifting uncomfortably under the man's inhuman gaze.

"Lowell," Agnes nodded in greeting to the wolf. "Where are they?"

"The cookbooks?" Lowell asked, his eyes dancing with humor. "Follow me."

The dark-haired man turned on his heel to walk deeper in the store. Roy let out a choked sound. Following his gaze, Agnes found a tufted gray wolf tail wagging merrily from the back of Lowell's trousers. Agnes chuckled darkly.

"A shepherdess makes a quite a mess," the wolf sang under his breath as he walked, "but little lambs are lovely."

Agnes followed behind him, not waiting for Roy to regain his composure. When the young agent finally caught up, he nearly toppled a stack of books in his rush to not be left behind. Lowell led them to a cramped back room, and there, at the tiny table, sat Persinette and Manu sipping from chipped, mismatched teacups.

"Agnes," Persinette chirped. It looked like it was taking everything she had not to hop up and hug him. Agnes was grateful she didn't.

"I'll leave you to it then. Kettle's on the stove if you want it." Lowell shut the door behind him.

Roy stood awkwardly by the door, rocking on the balls of his feet.

"Sit," Agnes ordered before he flopped down into one of the little chairs himself. Roy complied almost robotically.

"Who's your friend?" Manu asked, his unseeing eyes flicking vaguely toward where Agnes was seated.

"Roy Buck—Roy . . . Roy Bucking—Buckingham, sir," Roy said holding his hand out to Manu.

When the Captain didn't take the extended hand, Persinette reached out to shake it, offering the man a smile. "Persinette. I think I saw you around MOTHER while I was there."

Roy's shoulders relaxed as he shook Persinette's small hand, and Agnes thanked the gods for Persinette's unending niceness—as annoying as it was most of the time.

"This is Captain Manu Kelii. We're here to help"

"Thank you," Roy said, smiling a little.

Persinette nodded, settling back in her chair, her hands wrapping around the chipped teacup again.

"So, Agnes, how are things progressing?" Manu asked.

"Slowly," Agnes offered, releasing a sigh. "I don't know how much longer Sully can hold on with how things are going. I've made sure a medic sees him, but he's lost a lot of blood." The vision of Sully bleeding and panting caused an ache to radiate through Agnes all the way to the knuckles in his fingers. He clenched his fists.

"It'll be over soon," Persinette said, presumably to console him. "Would you like some tea?"

"No, no time." He waved the offer away. "I'm just here to facilitate the meet between you two and Roy. I hope you can save the Enchanted embedded in Headquarters before MOTHER gets it into its head that they pose a danger."

Manu and Persinette nodded.

"We'll have to reach out to some of my other contacts." Manu tapped his fingers on the blue cup, right along the crack where it had been glued back together. "I already have Benard compiling a list of people who would be willing to help us."

"The list will likely be very short," Agnes murmured tiredly. "Reach out to the Hunter family. See if they remember me. Maybe they'll help a little. They were always on the fringes of this."

"We'll have to do it slowly anyways," Roy added. "If too many Enchanted go missing too quickly, MOTHER will realize we're up to something. And it'll take me time to get them all out into the field."

"Then you have your work cut out for you," Agnes said, washing his hands of the whole thing. "For my part, I'll be on trial."

"We'll make it work." Persinette offered Agnes and Roy another reassuring smile. Agnes had no doubt that she believed that they would, but he, for one, wasn't sure how.

Manu pulled a small compact from his pocket and slid it across the table so hard it nearly fell off the opposite edge. Agnes caught it and passed it to Roy. "This is how you can get in touch with us. Just say *Defiant Duchess*, and it'll ring us. We'll need to know when and where you'd like us to provide an out for your people."

"And what camp they send Agnes and Sully to," Persinette added. "Hopefully, it'll be the same one." She lifted her cup to her lips, and took a slow sip, as if she needed something to steady her.

Roy nodded, tucking the compact into his pocket. "We'll start next week. One of our gnomes and I have been put on the docket for a recon mission in Kristoff, again. If your people could provide a distraction, that is."

Manu grinned. "Distractions are what we do best. I believe you have a safe house around there where we could take them, Agnes?"

"Yes," Agnes replied. "See Lowell for the details. He has

a definitive list of all the safe houses in this province, and he'll be able to tell you who to see about a list for the others." His shoulders relaxed from where they'd been hunched around his ears for what felt like months.

Roy had been the right choice. This would work.

"Wait." Confusion clouded Roy's face. "Won't they be housed on your ship until they can be transported to the Waste?"

"We don't have room, I'm afraid." Persinette sighed. "If we're going to be clearing out a labor camp shortly, none of them can be housed in one of the Uprising safe houses. Especially not if we're going against Uprising orders. We're close to full as is and will have to have a second ship help us on that mission. But don't worry: we'll make sure they're safe."

Agnes marveled for a moment at how calm and sure Persinette was. Where had the stuttering mess gone? The one who had been a doormat for him and half the MOTHER agents in the compound? When had she become so self-assured?

Agnes checked his watch. "We should go. We still have to pick up food."

Roy nodded in agreement, and the two men left the way they had come. They purchased food and made their way back in time for the Collection later that evening, much to Kore's annoyance.

The coming days were full of intentional little mistakes. Sully could see Agnes trying—perhaps a little too hard—to make himself seem incompetent. The agent in charge of him must have been dense if Agnes had to work so hard.

"I'm going to let you off the chains," Agnes whispered to him, "and then I need you to attack me when my back is turned."

"What?" Sully choked out, eyes wide with horror. Agnes couldn't mean . . . surely he didn't really want *that*! That was going a little too far, wasn't it? There had to be another way.

Pain lanced from his heart up his throat, nearly strangling the words. "No, I can't hurt you."

Agnes blinked at him in confusion, then shook his head. His deep blue eyes pled with Sully. Begging him, *Just do this, please.* "You have to. This is just the thing to push her over the edge, and we're running out of time."

"Aggy. I can't," Sully tried to explain, his voice breaking. "I can't hurt you."

He never could, even if he'd wanted to. Even if sometimes he had been so furious with Agnes that he'd longed to shake him until his teeth rattled.

"You will do this, or we will both die here." Agnes's voice cut dangerously through the silence. "Tonight, I'll forget to chain you back up, and tomorrow when I return, you'll attack me. This is not open for discussion, Sullivan."

With that, Agnes reached down and unlocked the shackles that attached Sully to the wall on the far side, keeping him from running for the door.

"Aggy," Sully all but whimpered as he watched Agnes stand and straighten his clothes.

"Kore will be with me. Make it look good."

Sully's heart stood still as Agnes leaned down, brushing his fingers along Sully's jaw gently in a gesture that was all too familiar.

"This will all be over soon, I promise," Agnes whispered. "Just do as I say."

Sully lifted one large dark hand to hold Agnes's smooth fingers against his cheek a moment longer. "All right, Aggy. I'll do as you ask."

Agnes nodded, stood, and left Sully to the dark and lonely cold of his cell. Sully let his mind drift to the last time Agnes had made him this angry.

Years and years prior Agnes had surprised Sully with a tiny cottage on the outskirts of Crickee. During that time, they had spent countless nights and days hiding away from the world that raged around them there. It had become their refuge away from the Uprising, MOTHER, the war. With Sully's parents long gone, he'd begun to think of that little cottage as his home.

It was there, in that one-room place, that he'd realized that Agnes felt just as deeply for him as he did for Agnes. Sully had known happiness, true happiness, for a few brief months, and so had Agnes.

"This has to be the last time," Agnes whispered, breaking Sully from his reverie as his rough fingertips ran a well-practiced line over the Agnes's chest.

"What?" Sully asked, only half paying attention to the words.

Agnes's long, graceful fingers gripped Sully's wrist, drawing his attention to his face.

"I said this has to be the last time," he repeated patiently. "We have to sell this place. This has to be it, Sully."

Sully shook his head, pulling his hand away. "You can't mean that."

"I do, it's getting to be too dangerous. We can't keep doing this. One of these days, someone is going to see us coming here, and they're going to figure out not just what's going on, but that I'm a MOTHER asset, and you're in the Uprising." The heart-shattering feeling that had settled into Sully's chest was reflected in Agnes's eyes, but it would seem Agnes had made up his mind.

"And what if they do find out?" Sully asked recklessly. "Who the hell cares?!" He was on the verge of shouting then. His voice raising dangerously as he felt his grip on the beast inside of him loosening. He could already feel tiny drops of water dripping off his hair and onto his shoulder.

Agnes sighed, rubbing at his face. "Please. Don't be angry," he whispered tiredly. "I just . . . I couldn't stand it if you got hurt because of me. And that's what will happen if we keep this up."

Sully took a deep breath, forcing himself to regain control before he continued. "But we've already been doing this so long."

"I know we have. But things are getting more serious. MOTHER is keeping better track of our movements. It's just too dangerous." Agnes's eyes pleaded with him to understand.

There was a large part of Sully that wanted to reach out and shake Agnes. It wanted to scream at him and tell him that it didn't matter if Sully got hurt. That's what Sully had signed on for—danger. And he'd done it all for the beautiful rainbow-haired unicorn who lay beside him. But there was another part that couldn't stand the pain in Agnes's eyes and would do anything to make it go away. That latter part won out.

"When will I see you again?" he asked, a part of himself breaking at the thought of not seeing Agnes for perhaps years to come.

"I don't know," Agnes said. His well-manicured, trembling fingers brushed over the stubble on Sully's chin. "But I can feel it, this will all be coming to a head soon."

Sully resisted the urge to pepper Agnes with more questions; instead, he let himself enjoy what little time he had left with his Aggy.

That had been over twenty years ago—Sully wasn't sure exactly how long it had been anymore. The years without Agnes had bled together in a sea of black, white, and gray nothingness. He fought, still. He did his job for the Uprising, still. But in the end, it was only so that he might see Agnes again, and it often felt hollow. There had been nothing left after his family died, just Agnes.

And even that he'd lost in the end.

WHAT SHOULD HAVE BEEN a simple task—one that Sully had done more times throughout his life than he cared to count—was rapidly becoming a source of anxiety. There was one single difference between those events, and this one, this was real. He'd hurt several people who were on the opposing side over the years, but when it came to someone who was on his side? Someone who he liked? Well, that was always faked. An act to convince the enemy they weren't working together.

Also, this was *Agnes*. Dear, sweet Aggy. Sully's heart clenched at the mere thought of causing him pain.

"I don't want to," he muttered to himself, taking another round from one wall of his small cell to the other. Large dark hands gripped his tightly curled hair and gave it a yank in frustration. This was going to hurt Sully far more than Agnes, as cliché as that sounded.

"Make it look good," he repeated over and over again. "Make it look good."

But how could he make it look good without causing Agnes permanent damage? Sully was such a large man, broad shoulders and sizable muscles. It would be too easy to break something he didn't mean to on the fine-boned unicorn. Even if he tried to be gentle with him.

"Oh Aggy, what have you gotten us into?" he asked too loudly in his anguish.

"It'll be all right," a voice drifted through the bars. Sully stilled to look at the guard whose back was turned to him — Roy, he thought his name was — as if he hadn't spoken at all.

"What?" Sully asked, brushing one large hand over his face, and pacing over to the cell door to peer out at the much shorter man.

Roy glanced over his shoulder, offering a comforting smile. "It'll be all right. Agnes is a lot tougher than he looks, and he knows what he's doing."

"I know that," Sully snapped. Then he took a deep breath to calm himself again. "I'm sorry. I didn't mean that."

It wasn't Roy's fault that all of this was happening. If it

was anyone's fault, it was Sully's. If it weren't for his insistence that Agnes come with him, then they wouldn't be in this mess. Agnes could remain safely behind the protective walls of MOTHER, and Sully could continue to fight them from the outside.

No, Sully told himself, *he can't continue to go on as we always have. Something has to give.*

"Right, of course," Roy mumbled awkwardly, turning back to the vast empty corridor. "I was just trying to—"

"Be comforting," Sully finished for him. "Thank you. That's very sweet."

The young man nodded, his shoulders relaxing, and was quiet for several seconds before asking, "How long have you been together?"

"I'm sorry?" Sully's eyes narrowed, peering out at the guard's back, trying to sort out what sort of man Roy really was. It was always hard with the humans who fought alongside the Uprising. What were their real motives? Were they double agents? Sully had learned to be wary.

"You and Agnes," Roy clarified. "How long have you been together?"

Sully quirked a brow, eyeing the young agent suspiciously. "What makes you think we're together?"

He couldn't see Roy's face, but a flush crept up his neck, and he ducked his head in embarrassment.

"I'm sorry, I didn't mean to assume," he muttered. "I just . . . in all the years I've known Agnes, I've never seen him sacrifice his pride for someone else."

"Oh." Sully hadn't thought of it that way before. He hadn't thought of how proud his Aggy was, and how this part of the plan would eat at him. How he would have to pretend to be useless, incompetent, stupid. All of the things Agnes prided himself on not being. Without his pride, what would Agnes be? Sully supposed he'd find out.

"We go back quite a ways," he answered finally. "But haven't you heard, it's rude to ask an immortal their age?" A smile tugged at Sully's lips for perhaps the first time in a month.

Roy laughed, shaking his head. "No, but I guess I know better now."

A companionable silence settled between the two, and Sully decided he quite liked Roy. He was a good enough guy. It was almost a shame this was the last time he'd likely ever speak to him.

The young man pulled out his pocket watch to check the time and nodded to himself. "They'll be coming soon. You better get yourself ready, whatever you plan to do."

"Right." Sully sighed heavily.

The familiar twinge of anxiety settled into the pit of his stomach. He slunk further into the darkness of the cell, away from the light of the hall and prying eyes. Not but a few minutes later, he heard the approach of two sets of footsteps. Agnes's voice echoed off the empty corridor walls, but Sully's ears rang so loudly that although he knew it was Aggy, he couldn't make out the words.

"You're free to go, Agent Buckingham," a woman's voice filtered through the noise.

Sully looked out to see the guard known as Graham. He nodded to himself. Wise. A witness who was not on their side.

"Right. I've got Collection prep to see to." Roy lingered for a moment, perhaps to make sure that someone was there to save Agnes from Sully? Sully couldn't be sure.

Agnes opened the door, stepping through with his head still turned to eye the guards over his shoulder. "You've got a couple new assets to train, don't you?"

"Yeah," Roy nodded, running a hand through his short dark hair. He looked nervous. And the conversation *almost* sounded scripted. Sully hoped the other guard didn't notice.

It all happened in a heartbeat—that was how it had to be. Sully tackled Agnes to the ground. Using his full weight to press Agnes into the cold stone floor in a way that was familiar and different all at once.

Agnes's hands flew up to protect himself, but not quick enough.

Sully didn't waste any time, his punches landed hard and fast to the elegant line of Agnes's cheekbone, feeling something break beneath them.

Damn it.

"Get it off me!" Agnes shrieked, feebly fighting back. He wasn't even trying! Why wasn't he trying? Another blow landed to Agnes's jaw, and Sully had to hold back a wince. Those graceful features were going to be black and blue by the time he was finished.

Make it look good, Sully reminded himself, driving his fist into Agnes's shoulder. He kept hitting him until he felt a shock of electricity rush through him, causing every muscle in his body to jolt and shiver. He jerked, and rolled onto the cold floor, looking over at Agnes who was panting for a moment.

Then . . . darkness.

Blissful darkness.

Cold radiated from the ice pack on Agnes's cheekbone as it left behind a wet patch of skin. A medic tutted, pacing around the chair.

"You should never have been left alone with that beast." Her voice was high and nasal, and it made Agnes's ears ache. "You're lucky to be alive."

"Right. Lucky," Agnes muttered, wondering if this is what lucky felt like. He supposed he couldn't be too angry with Sully. After all, Sully was only doing as he'd been told. Make it look good, that's what he'd told Sully. And a broken cheekbone definitely made it look good.

I should have told him not to go for the face. It was too late for such thoughts now, so he merely laid back on the hard cot and let the medic fuss over him. It wouldn't take long at all to recover. When properly treated, a creature with as much magic as he had could heal in under a week. It was merely a matter of letting the medic clean him up and getting whatever tinctures she thought necessary applied.

"Honestly, I don't know what the hell you were thinking." She was clucking still, her magic weaving in glittering waves through the air. "Were you trying to be some kind of hero?"

Agnes snorted, then winced when it irritated his sensitive nasal passages.

"Him? A hero?" Kore called from the door with a snicker. "As if 95 could be anything of the sort."

"Kore, how kind of you to come and check on me." Agnes sat up so that he could get a better look at her.

"You look like shit." Agent Kore positioned herself at the side of the cot, towering over him as best she could.

"Always a delight, Agent Kore." Agnes's eyes flicked over her, drinking in the smug expression on her face. "What do you want?"

She waited a beat, and when she finally spoke, it was in a tone of superiority. "Word just came down: you've been deemed incompetent. You're no longer in charge of questioning the kelpie. That honor will be left to me."

Incompetent. Even if that had been the plan all along, Agnes's pride chafed at the word.

"Well, if you think you can do a better job," he grumbled begrudgingly.

"I know I can," Kore's eyes flicked over him once more. Assessing, and finding him wanting. She patted the bed beside his leg. "You get some rest, 95."

Agnes nodded, slumping back onto the cot again as Kore turned to leave.

"Agent," he called after her as if maybe he'd just realized something. She stilled and waited. "I'd like to be there when you question him."

She turned to him once more, her eyes narrowing on him. Her pink tongue flicked out to lick over a dry lower lip before shrugging. "Be my guest. We start in a few days. I hope you're better by then."

Without another word, she turned to leave him to the medic's care again.

"DID he have to hit you quite so hard?" Penny asked with a wince, her fingers brushing lightly over his bruised cheekbone.

Agnes swatted her away, growling. "Leave it."

Penny huffed and crossed the small sitting room to sit beside Gladys who stared into the crackling fire. The old pixie's wings fluttered reflexively.

"You don't need to be nasty to her, Agnes," Gladys chided.

He grumbled, crossing his arms over his chest. "Tell me what's going on with Sully," Agnes demanded.

The two women shifted.

"What is it?"

"He's not doing well," Penny blurted.

Agnes felt his heart constrict, his mind filling with images of a bleeding Sully.

Gladys sighed, finally turning her sympathetic gaze from the fire to Agnes. "Kore has removed the cot you gave him. He's not being allowed to bathe."

"No food, or water," Penny added unhelpfully.

Gladys nodded. "And they're leaving the light on in the cell to try to keep him from sleeping."

"Have either of you seen him?" Agnes was surprised by how tight his voice sounded.

They shook their heads.

"Roy says he's holding up all right," Penny murmured in a half-assed attempt to comfort him. "In spite of it, he says Sullivan's spirits are high."

"I'll be in to see him tomorrow," Agnes said, mostly to himself.

"That'll help." Gladys smiled. She reached one wrinkled

hand to give Agnes's a comforting squeeze. "You'll both be out of here soon, Agnes."

Agnes nodded and fell silent. He stared into the fire, doing his best to keep the images of Sully hurting from his mind.

MORNING CAME MUCH TOO EARLY for Agnes. He pawed at his face, wincing when he irritated the bruises.

"Damn it." He wanted nothing more than to curl back up in his bed and sleep off the pain. That wasn't an option. He rolled out of bed and dragged himself into the bathroom to get ready for the day ahead.

The vindictive child waited for him outside Sully's cell. Her fingers jerked in excitement while she donned an almost-pleasant smile.

"What're we waiting on?" Agnes asked.

Agent Kore turned her eyes up to him, a horrible glint in their insipid depths as the grin on her face spread into something manic.

The ticking sound of clockwork announced the arrival of a tiny droid. In its outstretched arms was a tray laden in sharp instruments from knives to scalpels. Agnes felt his stomach give a harsh twist and thanked the gods he hadn't eaten breakfast.

"We've tried your way." Kore's voice was barely above a whisper, excitement in every breath. "Now we'll try mine."

Agnes swallowed roughly, maintaining a careful mask of indifference. "Right then. I suppose we ought to get started?"

Kore took no further prompting, she headed into the cell with the robot hot on her heels. The instruments on the tray jiggled noisily as it walked, putting one unsteady foot in front of the other.

Agnes filed in behind them, taking up a position close to the door so that the light didn't shine quite as well on Sully.

Sully had been chained to the chair again, vulnerable and unable to protect himself. *Surely, there has to be another way*, Agnes thought. No, he knew it had to seem like the information was hard to get out of Sully. If it didn't, then it wouldn't be accepted as true. He took a deep breath and tried to brace himself.

Kore pulled a serrated knife from the tray, pressing her finger to the blade to draw a pinprick of blood.

"Sharp," she murmured—almost to herself, but her eyes pinned Sully to his chair.

Sully, for his part, lifted one black brow, a smug grin settling onto his handsome features. "Yes, knives generally are."

"Oh, it wants to talk now?" Kore laughed hollowly. She took a step forward, pressing the point of the blade lightly to Sully's forearm—not hard enough to draw blood, yet, but enough to get her point across. "What is the Uprising plotting?" she asked in a childish sing-song tone.

Sully merely laughed, his eyes dancing with derision and amusement. "Am I supposed to be afraid of you and your knives, little girl?"

With a wicked glint, the knife slashed through the air and into the skin of Sully's forearm. Agnes's gut twisted, his heart pounding in his ears as his eyes fell upon the pooling of blood atop Sully's skin. It oozed slowly from the cut, over his arm, and down to the floor. Agnes felt the bile rise in his throat and blood pool in his mouth from biting his tongue to hold back a whimper.

Sully didn't flinch. His expression remained bemused, unfazed by the blood slowly seeping from his skin.

"What are they planning?"

Sully's deep, rich chuckle filled the cell again, his eyes twinkling with humor. "Why? You looking to join up? We are always looking for fresh meat."

The second slice of the knife crisscrossed the first, leaving another jagged line.

Two. Agnes counted in his head, his hands clenching at his sides.

Sully continued to meet Kore's eyes with an expression of sheer indifference. Agnes wished Sully would just give her what she wanted. Get this all over with. But he knew better; Sully had to make this look good. Which meant withstanding as much torture as possible.

"This will go a lot more smoothly if you just tell me," Kore said. She seemed uninterested in actually getting an answer. The cuts on his arm weren't particularly deep, but they didn't need to be if they bled plenty.

Sully's only response was to shrug.

Three. The next cut, closer to the bend in Sully's elbow, and a little too close to the vein pulsing under the skin for Agnes's comfort.

Four. This cut was on Sully's well-muscled upper arm. The blood trailed down to meet the pool at the bend in his arm.

Five. Kore sliced into the bulge of his shoulder muscle, but Sully continued to eye her impassively. Agnes's ears rang, making it hard for him to hear Kore's questions.

Kore got sick of repeating the same question over and over, it would seem. "Where is their next target?"

"Wouldn't you like to know?" Sully countered cheekily and winked.

Six.

Seven.

Eight left a crimson star on the spot where Agnes had

once kissed Sully's heart. He felt his own heart clench, wishing he could reach for Kore and put a stop to this. But it wasn't time for that yet. Soon it would be, but not yet.

Nine cut a jagged line across Sully's well-defined collarbone. Agnes remembered brushing his fingers over it lovingly not but twenty years ago.

Ten. The opposing chest muscle where Agnes had once rested his head was flayed open, and gushing. Agnes's throat was already raw from the bile, and the excessive swallowing around a dry mouth. He felt the sting of his nails leaving crescent-shaped cuts in his palms. It took everything he had in him to maintain in control enough not to snatch the knife from Kore's hand and drive it into her instead.

"Who's the mole?" Kore asked, changing tactics once more.

Sully laughed in response. "You mean you don't know?"

Agnes tried to meet Sully's eyes, he wanted to tell Sully to just give him up. Just tell her what she wanted, so this could all stop. But Sully kept his eyes firmly on the girl with the knife tip pressed to his stomach.

Eleven and *twelve* slashed across Sully's muscled stomach. Agnes followed the lines of the blood weeping down over his bare torso and could see sweat beginning to coat Sully's dark skin. The torture was starting to get to him, even if Sully wasn't showing it. How much more of this could he take?

"No. Why don't you share?" Kore continued conversationally. She pulled the blade away, brushing the blood from it onto her brown pants, leaving behind a dark stain. "I'll have to burn these later," she muttered to herself disinterestedly before she returned her attention to the kelpie. "If you tell us, I'll leave you alone. We can send you down to the camps, and that will be that."

It sounded like a bargain to Agnes. Turn him in, end this now. That's where this was going, after all, Sully would have to turn him in. Why not do it now? Before Kore got it into her head to leave less than superficial cuts on Sully's skin. Sully wouldn't meet his eyes.

Sully quirked a brow at her. "Oh, really? That easy, huh?" He tilted his head, pretending to think about her offer. "Nah, I think I'm good."

Lucky number thirteen.

Kore leaned in close, almost on her tiptoes to press the tip of the serrated blade to Sully's temple. Agnes flinched, his eyes squeezing shut, as she dragged the blade from that point down over Sully's cheekbone toward his jaw. A sob ripped Agnes's eyes open in time to see the rough *L* gushing angrily.

Sully sobbed again, and Agnes felt something within him break. He couldn't do this anymore. He couldn't sit back and watch Sully be sliced to ribbons.

"It's me," Agnes rasped. "I'm the mole. It's me."

Kore whipped around, her hands still tightly gripping the hilt of the blade. "What was that, 95?"

The room stilled.

The robot, who up until that point had remained utterly motionless, turned its glowing gaze on Agnes. And Sully —*Oh gods, Sully*—his chest was heaving, but he met Agnes's gaze fiercely. This was it.

"I am the Uprising's mole," Agnes said calmly and clearly. "I have been for a very long time. Since before you were born, even." He let his tone drift into the casual. As if it didn't matter.

A scream of rage reverberated off the stone walls, the knife flashed in the dim light, and then Kore was on him. She knocked him to the ground, the cold floor pushing the air from his lungs. Pain shot through him as she plunged the wicked knife into his shoulder, the skin tearing beneath its jagged teeth. *Once. Twice. Three times* —he counted before Graham could rip Kore off him and drag her away.

"You're going to die for this, 95!" Kore screamed shrilly. "I'll make sure of that! I'll make sure they flay you alive!" She kept screaming even as Graham dragged her from the cell, and out into the hall.

Agnes sobbed, his eyes blurring with tears from the burning pain in his shoulder. Distantly, he could hear Sully shouting and asking if he was all right. Somewhere in the back of his mind, he felt the blood staining his elegant waistcoat. *Well, that's one outfit ruined.*

A pair of MOTHER agents rushed into the cell to drag Agnes to his feet and lock his wrists in irons. Agnes looked over at Sully, whose cheeks were inexplicably wet—had he been crying?

"It's going to be all right now," he promised just before they dragged him out of the cell and down the corridor.

IN RETROSPECT, Agnes realized, perhaps that hadn't been exactly true. His gaze flicked around the cell they'd locked him in—it was much like Sully's except maybe smaller. Cold stone walls, a hard floor, and no furniture in sight to relax upon. He sunk to his bottom against the wall with his knees to his chest. Perhaps he should have fought the guards and tried to wait to see if Sully received proper medical care before he was carted off. But what was done, was done.

Now, locked away in his own cell, he was in the dark in more ways than one. Worry gnawed at his belly, making him feel a little sick. Or maybe that was the blood dribbling from the jagged wound on his shoulder. Either way, he felt light-headed and nauseous. The darkness of the little stone room didn't make it better. Without any light to act as a place marker, the room spun around him, and he couldn't quite gain purchase.

So, he waited, hoping and praying that soon, one of his assets would come and see him. Penny, maybe? Or Gladys? Someone who could give him an update on Sully's condition. Minutes slipped into hours, and hours into what felt like days.

"Agnes," someone whispered, finally, through the barred window on the cell door. "Agnes?" the voice asked again, drawing Agnes out of a dream-like state of half-consciousness.

"Yeah. I'm in here. I'm alive," Agnes slurred. He stood, wobbling on his feet, to make his way to the door.

Upon peering through, he found the earnest gaze of Roy staring back at him.

"Good ol' Roy," he muttered to himself.

Roy frowned deeply as Agnes came into the light, his eyes flicking to the stain of blood on Agnes's waistcoat.

"It's not as bad as it looks."

The young agent shook his head. "Have they had a medic in to see you?"

A hollow laugh left Agnes at the ludicrous question. "No, and I don't expect they will. I'll be surprised if Kore even lets me live till trial."

"Yeah . . . she was really pissed." Roy sighed, rubbing his face. "Agnes, she wants you dead."

Agnes giggled manically at the thought. "Well, she might not have much longer to wait."

Blood loss. Infection. The noose. One of them would kill Agnes sooner rather than later.

"I could—I could bring you a medic. You ought to at least have that cleaned."

Agnes shook his head, slumping more fully against the door. Roy was a good man—too good—even before he'd fallen in love with Penny and joined the Uprising. Their people would need him. "There's no sense in you getting yourself into trouble. You've got work to do. Get our people out."

"What about . . . what about you?"

Agnes resisted the urge to snort and ask, 'What about me?'

"Keep your ear to the ground, and find out where they're taking us. Once you know, give Manu and Persinette any information you have. They'll take care of the rest." Taking a deep breath, Agnes met those earnest eyes levelly. "But don't get too caught up in what happens to Sully and me. You focus on your work. You get our people out, make sure they're safe. I promised them that, and you're going to have to deliver."

Roy nodded. "Yes, sir."

With that out of the way, Agnes moved on to what he really needed to know. "Sully?"

A frown etched Roy's face, and he took a deep breath. "He's in rough shape, but at least he's been seen by a medic. We had someone in there the moment you were dragged out. I convinced my superiors that it wouldn't do us any good if he bled out, and he'd be more useful at the camps. He should be all right."

Relief washed over Agnes, his muscles relaxing, and a deep exhale leaving him.

"Good." Now, maybe, he could die in peace.

"Can I get you anything?" Roy asked.

"No. Thank you, Roy. I'll be all right. It'll all be over

soon," he whispered, slinking back into the darkness of the cell, to sink to the floor again.

Sully would be safe.

Whatever happened to him now didn't matter.

Not so long as Sully was safe.

"He's late," Benard said, tapping a fingernail on the windowsill of the empty shop they leaned against.

"Only by a few minutes." Persinette checked her pocket watch.

"What if this is a trap?" Owen asked, his arms crossed over his chest, eyes sharp as he scanned the empty street.

They'd parked themselves there in the shadow of a tattered gray awning of the empty building, far enough away to not be bothered, but not so far that when Roy 'happened' upon them, it would look suspicious.

Benard didn't like it, and he'd said as much, being out in the open like this. Persinette felt exposed, but she swallowed down the feeling in favor of putting on a brave face. Manu should have been here with them, but they had all agreed it was too dangerous, and all he'd do was draw more attention. She tugged the newsboy cap she'd stolen from Derek, the deckhand, further down over her ears to hide her short lavender hair.

"Don't worry too much," Drea said, bumping her shoulder against Persinette's. "You've got plenty of manpower with you. Nothing's gonna happen."

Persinette nodded, offering Drea a weak smile. It was nice to have her along, even if she was still a little too young in Persinette's mind. But Drea had been loyal since the beginning. Manu referred to Drea as Persinette's personal Owen, and she seemed to live up to it. Drea was strong, and steady, and a fighter. Where Felicity was happy to tinker away with the engineers, Drea preferred to spar. Still, they'd become close, like sisters. A family the likes of which Persinette had never hoped for before.

"Here he comes," Owen said, calling their attention back to the people milling about further up the road.

With his hands stuffed into his pockets, and shoulders hunched a little, Roy made his way through the crowd. He didn't make eye contact with them as he passed, just kept walking, with an almost imperceptible nod to no one in particular.

Drea grabbed Persinette's hand and let out a giggle like they'd been doing something they shouldn't have, hidden in the shadows. Then she dragged Persinette along behind Roy, racing ahead for a moment, but not far enough to lose sight of the MOTHER agent in the neighboring shop windows. The fading light of the evening was perfect for this, Persinette realized, and she had to acknowledge that between Benard and Roy, they really seemed to know what they were doing.

She didn't see them, but she knew that a few minutes later, Owen and Benard would slink from the shadows and duck down into the alley. Then they would follow them along the parallel street, to keep from drawing attention to themselves.

"I think we're clear," Persinette said as she looked back down the street.

They had gotten far enough away that the foot traffic behind them was but a blip. Amongst the abandoned buildings on the outskirts of Maximus, they could speak more freely.

"I only have an hour." Roy pulled his watch out to check the time and cursed under his breath. "Scratch that—forty-five minutes. Kore is already in a mood, if I'm late getting back to the mission, she'll skin me alive."

"Why? What happened?" Persinette felt something sour in her stomach. She didn't know anything about Kore aside from what Roy had been able to tell them. Although the girl was young, younger than even Felicity and Drea, she was ruthless, and Persinette feared what Kore would do to any of their people on the inside.

Roy's steps stuttered a little, as if he'd tripped over his own feet. He closed his eyes, inhaled deeply through his nose, and then opened them again. "Sully told her Agnes is the mole. Er—rather . . . I guess Agnes confessed to being the mole."

"Shit," Drea breathed.

"How is he?" They weren't friends, Persinette knew that. She knew that Agnes didn't even like her. Their relationship was purely one of necessity. He needed her to help him get his agents out and keep them safe. He needed her to save Sully. That was all there was to it. But she still worried.

"Not great?" Roy said it like it was a question, but it felt more like a punch, right to the stomach. And even that wasn't as bad as what he said next. "She stabbed him, and they're refusing to let him have medical treatment."

"Shit," Drea breathed again.

Persinette could only nod. She wasn't one for foul language but that word seemed to encompass how she felt in that moment.

"Anyway," Roy continued at length. He let out a whistling breath as his shoulders slumped. "We need to move fast, I think. I don't want them looking too closely at the people he associated with while he's on trial."

"Right." Persinette turned to head down the street again. "How many are we taking this time?"

"Just the two. I worry if too many escape at a time they'll start to notice what we're doing. But Violet and Henry are both out for Collections tonight."

"Won't someone notice when your Enchanted assets start going missing while on Collection missions?" Owen asked as he and Benard joined them on the main street again.

Roy stopped in front of an old apartment complex. It was all clean lines and big windows, which had since been boarded up when it fell into disrepair.

"Maybe, but Agnes was kind of counting on the fact that the agents they're in the field with will be too scared to report that an asset escaped." Roy tugged at the door, trying to get it open. "Help me with this, would ya?"

Between Drea, Owen, and Roy tugging at the door, they managed to get it open. Inside was a cold marble lobby, covered in a thick layer of dust, with two faded wingback chairs huddled together. In those chairs sat a fairy, his wings twitching nervously, and a green-skinned elf. They both startled at the noise but relaxed when they saw Roy.

"All right, Henry? All right, Violet?" Roy asked, and they both nodded wordlessly. "Great. This is Persinette and her crew. She's going to take you back to the *Duchess* and get you on your way out of here."

Persinette smiled and gave a little wave.

Roy nodded, tucking his hands back in his pockets. "Right then, I'll leave first. You lot should go out the back way. I think there's an alley that leads back toward the docks. You are at the docks, right?"

"Yeah, we didn't want to draw any more attention to ourselves than we needed." Benard cleared his throat. "Although someone fought us on the cloaking spell."

"He was just worried about that the magic would—" Persinette tried to argue.

"No." Benard clicked his tongue. "He was worried his *girl* would look ugly. Don't sugarcoat it, Persi."

Persinette shrugged. "The *Duchess* is cloaked now, isn't she?"

Benard grunted, but didn't say anything else.

"Owen and Drea, go check out the back exit. See what our route looks like. Roy, thanks for meeting with us." Persinette turned a bright smile to him. "Have a safe trip back to HQ."

"Fly safe," Roy said with a nod, and then he disappeared back out into the slowly darkening city. Drea and Owen slipped further into the lobby to check their exits.

Persinette clapped her hands lightly and turned to the awaiting Enchanted. "Okay then. Violet and Henry, let's get you two out of the city safe and sound, shall we?"

"Where are we headed?" Henry asked as he stood. He tucked his hands behind his back to hide their shaking, but Persinette had caught it.

"We've gotten a house set up for you in Ludo. You'll be safe there until we can find a more permanent solution," Benard said, all business.

"Are we just supposed to . . . hide?" Violet's voice shook a little.

"No, of course not." Persinette smiled. "It's not a very big place, and most of the people who live there are either in the Uprising, or they're Enchanted sympathizers. No one will turn you in. You'll be free."

"Free?" Henry said the word like it was a foreign concept to him.

"We know it's not much." Persinette sighed. "I wish we could offer you more than a village. But right now, we can't. To keep MOTHER from finding you again, it's either we tuck you away in small, sympathetic places or we take you to the Waste."

Violet let out an involuntary whimper, and Henry jerked as if she'd slapped him. Persinette shook her head.

"I didn't think that's what you'd want. But this is temporary, I promise."

"Temporary." Henry sounded doubtful. Persinette couldn't blame him for that. She would be doubtful too. As the world stood, it seemed there would never be a safe place for their kind.

"Things are changing." Benard moved to her side, putting a comforting hand on her shoulder. "We're making sure of that."

Persinette nodded her agreement.

"We found the back exit," Drea called, her voice echoing off the marble floors, before any more could be said. She brushed her dusty hands onto her trousers as she came back into view. "Let's get a move on before MOTHER calls out the dogs."

Violet rose from her chair, her hands pressed tight to her sides, her movements jerky.

"Hey," Persinette said quietly, drawing the girl's shining amber eyes to her. "It's going to be okay now."

Violet gulped but took Henry's hand and fell into step with the others as they headed through the lobby to the employee entrance in the back. Once there, Persinette ducked out into the alley to get a better look at what they were dealing with. Then she turned back to her small retinue.

"Everybody got their glamours on?" She waited as Violet

and Henry's faces changed like a sheet falling over them. Once they looked entirely human, Persinette nodded in satisfaction. "We're going to split up. Violet, you're with me and Owen. Benard and Drea will go with Henry. You have your routes?"

"Yes, ma'am," Owen and Drea said in unison.

"Good. Let's get a move on. If we're much longer, Manu is going to send out a search party."

Benard scoffed, rolling his eyes.

"He worries. It's sweet," Owen argued, nudging Benard lightly with his shoulder.

"It's ridiculous." But there was a little smile on Benard's lips that told Persi that he was secretly pleased.

"Less flirting, more walking," Drea grumbled, trying to push Owen toward Persinette and only managing to let out a grunt of frustration.

Owen laughed, ruffling Drea's hair. But no more was said as they broke off into their groups to head back to the ship, each group taking a different winding path back to the docks.

BENARD AND DREA'S group was the first to arrive back at the ship. Manu knew, because he was waiting for them at the loading platform with his hands raking through his impossibly mussed hair.

"Where is she?" he asked, the worry making his words break a little at the end.

"She's right behind us, Cap'n. Relax." Benard patted Manu's shoulder. "Owen is with her. She'll be here in no more than ten minutes."

"Felicity, go get our new guest settled in!" Manu barked

—perhaps a little harsher than he ought to, but Felicity didn't argue.

"Yes, sir." She jerked her head toward the platform, indicating for Henry to follow.

"I'm coming with," Drea announced, leaving Manu and Benard to wait for the others.

"I don't like this," Manu said once he heard the platform descending again toward them on the ground. "She shouldn't be out there without me."

"You're not exactly stealthy right now, sir."

"I know, but I'm supposed to have her back. That's the deal." He grabbed at his sleeves, shoving them up to his elbows in his agitation.

"Perhaps you should head inside, sir."

"No. I'll wait here. We aren't taking off without her." Manu's hands shook, so he stuffed them into his pockets to hide them away from Benard's knowing eyes.

"You know she can take care of herself, sir."

"I know that! Do you think I don't know that?"

"I think you forget, sir, that Persinette broke her hand to get out of that cell, and was ready and waiting for us with an army behind her when we arrived. Besides, imagine how angry she'd be if she found out you were underestimating her." Benard's lip settled into a frown, and he shuddered a little. "I don't think I'd want to be on that girl's bad side."

"On whose bad side?" Persinette asked, skipping up to them with a bright smile stretching her freckled face.

Before Benard could open his mouth to incriminate him, Manu said, "No one. Run into any trouble?"

"None at all. It was almost too easy. But I imagine the next pick-up won't be." Persinette loaded onto the platform with the others, before it rose slowly into the air toward the *Duchess*. "Once MOTHER catches on to what we're doing, they'll be more cautious."

"We'll have to work fast," Benard hummed in agreement.

The platform ticked into place, and the group moved toward the stairs out of the cargo hold.

"Benard, why don't you take our new guest to find Felicity and Drea?" Manu asked, and waited until he heard Benard's retreating footsteps to take Persinette's hand and give it a tight squeeze.

"I'll go make sure everything is tied down for take-off," Owen offered with a chortle.

"You do that," Manu grumbled, feeling distinctly like he was being made fun of.

Once they were gone, Persinette leaned in to brush a quick kiss to his lips. "I'm okay, really. Promise."

"I wasn't worried." Manu had always fancied himself a good liar, but he guessed that his face gave him away because Persinette just laughed.

"Of course not. Come on, let's get the course plotted. I don't want to be around here when those agents realize their assets are missing." Persinette tugged him toward the helm.

"Aye, aye, Captain."

If it weren't for the man's well-worn shoes covering the red stain on the floor, Sully wouldn't have noticed he had even entered the cell. Even as blood dripped from the cut at his temple into his eyes, he couldn't seem to drag his gaze away from Agnes's blood on the cold stone. In all their long years together, he'd never seen Agnes bleed.

"Kore really did a number on you." Sully could just barely hear the medic *tsk* over the ringing in his ears. The lanky man moved closer to get a better look at the wound on Sully's face, further blocking Sully's view of the bloodstain. He forced himself to look up at the tan face, half-covered in thick glasses and untidy hair.

"They're just flesh wounds," Sully croaked, barely caring about his injuries. The medic lifted an antiseptic soaked cotton ball to Sully's face, drawing a wince at the sharp sting. He squeezed his eyes shut to ward off the pain, but behind his lids, he could see the knife plunge into Agnes again and again. His eyes flew open with a gasp.

"Sorry," the medic muttered as if perhaps it were the bite of the needle tugging the wound shut that had caused the gasp.

Sully merely grunted. He held still, letting the man get on with his work. The sooner he was done, the sooner he'd be out of there. Then Sully could begin to formulate a plan. He needed to get to Agnes, make sure he was all right, and get them both the hell out of there. How he was going to manage such a feat, he had no idea.

"It's a real shame about Agnes," the medic tutted thoughtfully as he finished stitching Sully's face.

Sully's heart hammered in his chest at those words. He looked up to the medic's face once more, fear choking off the breath from his lungs.

"What?" Sully asked as if coming out of a deep sleep. "What about Agnes? Have you seen him? Is he all right?"

Almond eyes blinked behind his spectacles as the medic pulled back a little. His thin lips turned down into a frown, and he shook his head.

"No, I haven't," he said gently as if perhaps he realized what that meant to Sully. Maybe he did. Sully wasn't above showing how he felt at this point.

Helpless. That's what Sully was. He couldn't get to Agnes; he couldn't even stand up. There was no way for him to comfort or care for his Aggy. The realization settled into his stomach like a lead weight. He might never see Aggy again.

"But you will?" Sully asked—begged—his heart thundering in his ears.

The medic's thin lips twitched further down; he shook his head again. "I'm afraid not. Agent Kore has forbidden any medic to treat him."

A sob choked Sully, his gut twisting violently. "She can't *do that!*"

Sympathetic eyes blinked back at Sully, and the medic sighed. "Until the Council says otherwise, she can. But I wouldn't worry too much about it, they'll want him in decent shape for his trial. I'm sure they'll order someone to at least treat him to prevent infection and stop the bleeding. If nothing else."

Trial.

The word echoed in Sully's ears. Agnes was going to stand trial. And not just for a minor offense—for *treason*. Treason was a hanging offense in any province of Daiwynn.

Sully swallowed a lump in his throat that threatened to rip another sob from him. Maybe they would go easy on him. Maybe because Agnes had worked for them for so many years, he would be shown some mercy. Or perhaps that would make things all the worse. MOTHER did not like to be fooled, after all.

"I wouldn't worry too much about him," the medic said, not unkindly. "You've got yourself to worry about now."

He was just trying to help, Sully knew that. He saw the logic in the man's words. But still, Sully felt his heart clench, and his eyes burn with unshed tears. How could he lose his Aggy before he'd even really had him? Aggy was immortal—as all unicorns were—but he was not invulnerable. He could die.

"Guard," Sully called, his voice a rasp of what it had once been. When no one peeked in, he shouted, "Guard!"

Bright eyes peered at Sully from around the corner. A guard he didn't recognize frowned at him.

"What do you want?" the man snapped irritably.

"The unicorn. When will he be seen by a medic? What has the Council had to say about him?" Sully asked, desperate for anything.

The guard's only answer was a snort before he ducked back out into the hall—seeming intent on ignoring anything else Sully had to say.

"Can't you ask for me? Can't you find out?" He was begging now, there was nothing left for him. He needed to know. He needed an answer. What if Agnes was dying? Sully's chest tightened in panic, his mind reeling on the verge of hysterics. Oh, gods. What if . . .

The guard didn't answer; he just stared ahead blankly.

"Guard!" Sully shouted, voice breaking. "Guard!"

Nothing.

The medic sighed, pressing a calloused hand to Sully's shoulder. "You need to relax," he whispered just loud enough for Sully to hear. "You're going to give yourself a heart attack. I'll see what I can do about getting you some information. But please, rest."

Sully nodded, trying to will the panic to settle, but it didn't seem to want to. With it came rage like he'd rarely known before. A terrible, terrifying rage that if he weren't shackled with iron, he knew would release the demon inside of him.

"Thank you," he whispered.

"I'm Harrison," the man offered.

For a moment, it looked as if Harrison might offer his hand to shake, but then he seemed to realize the ridiculousness of such a thing.

"Now please, rest," he insisted as he finished up bandaging Sully's wounds.

"Yes, rest," Sully whispered.

When Harrison left, taking his medical bag with him, Sully tried to do just that. But peace and sleep would not come to him. Every time he closed his eyes, he saw Agnes going white with blood loss again and again.

RAGE SLIPPED AWAY from Sully as the minutes ticked by, leaving behind only a deep, empty, all-consuming sadness.

Agnes was hurting, and Sully wasn't there to help him. There was nothing in this world Sully wanted more than to hold his Aggy, stroke his hair, and take the pain away. But he was trapped in that tiny cell, chained to that uncomfortable chair. Still, he would bide his time—someday soon they would pay for hurting his Aggy.

Noise filtered down the empty corridor. Sully flexed his hands in the iron cuffs, trying to get blood flow back to his fingertips.

He lifted his head at the sound of approaching footsteps. "Oi, have you brought me dinner?"

"No," came a sharp voice from beyond the door. Then there was a face on the other side of the barred window, backlit by the lights in the hall. Something rattled, out of view, but Sully paid it no mind as he squinted to try to make out the face.

"Then what?"

"We have some more questions."

Ah. Now the rattling made sense. They were going to torture him again. "Bring it on."

"Very good. Very good. Let's hope that can-do attitude continues." The man tutted as the door to Sully's cell opened with a creak. He pushed a little cart with a tray full of instruments into the room, metal clattering against metal.

"Oh look. You brought toys!" Sully said with mock cheerfulness, sitting up a little straighter in his seat. "Hi, I'm Sullivan Hunter. I'd shake your hand but . . . well . . ." Sully laughed, his eyes not straying to the tray of instruments. "I'm a little tied up."

"Andrew Gothel. But you can call me Andrew." Andrew didn't meet his eyes. His focus remained solely on reorganizing the items on the tray, straightening them into neat little rows.

It was a gesture so similar to Agnes, it made Sully physically ache. He swallowed it down, squeezed his eyes shut for a moment, and centered himself. He had to be ready for this, whatever this was.

"Ask me no questions, and I'll tell you no lies."

"Is that how you're going to play it?" Andrew asked, tone conversational more so than threatening.

Sully nodded.

Andrew sighed, his hands falling limp on the edges of the tray so as not to disturb the instruments upon it. "I don't suppose I could persuade you to change your mind?"

Sully shook his head.

"I thought as much. I heard about your resistance to Agent Kore's torture. And then the way you lunged to protect that *unicorn* . . ." Andrew shook his head, clicking his tongue in admonishing disapproval. "No, I didn't think you'd be easy to turn on him."

Sully snorted, rolled his eyes, and held his tongue. He didn't particularly care for the way *Andrew* was talking about Agnes, but it wouldn't do any good to get the man angry. That would just make the torture worse, and Sully wasn't so sure he'd survive another bought of blood loss like the one he'd suffered at the hands of Kore. And he had to. He had to survive. Otherwise, who would save Agnes?

"And what if he's turned on you already? What if he's told us everything we need to know?" Andrew asked, lifting a wicked looking instrument up to the light as if to see how sharp it was. It looked like a potato peeler, but Sully didn't have to be a telepath to know that Andrew wasn't planning to use it on potatoes. "If I were you, I'd get ahead of him. Give us what we want, and they'll go easier on you down at the camps."

"No."

"So loyal." Andrew shook his head, setting down the

device with a decisive click of metal on metal. Then he picked up another—a scalpel. "But how loyal is he to you?"

"Look, if this is some new torture tactic, it's not working. Get on with the pain and put us both out of our misery." Sully slumped back into his chair, doing his best to look relaxed and bored even as his eyes remained trained on Andrew.

Andrew laughed, but the smile splitting his handsome face didn't quite reach his eyes which remained unwrinkled and too sharp. "So eager."

The scalpel was sat back in the neat little row with a *clink*, and Andrew turned from his instruments to meet Sully's eyes at last. Sully knew him, though he wasn't sure from where exactly. Perhaps he'd been one of the agents who'd helped bring him in. Or maybe he'd been a guard at some point. It didn't matter. What mattered was that where Kore was all hot fury, threatening to burn them both alive, Andrew was cold and detached. Andrew was *dangerous*.

"What do you want to know?" Sully asked, lifting a brow in curiosity.

"Will you answer my questions honestly?"

"Maybe. Maybe not. Who's ta say." Sully got sick satisfaction from the way Andrew's eye twitched a little. A moment later, the impassive mask was back. But it was enough of a crack for Sully to see the man underneath. Enough to know what buttons to push to frustrate Andrew into leaving.

"Don't be impertinent."

"Why not? It's so fun!"

Another twitch. Almost imperceptible if Sully hadn't been looking for it. Just above the mole under Andrew's right eye. Sully wondered how much longer Andrew would be able to keep this up before he lashed out.

"Unless you're ready to get down to it," Sully offered,

flashing a cheeky smile. "Because like I said, the sooner you do your thing, the sooner I get to take a nap."

"You know there are no doctors in the camps. Just med droids, if those are even still working. I don't know, I haven't been to one since I was a child."

"You're still a child." Sully snorted. It was true, Andrew looked to be no older than thirty, if he was a day over twenty-five. In every way that mattered, he was a child.

If Sully hadn't been looking for it, he would have missed the subtle clench of Andrew's hands on the tray as his knuckles turned white. "What relationship do you have with the unicorn?"

Sully flinched, whether visibly or not, he wasn't sure, but he flinched. This seemed to satisfy Andrew as his smile stretched a little more toward something genuine causing the corner of his right eye to wrinkle just a little.

"We don't have one."

Andrew sighed, reaching for a book of matches that Sully hadn't noticed before on the tray. "No?"

"No."

"You know what I hate?" Andrew struck a match, his dark eyes glittering in the flame as he watched it burn down toward his fingers.

"No. Why don't you tell me?"

"Liars." Andrew tossed the match at Sully's chest. It went out before it hit his skin, but the embers stung.

"Then I hate to break it to you, sweetheart: you're in the wrong line of work." Sully barked a laugh.

Andrew lit another match this time pressing the still lit tip dangerously close to the tender skin on the inside of Sully's wrist. "Do you love him?"

"Do you even know what that word means?" Sully shot back, grinding his teeth to force his hand from clenching as

Andrew pressed the match to his wrist, burning a neat circle into the tender skin.

"I'm asking the questions here." Andrew shook out the match and grabbed another from the little book.

"I think I told you that if you asked me no questions, I'd tell you no lies." Sully forced a smile, pressing his back molars together to keep from panting against the pain.

"So cheeky." Andrew shook his head, lighting another match. "95 had men inside. I want names."

"Don't let your wants hurt you."

Andrew pressed the match into the skin just above the other burn, creating a searing line of bubbling flesh that left Sully's heart pounding against his ribs.

It went on that way until the matchbook was empty. When it was, Andrew looked down at the folded cardboard as if it had disappointed him somehow. Then he shook his head. "You aren't helping him by staying silent."

"I'm not hurting him either." Sully breathed through clenched teeth.

"He doesn't love you, you know," Andrew said as he pushed the tray over toward the door.

"And you'd know that how?"

"Unicorns aren't capable of love. No Enchanted is." He shrugged, as if it were the most obvious thing in the world. "I'll see you tomorrow, Sullivan. Till then, get some rest."

The door slid shut quietly, leaving Sully with just the ache of raw skin and the dark. He closed his eyes and tried to force himself to sleep.

The blood was still oozing from Agnes's shoulder, but it had slowed, and cooled, leaving a trail of slimy congealed grossness. Agnes had become numb to the sensation hours ago.

Or was it days?

He couldn't be sure anymore.

They hadn't bothered to turn on any lights in his cell, and the darkness distorted everything around him from his perception of time to the sounds in the corridor beyond.

He was probably going to die here.

Alone.

Cold.

Bleeding.

But then he'd always known that would be his end, hadn't he? There was no good way out of this game of chicken he was playing with MOTHER and the Uprising. One would think that Agnes had come to terms with his own demise decades ago. Still, it came as a surprise. Perhaps it was the nature of the situation. How it had been a girl — not much older than a child — to drive the knife into his shoulder, a little too close to his heart. Or maybe it was the expression on Sully's face as he'd watched, helpless to do anything to stop it.

Agnes shook the image away. That was not how he wanted to remember Sully in his final moments. No, Agnes wanted to remember Sully laughing, and smiling. The way he had in that little cabin all those years ago. Agnes wanted to remember their short time in that oasis, the one Agnes had carved out for them in a world that was threatening to tear them both apart. It had been so nice. Peaceful, in its way. Warm.

He wasn't sure how long he lost himself to those thoughts, but it seemed an abrupt shock when the door to the cell opened. Light burned his eyes as someone flicked the switch on the outside of the wall. Agnes squinted to try to make out the face, but it was a struggle.

"Still alive?" the man asked, dropping what sounded like a duffle bag to the floor.

"If that's what you want to call it," Agnes croaked around a dry throat. Honestly, he was surprised he hadn't gone into shock, but he supposed his own stubbornness wouldn't let him. That oblivion would have been preferable, but he'd always been a mule about things.

The man snorted but said nothing else as he crouched in front of Agnes and pushed his soiled shirt from his shoulders to join the waistcoat on the floor.

"I thought I was going to be left here to die."

Maybe you still will be, Agnes's mind supplied helpfully.

The man hummed, pulling gauze from the bag. "Kore would like that. But you have to stand trial."

"Oh, so you're here to treat me so I can face the executioner's block?" Agnes rolled his eyes. There was something hilariously poetic about the idea that they'd send a medic down just so that they could then execute him. "How kind."

"Something like that." The man chuckled, and Agnes

found his eyes finally focusing a little. He didn't recognize the man before him, all thick graying beard, and shining hazel eyes. That was probably done intentionally. Lest he convince the medic to let him out, or pass along a message for him.

"Who are you?"

"Grayson."

"You gonna stitch that up, Grayson?" Agnes asked, studiously avoiding looking the gaping wound in the face. It would be easier to ignore it if he didn't see it, or so he told himself anyhow.

"That is not on the agenda, no." Grayson finished cleaning up the wound, and wrapped it with a bandage.

"You're just going to leave it all . . . gaping open and gross? It won't heal right that way." Agnes clenched his jaw as Grayson pressed perhaps a little harder than need be on the wound.

"My orders were to not stitch you up." Grayson shrugged, putting his supplies back into the bag at his feet.

"Yeah, but what about your Hippocratic oath? Surely you can't leave a person just bleeding out like I am." Was he begging? Gods, Agnes hoped he didn't sound like he was begging. Begging was pathetic, and he was not pathetic. But at the same time something vicious and disgusted squirmed inside of him at the thought that the wound would be left open. What if something got in it? All of the germs in the cell would surely infect him. He'd wind up dead before they'd even reached a verdict.

Grayson stood, slinging the duffle over his shoulder. There was a hard light to his eyes that hadn't been there a moment ago, something dark and twisted that Agnes had seen too many times in his years with MOTHER not to recognize.

Hatred.

"You're not a person, 95. My Hippocratic oath does not apply to things like you. My conscience is clear." He nodded to himself, as if that made the whole speech that much more valid. It did not.

"You're deluded." Agnes laughed, wheezing, as the manic fear twisted up his throat threatening to take him over. "You all are! Delusional children!"

Panicking.

That's what he was doing, panicking. That wasn't good. Agnes drew in a wheezing breath to try to calm himself, but it didn't do anything.

Grayson narrowed his eyes. "Children? At least we don't play with people's lives like you *creatures* do."

Agnes snorted, choking on another hysterical half-sob of laughter. "Play with people's lives? I've been alive for over a hundred years, boy, and let me tell you, the only *creatures* I've seen toying with others' lives is your kind."

If it weren't for the shaking of Grayson's hand around the leather handle of his duffle, Agnes would have thought the man was completely calm. But he wasn't. No, Agnes was getting to him. Agnes wasn't sure what he was trying to accomplish in doing so. Maybe he just wanted to hurt someone before he didn't have a chance to anymore. Maybe he just wanted to take one more MOTHER agent down with him. He couldn't tell, and he didn't care to dig too deeply to find out.

"So next time you get all sanctimonious, remember that almost every being you've hunted has seen more of the world than you could ever imagine. There is more history flowing through their veins than you could ever hope for. And long before humans started a war with us, we were just trying to live in peace. Think about that when your head hits the pillow tonight!" Agnes spat the words, his heart pounding in his ears. He could feel the wound on his shoulder bleeding more, but he didn't care—he was going to leave a mark.

The sharp sting of Grayson's meaty hand on Agnes's cheek wasn't a surprise. He'd been expecting it. He was just impressed the man had maintained enough control to hit him with an open hand. It wouldn't leave a bruise the way a fist might.

Another high-pitched laugh ripped its way out of Agnes's throat. He threw his head back, letting it vibrate around the dank cell.

And Agnes kept laughing, even as Grayson slammed the cell door behind him. Even as tears streamed from his eyes. Even as his throat was left raw and aching. Even as every part of himself told him to stop.

He couldn't stop.

He laughed.

AGNES STARTED COUNTING his time in meals, as there was no other way to determine its passage.

Six meals of molded cheese, stale bread, and some sour, mushy substance that once might have passed for porridge. Whether that meant it had been two days, or six, or even ten, he wasn't sure. But he knew there had been six meals.

The door opened with a creak, and then something coarse and light smacked Agnes in the face.

"Put it on," a gruff voice ordered. "We can't have you showing up for your trial half naked."

Agnes struggled with the shirt for a moment, wincing when the motion pulled at the still-healing wound on his shoulder. He carefully avoided looking down at the bandage, knowing it was probably caked with blood and dirt at this point.

"Not naked, but it's okay if I'm bleeding to death, right?" Agnes snarked, his head popping out from the shirt to glare at the shadowed, blurry figure in the doorway.

"Stand up," the figure ordered.

With trembling legs, Agnes forced himself to his feet. But the moment he stood, his knees gave way and he flopped back down onto the hard floor with a groan. Maybe it *had* been six meals in ten days? He hadn't been this weak when he'd been thrown into the cell.

"I said stand up!"

"I would if I co-uld." Agnes's voice came out weaker than he intended it to, breaking on the last word. "S'tired."

"Useless." The figure lumbered forward and hefted Agnes up by his uninjured shoulder. *Small mercies.* "Ugh, it stinks."

"I'm sure you'd smell like a daisy after being locked in a cell for . . . how long's it been?" Agnes's head listed to the side as the figure dragged him out into the brightness of the hall. He squeezed his eyes shut to keep the light from burning his retinas any more than it already had.

"We've gotta throw it in the showers before the trial. No one is going to want to even look at it like this."

"Yeah, sure. There's about half an hour till the trial. That enough time?" another blurry figure asked in a higher-pitched voice. Likely a woman. But Agnes's vision was so hazy he couldn't make anything out through the crack between his lashes.

"It'll have to be." The first figure clicked their tongue in disgust. "Help me get it to the showers."

What followed was a painful ordeal of being dragged along as his feet stumbled to keep up. Neither of the

MOTHER agents seemed keen on slowing their pace just so Agnes could walk for himself. His feet tripped over each other uselessly half the time, and the other half his toes dragged the floor.

What felt like seconds later, he was sat on the hard floor of one of the big shower rooms, and cold water pelted him from above. Rainbow hair clung to his shoulders, but Agnes didn't even try to scrub himself. That was too much work, and between the shivering from the water, and his trembling from lack of food, it would be useless anyhow.

The water still wasn't running clear when it was turned off abruptly, and Agnes was dragged to an upright position again. Better than nothing he supposed.

"It still stinks," the first guard complained again.

"Whatever. We're out of time. Besides, if they're just going to put it down, it doesn't matter."

No, it didn't matter. If MOTHER was going to execute Agnes for his crimes, then what would it matter if his hair was greasy and knotted? What would it matter if he'd been in the same clothes for days? It wouldn't.

Still, he could feel the dirt clinging to him. The germs slowly but surely seeping into his skin where they would infect him. It was like a thin layer of something crawled across his skin.

The room was silent when the two guards dragged Agnes inside, and threw him into a hard wooden chair in the box. He'd seen only a handful of others like himself thrown into this box after they'd gotten caught. But he'd never seen the tiny courtroom so full before. Even without being able to make out faces, the vague shapes of bodies were enough to tell him that the room was packed to the brim.

"Asset 95, you are charged with treason in the first

degree," someone said—the judge he supposed, as the voice came from the front of the room. "How do you plead?"

That same manic laugh from before crawled up Agnes's throat, threatening to choke him if he didn't let it out.

So he did.

FIFTEEN
SULLY

Sully wasn't too sure how long it had been since Andrew had left, and was even less sure how long it had been since Agnes had been dragged away. Was Agnes even still alive? Had he been seen by someone? Would they make sure he was healthy enough before sentencing him? Would Sully ever see him again? Or was . . .

No. That couldn't be the last time.

The fall of footsteps outside his door drew Sully out of his melancholy. His eyes flicked to the barred window as two hulking guards came into view.

"Something I can help you gentlemen with?" Sully asked.

All he received for his trouble was a grunt of annoyance as the door opened.

"Yes, my day is going quite well," Sully said, half wondering if he could annoy them enough that they'd throw him in whatever hole they'd thrown Agnes down.

No such luck. The guards flanked him, and dragged him to his feet, where Sully swayed precariously on legs made of jelly. How much blood had he lost over the last month? He supposed it didn't matter now; it was over. It was all over.

They didn't say as much, but Sully knew that wherever they were taking him now would be his final destination.

They dragged him from the cell, supporting much of his weight between them.

"Where are we headed, guys? Am I going to get some fresh air and sunlight finally? I must say, that will be a treat." He snickered.

Neither guard seemed to pay him any mind, dragging him with his feet skidding against the floor.

"So, do I get a name from my rescuers?" Sully didn't expect any answer, but he was enjoying being sassy far too much, so he chattered on. "If I'm going to write a thank-you note, I ought to have a name to use on it."

The guards continued in their stony silence, giving him nothing—not even a glance—in response.

"You know, if you're taking me to be executed or something, I think I get a last meal. Right? Isn't that a thing MOTHER still does?"

All the while, Sully's eyes surveyed the changing landscape. They traveled past empty cell after empty cell—the corridor where they had held him remained silent but for his chatter. No sign of beautiful rainbow hair was anywhere in sight.

"I mean if it's up to me—I think I'd like a steak. Rare, if you please. With a side of cheesy scalloped potatoes, and a nice cold pint." He continued to yammer, and they dragged him down another long hall to an elevator. "Oh, or maybe a cheeseburger. I always did fancy those things. With a brioche bun and smoked gouda. Yummm."

That, it would seem, was too much for the guard to his right. For in the next moment, the large man clocked Sully over the head with his closed fist.

"Shut up," he growled.

"Right. Shutting up," Sully muttered, his eyes squeezing shut to prevent the room from spinning.

After a moment, Sully forced them open again, for fear he might miss a sign of Agnes on his way, but there was none. Not a single strand of brightly colored hair. Just gray, brown, and more gray. By the time they made it to another gray room, Sully felt his heart pounding in his chest. What if they executed Sully? What if the last time had been the *last* time he saw his Aggy? He swallowed roughly and told himself not to think on it, at least not for now.

The door to this new cell swung open to reveal a slightly larger room. Along the walls were metal tables lined with nasty looking instruments. Perched in the middle of the room—beneath a glaringly bright spotlight—was a metal chair with iron restraints attached to both armrests, and the front legs. In a dusty laundry bin near the door were stacked shabby uniforms that may have once been white.

Sully didn't fight—what point would there have been?

He let them drag him to the chair and strap him to it. Both guards moved to stand just outside the door, leaving him to the hands of two other agents. A buzzing electric razor was brought forward, and one of the agents shaved away his tightly curled hair and the stubble on his face, leaving him bare for perhaps the first time in all his life. When the buzzing of the razor died away, a humming sound replaced it. Sully's dark eyes fell on the tattoo gun as it moved closer.

After a few minutes, it left behind a number that burned like a brand on the tender skin of his forearm.

An agent released him from the chair while the other thrust a dingy uniform into his lap.

"What's this? Pajamas? Do I get a nap now?" Sully asked with a slow grin. Was it a good idea to be testing his captors? Maybe not, but Sully needed a minute with their backs turned to tuck his pocket watch away someplace safe.

He didn't get that minute. What he got was a harsh smack to the unstitched side of his face, hard enough to jar his stitches, eliciting a wince.

"Change. Now," the guard ordered.

The small trinket had never felt so heavy in his pocket before. It seemed to weigh at least ten pounds, reminding him that if he lost it, he'd be breaking a promise to Agnes. It was silly—Sully knew that—but he'd kept the little watch for this long, and he wasn't willing to part with it.

"Nah, you know, I think I'm good. I'm kind of attached to this outfit." Sully gestured to the torn and bloody pair of pants and nonexistent shirt.

The younger guard blinked wide green eyes at him as if she were confused—maybe she didn't know what sarcasm was. The male guard was unamused. Sully heard the drag of something hard and metal across the table behind him. He didn't pay it much mind, until that piece of metal connected with his head. Sending him reeling to the floor, his ears ringing. Sully lifted a hand to the back of his head, wincing at the welt he found forming there.

"No more games," the guard barked at him over the ringing in his ears. "Put on the damn uniform."

Sully nodded too quickly, the motion making his head spin. Still, he pulled the uniform top over his bald head, tucking the watch into the folds of the dingy fabric, then undid his pants, and kicked them toward the tufts of tightly curled hair. He took his time—carefully hiding the watch in the folds as he tugged up the pants.

"Don't make me bust open that pretty face of yours again," the guard threatened, still brandishing a heavy-looking metal pipe. That must have been what had left Sully's ears ringing.

In a movement clumsy from blood loss and one too many blows to the head, Sully tried to tuck the watch into the pocket of his new uniform without the guards noticing. It slipped from his fingers into what he thought was a pocket, but was actually just a fold in the pants, and clattered to the floor.

"What's that there?" the guard called, stepping forward to get a better look.

"Nothing," Sully lied. It sounded pathetic even to his own ears. He scooped up the watch quickly.

"It'd be better for all of us if you just handed it over," the woman murmured, biting her lip.

"I don't have anything," Sully said, squeezing his hand around the metal so hard he feared it'd give. He wanted to tell her that it was easier said than done to hand over the little watch. It wasn't as if the item was particularly valuable, or even beautiful as it once had been. But Agnes seemed so far away now, and a foolish part of Sully thought he needed to cling to this last piece of his unicorn.

The male guard had had enough; he swung the pipe hard and fast at the knuckles turned white from Sully's tight grip. With a yelp, pain shot up Sully's arm, making him drop the watch.

It fell to the ground with a hollow echo that Sully felt deep in his bones. There it went, his last piece of Aggy. Sully squeezed his eyes shut, forcing back the tears burning there.

"Well, well, well," the guard clucked, clearly pleased with himself. "Will ya look at that. It's got itself a pretty bit o' jewelry. Prolly its girlfriend's." The wide-set, snaggle-toothed man squatted to examine the watch more closely. In his grubby fingers, the worn gold glistened brighter than ever. Sully felt his heart clench. "Hey, Sammy, ya think Jenny will like it?"

She shrugged, uninterested in the watch. Both seemed to ignore Sully, who made a reach for it, his stitches screaming at the quick action.

Once.

Twice.

The third try was almost the charm; he felt his fingers close over the smooth gold surface before a jolt of electricity sent him to his knees. He looked up at the small woman—Sammy—holding the stunning pistol blearily.

The man laughed, clapping her on the shoulder and sending her stumbling.

"Well done, Sammy. I didn't think you had it in you!" He moved to Sully's side, dropped the watch beside him on the ground. "Ya know what? Jenny wouldn't like it anyway. It's ugly." He pushed the toe of his grimy boot over top of it.

Slowly, he pressed harder and harder until the watch gave way with an agonized *tink* of broken glass and bent metal. When his boot came away, the tiny trinket lay in pieces beside Sully. Glass shattered, gears exposed, and the embossed unicorn twisted beyond recognition. Gone. His beautiful gift from Agnes was gone.

Sully couldn't help the sob that left him, his fingers shaking as he reached to touch the broken pieces. "Oh, Aggy."

"Nothin' more than a bit of trash," the guard sneered, his eyes gleaming at Sully's pain. "Get up."

Sully didn't hear the guard's order past the pounding of blood in his ears. He stared at the broken pieces of the watch, his heart aching. Was that it? Would that be the last of Agnes he had? And now it was gone? What was left for him without Aggy?

"I said, get up!" the guard shouted, rearing one scuffed

boot back to kick Sully hard in the ribs. Sully yelped, moving away from the boot to roll onto his side. "Get up, or I'll kick you again. They didn't say nothin' about you being in one piece when you got there."

"All right," Sully wheezed, his throat raw from pain and sadness. "All right." Pushing himself up into a seated position, he winced at the aches settling rapidly into his body.

"Hurry the hell up, kelpie."

He saw the boot still poised to strike again.

"I'm moving." Sully moved onto his knees and slowly to his feet. One hand reached to hold his already bruising side. "Gods, I'm getting too old for this shit."

"What was that?" If it weren't for the iron clamped around his wrist, Sully would have fought back. He had had enough of being kicked around, and the guard that stood beside him had pushed just the right buttons. But when his eyes fell to the ruined watch on the floor, he felt something inside of him break.

"He's ready," Sammy called, crossing the room to open the door. In came the silent thugs again. They flanked Sully and dragged him down a much shorter hall with doors on both sides. He stumbled, struggling to keep up with them.

"Oh, Aggy," Sully whispered to himself again. His gaze searched from one door to the next, but all of the windows were shut, so he couldn't see inside. He wondered if Agnes was here. Or perhaps they were keeping him in a special cellblock. Somewhere there was no hope of escape.

One of the burly men gave him a hard shove, and Sully stumbled to his knees in an even smaller cell. The slam of the door behind him rang through the space. Closing his eyes, Sully let himself cry for perhaps the first time since his parents had died. Curling onto his side on the cold, damp floor, he tried to envision Agnes's face as he presented him the small velvet box again, but the memory was dull and faded with age.

EVENTUALLY, the tears dried up.

Sully's throat was scratchy, and the salt made his face itch. He choked out a dry sob, scrubbing at his cheeks tiredly. How much time had passed? The pitch-black cell gave no indication.

Despite his exhaustion, his mind gave him no peace. For when the questions of what could or would be dried up with his tears, images replaced them.

There.

There he was.

With his back to Sully, Agnes trembled. His beautiful rainbow hair clung to his elegant neck with sweat, and he shook with cold. A sob wracked his lithe form, as a severe fever clung to his skin from the infection. Blood oozed slowly from the gnawing gash in his shoulder. Sully reached for him—more out of habit than thinking the image before him was real—and his fingers brushed only air.

A whimper left Sully as he scooted across the cold floor to try to reach Agnes, but each time Agnes seemed further and further away.

A mirage. Nothing more than a trick of his exhausted mind.

But that didn't mean that that wasn't what Agnes looked like right then. For even if Sully couldn't see Agnes, he knew that his unicorn was in pain, wherever he was. In agony, and alone—Sully's heart clenched at the thought. What would he give to be there with Aggy right then? Anything.

Sully pulled his hand back finally, swallowing roughly. He had failed—not that there was any real chance of him succeeding in this. The game was stacked, and MOTHER held all the cards. The only move he ever really had was to sacrifice himself, and even that move would have consequences. He just hadn't thought they would be so heavy.

Hours—or maybe days, for all Sully knew—passed him by in that black cell before a fresh set of thug-like MOTHER agents came to retrieve him. Sully's belly growled with hunger, the only real indication of how much time had passed. They moved to him and tugged him to his feet heedless of whatever injuries he might have sustained during torture and his processing.

"What time is it?" Sully slurred the question. They set him on his feet, and he wobbled unsteadily.

All the answer he got was a grunt, and a kick to the back. It forced him into the hall and to his knees again. Sully felt the rough floor scrape the skin of his palms.

"Get up," one of them growled, his words accompanied by the threatening buzz of a stunner pistol.

"Right, no questions." Sully laughed hoarsely. He pushed himself to his feet again, with another wobble. One unsteady footstep followed the other, making slow progress of the hall before him.

"Hurry it up," the guard growled again, jabbing him with the stunning pistol in his lower back. As if Sully needed the reminder.

Sully was given no opportunity to gather himself and move more quickly. The guard jammed the stunning pistol between his shoulder blades and sent a jarring shock through his body. Sully sank to the floor as his muscles jumped and jittered with electricity.

One of the guards kicked him, growling, "Get up."

To which Sully responded with a pathetic moan.

A disgusted snort preceded one of the burly men crouching down and forcing Sully to his feet again. They both flanked him, then without any more words, dragged him through the hall of holding cells. He was left no time to look into the other cells to search for Agnes again before they pulled him into a large loading bay and propped him up on his feet.

He blinked at the brightness of the room as he looked around. Two large zeppelins had been parked on either side of the loading bay. Their cargo holds were open, and in front of the ramp into them were serpentine lines of people. Each had their shaved head hung in submission and fear as they were marked off one at a time, clamped together with chains and loaded onto a ship.

Sully's heart sped in horror as the enormity of what he was facing came into harsh focus. Never before had he considered that MOTHER was operating on this scale—after all, it always seemed like they barely made a dent in the Enchanted community. He'd been naive to think that this was a small battle. Now—as he faced the sea of bodies being carted to inevitable death—he couldn't silence the voice in his mind that whispered, *That's right, you fool. You're fighting a losing battle.*

Another harsh shove to his back sent him stumbling toward one of the lines. Once there, the two guards left him, seemingly uninterested in if he'd put up any further fight. He looked around, wondering if there were any way to escape from here.

There was none.

The doors to the bay were tightly sealed, presumably until one of the zeppelins took off. He could see one exit—the door he'd come in through, and in front of it stood no less than five guards all armed to the teeth. Sully wasn't getting out of that hangar alive unless it was on one of the ships.

He shuffled forward as the line moved, and more people joined it behind him.

He watched with morbid fascination as the people before him stopped before a pair of guards standing at the bottom of the cargo hold ramp. One guard would force each person to bare their forearm to the other, presumably to check the tattooed number on their skin. The other would jot the number down onto a list. Finally, the original guard would clap a set of irons on the person—connected to the person who had preceded them—and shove them up into the hold.

Over and over and over again—like an assembly line—until Sully found himself crammed into the cargo hold.

He inhaled deeply, closing his eyes, as he felt the walls close in around him. There were far too many people in such a small space. He felt every subtle shift, and jostle of those around him as they bumped into him.

Everyone winced as the machinery of the clockwork ship screeched to life. Then came a hard jolt that knocked several of his fellow prisoners off their feet as the ship lifted off the ground. Another deafening noise permeated the air; he guessed that was the hatches of the bay opening above them to let the zeppelin drift out into the open sky.

Sully closed his eyes, his stomach dropping as they climbed higher and higher into the atmosphere. Leaving MOTHER and probably Agnes behind.

When his stomach had settled again, he knew they had leveled off. With the takeoff behind him, his dark eyes flitted around in search of Agnes. He hoped they had decided to send them to the same camp. What would he do if they hadn't? He didn't know. Sully quickly pushed the thought from his mind—fate couldn't be so cruel. He swept the crowd in search of a beautiful rainbow head, but all he saw was pale bald head after pale bald head.

Somewhere in the hold, a child cried; no one bothered to shush it. Soon, a second, and fifth cry joined the chorus.

And still, he saw no signs of Agnes. How would he even know him like this? With no hair or fancy clothes to indicate Aggy, there was no way to tell if he were among them.

Sully's heart sank further in his chest. Hope slipped through his fingers like water. He reached for the pocket watch at his side, needing the solid comfort of something.

No pockets. No watch. Sully had to bite his cheek to restrain a sob. Agnes's words echoed in his mind: *Don't break it.*

Squeezing his eyes shut, Sully forced himself to breathe through the pain that threatened to overcome him entirely. When he had control again, he formulated a plan. He would bide his time, for now, and search for Agnes when they reached the camp. It would be easier to pick Agnes out without a crush of people closing in around him. Until then, he closed his eyes and forced himself to breathe.

Soon enough, more shouting filled the air, and Sully felt his stomach drop as the zeppelin descended to the ground. They were landing.

Just outside the city of Pascal—far enough away so that the humans of Pascal didn't have to see or think about what was going on there—lay the barbed-wire-topped fence of labor camp 9C.

Behind the chain-link was a barren field of angry-looking wire grass. Beyond that browning grass stood a collection of pale, depressed, dilapidated buildings. A swirl of dust and tiny pebbles formed as the zeppelin lowered itself to the ground. What had once been a recreation field —long ago when MOTHER still cared about the health and happiness of their inmates—had turned into a landing pad. With a thud and a loud bang, the zeppelin set down and opened the cargo hold.

A guard was already waiting for them. He peeked into the hold before he started shouting. Sully couldn't quite make out the words, but he supposed they were ordered to vacate the ship. The crowd around him shuffled collectively toward the opening—one or two of them stumbling and nearly falling out of the open hatch.

"One at a time!" the guard barked.

This order ceased progress entirely as they all looked from one to another, trying to decide who would go first. Then they all moved at the same time again.

"No! No! No!" he shouted, then climbed up into the hold with them. "Who has the end of the chain?"

There was a long moment of muttering as they tried to figure this out. Confusion and upset traveled through the crowd as it seemed that there was no end. Sully frowned a little, looking around. There was no way to tell, and no one was speaking up.

Another guard joined them at the edge of the hold and shouted inside, "What the hell is taking you so long?"

"The cargo shifted in transit," the original guard muttered irritably. "Give me the damn cutters."

Once the guard outside had handed the guard inside a set of bolt cutters, he cut two Enchanted apart.

"You're the end." He cut the young woman a glare. "Now get out." Then he gave her a harsh shove, and she stumbled down the ramp to the dusty ground.

From there, the rest filed out after her. They were herded into a neat line that snaked toward a squat building on the edge of the compound.

Sully's eyes swept the group as they separated, searching for the tall, aristocratic features of Agnes. It was no use; those around him moved too quickly, and they kept jostling him. Soon he too was in the single-file line, and there was no hope at all of seeing anyone's face. He focused on not stepping on the heels of the person in front of him.

Inside the small building was a large wooden desk where a MOTHER agent glared at them all in disgust.

"Number!" she shouted into his face, spittle flying.

Sully blinked at her for a long moment in confusion. He had half expected she'd ask his name, and species to categorize him. That was MOTHER's habit, after all.

"Number," she repeated. Her face turned red with irritation the longer he blinked at her. Finally, she let out an aggravated sigh and hissed, "Show me your damn arm, you moron."

When he held it out to her, she checked the chart before her, scribbled something down on paper, and held it out to him. Then her eyes flicked to the person behind him.

"Next!"

Sully blinked down at the slip of paper and his forehead creased in concentration, doing his best to make sense of the chicken scratch.

"I'm sorry, but I can't read this."

She stared at him blankly. "That's not my problem," came her nasty reply. Then she looked at the person behind him again and shouted, "Next!"

A yank on his chain gave Sully no chance to argue further. He was forced to move along, dragged by the shackles at his wrist to another small building. There, a set of threadbare—but, thankfully, *clean*—sheets were thrust into his arms along with a thin blanket. More dragging, and Sully found himself in a small room where a guard moved between him and several others to unchain them. They left the iron shackle on his wrist, of course. It was the only thing preventing the Enchanted from using their magic to fight back. Once that was done, someone stood at the front of the room and droned on.

"You all have been assigned to the mine. You will report to building 15H in the center of the compound every morning after the bell rings. Once there, you will be assigned whatever job is needed." The young woman didn't lift her eyes from the clipboard in her hands. Presumably, she'd been given a script to stick to during these things, but Sully had no way of really knowing. "Laundry day for your group is the fifteenth of the month. You will not be given clean sheets or uniforms before that date, and if you miss it, you'll go another month without clean things."

Sully wondered how people kept track of the date in a place like this. Where everything was gray, and it looked as if the days would all bleed together, but he didn't bother to ask. He doubted MOTHER would give them calendars for such a thing.

"Go to your bunks and get settled in." That seemed to be the end of her speech, for the next thing Sully knew he was ushered out of the building. The others from his group rushed toward their bunks. He supposed they could read their slips of paper.

"Umm . . . excuse me," Sully offered, approaching a guard as slowly and politely as possible. "I can't seem to read my bunk slip."

"Move along!" the man shouted into Sully's face.

Sully winced, frowning. "I would, but I can't read the other guard's handwriting."

"I said. Move. Along."

"I'd like to," Sully said, his eyes narrowing. "But I can't read her handwriting. If you could —"

"Got a smart mouth on you, do ya?"

"What? No. I just can't read that woman's chicken scratch. I'd be —"

Sully didn't get the chance to finish that thought as a moment later a jolt of electricity ripped through him, tearing him from consciousness and plunging him into darkness.

Again.

Great.

"He's clearly guilty!" Came the shrill shout of Kore from somewhere to Agnes's right.

Ah, Kore. Reliable, that one.

Agnes snickered some more.

"Don't let him try to use insanity as a defense. He knew what he was doing!" Kore sounded genuinely afraid that Agnes would somehow weasel out of this. "He should be executed right away! He killed my parents!"

"Now, now, Miss Kore. Er, *Agent* Kore, that is. There is no proof of that," the judge argued.

"Then what?" Kore demanded, her fists banging against something, perhaps a table? Agnes couldn't be sure. There was a table shaped blur in front of her, but maybe it was a bench. He squeezed his eyes shut for a moment to try to clear his vision, but it did nothing.

"I hope that's not permanent," Agnes muttered.

"What?" Kore snapped, and Agnes could feel the glare burn into the side of his face.

"Nothing." Agnes let out a breath, his shoulders sagging as he slumped further back in his chair. He scrubbed at his eyes, ignoring the clank of chains on his wrists. Why bother? He could hardly see, and he definitely couldn't walk on his own. What use were they? "Are we done yet?"

"Are we boring you?" Kore's tone had an edge to it, something sharp and serrated like the blade she'd used to carve up Sully's face.

"Little bit." Agnes pretended to hide a yawn behind his hand, just to annoy her. Was it wise to irritate one of the people who'd help decide his fate? Probably not. But at that point Agnes was fairly sure he was going to die. What use was there in delaying the inevitable?

The judge choked on a sound that might have been a laugh, but Agnes wasn't sure. "Then let's get on with it, shall we? How do you plead?"

There was a noise like someone had opened their mouth to speak, but it was cut off by a sharp glance.

"Let him speak, Kore," the judge said.

Agnes thought to say something snarky again, but swallowed down the words. "Guilty."

"See?" Kore crowed. "He knows what he did!"

"Well of course I do," Agnes sniped. "I'm not an idiot. I knew I was a spy."

"And you know that the punishment for treason is death, don't you, 95?" the judge asked, a little too gently. Agnes wished he could see the man's face. Perhaps it was someone he knew.

Squeezing his eyes shut again, Agnes nodded.

"So, let's get the firing squad ready!" Kore sounded absolutely delighted. Agnes imagined her rubbing her hands together in glee.

"Surely," someone spoke up. Roy. Thank the gods for Roy. He cleared his throat, probably straightening his waistcoat nervously as all the eyes in the room turned to him.

Agnes resisted the urge to shake his head. It wouldn't

do for Roy to draw too much attention to himself, not now. But what was done, was done, Agnes supposed.

"Surely," Roy continued at length, "it would be more of a punishment to have him sent to the camps where he'd die slowly, suffering. An execution for this level of treason is too quick. Isn't it?"

Agnes's breath caught, lodging in his throat hard enough to near choke him. He'd thought he was going to die, but this was an out. A possibility for survival that he hadn't hoped for, even as it had been the plan.

A rumble of murmuring started, slipping through the courtroom as some voiced their agreement, and others argued against. Agnes wasn't sure who was winning, but a small sapling of hope took up residence in his heart. Maybe, just maybe, he'd be able to escape his fate. Maybe he'd see Sully again.

"All right, quiet down, everyone," the judge called, bringing silence to the room.

Agnes wondered what would come next. Would they take a vote? Would Kore get the final say as she'd been his handler? Would they ask his opinion? Should he look suitably worried that this option was now on the table? He had no way of knowing. And without any cues from the faces around him, there was no way to tell which way this would go.

"For crimes against the crown, Asset 95 will be charged with a lifetime in her service —"

"NO!" Kore screamed over the judge. There was some crashing of furniture—a chair, maybe? Or a table? And then the blur that Agnes assumed was Kore flew across the room toward him, arms outstretched as if to choke him. Someone grabbed her around the waist, yanking her back just as her nails scraped the tender skin of Agnes's neck. She thrashed, making a sound that was more beast than person. "You can't let it live! It killed them! It killed my family!"

"Please escort Agent Kore out," the judge said calmly.

Kore's screaming faded as she was pulled from the room. The slamming of a door signaled her exit, along with whatever agents dragged her along.

The judge cleared his throat. "As I was saying. For crimes against the crown, asset 95 is charged with a lifetime in her service at the labor camps. Asset 95 will be taken away immediately for processing."

The sounds of movement followed, and Agnes was lifted from his seat again to be dragged out of the room. His boots scuffed against the tiled floor, they'd never be right again, no matter how he shined them.

With his vision still blurry, Agnes felt strangely detached from the proceedings that followed. He knew what processing meant. He knew he would be shaved bare and have the numerals 95, the number he had always been known as to MOTHER, carved into his skin with a needle. But he found himself unable to feel the sting of the needle or hear the buzz of the razor as his long rainbow tresses joined the layers of hair on the floor. With so many different colors there, it was hard to tell which chunks were his own anyway.

The pocket watch was lost in the shuffle as he was forced into a new uniform and thrust out the door toward the landing bay.

"You look even uglier than I remember." Kore's voice floated on the air, grounding Agnes into the chill and the agony that came with everything, dragging him back into his body when he'd been happy to just ignore everything. His arm stung. His head was cold. A chill had settled so deeply into his skin that he felt it crawling along his bones.

"Come to say goodbye?" Agnes asked, voice tight and

tired. No, that couldn't be his voice. That had to be someone else's. And yet, he'd felt the words leave his throat.

Kore snorted. "That kelpie isn't going to want you now. You're hideous."

The words echoed, strange and hollow in Agnes's mind. Like they hadn't been spoken at all, but had simply appeared there. As if they were his words. She was right, after all, Agnes was ugly. Sully wouldn't want him now.

"Pathetic."

Someone shoved Agnes, and he stumbled forward into the loading bay. Kore's voice, and face faded from his view, but the words stayed. Echoing around in his mind like they would off the walls of his cell.

No one else stopped them. No one else came to say goodbye. Agnes didn't know what he had hoped for. His own people couldn't show their faces around him, not now. It would look suspicious. Roy had already stuck his neck out in saving Agnes's life. He couldn't ask for any more from them.

Distantly, he felt the shift of the zeppelin as it lifted out of the bay and into the air.

You're hideous.

The words drowned out the sounds of flight.

You're hideous.

The zeppelin touched down, almost causing Agnes to lose his footing. Somehow, he managed to stay standing. A box beside him rattled, probably full of weapons or supplies, or some such for the MOTHER agents at the camp. He knew they weren't full of supplies for the people kept there.

You're hideous.

There was some shouting outside as the MOTHER agents unloaded the cargo. Agnes was unloaded right alongside a crate of expired grain.

Someone, somewhere, shoved a pile of rough sheets into his arms, and shoved him out a door into a narrow alley. There was a crumpled piece of paper in his hand, a number scrawled across it. But Agnes didn't have it in him to look down and read it. So, he wandered.

You're hideous.

He let his feet scuff across the dirt pathways through the camp. No one was around, he noticed, although the reason didn't really register. Nor did it seem to matter. In fact, he preferred this. He'd rather no one see him this way.

At some point someone came from one of the buildings. A small fae boy.

"Can I help you find your bunk?" the child asked, but the words got garbled and hazy on the way to Agnes's mind. And his response got lost somewhere between his brain and his tongue. The child shook his head, looked down at the paper, and led Agnes to his bunk. "It's all right. Lots of folks are like this when they first come."

Agnes nodded, whether to express his thanks, or to agree, he wasn't sure.

"You'll get used to it. Everybody does," the child said sagely, like he was much older than he appeared. He patted Agnes's hand gently. "Those two bunks are free. You can take the top or the bottom, whatever makes you feel best. I'm Benji, by the way."

"Agnes," Agnes managed to force from his lips. It was a struggle, but it would be rude not to introduce himself, right?

"Nice to meet you, Agnes." Benji said with a bright smile. "You get yourself comfy. Dinner is in an hour."

Agnes nodded again and went to the bunk.

"Right, I'll see you," Benji said by way of farewell, and turned to leave.

Once he was gone, Agnes threw the rough sheets onto

the floor, and climbed into the top bunk. He rolled onto his side, to face the wall, and just let his mind drift. That was easier. Anything had to be easier than adjusting to his new circumstance.

You're hideous.

No one came to drag him to dinner, and when his bunk mates filtered in, they ignored him too. Agnes was grateful for that. He'd rather drift away than deal with other people right then.

You're hideous.

Days passed by in the same fashion. He started to count the time by his interactions with the guards who dragged him from his bed to shower, eat, or change, not really sure how often they happened.

You're hideous.

It was three forced feedings later when that voice filtered in through the haze.

"Hey, you mind if I take the bottom bunk?"

Sullivan.

At least there was a window in the isolation cell they dragged Sully to, he could say that much. He could look out and gauge how long it had been. He watched the sun move across the sky throughout the day and kept track.

A week.

It had been a week since they had thrown him in that cell. A week and seven meals. He supposed they didn't want him to die, but they had no desire to ensure that he was as strong as he once had been. Or maybe that was just as often as they fed the Enchanted of camp 9C. He had no way of knowing, and he certainly wasn't about to ask the man who slid a meal of sour-smelling mush through the slat in the door.

Sully caught a shadow flittering across the dirt outside. Someone made their way to his door.

"Supper time already?" Sully asked, slouching back against the wall and nudging the tray from yesterday's meal toward the door. "I haven't finished last night's gruel."

There was a grunt from the other side of the door. Instead of sliding open the little hatch, Sully heard the scraping of a key in a lock, and then the door to his cell was flung open.

"Get your ass to your bunk."

"Love to. Would you mind telling me where I'm head-ed?" Sully pulled the still-crumpled piece of paper from where he'd set it on the floor. He stumbled a little toward the light to get a better look at the handwriting. "I still can't quite make this out."

Without glancing at the paper, the guard grabbed Sully's wrist and yanked him along down the alley. After some initial stumbling, Sully regained his footing, and trudged after the man.

When they finally stopped it was before a lopsided building, more shack than cabin. "This is your bunk."

Then the guard turned, and lumbered off back from whence he came.

"Uh . . . thanks?" Sully frowned, looking at the door to the "bunk." There was at least an inch gap underneath the door that probably let in a cold draft in the evenings. And either the shack itself wasn't level, or the door hung on the hinges askew.

"You need to be more careful," someone said as they came around the corner. "The guards don't like it when we ask questions."

Sully cocked his head at the woman, trying to place her face for a moment. "Do I know you?"

"Just keep your head down and pretend you know what the hell is going on until you do." Her tone left no room for argument.

"Right . . . thanks. I'm Sully?" he said it like it was a question, holding his hand out to her.

Hazel eyes narrowed on the outstretched hand for a moment. Then she held up the armful of sheets and blankets she'd been balancing. "These are for you."

"Oh, of course!" He rushed to take them, scrambling a

little to keep the tangle of rough fabric from falling into the dust. Once he had everything in his arms, he tried again. "I'm Sully."

"I heard you."

"This is usually the part in an introduction where you tell the other person your name," Sully prompted, flashing a winning smile.

"Is it?"

"Yes, it is."

"Would it be rude if I didn't?" She pushed a pair of wire-rimmed glasses further up her nose.

"Didn't what?"

"Introduce myself," she said plainly, crossing her arms over her chest.

Sully blinked at her, dumbfounded, before he let out a startled laugh. "Yeah, I think it would be a little rude."

"Rose."

"What?"

"That's my name. Rose." She still hadn't held out her hand for him to shake, and at this point, Sully figured she wasn't going to.

"Nice to meet you, Rose." Sully smiled.

Rose rolled her eyes. "You always smile that much?"

"So I'm told." He shrugged.

"Go in and get your bed made. If you're not ready for dinner when the bell rings, they won't hold it for you, and you'll just go hungry."

"Thanks! I'll see you around?"

"Yeah. Maybe." Rose turned to head back the way she'd come. "And remember what I said: keep your head down."

"Yes, ma'am." Sully turned back to the door, inhaling deeply through his nose and out through his mouth to steady himself for what he would see on the other side of the door. "It can't be any worse than what I've seen so far," he told himself.

But couldn't it?

The door opened on creaking hinges, loud enough to wake anyone who might have been sleeping on the inside.

Fluttering blue wings drew Sully's eyes to where a little boy stretched out a fitted sheet on one of the bunks.

"You gotta make your bed," the boy said, without even turning back around.

"Yeah, I'll do that." Sully nodded, eyes flicking around the dimly lit room. There were no tables. No chairs. Not even floor space to store their shoes. Just bunk after bunk stacked one on top of the other to pack as many people in as could fit into the tiny space. Ten bunks total. Twenty beds. All pressed so close that a person could reach out and poke their neighbor in the cheek if they wanted.

"That one's free." The boy pointed one pale blue finger over to a lower bunk in the corner. "Just don't bug the guy on top."

"Why? What's wrong with him?"

The boy shrugged by way of answer, and instead moved on to introductions. "I'm Benji."

"Nice to meet you, Benji. I'm Sully." Sully offered him a smile, and Benji returned it a little hesitantly.

"I wish I could offer you another bunk. That guy . . ." Benji huffed out through his lips, shaking his head. "He isn't nice."

"I'm sure I'll be all right. I'm a big guy. I can handle myself." Sully hoped this would ease some of the tension wrinkling the boy's face. "Don't worry about me."

"Right. Dinner bell rings in two hours. You got till then to make your peace." Benji's eyes flicked toward the back corner of the room, looking skeptical. "I've gotta get back to the laundry."

"Don't let me keep you. I don't want you to get in trouble."

Benji's eyes flicked between Sully and the back corner again, unsure.

Sully winked.

Benji huffed a laugh, and then turned to leave. "You be nice to this one, you cranky old goat!"

There was a grunt of annoyance from the back corner, but no other response came. Then Benji left Sully alone with his new bunk mate. Clutching the bedding closer to himself, Sully turned sideways to shimmy between the bunks and make his way to the back corner.

The bed in question was a lower bunk. The person on the top was laying facing the wall on the bare mattress, their bedding kicked carelessly to the dirt floor.

"Do you need help making your bed?" Sully's voice was low, amiable. He half hoped the "cranky old goat" wouldn't hear him, and then he could just flop down onto the hard-looking cot below and not be bothered with it. But when he got another grunt in response, he sighed. That probably wouldn't do. He didn't need more enemies in this place. "Hey, you mind if I take the bottom bunk?"

The person on the bunk shifted, their shoulders tightening when Sully's voice broke through the silence of the cabin.

"I thought you liked to be on top," the figure said in a voice that was rough, weak, and all too familiar. A voice Sully would recognize anywhere.

"Aggy?"

"Oh good, they stuck us together. Now I can listen to you snore all night," Agnes snarked in that same hoarse voice, but he didn't roll over to face Sully. It left Sully aching in a way he didn't quite understand.

"Look at me, Aggy," Sully pleaded, his eyes flickering

over the way Agnes was laying. Cataloguing all the hurt, and the thinness, that he could see in Agnes's tightly curled figure. Agnes had curled in on himself, his bald head resting on his arm instead of the flat pillow he'd been given. There was a stain on the shoulder of his uniform, but in the low light Sully couldn't make out if it was blood or something else.

"No. I don't think I will." Agnes's tone was hard, harder than it had ever been, and laced with ice. "Just make your bed, and shut up."

Sully scowled, shaking his head a little. He knew better than to push. Pushing Agnes when he got like this was like trying to push a boulder up a hill. It hurt like hell, and you got nowhere. Sully just nodded, and dipped down to make up the little cot underneath Agnes's as quickly as he could. His fingers itched to reach out to Agnes, to tell him that everything would be all right. To hold the broken pieces of his unicorn together until they could mend themselves. But Agnes needed space, and Sully would give it to him.

When he was done, he curled up on his cot and let himself drift for a while. He let the sounds of Agnes's shallow breaths lull him into something not quite sleep, but not quite awake either.

Agnes was here. He was in one piece, for the most part. And soon . . . soon they would escape. They would be free. So long as they were together, nothing else mattered.

An alarm jolted Sully from his thoughts, making him sit up abruptly and bang his head on the bed above him with a yelp.

"Shit," he hissed, rubbing at the already bruising skin. Gods, he missed his hair. It would have cushioned the blow at least a little.

The door banged open, light streaming in from the outside to burn at Sully's eyes again.

"Supper's up. You better hurry if you want to eat," Benji called, winding through the bunks to stand in front of Sully. "Come on, I'll show you where the mess hall is."

Sully nodded and rose. He looked back to Agnes, reaching for him to pull him along. "Aggy . . ."

"Leave him." Benji ordered sharply, taking a hold of the corner of Sully's sleeve and tugging him toward the still open door.

"What? Doesn't he need to eat?"

"He should, but no one can make him. They'll be by to force feed him tomorrow. Come on."

Sully looked over his shoulder at the monochrome lump that was Agnes on the cot in the corner. There was something tight and sharp in his chest that he could only assume was his heart breaking for Agnes. It would be easy to go back, pick him up, and take him along. But would that be better or worse? Would that draw too much attention to Agnes's weakness? The guards had to know he was weak already. Still, Sully just . . . he wasn't sure what was right here.

"How long has he been here?" Sully asked instead as he let Benji drag him out into the fading light of the evening.

"About a week. He hasn't left his bed except for when they drag him to the showers, or off to make him eat." Benji's young face was set into a frown, like he didn't quite understand the instinct within Agnes to give up. But Sully did. That instinct had lived within Agnes for so long, and something had finally snapped to make it take over. Something had finally pushed him over the edge. If Sully didn't do something, Agnes would fade away.

"Has he been to see a medic? Last time I saw him, he was pretty seriously injured. He probably needed stitches."

"No. He won't leave the bed. We offered to take him down to the first aid shed, but he won't. He won't even talk to anybody." Benji shrugged, and he seemed to be trying to carefully compose his expression into something neutral, but it wasn't quite working. There was a cross between confusion, frustration, fear, and anger resting there that made his young face look so much older than it was. "He just . . . he just *lies* there, and stares at the wall."

Sully sighed, shoulders sagging, and feet kicking up dirt where he didn't have the energy to lift them much anymore. How was he going to fix this? How was he going to pull Aggy out of this? Agnes had never been this bad before.

"You know him?" Benji asked, looking up at Sully with an expression that could only be described as a cross between hope and curiosity.

"Yeah. He's . . . we're . . ." Sully struggled with the words. What were they? "His name is Agnes," he said when all else seemed to fail him.

That seemed to be enough for Benji, who nodded. "Well, I hope you can get your Agnes to get out of bed. I don't know how much longer he'll be able to survive like he is."

"I'll try," Sully promised.

Benji tugged him into a better lit hall with a long line winding from where two automatons served the prisoners along the walls to the door.

"Shit, this is gonna take forever." Benji huffed, but didn't say anything else as someone from further up in the line turned to give him a dirty look. He made a gesture of sealing his lips and shot raised brows back at the person who turned around, satisfied. "No talking," Benji whispered through barely opened lips.

Sully frowned, looking around. Benji was right: everyone was silent, or as close to it as they could get. There was some whispered conversation, but it seemed everyone was afraid to talk much beyond that. Instead, the hall was full of the sound of silverware scraping against plates, and chewing. It was eerie.

Sully waited in line, took his tray of mushy gray something or other, and sat beside Benji to eat in silence.

The news that Agnes had been sentenced to a lifetime of hard labor in the service of the crown should have been a relief to Persinette. It meant that, at the very least, he was still alive. It was the best possible outcome they could have hoped for.

"Do you know where he was sent?" Manu asked, giving voice to the question that clung heavily to the inside of Persinette's throat.

Roy's shoulders sagged with a heaved sigh. "Not yet. I put in a request to have him transferred to 9C."

"Where's that?" Benard called from where he sat at Manu's desk, scouring a map of Daiwynn for their next safe house.

"Just outside of Pascal. It's where the records say they sent Sullivan."

"Good call." Manu nodded. "Then we only have to break into one of those damned places."

Persinette frowned, her hands shaking where they sat in her lap. She'd been silent for the last few minutes, processing what would be happening to Agnes at that moment. He'd be processed. He'd be processed and sent to the gray toil of the labor camps. Would he even survive that?

It had been the plan all along, but it had never really felt real until that very moment.

Manu seemed to sense the inner turmoil and fumbled for a moment, taking her elbow, and then traveling down along her hand until he could give it a firm squeeze.

"For the time being," he said the words like a promise.

Persinette nodded, smiling a little as she leaned in to kiss his cheek. "Right. Soon we'll get the others out."

"Right."

Benard glanced at them, but didn't say anything, shaking his head.

"Thank you," Persinette said to Roy. She inhaled deeply and sat up straighter, shoulders back, chin up. She was a captain, not a little girl. She needed to start acting like it. "For keeping Agnes alive."

Roy blushed under the praise but shook his head. "No need, Captain. It's my job to make sure my people are safe."

"Speaking of which," Benard interrupted, coming over to them with a folded map. "I think Didymus might be our next best bet. It's not as insular or secluded as some of the other towns we've used, but we also don't want them all in one place."

"Didymus is right next to Labor Camp 6G." Roy frowned. "I don't think that's a good idea. Those towns are usually more heavily patrolled than others in case someone escapes."

"Usually," Benard agreed. "But the camp there is largely defunct, isn't it? No one will be looking for them there."

Roy shook his head. "I'd rather we take them to Fizzi-gog. I know it's a little farther out, but it's safer."

Benard looked down at the map in thought, his fingers

tracing the path. "That's at least twenty miles in the wrong—"

"Roy is right," Persinette said, ending the conversation there. "I don't want to take them anywhere near a labor camp, especially with what's on the horizon. MOTHER is going to crack down on the territories outside the camps. We can't take the chance that they'll find their escaped assets there. Roy, the next Collection site is?"

"Gelfling."

"Right then. Benard, set a course. We have three days, and I'd like to be there a little early, so it doesn't look suspicious." Persinette's voice grew stronger as Manu clasped her hand more firmly, offering her the support she needed.

"And when you've done that, we want that list of captains," Manu added.

"Yes, Cap'n." Benard gave them both a curt nod and then left for the helm. The door to Manu's quarters shut behind him, and Persinette returned her gaze to Roy.

"How is he?"

Manu snorted beside her, but didn't say anything. She knew that Manu didn't agree with her worry for Agnes. Agnes had been cruel to her when she'd been under MOTHER's roof. But he was still one of them. He was on their side. And they needed as many people on their side as they could get.

Roy's eyes flitted from Manu's annoyed expression to Persinette's sincere gaze. "It's not good, Persi. He wasn't in good shape last I saw him. And you know they don't give them any kind of medical attention down there."

"Then we need to hurry," Manu said, firmly. Persinette's head jerked to look at him in surprise, and she wasn't sure if he heard her clothes rustle, or if he'd felt the movement but he smirked in return. "I'm not completely heartless."

"I never said—"

"So, how long before they'll get us a message?" Manu asked, ignoring Persinette's protests.

"I don't know that they will. 9C is a mining camp, so they don't exactly have access to a whole lot of technology there. We might get lucky, and they might find some way to contact us, but I wouldn't wait around for it." Roy's tone was neutral, but Persinette could see that the thought bothered him more than he was letting on.

It bothered her too. They would be going in blind if they couldn't get Agnes and Sully to give them some information from inside the camp.

"Can we get someone to recon it for us?" she asked hopefully. Maybe they could have one of their MOTHER assets transferred there and that person could leak information. Or maybe Roy could get his hands on some records. Something. Anything. Would be better than going in without any knowledge of the place.

"I'm afraid not, Captain." Roy passed a hand over his face. He'd aged since their first mission together. Tiredness lined his face in a way that was all too human, reminding Persinette that that's exactly what he was. Roy was just a human doing his best. She couldn't ask him to sacrifice himself any more than he already had for this mission.

They sat in silence for a beat too long, Persinette fiddling with the tips of Manu's fingers and Manu stroking his thumb along her knuckles in a gesture that was all too familiar now.

"I have a favor to ask," Roy said, breaking the silence. She watched as the reflection of the man leaned back from his mirror and looked over this shoulder as if making sure no one was listening to him. Then he leaned in close to lower his voice. "A big favor."

Manu quirked a brow and Persinette found herself leaning in closer to hear the near-whisper.

"What is it?" she asked in a hushed tone.

Manu bit back a laugh. "This is a private line, you two."

Roy rolled his eyes. "Right. I need help getting Penny out. I know she's not going to want to go but I . . . well . . . I need to know she's safe."

"You want us to abduct your girlfriend?" Manu asked, choking on a surprised chortle.

Persinette paled. "Roy, if she doesn't want to go, we really can't make her. That's not—that's not right."

"Not abduct," Roy argued. "Just . . . you know . . . take against her will for her own good."

"Abduct," Manu repeated.

Persinette hissed, swatting Manu lightly on the shoulder.

"What? It is!"

"If she doesn't get out of MOTHER soon . . . I don't think she'll make it." Roy's shoulders had sunk, and he wasn't looking at them anymore. He seemed to be looking down at his hands. "There have already been talks about . . . about . . ." His throat bobbed as he nearly choked on the words. "About thinning the herd of Enchanted. That Agnes probably had some others working with him. They're going to be looking at us so much more closely now. And Penny isn't exactly subtle."

"We'll help. Of course, we'll help. You worry about getting her to Gelfling, and we'll worry about keeping her safe."

"Pers, I don't—"

"Manu, we're doing this. We're helping them."

Manu let out a long, loud groan, but nodded as he lifted a hand to rub at his face. "Fine. Fine. Fine. It seems the captain has made up her mind."

Roy's answering smile was wide enough to crinkle the

crow's feet around his eyes. "Thank you. And one more favor?"

"One more?" Manu threw his head back in an exaggerated motion of being put out.

Persinette laughed, patting Manu's hand lightly.

"Keep her on board with you. I know you don't have much space, but that way I'll still be able to talk to her sometimes?" Roy said, hopeful.

Persinette couldn't help but nod her head in agreement. The communication ended there, with Roy swiping at his mirror to close it off and Persinette's end turning naught more than a reflective surface.

"All in the name of true love?" Manu asked, not lifting his head. His pale eyes stared blankly at the ceiling.

"Don't be dramatic. If you could have seen his face, you'd have agreed too."

"Such a soft touch." Manu laughed, bumping his shoulder against hers, and bringing a blush to Persinette's cheeks as he did.

"Stop it."

THE DAY of the mission came, and it was an absolute disaster. With Penny, Roy had ferried four other Enchanted from the MOTHER compound, making a total of five—more than they'd ever helped escape before. One of which wasn't more than ten years old.

"Roy," Penny growled, her eyes narrowing on Persinette as Roy led the small crew into an abandoned factory. "This is not what we agreed."

"I know it's not," Roy said. His tone was strained, but

there was a hard line across his shoulders that spoke of determination.

"I'm not going." Penny crossed her arms over her chest and dropped down to sit with her legs crossed on the floor.

"This is not up for debate." Roy's voice rose, his face turning a little red. "We talked about this. You have to go."

"Then you can come with me."

"I can't. Not until they're all out."

"Then I won't either."

Persinette frowned, looking around the small band of Enchanted Roy had brought. "We need to get moving."

"Well, I'm not," Penny argued again, seeming to plant her weight further into the hard floor beneath her.

"Pen, we can't do this right now. If we take up any more time, you'll put all the others in danger." Roy tried to reason with her. But he forgot that fairies could have a distinctive bratty streak, and all he got for his trouble was Penny blowing a loud raspberry. The noise made the ten-year-old giggle.

A ringing started in Persinette's ears, quiet at first, but steadily growing louder. She frowned, shaking her head. Drea moved quickly to her side, resting her hand on Persinette's shoulder.

"Captain?" Drea asked, voice hardly loud enough for Persinette to hear over the growing noise.

"You and Owen take the others. Leave Penny to me. We don't have much time." Persinette rubbed at her temples, trying to force away the sound, but it was no use. Not when she knew what it meant. With the growing ringing came the cold shiver of *knowing*. Someone was coming. Someone had already tripped the first ward she'd set up three blocks back. They didn't have time for this. Every second they wasted, whoever it was got closer.

"Captain, I don't think —"

"Did I stutter?" Persinette asked, her voice harder than she meant it to be. "Take the others and go. Penny and I will be right behind you."

"Captain Manu said not to leave you without protect—" Owen tried, his voice laced with something like fear.

"Owen, I gave you an order." The words felt like grit against her throat. Persinette hated pulling rank. It wasn't who she was. But there wasn't time for this. Whoever it was had tripped the ward two blocks back now. They were moving faster, and soon they'd be on her crew's tail. She couldn't take the chance. Not with a child amongst them. "Go out the back. Make sure Benard and Manu have the *Duchess* ready to leave when we get there."

Owen nodded quickly, scooping up the child, and between himself and Drea they herded the rest of their small group of escapees through the factory to the back entrance. Once they were out of earshot, Persinette turned her attention to Penny.

"Listen up, little miss, we have about a minute before whoever tripped my wards breaks through that door. It might not be MOTHER, but I don't have much hope for that. We can run and get the hell out of here or stay and fight. But in the end, you will be coming with me, and I won't put up with another tantrum. Am I understood?" Persinette's hands rested on her hips, magic simmering in the air around her in her frustration.

Penny looked up at her, nose wrinkled, before she snorted. "Yeah, all right. I like you, Captain."

Roy held out a hand to help Penny to her feet. "I'll stay, and make sure they don't follow you."

"Thank you, Roy. Make sure you don't get caught. We need you." Persinette reached for Penny, dragging the girl with her toward the back of the factory.

"Aye, aye, Captain." Roy gave her a cocky salute and pulled a pistol from the holster on his belt.

Persinette tugged Penny around the corner, just as the front door slammed inward, rattling the old building with its force. With a murmur, Persinette threw down a spell to hide their trail.

"Roy!" Penny shouted, but Persinette dragged the fairy along behind her.

The sound of gun shots ricocheted off the cement walls. Persinette kept running, skidding along the smooth tiles of the floor. There was no time to look back. No time to stop and mourn. They had to go. Persinette threw back another spell, sending up a silent prayer to whatever gods there were that it would hit home. Shield magic was tricky like that, and without eyes on Roy, all she could do was hope.

"We have to go back for him! We can't just leave him! They'll kill him!" Penny was sobbing now, her feet tripping over themselves as they broke out into the alley behind the factory.

Persinette didn't bother to argue as there was no point in it. No point in wasting the valuable energy she needed to run, to do magic, to flee. Whispering another spell, she levitated Penny off the ground before the girl could think to dig her heels into the dirt.

"Take me back! Take me back right now! Roy! Roy!" Penny's words had lost all their fight. She wasn't even struggling anymore. She just looked back as Persinette ran on.

Ragged gasps were all Persinette could manage by the time she reached the loading platform. No one was waiting for them, just like she'd instructed. Slamming her hand down on the button to lift the platform, she looked back just in time to see five figures in the distance. She couldn't be sure who they were, whose side they were on. They could have been MOTHER. They could have been Uprising. It didn't matter.

"Persinette, are we all clear?" Benard asked through the crackle of a speaker on the platform.

"Go! Don't wait for the platform to fully lift! Just go!"

Penny was crying, sobbing, wailing into Persinette's shoulder. Persinette held her, stroking her back as they rose into the air.

The *Duchess* set sail without any hesitation, leaving Gelfling behind.

The platform rattled as it finally settled into place inside the loading bay. Owen was waiting for her, looking concerned.

"Take Penny to a room, get her settled. I need to speak with Benard and Felicity about a cloaking spell." Persinette held the still gasping girl out to Owen. "Go with Owen now," she said to Penny gently. "He'll take care of you. We'll . . ." She swallowed roughly, not wanting to say the next bit, but knowing she needed to. "We'll be in touch with our contacts in MOTHER tomorrow and see about Roy."

Saying his name brought another wave of sobbing from Penny, but the fairy didn't fight as Owen led her up the stairs into the main part of the ship. Once Persinette caught her breath, she followed them up, heading for Felicity's room instead of the helm.

"Felicity," Persinette called, knocking on the door lightly. When she heard a muted bang, she sighed and pushed inside. "What are you blowing up now? I thought Manu asked you to stop it with the explosive chemicals?"

"He's not the boss of me." Felicity giggled, lifting her goggles to her head to reveal that her face had been smudged in ash. "What'd you need?"

Persinette opened her mouth to argue the point that Manu *was* in fact the boss of Felicity, but then closed it again deciding such an argument simply wasn't worth the trouble. "We need to hide the ship. I need you to do some digging on long-lasting, low-impact cloaking spells, and to gather up anyone who can perform them."

"Can't we just have Benard do it?" Felicity whined. "That'd be so much easier."

"No, we can't. I might need him out on missions, and goblin magic doesn't work when he's not touching the thing he's hiding. Plus, you know it's not as effective on inanimate objects."

Felicity huffed, carding a hand through the short blue hair on top of her head.

"And while you're at it, I want you and Drea to check in on our new passengers. Some of them are pretty young, and as the youngest members of the crew, it's your job to get them settled in. Especially Penny." Persinette reached over to grab a pen from Felicity's desk, scribbling down Penny's room number on it. "This is where Owen set her up at. You two need to be extra nice."

"I'm no good at making friends. It only worked with Drea because she thinks I'm pretty." Felicity pouted, her lower lip poking out in an exaggerated gesture.

"You've been spending too much time with Manu. Quit complaining and get to work. And tell Drea when she shows up that I want to see her in the helm. Manu, Benard, and I are going over the list of potential team ups once we're in free air space, and I'd like her opinions on them."

"She doesn't know anything about any of the other pirates."

"I know, but Benard has been working up dossiers on them, and her instincts are always good."

"Aye aye, Captain!"

The gnawing open wound on Agnes's shoulder wasn't that bad. It hurt, yes, and despite the bandages that had been applied at MOTHER, it hadn't stopped bleeding yet. Probably because Kore had cursed her knife somehow, but he was immortal, it would take a lot more than just a shoulder wound to kill him. He'd lost count of how long it had been since the bandage had been changed last, and at this rate, infection was inevitable. That would be what killed him.

Still, he couldn't find it within himself to care. What did it matter if he died of an infection now? He was ugly anyhow. Kore had been right. Sully wouldn't want him now that he was ugly.

Agnes appreciated the space. He appreciated the silence that fell between him and Sully, but there was a coldness to it. Like the longer it stretched, the further and further away Sully got from him. He was grateful when the supper bell rang, taking Sully from him completely. At least without Sully in the room with him, Agnes didn't have to think about the ever-growing distance.

Silence blanketed the room, and Agnes did his best to go to sleep. Maybe if he was asleep when Sully returned, they wouldn't have to talk about it. Maybe then they could just ignore this whole situation until the infection took over, and Agnes faded away. It would be preferable.

It occurred to him that this wasn't over. Sullivan would stop at nothing to get Agnes to come around. He'd proven just how stubborn he was time and again. He wouldn't—or maybe he couldn't—give up. That meant that eventually—probably very soon—Agnes would have to face him.

The thought struck Agnes hard as he realized that for the last few days, he'd been hanging on to what he and Sully had like a lifeline. A bond he'd always thought so strong now seemed fragile, and brittle as Agnes reassessed it. How well did they really know one another?

It had been years, yes, but over the years there hadn't been much time for them to get to know one another. Agnes was confident that the reason Sully had fallen for him was that he was beautiful. Now that that was gone, Agnes would not be able to hold his interest. Another sob left him, and then the urge to destroy settled in.

There was nothing Agnes wanted more at that moment than to rip the cabin apart. To tear the paper-thin stuffing from every mattress. To break the bunks down into timber and set the whole thing ablaze. If just to feel in control of the situation again.

What he did instead was wander out of the cabin and search for the washroom.

"Hey! Hey, you!" a guard shouted from further down the dirt walkway.

Agnes turned to watch a burly man stride up to him with all the unearned confidence of a bully on a playground. It took a moment for Agnes's brain to fit the face with a memory of a man shoving a tube down his throat to force feed him mush. Agnes shuddered.

"Oh, it's you," the man leered, eyes flitting over Agnes for a brief moment. "Up and about, I see."

Agnes shrugged, his shoulders curling inward to make himself as small as possible. He did not want this man's attention, and the sooner he was able to get away from him the better.

"So, it would seem," Agnes croaked, voice rough from disuse. He cleared his throat and turned to head back in the direction of where he thought the washroom was. Maybe if he just kept walking, this man would leave him alone. Agnes could hope.

"Lookin' for somethin'?" the guard asked, taking a step closer, invading Agnes's personal bubble enough to almost make him step back. He may have been able to refrain from that urge, but he couldn't help the flinch that jerked his wounded shoulder.

Damn it.

"I was just . . ." Agnes swallowed thickly, feeling the hairs on his neck stand on end. "Just looking to see where I could get a new uniform, and a shower?"

Muddy brows raised into the man's frankly hideous hair cut—what man had bangs that shaggy and thought them fashionable?—and his lips tugged into something more. . . Something Agnes couldn't place but that turned his stomach.

"We only issue new uniforms once a month. But I think I can make an exception for *you*." The word 'you' rolled off his tongue in a way that threatened to make Agnes vomit the empty bile of his stomach. "This way." He tilted his head for Agnes to follow him.

It was a struggle to get his feet to move, but ultimately Agnes forced himself to follow in the man's wake. If he wanted to make himself somewhat presentable for Sully, what other choice did he have? Besides, cleaning the wound on his shoulder would probably be a good start to getting himself together. He knew Sully was going to have something to say about his current circumstances, and to be honest, Agnes could do without the lecture. So this was probably for the best.

The sound of hinges squeaking drew Agnes out of his thoughts. His eyes landed on the form of a woman sitting behind a desk, a book held up in front of her eyes to block any distinguishing features.

"What do you want, Wilson?" she asked without lifting her eyes from what Agnes assumed was a trashy romance novel, given the shirtless man on the cover.

The guard—Wilson—leaned against the desk, pressing his hip into the corner as he arched over to meet her eyes behind the book.

Flirting, Agnes's mind supplied, picking up the gesture from his own repertoire. *Gross*.

"I need a fresh uniform for this one here."

"We only issue fresh uniforms on the first Monday of the month," the woman replied curtly, pointedly turning a page. She was clearly unimpressed by Wilson, and Agnes had to say, he agreed with her. Compared to the muscular figure on the cover of her book Wilson was . . . well . . .

"Oh, come on, Yasmeen, don't be like that. I know you guys can issue a new uniform for special circumstances."

"It's not a special circumstance, though, is it?" Yasmeen asked, finally setting the book down, but not before carefully marking her page with a bookmark. "That uniform," she said with a gesture to it as if it weren't on a person at all, "is still in one piece. So, no. It is not a special circumstance. No. I will not be issuing it a new uniform. Whatever fancy you've taken to it."

"But, Yasmeen," Wilson pleaded, leaning in closer so their noses were a hair's breadth apart. "This is a unicorn.

You remember? We were instructed to take special care of it."

Agnes felt a pin prick of panic settle into his gut. That wasn't right. That couldn't be good. Who had instructed that? Why? What did 'special care' mean? He shook himself, clasping his hands behind his back to hide their shaking. It didn't matter. He could worry about that later. Right now, his focus was to get clean, and go back to Sully not smelling like he hadn't bathed in a month.

Yasmeen's eyes flicked from Wilson to Agnes thoughtfully. Finally, her nose wrinkled in disgust. "Fine. Whatever. Just get it out of here. It smells."

She rose from her chair and moved to the closet behind the desk. When she returned, she had a neatly folded uniform in her hands that she handed to Wilson before shooing him out. Wilson turned for the door, and Agnes followed behind. Once outside, Wilson led him through to the long and squat building made of cinderblocks that housed the showers.

The room inside was one long shower of yellowing tiles, dotted with shower heads every couple of feet and drains on the floor to match. It was dank with the heavy smell of mildew.

"Go on, then," Wilson said his hands still holding the fresh uniform as he leaned against the dry wall near the door.

"Can I get some privacy?" It was a stupid question, Agnes knew. He'd given up his privacy the moment he'd sacrificed himself for Sully's safety. But the hope was still there that maybe, just maybe, he'd be allowed some dignity.

"Do I make you uncomfortable, unicorn?" Wilson asked with a snort. Then he took another step into the room of showers, closing the space between him and Agnes.

Agnes stepped back automatically, skidding against the

damp tile floor. He felt every weakness in his body—the nights without sleep, the days without food, the blood loss —he didn't have it in him to fight. He knew if the guard got any closer, though, he'd be left with no choice. It would be fight, or accept whatever desire lay beyond those gleaming eyes.

"I would just like a little privacy," he repeated. Tone quiet, head ducked in obvious submission. The best way to keep a dog from biting was to not look it in the eyes.

"What for?" Wilson asked, taking another step into Agnes's personal space. And then he was close enough that Agnes could see his polished boots against the mold growing in the grout from where his head was ducked.

"No reason," Agnes continued, refusing to lift his head.

Leave me alone. Leave me alone. Leave me alone.

He bit his tongue hard enough to draw blood, swallowing down the words. There was a shout on the tip of his tongue. A desire to trod on the man's instep, and break his nose with one decisive strike, just as Agnes had taught Persinette. But he remained frozen, half from disbelief, and half from lack of strength to fight. He was losing it.

Wilson moved quickly—or maybe Agnes's brain had just slowed down from what little he was doing to take care of it—grabbing the wrinkled shirt to rip it from Agnes's body. The gash on Agnes's shoulder pulled angrily at the harsh movement, drawing a wince. But that didn't stop Wilson.

Agnes felt the cold, slimy tiles brush the skin of his back, though he didn't remember being pushed, and then Wilson was on top of him.

There was a moment of dissonance, where it didn't feel like this could possibly be happening to him. Surely, this had to be happening to someone else, as so many bad things in life seemed to. Agnes was watching it from the outside as

Wilson tugged at the elastic keeping the uniform pants on his hips.

No. No. No. No. No. No.

This was real. This was happening to him. Agnes came back to himself as he felt the weight of Wilson press against his hips.

No, no, no, no, no, no.

"Get off," Agnes begged. His hands shoved at Wilson's shoulders, but he couldn't press the man off of him, no matter how he tried.

No, no, no, no, nononono.

There was a bang, Agnes only just heard it over the sound of the pounding of blood in his ears. Light filtered in through the open door, a shadow falling over Wilson's back.

"Wilson! What the bloody hell are you doing in here? Stop fooling around and come on! Ava got two of them to fight in the yard!"

"I'm busy!" Wilson growled over his shoulder, his hips still forcing Agnes's down into the hard floor. Agnes didn't have time to register the pain it caused until that moment. He was going to have bruises.

"You can have the unicorn later! Come on! You're missing all the good bits!"

Wilson grumbled, but pushed himself to his feet. He gave Agnes one last long look. "I'll see you around, unicorn."

And then he rushed out the door, leaving Agnes struggling to breathe as he trembled on the hard tile floor. He didn't know how long he lay there, trying to regain control of his body, but it felt like too long. It probably *was* too long.

"Get up, Agnes," he told himself, rolling over to push onto his knees. He needed to get up, get clean, and get the hell out of there before Wilson could come back.

It was a struggle to crawl to the wall, and reach the

knob from his knees, but he managed. He didn't waste time kneeling beneath the water; instead, he slipped out of his wet and clinging clothes and scrubbed himself down with them. There was a bar of soap on the wall, but he didn't know how long it had been there. Agnes scrubbed, and scrubbed, and scrubbed until his fingers were raw, and the cold spray had turned his toes blue.

Wilson's touch crawled under his skin like bugs. Making his fingers tremble over the places where the bruises were already darkening. But Agnes forced himself to focus. He forced himself to hurt. There wasn't time enough to scrub away the feeling of his touch, there never would be. And he needed to go before Wilson decided to finish what he'd started.

Without a towel, he pulled on the thin uniform, ignoring the way it stuck to his still wet skin, then slipped on his shoes and headed to the door. He took a moment to steady himself, peeking out of the building in both directions to make sure there was no sign of Wilson, and then he sprinted back to his bunk.

Once tucked away safely in the back corner of the little room again, Agnes curled his arms around himself, and pressed his back to the wall. All at once what had happened crashed down onto him. The crawling started again. Buzzing under his skin like beetles.

How could he face Sully now?

Agnes didn't sleep, just let himself drift. So he was aware when the inhabitants of his little bunk returned from their supper. He sucked in a breath, tracking Sully's progress through the bunks back to their corner. Just as

Sully turned to meet Agnes's eyes, Agnes squeezed his shut, feigning sleep.

"Aggy," Sully murmured, his hand resting on the bed beside Agnes's arm. They were at eye level like this, with Sully being so tall, but Agnes didn't have it in him to meet Sully's eyes. Not now. Not after everything that had happened. If it weren't for the crawling still under his skin, he would have turned his back on Sully to face the wall.

"Go to sleep, Sully." Agnes let his body sag more against the mattress, the exhaustion catching up with him now that the safety of Sully was within reach.

Agnes didn't have to see it to know that Sully's lips had settled into a frown, and a wrinkle had pinched between his brows. A look of upset, and determination that Agnes was all too familiar with.

"No. I'm going to stand here and wait until you look at me."

Ah, there it was. That unmovable will. The same stubborn tone Agnes had fallen for all those years ago. Under different circumstances, it might have been enough to make Agnes smile. Not tonight.

"Then you're going to be standing there an awfully long time," Agnes said without any of his usual bite or wit. The words felt hollow, all of the fight having been drained out of him. If he was looking, he was sure Sully would have started to look more concerned. Those kind dark eyes of his pleading with Agnes to let him in, to let him help.

Agnes curled up tighter, huddling in on himself, but still stubbornly refusing to move his back from where it was pressed to the wall. He needed to be able to see if Wilson was coming for him. Not that he'd have anywhere to run.

"I'm taking you to the medic shed," Sully said, reaching out to brush his fingers across Agnes's injured shoulder.

When Agnes didn't flinch back, Sully rested his hand there. "First thing in the morning, we're getting you patched up."

"Whatever blows your dress up, darling," Agnes said blithely, shrugging his shoulder to displace Sully's hand. It didn't work. Sully held on firmly, and all he got for his troubles was another pull at the stab wound and a hiss of pain.

The bed dipped beneath Sully's weight as he climbed up into the bunk with Agnes. There was a moment where Agnes thought to shove him away. To keep him at arm's length as best as he could. But Sully was warm as he wrapped his arm around Agnes's waist, settling the blanket over top of them, and warding off a bone-deep chill that Agnes hadn't noticed till just then. He couldn't do it. Agnes was weak. He let his body relax into the warmth of Sully's chest, let himself begin to settle down for the first time in what felt like months.

"We'll be all right, Aggy. They're coming for us," Sully promised, and Agnes squeezed his eyes shut to fight off the threatening burn of tears.

How soon? Would they get here fast enough? Manu and Persinette had promised it wouldn't be much longer than a week after they were sent to the camps. But it had already been that, hadn't it? He couldn't be sure. Time had become a strange, twisted thing that made no sense to him anymore.

And he wasn't sure how much longer he'd last in this place. The cold, colorless walls, the thin, colorless clothes, the lack of grass on the ground—it was all too much. Agnes could feel the walls closing in on him. Unicorns were not meant for this kind of life. They were built for color, and vibrance.

Still, Agnes would hold on to what he could. He would rebuild his strength the best he knew how. He needed to be ready for when Manu and Persinette came, and he would be. He would be prepared to fight, to save Sully and the others.

He lay there—listening to Sully's peaceful snores—and vowed to do just that. He soaked up Sully's warmth and promised to rebuild what had been burned to ash. He would rise from it all, and he would make sure he took Sully and the others with him to safety.

With his mind made up, and the solid weight of Sully's arm around him, Agnes finally—*finally*—drifted off to sleep.

In the morning, there wasn't time to drag Agnes from the bed to the medic shed. The work bell rang, and everyone in their small bunk scuttled to the door.

"We have to go," Benji said, frowning when he noticed Sully hesitating. "He'll be safe here until after dinner. Then we can see about getting him some help."

Benji's words made sense. They didn't really have time to hunt down medical attention now. If Sully was late to the mines, he'd be in trouble.

"You don't want to be locked back up in solitary, do you?" Benji hedged, his little hands tugging at Sully's sleeve.

"No." A shiver ran down Sully's spine, not at the thought of being locked up again, but at the thought of being away from Agnes for that long. "I do not."

Benji nodded, and pulled on Sully's sleeve until he was moving again. Taking slow steps toward the door. Once they reached it, Sully frowned, and shook his head. He yanked his sleeve from Benji's grip. The boy opened his mouth to protest but Sully just turned back to the bunk.

"Give me a minute. I'll be right out for breakfast," he

called over his shoulder as he dodged one of their other bunkmates who was swinging down from his bed.

"Fine," Benji sighed, shaking his little head and stepping outside.

Sully crouched, quickly scooping up the blankets from his bed and draping them over Agnes's curled up form. "I'll be back in a few hours, then I'll take you down to dinner with me. After that we can go to the medical shed."

"Mm," Agnes mumbled. Whether it was in agreement or not, Sully couldn't tell. But it didn't much matter. It was more of a response than he'd been expecting.

"You'll be all right. We both will be," Sully promised, repeating the words he'd said last night as he curled around Agnes protectively. "Benji says you're safe here."

Agnes opened his eyes, thick lashes fluttering a little, to look skeptically at Sully. As if asking, *Am I really?* And he was, perhaps, right. Sully could make no guarantees that either of them would be safe here. But it was better Agnes remained tucked up in the bunks than drag his injured body to the mines.

"As safe as one can be, in a place like this," Sully amended.

That seemed to appease Agnes, for he merely huffed a breath and shut his eyes without another judging look. Sully wasn't sure if that was acceptance or not, but as Agnes hadn't fought him on anything, he was willing to count it as a win.

The rustle of everyone getting ready and heading out had died down. Leaving just Sully and Agnes and the quiet of nineteen empty beds. It was eerie, but Sully forced a smile to brush the feeling aside, ignoring the way it made the skin at the back of his neck prickle like something wasn't quite right. Things might never be quite right again, not if they didn't get out of here. He knew that. The gray of the labor camp would suck away the color of Agnes and leave nothing but a shell. It was Sully's job to make sure that didn't happen.

"I'll be back after work," he said again, although he knew Agnes had heard him the first time. Then he leaned in to brush a kiss to Agnes's wrinkled forehead, hoping to smooth it. "Get yourself some rest. Okay?"

Agnes exhaled a long, put-upon breath through his nose, but he opened his eyes to meet Sully's again and nodded.

"Good." Sully's smile wrinkled a little into something more genuine.

"Go, or you'll miss breakfast," Agnes rasped.

Sully took another moment to burn the image of Agnes into his mind. Something to keep him going throughout the day, something to look forward to when he got back. And then he nodded, and turned to leave.

The clatter of spoons on bowls was the only sound in the mess hall, but Sully found it strangely relaxing. It was nice to hear the sounds of life around him. What wasn't nice was the cold and slimy mush that the labor camp's cooks dared to call porridge.

Twenty minutes. That's how long they were given from the breakfast bell to the work bell. It took at least two minutes to walk from each person's bunk to the mess hall. Another five to eight minutes in line. Leaving each of them a maximum of thirteen minutes to force down the cold porridge that felt more like worms sliding down than food. Some of the others had this down to an art, they'd been there so long.

Sully watched as one particularly wrinkled old imp tipped his head back and took it all in one great gulp.

"I guess that's one way to do it," he mumbled, swallowing down another spoonful that wriggled the whole way before settling like cold sludge in his gut.

"It's not so bad once you stop thinking of it as food," the old imp said, offering Sully a wry smile.

"And what should I think of it as?"

"Survival."

Sully nodded, lifting his bowl to take a long gulp. He struggled to choke back a gag, as his throat and stomach rejected the oozing feeling, gurgling slowly down his throat.

"That's the ticket!" The imp slapped him on the back, almost bringing the food back up again. "Tobias."

"Be quiet," someone hissed from across the table. Sully looked over to see the dark, sharp eyes of a goblin glaring back at him. "No talking during meals."

Tobias winked at her, his light eyes shining. "Sorry Delilah. We'll hush up."

Delilah gave him one more long, withering look, and then returned to her own porridge. Tobias waited until she was absorbed in her meal again to return his bright smile to Sully. "Like I said, I'm Tobias."

"I'm—"

Just as Sully held out his hand for a shake, the work bell rang.

"Everybody out! Off to work," a guard shouted, banging a baton on a table full of children that seemed to have banded together. Benji was among them. They all squeaked loudly and jumped from their seats, nearly abandoning their dishes. But a sharp look from the guard reminded them of their duties, and they grabbed their bowls and utensils to drop them in the bin by the door.

"Time to get to work," Tobias said jovially. He moved easily from his seat, with the smoothness of a much younger man.

Sully nodded, scooped up what was left of his meal, and

followed Tobias to the bin at the door to dump his half-finished bowl into the trash with the others.

Wind howled against the opening of the mines, making the dark hole look even more like a mouth waiting to swallow them all. Sully followed the steady line to pick up his lantern and head deeper within.

"You, you, and you, you're in sector eight," a guard said, pointing to Sully, Tobias, and Delilah. She didn't wait for them to nod their understanding before turning to a group of five children, and assigning them to sector ten. Sully and his little group moved deeper into the caves, following the signs to their section. Once they seemed to be out of ear shot of the guards, Sully turned his smile on Tobias.

"Like I was saying, I'm Sully." He set the weighty pickax down beside the wall to hold his hand out for Tobias to shake. "It's a pleasure."

"Pleasure's all mine." Tobias's lips split into another wide grin as he took Sully's large hand into his own and gave it a firm shake. "The old crone we got grouped with before you was a bear."

For a moment, Sully thought to ask what had happened to her, but then he thought better of it. She'd died. Of course, she had. There was no other way out of a place like this. He swallowed down that thought, forcing it somewhere deep inside so that he wouldn't have to imagine that happening to Tobias, or Benji, or Agnes, or even Delilah.

"I'll endeavor to be better company, then," he joked back. It felt strange to laugh and make light of a situation this dire. But what else was there to do? Sulk? Accept defeat? Let the inevitable take not just their lives but also their spirits? No. That wasn't an option.

"You do that." Tobias winked, tapping the side of his nose in a gesture of mischief.

"No talking," Delilah hissed again, her eyes narrowing on them both. "Get to work."

"Yes, ma'am." Tobias nodded with a faux seriousness that didn't match the light in his eyes.

Silence fell between them, broken only by the clank of metal on rock, and Tobias's off tune humming. It was nice—relaxing, almost—to focus on the work, and not worry about what would happen later. Sully let himself drift with the work. Let his mind think solely of the rocks, and the dirt, and not of whatever they were breathing in that would no doubt settle into their lungs, or the deep cough Delilah had.

Hours passed that way, with only a break for water and to use the facilities around lunch time, and then they were at it again. By the time the dinner bell rang, Sully was vibrating in his boots to get back to Agnes. To scoop his unicorn up in his arms and carry him off to get food.

He raced out of the mines, throwing his helmet and lantern at the guard at the entrance hard enough that she looked like she wanted to beat him with it. But she wouldn't stop him. She couldn't. He had someplace to be.

"No running!" he heard someone shout at his back, probably Delilah. He didn't care. Sully's worn boots kicked up dirt, leaving a trail of dust in his wake as he ran to the bunk. Once there, he found Agnes just where he'd left him. Although he looked more alert, even pushing to sit up. "Don't strain yourself. I'll help."

Sully reached for him, but Agnes knocked his arms away, glaring. "I can do it."

"All right." Sully nodded, but didn't pull his arms back, just let his hands hover in case Agnes needed him. "We'll head to dinner first."

"Joy," Agnes muttered, swinging his legs around to the edge of the bed. He pushed himself forward until he could slide off and drop down onto his feet. But when his feet hit the ground, his knees gave out a little, and Sully swooped in to help him up again.

"Careful. You're still—"

"I can do it!" Agnes growled, lifting his head to narrow his eyes on Sully's face. Sully swallowed down any more protests and nodded. "Let's go."

"Right. Yeah. We only get about forty-five minutes to eat dinner," Sully chattered, trying to fill the silence as he walked behind Agnes who took his time in shuffling between the bunks but didn't stumble again. "And the line gets longer than the breakfast one."

The path that led to the mess hall was a crush of people making their way to dinner. Everyone was moving at their own pace, and somehow managing to not jostle each other in their relative hurry. Agnes's boots scuffed at the ground, and Sully settled into an easy pace beside him.

Once they were in the hall, they headed straight for the line.

"I'd offer to get your tray for you, but we aren't allowed to do that," Sully whispered.

Agnes clicked his tongue in disgust, but didn't say anything else.

Dinner was a meal of bread hard enough to use in an uprising against the guards, and some kind of meat mixed into rice that had congealed into something more akin to Jell-O than stir fry. They found a table away from everyone else and ate in a silence more companionable than the room would normally allow.

It was good to see Agnes eating. Good to see the way the warm food, as disgusting as it might be, heated his cheeks into something closer to healthy. He looked so pale, and hollowed out, but Sully was sure he could get Agnes back to where he needed to be. Back to fighting fit. His hope was just that he could do it quickly enough that Agnes would be ready when Persinette and Manu came.

A chair scraped along the cement floor, drawing Sully's thoughts and eyes away from Agnes to the lumbering form of a guard across the room.

Silence fell over the mess hall. There was no clatter of utensils on bowls. No whispered chatter. All that Agnes could hear above the pounding in his ears was the rustle of fabric as people turned to follow the progression of whoever's heavy boots paced across the room. Agnes held his breath, too afraid that if he didn't, everyone would hear the panicked scream that clawed its way up his throat.

"You look like you're having a fine evening, little unicorn," Wilson cooed, leaning onto the back of the empty chair next to Agnes.

Agnes stiffened, tilting toward Sully as subtly as he could manage. His eyes flicked around for someone, anyone to help, but the others in the room ducked their heads as soon as he looked their way, focusing instead on their food.

"Leave me alone," Agnes hissed, scooting his chair across the floor in another horrible screech. Out of the corner of his eyes, he saw Sully's hand gripping tightly onto a metal spoon. He wondered how much pressure it would take for Sully to slam that spoon into Wilson's eye socket.

"And why should I?" Wilson asked, a dark chuckle turning his words into twisted joviality. He was having fun.

"Because I said so." The words came out stronger, and

more like himself than Agnes thought himself capable anymore. But how long could he hold onto that? How long before he caved again to the fear and disgust that crawled like insects under his skin? He didn't know. He prayed it was long enough to keep Sully from doing something stupid.

Wilson snorted, grabbing Agnes's chair to yank it close to his side, his arm flopping across the back of it in a manner much too possessive. "Come now, don't play hard to get, little unicorn. I don't like games."

"Go. Away. Wilson." Agnes forced the words out past his teeth.

Wilson's smile turned sharp and predatory as he pressed himself into Agnes's personal space. So close that Agnes could feel the heat of Wilson's breath against his cheek. "Or what?"

Sully jerked. The movement too small for anyone but Agnes to see. Agnes reached over beneath the table to give Sully's knee a firm squeeze. *No violence*, the gesture said. *Don't get into trouble*, it pleaded.

"Agnes, I think we need to be getting along to the medic now." Sully's voice sounded loud and firm, ripping Wilson's attention from Agnes to the man sitting beside him. There was a moment, a heartbeat, where Agnes could see the rage on Sully's face. He could see the kelpie swimming beneath the skin, fighting to come to the surface and lure Wilson to whatever water was closest.

Agnes squeezed the knee in his grasp a little tighter. Keeping Sully sitting even as he felt the muscles in his leg preparing to stand.

Wilson's eyes flicked from Agnes to Sully and back again in a moment. Then he laughed, as if this was all just some big joke. As if Sully couldn't stop Wilson from getting at Agnes if he wanted to. And maybe he couldn't. Wilson's eyes narrowed in a leer. "I'll see you around, little unicorn." He rose to his feet. "Get well soon."

The words themselves may not have been particularly threatening, but the tone was clear.

You cannot run. You cannot hide. You are stuck in here. With me.

Agnes swallowed, forcing down whatever bile and food threatened to choke off his breath and make themselves known to those around them. For a moment, his grip tightened on the table and Sully, grounding himself once more to where he was, and who he was with. Sully was there. He was safe. For now. Sully would protect him.

Sully carefully peeled the fingers on his knee away and threaded them through his own, returning the grip. Strong and comforting. Then Sully helped Agnes from his seat, leaving behind their dishes, without another word.

It wasn't until they were outside in the fading light of the camp that Sully finally asked, "What was that about?"

"Nothing." The lie felt like lead on his tongue, but Agnes didn't hesitate in forcing it past his lips. He knew, probably better than anyone who had ever known Sully, what would happen if he were to tell Sully what had almost happened in the showers. He knew that if Sully learned of what Wilson had done, Sully would flay him alive, and Sully would either be locked in solitary or worse. A kelpie's rage simmered always, just below the surface. Sully's was just under his happiness, and his bright smile. It would be easy enough to draw it out, especially given how protective he'd always been of Agnes.

To protect them both, Agnes lied.

"Nothing?" Sully insisted as he looked down at Agnes skeptically.

That head and a half in height Sully'd gained with age

had never felt like so much before. Agnes resisted the urge to walk on his tiptoes just to minimize the difference.

"That didn't look like nothing."

"Look"—Agnes stilled, pulling Sully to a stop beside him, and looking up to meet his eyes firmly—"do you want me to be treated, or do you want to have an argument over what some stupid guard said?" His tone was deliberately irritated, and tired. Agnes wasn't angry—he didn't know that he could be at this point. But he also knew that the best way to get Sully to stop questioning him was to play on his emotions. Agnes had always been good at manipulating others; Sully was no exception.

Sully's dark eyes narrowed on him, a frown tugging at his lips. Agnes waited a beat, watching his mind move over those words.

"That's what I thought," Agnes said at length when Sully didn't argue any further. He gave Sully's hand a tight squeeze and moved them along again. Sully didn't resist.

Agnes pressed his shoulder to Sully's, letting his weight rest there. Letting himself find comfort and warmth, and even allowing Sully to take some of the crushing weight for him as they crept through the decrepit maze of buildings, the darkness sinking around them, until they reached one that was smaller than their bunk. It was clear by the size of the building, and the thorny vines growing up the walls, that not many people had been to see the medic. And if they had, it had been quite some time since then.

"Well . . . this is cheery," Agnes said, hiding the fear that weighed down the pit of his stomach, threatening to drag it to his feet.

Sully sighed, his shoulders relaxing a little against Agnes's. "Maybe it's not as bad as it looks."

"Right." Agnes snorted. "You think they provide

medical treatment to the inmates regularly?" He rolled his eyes, looking up to meet Sully's.

Sully opened his mouth to argue, but Agnes cut him off.

"They don't. They let them die." Agnes's tone had taken a hard edge, no longer sarcastic, or playful. That was the truth of it. The truth of a life in the labor camps. It would be hard. It would be dull. And it would be short. "What kind of hatchet job do you think they're going to do on my shoulder?"

Sully shook his head, biting at his lip in thought. He took a long moment to put together whatever words he planned to say, and Agnes gave him that time willingly. "As long as they're able to stitch you up . . . anything has to be better than an infection, doesn't it?"

"Says you."

Agnes felt more than heard Sully suck in another breath. Then he shifted, moving to stand in front of Agnes, reaching forward with his free hand to gingerly tilt Agnes's chin up. Their eyes met and Sully's turned soft, pleading.

"I won't let anything bad happen to you." The words left him like a promise. A vow. "We'll get you stitched up, and then you can go back to bed and get some rest."

Denying Sully had always been a struggle for Agnes. But when he asked like this? It was impossible. There was nothing Agnes could do to stop the nod of his own head, and the flow of his words. "Fine. Let's get this over with."

Behind the thin door that moved on screeching hinges, they found a building with flickering lights, an empty wood stove, and not a soul in sight. There was no medic. Just wooden cabinets full of unused medical supplies, and a rusting medical droid sitting dormant in the corner. A thick layer of dust covered everything, evidence that no one had been inside of the medical shed in years.

"Well, this is . . . underwhelming." Agnes ran a finger

along the top of the cupboard, cutting through at least a centimeter of grime. There were no other doors, and the whole room was open, leaving no room for a doctor to hide. "Guess you're just going to have to stitch me up yourself, Sully."

"I . . . I can't—I can't do that, Agnes." Sully's voice went up an octave higher than it had been since he turned twenty.

Agnes shrugged, moving to clamber up onto the examination table. It wobbled precariously, with one leg slightly shorter than the others.

"I've never had any training. I don't know anything about stitches."

"It's just like sewing," Agnes said, unaffected. He ignored the subtle twist in his gut. "I know your mama taught you how to repair a shirt. It's just like that. Besides, the medic who fixed up your face didn't do a great job either. We'll match."

Sully's frown deepened, the stitches on his face pulling a little as he thought, then nodded. There wasn't much choice, and they both needed to be in near peak form to escape. Sully knew that. Agnes watched Sully tighten his hands into fists to steady them, and then turn to dig through the cabinets to find what he'd need.

"It doesn't look that bad, does it?" Sully's voice was quiet, his head ducked as he dug through a drawer. Agnes couldn't see his expression, but he could hear the self-consciousness.

Agnes bit his tongue to keep from replying with something inevitably snarky. Had Sully not seen himself? Did he not know how handsome he was? In Agnes's firm—and correct—opinion, all a couple of stitches did to Sully's face was made it that much more handsome. A scar would do nothing to detract from the ruggedly dark beauty of Sullivan Hunter. If anything, it would add to it.

Agnes frowned, watching Sully's shoulders hunch forward, as if trying to make less of himself for Agnes to ridicule. The table made a *thunk* when Agnes slipped from it, but Sully didn't turn around. He must have been too wrapped up in his own head, his own doubt. Agnes moved without a word, pressing his chest to Sully's back, and wrapping his arms around Sully's waist. With a squeeze, Agnes pressed his face into Sully's neck for a moment before hooking his chin over his shoulder.

"I think it makes you look roguishly handsome."

"Yeah?" Sully asked, turning his head to look at the side of Agnes's face.

"Definitely." Agnes nodded, digging his chin into Sully's shoulder. He waited, letting the sincerity of his words sink in. Sully had always been able to tell when Agnes was lying. Agnes pulled back and looked at him firmly, letting Sully see no trace of falsehood in his gaze. "You'll be the talk of the ship when Persi and Manu get here."

Sully flushed, rolling his eyes. "Stop flattering me and go sit on the table so I can work."

"Yes, sir." Agnes saluted, and then released Sully to return to the table. He climbed up once more, ignoring the way it wobbled, and pulled his shirt up over his head to make it easier for Sully to reach the wound on his shoulder. The skin around it was red with blood and inflamed from moving around. He knew he should have been resting it, but nothing had seemed to matter while he thought that Sully wouldn't want him. With renewed purpose, Agnes decided he would have to think more carefully about his actions. If he was to save Sully, and the others, he would need to be strong.

The cabinet shut with a *thump*, and Sully moved to the

table with an armful of supplies. "Are you sure you want me to do this? Maybe someone else in the camp is a healer? We could ask around."

Agnes shook his head, ignoring how the lack of hair made it feel strange. "There isn't time to search for one. I need to start getting better now so that when they come, I'm ready. Just . . . be quick. Don't worry about neatness. Just be quick."

Sully's eyes swept over the wound, a scowl pinching between his brows. "It doesn't look good, Aggy. I really think a healer should look at it."

"Well, we don't have a healer! We've got you and that kit that doesn't look like it's been used in twenty years. So, hurry up!" He should have felt guilty at the way his biting tone made Sully startle. He should have apologized. But Agnes just didn't have it in him anymore. He was tired, he was hurt, and he wanted this over with.

"This is going to hurt," Sully warned, taking a few breaths as he organized the kit along the table and seemed to rally himself to the task.

"No doubt." Agnes snorted.

With a nod—more to himself than to Agnes—Sully leaned in and began to work. He poured antiseptic over the wound. It seared worse than it had when Kore had dug the blade into Agnes's shoulder, and his eyes burned with tears, but he managed to swallow down a cry of pain.

That wasn't the worst of it. No. The worst of it was the first press of the needle into the skin—a tight pinch. Agnes felt the burn of tears abate, but only because they streamed, warm, down his cheeks.

Sully paused, looking up to check if Agnes was all right.

"Don't stop." Agnes forced the words past the raw feeling of his throat threatening to swallow his words.

What followed was the tugging of skin—one jagged

edge pulled toward the other. It was somehow less painful than the antiseptic, or the first pinch of the needle, but it wasn't exactly comfortable either. Agnes's breathing grew labored the longer Sully worked, hard pants causing his chest to heave.

Sully paused, reaching for Agnes's hand. Then he pulled it up to place it on his broad shoulder.

"Squeeze." He instructed, tone tender, and firm.

Agnes's grip tightened on Sully's shoulder, nails digging into the skin to leave crescent shaped wounds as the process began again. The wound had ripped itself open further in the days that led up to this. Meaning that what once may have needed fifteen stitches now required closer to thirty—all of which went painstakingly slowly as Sully did his best to pull the skin completely closed.

Minutes ticked away, and Agnes did everything he could to focus on the ever-present ticking of the clock on the far wall instead of the painful tug. He hoped that its rhythm would keep him still so Sully's work would move along unhindered. It seemed to work. Mostly.

When it was all done, Sully leaned in to press a lingering kiss to the jagged row of stitches. A gesture sweet in thought, but painful in execution as the area was still rather raw.

"Please"—Agnes winced, pulling away from the gentle press of Sully's lips—"don't touch it."

"Right. Sorry." Sully's face was carefully neutral as if he were trying to hide the sting of rejection. But Agnes didn't have the time to sooth Sully's ego. His head had started to swim somewhere around stitch twenty, and he felt at any moment he might pass out.

"I need to go lie down." The room was wobbling. Agnes squeezed his eyes shut to try to keep it from spinning out of control. Then he felt strong arms slip under his legs, and behind his back, lifting him easily in a bridal carry. "Sully!" He yelped. "What the hell are you doing? I can walk!"

Sully didn't respond nor did he let Agnes down. His grip tightened, and he kicked the door open lightly before they headed outside into the dimly lit camp. Agnes huffed a little, crossing his arms over his chest in a pout as he leaned closer into Sully's chest.

"Don't throw a temper tantrum." Sully seemed to be biting back a laugh.

"I'm not."

"You look like you are."

Agnes turned to glare at him, but didn't bother to say anything else to argue the fact that he was, very much in fact, throwing a bit of a temper tantrum.

"I've been thinking," Agnes said after the amused glint in Sully's eye had faded.

"About?"

"Well, the other day when I was out of my bunk, it was during work hours. I think that's the best time for them to come."

Sully's brows pinched in the center, creating an impressively adorable wrinkle. "What?"

"If Manu and Persi attack during work hours, there will be fewer guards on duty because they assume all the Enchanted are in the mine. They get lazy when they assume everyone is busy. It's early in the morning and in the evenings that they're worried about people escaping." Agnes turned his attention to nod at a small group of guards in the distance, chattering companionably beneath one of the few lights on this path.

"And everyone is too tired in the evenings after a full day of work without food," Sully continued, following that train of thought. "They'll be no good to us in a fight then."

"Right. Midday would be best."

Sully's lips pressed into a line, turning down another path toward their bunk. Once he was sure they were far enough from the guards they'd seen, he spoke again. "How do we get this to them?"

Agnes thought for a moment and then his lips pulled into a smile. *The med droid.*

"Ask around. There has to be an engineer here some-where, right? They should be able to rewire that old droid in the medical shed to send a message."

It was a long shot. Not all droids could send messages out to others. And even if that one could, who was to say that it wasn't so corroded that it'd be unusable. But they had to do something. And someone with a knowledge of magic and mechanics would only help their chances in making this plan work.

The small, confident smile that had inched its way up Agnes's lips must have given Sully hope. For soon after, his own lips spread into a wide smile as well.

"I'm sure we'll find someone."

All Agnes could pray for was that his hope would not be dashed.

When they reached their bunk, everyone stood outside in a cluster, the door held open by an irritable guard.

"What happened?" Sully asked, holding Agnes closer in a grip that should have been comforting but was a little uncomfortable. Agnes didn't fight to get down, though.

"It's that girl," Benji whispered, looking over his shoulder as if he were afraid the guards would hear him.

"What girl?" Sully prompted, bending down so they could both hear better.

"Gerlinde, I think was her name," someone else supplied.

"She was a gnome, wasn't she?" the woman from the bunk across from theirs asked.

"I don't know."

"I heard she'd been crying all day."

"Someone said she came back from work and her uniform was torn."

The whispers continued as gossip spread among the small group, but Agnes couldn't hear it past the sudden ringing in his ears.

Her uniform had been torn. Was she the one they'd forced to fight with another inmate? Or had another guard done to her what Wilson had tried with him? Agnes felt a wrenching from within his stomach, and all that kept him from throwing up was the grounding force of Sully's hold.

When they brought Gerlinde out, she was wrapped in a sheet and thrown over one of a big guard's shoulders like a used carpet.

Benji let out a sniffle and ducked behind Sully's legs, and Agnes buried his face in Sully's chest, unable to really look at the girl whose fate might have been his own. How old had she been? They talked about her like she was young.

"What're you all standing around for? Get to bed! You have work in the morning!" The guard who had been holding the door smacked her baton against her open palm with a slapping noise and waited as they all filed inside. "Sweet dreams," she crooned, and the door slammed behind her.

"I'd like to go on record as saying I think this is a terrible idea," Benard said from his perch on the arm of Persinette's wingback chair.

She blinked up at him with round green eyes, a frown creasing her forehead. "Why? Manu said they were friends."

Benard snorted and flicked his gaze to Manu, who shifted uncomfortably in his own chair before the fire. Benard looked as if he was about to say something, but his lips remained firmly shut. Waiting, it seemed, for Manu to elaborate so he didn't have to. Manu supposed that was fair.

"We may have been a little more than friends." Manu picked up the glass on the table beside him, then thought better of it and set it back down. He shook his head, picked up the glass again, and took the dregs of the drink from it as if fortifying himself, or perhaps stalling for time. Persinette couldn't tell which. "We dated for a time. But it ended completely amicably."

"She shot you, Cap'n," Benard said mildly.

Drea, who up until that point had remained silent, choked on a laugh.

"Only a little!" Manu huffed, setting the glass back

down with a *thunk*, and crossing his arms over his chest. Defensive. "It was a flesh wound!"

Benard just watched him.

"It didn't even leave a scar!"

Benard's response was a heavy silence, and a weighty look that, although Manu couldn't see, he could certainly feel.

"Well—okay, it did leave a scar," he amended finally, shoulders sagging.

Persinette watched the pair, her fingers turning a glass of water round and round in her hands as she listened. She'd never much thought about Manu with another person before, but the thought didn't bother all that much. After all, Manu was some five years older than her and had been out in the world. Of course he would have had other relationships. It only made sense. What bothered her was that Manu had failed to mention that little detail when the topic of Captain Stella had come up.

"You seem to have left that part out," Persinette said, voice low as she looked down at the swirling water in her glass.

She heard Manu fidget, the creak of the leather against his trousers giving him away.

"There was a reason for that." He cleared his throat nervously.

"I'd love to hear it," Benard chimed in with what seemed to be satisfaction at watching his captain squirm.

"I just didn't want to upset you," Manu said. His hands ran through his hair, making more of a mess of it than it'd been before. "I knew you hadn't been with anybody else, and I hardly want us to be comparing notes. You might— you might . . ."

He trailed off and reached for the glass again, but found it empty. Persinette waited. She gave him time to gather his words. It was only fair, after all; he'd been so patient with her.

"I didn't want you to think less of me for having been with more people," he finished.

Persinette snorted and leveled him with an incredulous look. "I'm not an idiot, Manu. I know you've been with other people. It's a part of life out here in the real world. Just be honest with me."

Soft and firm, that's what Persinette was these days. She may not have been as outspoken, and combative as Agnes had always been, but she was not a doormat anymore either. And there was one thing she would not put up with: lying. Not from Manu. Not from anyone.

Manu nodded slowly in understanding. "Of course."

"Right." Persinette sipped from her glass, sitting up straighter. "Now can we get back to the list of possibilities?"

"Of course, Captain," Benard said. His fingers smoothed the list out over his knee, eyes glancing over to Drea for a moment. She shrugged back at him. "As I was saying." Benard cleared his throat. "I don't think Stella is a good idea."

"She might not be a good idea," Manu agreed, rubbing at his face. He looked tired. More tired than he had in quite some time. But no one mentioned it. "But what other choices do we have?"

"What about Sebastian?"

One look at Manu's sour expression told Persinette that Sebastian was a non-option.

"I'm afraid to ask . . . what did you do to Sebastian?" Out of the corner of her eye, she could see Drea biting her lip, probably to hold in another chortle of laughter.

Manu's expression looked pained, like he didn't really want to say, but he'd just promised not to lie, so he got on with it. "We did a couple of competing jobs with the Uprising, and he lost. He's a sore loser."

"You may have rubbed it in his face a bit, sir," Benard reminded, which earned him a shrug from Manu.

"What about Felix?"

"No, sir, don't you remember? Felix lost his ship in a card game last month. He's out of the Uprising entirely."

Manu rolled his eyes, huffing. "Felix would lose his head in a card game if it weren't attached."

Drea and Benard shared a laugh, and Benard scribbled Felix off the list.

"Very true, sir. Charlie, maybe?" Benard offered hopefully.

"Charlie's ship isn't big enough for what we need. It's just going to have to be Stella. Face the facts, Benard."

Benard sighed, rubbing the bridge of his nose beneath his wire spectacles as if staving off a headache. "I don't know how you're going to convince her to work with you again, Cap'n."

"We don't have to convince her to work with Manu," Drea piped up, a wide grin across her lips as if she knew the solution to all of their problems. Maybe she did. She was barely seventeen, and Persinette would be the first to admit Drea was cleverer than it seemed anyone had ever given her credit for.

"What?"

"We just have to convince her to work with Persinette. And that should be easy enough. Everyone loves Persi." It sounded like the most natural thing in the world when said that way, as if it was obvious, and perhaps for Drea, it was. She gripped Persinette's shoulder, giving her a little nudge that nearly sent Persinette toppling from her chair.

Manu and Benard blinked. Perhaps this was the first

time they'd even thought about the fact that Persinette and Stella would have to meet.

"I don't think that's such a good idea, Pers," Manu said carefully, as if he were chewing on his words. "Stella is—well, she can be rather abrasive at the best of times. It's not that we don't think you can handle yourself—"

"It's just that Stella can be violent when she's angry," Benard supplied.

It was sweet, really, how both of them were concerned for her. Persinette was touched that neither of them wanted her to get hurt. But the thing they seemed to be forgetting was that this was war, and people got hurt in wars. Persinette had accepted the inevitability that she would not come out of this unscathed. All she could hope was that in the meantime she'd be able to do as much good as possible.

"Then Hiccup and Drea will protect me." Persinette looked up to Drea, who nodded firmly in agreement.

"Felicity added a taser feature to him just this morning." Drea's smile was smug. She was proud of Felicity, and she wasn't afraid of showing it.

"Felicity . . . put a taser . . . on the robot?" Manu asked. Persinette tried not to think about what the smirk on Benard's lips might mean.

"She said that he might need to protect himself from MOTHER agents." Drea shrugged.

"Or random tantrum-throwing captains kicking him for no good reason." Persinette's tone turned accusing, her eyes narrowing on Manu.

"That was one time! And I didn't even kick him that hard! He was fine! You were fine, weren't you, Hiccup?" Manu turned his pleading tone to the robot perched at his side.

Hiccup's only response was to blink the light bulb on

top of his head and let out a faint whistle that Persinette had begun to think of as a laugh.

Benard snickered beside her. Persinette had no way of knowing for certain, but she was sure he was imagining Hiccup tasing the captain. She nudged him with her elbow, shooting him a disapproving look which only earned her a wink.

"Still. The captain should go with you," Benard continued, when he'd regained control of himself. "Then if she gets angry enough to shoot at someone, she has a target."

"Exact—" Manu seemed to realize what had been said. "Wait. What?"

"So that's settled," Drea said cheerfully, standing up from where she'd been leaning against Persinette's chair.

Persinette nodded. "Set up the meeting for as soon as possible. And Drea, go see if Felicity has any other gadgets we could use?"

Benard and Drea ducked their heads and left to complete their assigned tasks. It wasn't until the door was closed behind them that Manu seemed to slump back in his chair more, a worried wrinkle between his brows.

"Do you really think you can persuade her to help?" He wanted Persi to succeed, she knew that, but he seemed terrified of her failure.

Standing from her chair, Persinette moved to take his hand and give it a reassuring squeeze. "I know you're worried about me, but don't be. We have to try, if we don't try, then we fail."

Manu nodded, sighing, and lifted his hand. Persinette took his wrist to help guide his deft fingers to her cheek. Once there, his thumb brushed lightly over her cheekbone, then he gave her jaw a little tug, an unspoken signal she'd learned to read weeks ago. She went where he led, letting him pull her lips to his until they met in a tender and thorough kiss that lingered.

It took time for the *Duchess* and Captain Stella's ship, the *Saccharine Sultana*, to be in the same place at the same time so that their captains could meet.

Four long days of fretting had put Persinette on edge. All she could do was worry about Agnes and Sully, and what could be happening to them while she took much too long to get to them. Manu did his best to distract her, but in the end, her mind always went back to them. Agnes had never been kind to her, but he didn't deserve to be there. He was good, at his core. Or at least she thought so.

Thus, it was a relief to more than just Persinette when the meeting finally came. Any anxiety felt by the ship's captains had passed on to her crew, and by the morning of, everyone seemed to be one spilled glass of milk away from a blow up.

"Too much," Persinette said, shaking her head at her reflection. She smoothed her gloved hands down the crimson silk of her floor length gown. Whose idea was it to dress up like this? She didn't look like a captain. She looked like she was going to a party.

"It'll make an impression." Felicity shrugged, her eyes examining the dress from where she sat on Persinette's bed. "That's what you want. Right?"

Persinette reached around to cinch the corset tighter, gathering the material of her dress into something more flattering. "Yeah. That's what I want."

Persinette wasn't sure why, but she felt it necessary to make an impression on Captain Stella. Perhaps it was because so much hinged on her ability to win the woman over to their side. Or maybe it was because she was one of Manu's ex-lovers. Persinette had been too busy to sit down and examine the feelings more closely.

"I wish my hair would grow back a little faster." She ran her fingers through the short lavender tresses. There was only so much magic could do when one had been shaved bald.

Felicity rolled her eyes, standing from the bed and digging around in the drawer of Persinette's small dresser. "You worry too much, Persi."

Persinette shot her an incredulous look as if to say, *I worry just enough, thank you.* But Felicity took no notice as she dug around until she found what she was looking for. When she came into view of the mirror again, a headband was in her hands, adorned with shining brass gears.

"I mean, you escaped MOTHER headquarters. You're pretty impressive." Felicity moved to stand behind her. She brushed Persinette's hair back with the headband carefully before stepping back and nodding, pleased. "You, my friend, are going to knock her dead."

A gentle and happy blush settled into Persinette's freckled cheeks. "Thanks, Felicity." She turned to kiss the younger girl's cheek on her way to the door. "Don't let them get out of hand while I'm gone."

"Aye aye, Captain." Felicity saluted, a proud and knowing grin stretching her lips.

Manu was waiting for her in front of the small dinghy that Benard had prepared. Hiccup huffed and puffed at his side.

The little robot let out a loud whistle when he saw her, and Persinette laughed, blushing brighter.

"Now, none of that, Hiccup. You can't be distracted flirting with me—we don't have time for it." Persinette wagged her finger playfully at him, and that earned a nod and a twitter. She took Manu's outstretched hand, giving it a firm squeeze.

"I can't believe I'm actually jealous of a robot," he grumbled.

"Soon," Persinette reminded, leaning in to kiss his cheek. "You'll be able to see again soon. Once we get Agnes and Sully free, we can get back to hunting down the Great Library. With all the spells ever written at my fingertips, I know I can find a cure."

Manu said nothing, but he seemed soothed by her assurances as they loaded into the dinghy. It disembarked shortly thereafter, with Hiccup in charge of navigating to their meeting spot.

Manu had suggested a neutral playing field, someplace neither group had the advantage. They had chosen one of the Uprising's small, abandoned safe houses on the outskirts of Pooka. Neither party could ambush it easily, but from what Persinette had heard, she wondered if that would stop Captain Stella.

They left nothing to chance, fitting Manu with a bullet-proof vest, and Persinette with a potion or two tucked up her sleeves. Enough to keep them from being injured, and to get them away as quickly as possible.

Captain Stella waited for them when they entered the small sitting room. She had splayed herself comfortably on a well-worn corduroy sofa that stood before a wall of dingy bead board. Her pistol rested in her lap, one hand laying across the handle lazily. She'd unbuttoned the powder blue jacket she wore to reveal a second pistol sitting peacefully in its holster. The implication was clear, at least to Persinette. These were just the weapons they could see.

"Kelii," Stella said to Manu, not bothering to move more than her eyes in assessing them.

"Moreau." Manu gave her a curt nod.

Then they stood there for a long awkward silence as Stella attempted to stare Manu down, and Manu tried to reciprocate with a glare of his own in the direction of her voice.

"I'm Persinette," she announced, her voice going up an octave with the awkward tension settling like a film on her skin. "I'm sort of Manu's—" She tried to think of the right word. Girlfriend? No. Perhaps it'd be best if she didn't say that considering Stella and Manu's history. "I'm Manu's co-captain."

This piqued Stella's interest. She sat up suddenly, elbows braced on knees as her navy brows lifted. Her dark eyes raked over Persinette, assessing her. And then Stella rose, the buckles on her boots jingling as she took one purposeful step after another to close the space between herself and Persinette. "That so?"

Persinette nodded, fisting her hands at her sides to keep from fidgeting under the woman's scrutiny. Hiccup nudged her, letting out a chirp of encouragement. Gulping down her anxiety, Persinette lifted her chin.

"Yes, that is so."

"What'd you say your name was again?" Stella asked, moving in a slow circle around Persinette like a predator might. Up close Persinette could see that Stella's eyes were dark, yes, but they weren't brown. They were a shade of caramelized amber, framed by impossibly long lashes, and brown skin free from freckles or age. And she was tall. Gods, was she tall. She was half a head taller than Manu, and Persinette had to fight to keep from shrinking in on herself.

"Persinette." She wished that Manu would say something. Anything.

"Come on, Stella," Manu scoffed, as if this whole thing

were ridiculous and Stella were some kind of puffed-up toddler. "That's enough posturing. Stop trying to scare her."

Click.

Wrong thing. Manu had said the wrong thing. Persinette realized when the faint sound of a safety being flicked off echoed through her ears, and then she felt the press of a pistol into the small of her back. Persinette shifted just enough so she could look over her shoulder to see the second pistol pressed into Manu's back. Manu, for his part, looked unruffled by this turn of events. How did he do that?

"I'll be the one giving the orders here, *Co-captain.*" She said the title like it was something ridiculous and silly. Like she couldn't ever dream of sharing her power with another person that way. And maybe she couldn't. Persinette was sure most captains wouldn't be willing to give up the control of their crew to another person. But that's what made Manu so interesting; for all his pompousness, he wasn't egotistical. At least not where that was concerned.

A small chirp of question came from Hiccup, and Persinette shook her head at him.

"No, Hiccup. It's all right. I'm sure Captain Stella just wants to chat. I'm sure she'll make the right choice and act like a reasonable person soon. Once she gets over her initial shock." Persinette kept her voice calm and had the audacity —because she had learned some cockiness from Manu—to quirk a fine brow in Stella's direction as the pistol dug into the skin of her back.

"No such luck. Talk, pretty girl, or I'll put a bullet right through that lovely spine o' yours."

Ah. So, they would be resorting to plan B, then. Persinette closed her eyes, inhaling, and let her magic hum through her blood to the surface of her skin, lifting the hairs on her arms. Once she'd gathered it close, she whispered a spell, and let that purring beast do the rest.

A loud yelp. Then the clatter of several pistols and a dagger or two on wood.

"See? I told you she'd get close enough to let you do that." Manu laughed. He looked too proud and pleased for Persinette to be mad at him as he patted Hiccup's head. He tipped his head up toward the ceiling where Stella hung from her bootstraps and gave Persinette a playful wink. "Find me a chair, would you, Hiccup? I think Pers's got this."

Hiccup chirped, the light atop his head glowing happily as he led Manu over to the couch. When Manu's shins hit it, he turned, and promptly sprawled himself out, in much the same posture as Stella had been. Stella still looked shocked, her long hair dangling below her head in a messy curtain of navy locks.

When the shock finally wore off, she started shrieking. "Let me down! You . . . you . . . you little witch!"

Persinette ignored her, bending to pick up the fallen weapons without a word. She set them on the water-stained side table, plenty out of reach from Stella, then arranged herself and her long red skirt on the sofa beside Manu, one booted ankle tucked neatly behind the other. It was a struggle not to lean into Manu's side, the instinct was so natural now, but she didn't want it to look like she was relying on him for strength.

"Not until you agree to be reasonable." Persinette folded her hands in her lap, and only once she was comfortably settled did she flick her eyes up to Stella's reddening face. She wasn't sure how long she could maintain the magic that had glued Stella to the ceiling, but she didn't think it would take much longer for Stella to give in, so it would be all right.

Being hung upside down by one's ankles wasn't a very comfortable position. Stella's dark cheeks were already turning a violent shade of purple as the blood rushed to her head. Soon enough her temples would be throbbing, and the headache that followed—well . . . Persinette didn't envy her that. Persinette swallowed down the bit of empathy that threatened to take over. Now was not the time to show weakness. She didn't want to hurt Stella, but there were lives at stake.

"I suggest you listen to her," Manu said with a proud smile. "She can be damn stubborn."

Despite Persinette's best efforts, a flush spread across her cheeks. She resisted the urge to lean in and kiss him, keeping her eyes firmly on Stella instead.

"As I was saying," Persinette continued primly, "if you agree to listen, I'll let you down."

Stella narrowed her eyes on Persinette and muttered what sounded like several obscenities in French. Persinette made a mental note to have Benard teach her French for later. Maybe they ought to start with the swear words.

"Fine," Stella said, when she seemed to have worn herself out, or run out of nasty names to call Persinette. "Let me down."

With a murmur, the spell released, and Stella floated gently down to her feet.

"Have a seat, please." Persinette gestured to the set of armchairs flanking the couch.

Stella moved to grab a chair, but Hiccup beat her to it. He scraped the chair along the floor until it sat facing Persinette and Manu, and then he stood there, looking up at Stella, unblinking, until she sat in it. Hiccup nodded his approval, and with clanking footsteps moved to stand next to Manu again.

"Thank you, Hiccup."

Hiccup twittered a reply.

Manu reached over to pat the little robot affectionately, and Persinette turned her attention back to Stella. She looked uncomfortable, her hair disheveled and face red. Persinette imagined she likely felt a little naked unarmed. But there was nothing that could be done for that.

"What do you want?"

"We're here to ask for your aid in rescuing a few of our operatives who have been sent to one of MOTHER's labor camps." Persinette wasn't going to beat around the bush with this. There was no time for it. Nor was there any time for pleasantries. Stella either got on board, or they found someone else. Simple as that.

Stella snorted, a disbelieving sound, as she leaned back further into the chair, crossing her arms over her chest. "You guys broke into Headquarters. What do you need me for?"

Manu barked a laugh, reaching out to nudge Persinette. "Word's gotten around quick, hasn't it? It's been what? A month? Maybe a month and a half? Look it, Pers, we're famous!"

Hiccup puffed out some steam approvingly in his approximation of a chuckle.

"That's right, Hiccup. Our Persinette is famous!"

Persinette pressed her lips together, and swatted Manu's hand away as he went to shake her gently again. "Manu. Be serious. Now isn't the time."

Manu huffed, and Hiccup did too in mild indignation before they both fell silent. With a nod, Persinette returned her gaze to Stella.

"Yes. We staged a coup on Headquarters. But that was only to save a few Enchanted. When we loaded up the ship that day, we came away with about twenty new crewmates. This time we plan on clearing out the camp. That'll be at least a hundred Enchanted who will all need a place to eat, and sleep until we can get them over the wall to the Waste. For that, the *Duchess* just isn't big enough. We need a second ship, and another captain."

Stella's amber eyes widened in surprise, mouth slightly agape.

"You're bloody mad, you know that?" Stella said, and though the words were offensive, the tone was awed. They'd won—Persinette didn't even need Stella to say it, not really. "This is completely bonkers."

"Are you in, or not?" Manu asked. His lips had turned up into that victorious smile he wore when he'd won a game of poker, which happened less and less with Persinette these days.

"If you aren't willing to work with us, we need to know now so we can find someone else." Persinette had to bite the inside of her cheek to keep from smiling. She knew the answer. It was obvious in that star-struck, mischievous look on Stella's face.

"For the chance to clear out a labor camp?" Stella pretended to think for about a half a second, but the expression was broken by a wide smile. "Where do I sign up, Captain Persinette?"

Persinette grinned back. She'd have to cling to this victory for a while—the gods only knew how long it'd be before they had another. She leaned forward, holding one freckled hand out to Stella, and was pleased to find Stella leaning forward in turn. With a firm shake, the *Defiant Duchess* and the *Saccharine Sultana* became partners.

TWENTY-THREE
SULLY

he air in the mines always turned stale around midday, Sully had learned. That's how he'd begun to track time, since lunch wasn't provided, and he worried that without a way to count down the hours until he was back with Agnes, he'd lose his mind.

Sully used the already dirty sleeve of his uniform to wipe sweat from his face, ignoring the grit that he felt scrape away at his skin. Tobias inhaled heavily, his lungs struggling to get a whole breath as he pushed his body past the point of exhaustion. It was like this every day, and Sully wondered how much longer Tobias would be able to put up with it. His kind wasn't exactly meant for hard labor. Imps were meant to be flitting about the fields, enjoying crisp sea breezes, and fluttering their tiny wings as they hopped from one hilltop to the next.

"You should get some water," Sully said, lifting the pickaxe again. The hollow *tink* of metal on stone echoed through their little sector of the mine. "Give yourself a minute of rest."

"No talking," Delilah hissed from where she sat sorting through the rubble that Sully and Tobias chipped away from the wall, pulling from the rock nuggets of iron and ore that could be used in MOTHER's weapons and machinery. They were helping to build an armory that would then be used to wage war against their own kind.

"You should get some water too, Delilah." Sully looked over his shoulder to offer her a toothy grin. The one that Agnes used to say would get him either out of trouble or into more of it.

She narrowed her beady eyes at him, as if considering him, and then huffed. Sully watched her, the smile plastered on his face still, and waited. When she'd finally had enough of it, she turned and headed back up the tunnel toward where the water was.

"I'll wait till she gets back to take my break," Tobias said between wheezing pants.

"She's gone. You can sit down for a minute." Sully took Tobias's elbow before he could lift his axe again and helped him to settle onto the ground with a groan.

"I don't know that I'll be able to get back up." Tobias laughed.

"I'll help." Sully smiled, brushing his hands on his pants and leaning against the hard stone, ignoring how it jutted out and scraped at his skin through the scratchy uniform.

Four days had passed, and they'd yet to find someone to help them fix the droid in the med shed. Sully had lifted it onto the examination table, and they'd taken it apart as much as they could without tools. But neither Sully nor Agnes knew what they were looking at. Sully was starting to feel he was at a loss, that they'd never get a message out. And then what? Would Persinette and Manu simply not come? Or would they come at the exact wrong time and cause more harm than good? Sully wasn't sure, and it was the not knowing that slowly chipped away at him.

"You've been awful quiet as of late." Tobias had started picking the dirt from under his fingernails but stopped to meet Sully's eyes with a look that was something too close to understanding. Sully always felt strangely seen with Tobias, but it wasn't a feeling he was uncomfortable with. After all, Agnes had the same penetrating stare. "What's the matter?"

"Who do I talk to about . . ." Sully trailed off, wondering if this was a good idea. He didn't think any of the other inmates in the camp would tattle on them for trying to escape, but one never knew. Still, he trusted Tobias. Probably almost as much as he trusted Agnes, and that was saying something.

Tobias's brows rose, but he waited for Sully to get his words out. He didn't push.

"Who do I talk to about finding someone in here?"

"What do you mean by finding someone? Is your girlfriend in here? I thought you were with that unicorn I keep—"

"No. Not a girlfriend," Sully rushed, cheeks flaring with heat at the insinuation of what he and Agnes were. Were they—was Agnes his boyfriend? It felt strange to think about and would probably be even stranger to say out loud. He opted against it. "I mean someone else. Someone like, say . . . a mechanic? Or an engineer? Someone good at tinkering."

Tobias's eyes narrowed as he looked Sully up and down, ever assessing, ever examining. He really was too smart for his own damn good. He was sure that if they got someone on their side in here, they'd want it to be Tobias. "What do you need an engineer for?"

Sully shifted, listening for any sign of Delilah. They likely didn't have much longer before she came back, and she was someone he didn't think they could trust. He needed to hurry this up. He sucked in a breath to steel himself, hoping he wasn't making a mistake that would get himself and Agnes killed, and took the leap. "I need something fixed."

Tobias's lips turned up in a sardonic smile, and he huffed a truly unimpressed breath out through his nose. "Well, if you can't tell me what you want fixed, I can't point you in the right direction, can I?"

Logical. That's what that was. It made perfect sense. And Sully had already decided to trust Tobias, hadn't he? So what point was there in being evasive now? His dark eyes flicked to the entrance to their sector, and he moved a couple of steps toward it to peek around the corner and make sure Delilah was nowhere in sight. When he returned to Tobias, the old imp sat there patiently.

"We need to fix up the old med droid in the medical shed so we can use it to get a message to our people on the outside." When he looked back to Tobias, the man's eyes had widened, and his mouth had fallen open.

They sat there in silence as Sully waited for an answer, his heart pounding in his ears, and Tobias looked as if the words he'd just said were gibberish. Maybe they were. Maybe there was no real way out. Maybe Sully and Agnes were just setting themselves up for a very messy execution. But they had to try, didn't they?

"So"—Sully shifted, one hand lifting to scratch at the back of his bald head—"who do I talk to about something like that?"

Tobias shook his head, seeming to pull himself from his stupor, a rueful smile wrinkling the corners of his lips. "Sorry. You're just the first Uprising agent I've seen in this place in a hundred years."

"What happened the last one?" Sully was pretty sure he didn't want to know as his gut twisted. But the words were out before he could stop them anyway.

"They broke her." Tobias's words were muted, sad, his

eyes distant. Then he sighed, passing a hand over his bald head, and nodded. "But you've got people on the outside?"

"Yeah." Sully nodded. "A pirate with a ship." He swallowed down a litter of other questions he had for Tobias about this other agent. Now was not the time. Still, it tugged at Sully to realize that Tobias and she must have been close. "So. Who do I talk to?"

"You're going to want to talk to Rosevelt. Don't you worry about it, though. I'll introduce you at dinner. Just finish up your work and get yourself back to your boyfriend." Tobias had a knowing look in his eyes, a twinkle that should have made Sully squirm. He reached out and helped Tobias to his feet. "I'm going to go get some water now. I'll bring you back some."

"Thanks."

THE REST of the day dragged on. Sully's excitement over their progress and his longing to be with Agnes made the hours tick by that much slower. By the time the dinner bell rang, his stomach was a pit of anxieties, each expanding into a bubble that that got bigger and bigger until it threatened to burst. Despite that, there was hope on the horizon. There was no guarantee, but there was hope. And where there was hope, Sully could find happiness.

"You look perky," Agnes said from where he leaned against one of the buildings between the mine and the medical shed. He'd taken to hiding out there, and that was probably safer. The door may have been flimsy, but there was a lock on it, and plenty of weapons inside. Sully felt better knowing that Agnes was at least somewhat protected when he wasn't around.

"I found us an engineer," Sully whispered, bumping his shoulder into Agnes's as they started toward the mess hall.

"You work fast." Agnes huffed a breath that bordered on an impressed laugh, and when Sully turned to look at him, a smile tugged at the edges of Agnes's eyes. Happiness. It'd been so long since Sully had seen it on Agnes's face, yet it was so recognizable it made his chest ache.

"I suppose I do." Sully returned the secret smile with a full-blown grin of his own. Then he took Agnes's hand and gave it a squeeze. Gentle. Reassuring. They were in this together, and they would make it out of this together. No matter what. "Come on. The sooner we meet this person, the sooner we can get you out of these god-awful rags and back into a proper suit. Maybe Manu will be willing to lend you something in the meantime."

The smile took over Agnes's face at that, crinkling around the edges. Blooming in a way that Sully had begun to wonder if he'd ever see again. He was grateful for it now. So grateful.

"Who *ever* said I'd willingly wear that man's garish clothing!" Agnes cried, all teasing as he nearly skipped along beside Sully. "No, sir. I'll be going shopping first thing. Get myself a proper cravat."

Sully laughed, shaking his head. "Of course. Of course."

It was a wonderful thought, Agnes in proper clothes again. It burst the bubbles of anxiety and replaced them with a swell of joy. The daydream of Agnes in a beautiful suit, his waistcoat neatly pressed and trousers fitted just so, was enough to make anything all right again. Agnes deserved to live a life of luscious fabrics, and only the most fashionable of cuts.

Sully was so caught up in the thought, he hardly noticed when they'd made it to the mess hall, and Agnes tugged him into line. But the musty smell of unwashed people and the sound of tonight's pureed meal flopping onto a plate pulled him back to himself. Dark eyes turned keen again, sweeping over the hall from where he and Agnes stood against the wall. He took a quick count of the guards and their positions. Four. And they all sat at a table together near the door, loud and jovial in that way only the truly free could be.

"Don't overthink it," Agnes murmured, giving Sully's hand a squeeze before dropping it to pick up his bowl from the end of the long counter.

"Huh?"

"I said, don't overthink it. That was always your problem when we played chess. You spent too much time thinking about all the possible outcomes, and not enough time acting. We can't hesitate." Agnes's bowl was filled with a wet thud, and then he moved off to the side to wait for Sully.

"Good advice, Aggy," Sully said through clenched teeth as he guided them across the room to the table where Tobias sat.

"Of course. I always give the best advice." The tone was so haughty, so wholly Agnes, that Sully had to choke back a laugh. Agnes smiled back, eyes sharp as they lingered perhaps a little too long on Sully's throat. He felt heat rise in his cheeks again but pushed those thoughts aside. Now wasn't the time. They'd have that later. Much later.

"Sully, good to see you," Tobias said, his eyes crinkling in his happiness as if they hadn't just parted ways in the mines. A wild-haired woman sat beside him, glasses perched on her upturned nose, and her hazel eyes assessed Sully and Agnes in one quick glance. He wasn't sure what she found, but he hoped she didn't find them wanting.

"Yes, a pleasure. Please, let me introduce Agnes." Sully moved to press his hand into the small of Agnes's back as he guided him into a chair. They kept their voices low enough, but in the quiet of the mess hall, they carried plenty for everyone at the table to hear one another. "Agnes, this is Tobias. We work in the mines together."

There was something morbidly normal about the conversation. Like Tobias and Sully were coworkers meeting in a cafe and introducing one another to their respective friends. It was weird, and Sully decided he didn't like it.

The woman beside Tobias leaned in to whisper something into his ear as Sully and Agnes sat down, glasses sliding down her light brown skin.

"I see, my dear." Tobias patted her lightly on the shoulder. "Let's discuss that rather than making assumptions, yes?"

"I'd really rather not," she said, loud enough for them to hear. Her eyes landed on Agnes in a hard look.

"Nice to see you again, Rosevelt." Agnes sat up straighter, meeting her cold look with one of his own. Sully winced at the hard edge to his voice. "So, this is where they sent you?"

"No thanks to you," Rosevelt spat, her eyes narrowing into something sharp and lethal, as if she were calculating how many seconds it would take to throttle Agnes and whether someone could stop her in time. "You were supposed to have my back, Agnes. Where were you?"

"I don't have to explain myself to you." Agnes tilted his chin up so he could look down at her in contempt.

Rosevelt's chair scraped across the floor as she stood, nearly hard enough to topple it. This earned her the attention of the entire hall, and the guards near the door, but she didn't seem to notice. Her fingers had fisted so tightly that her knuckles turned white. "You could have helped! You could have! But instead, you just sat there, like a coward!"

"Hey! Quiet down over there!" one of the guards shouted from where he sat, a piece of lettuce halfway to his lips.

Sully looked at Agnes, and what he found there surprised him. Agnes was biting back his words, jaw clenched. Maybe to keep from shouting back and insulting her further. When he finally swallowed down whatever bitter, angry things fought to the surface, what came out was, "It doesn't matter now. That was ten years ago."

"I haven't forgotten." There was still venom in the hiss, but Rosevelt settled back into her chair. She was giving them a chance. Not much of one, but a chance nonetheless, and Sully wasn't going to look a gift horse in the mouth.

"We aren't asking you to forget," Sully soothed, reaching under the table to take Agnes's hand and stroke his thumb across those pale knuckles.

"Nor are we asking you to forgive," Tobias continued for Sully, giving him a firm nod. "But this—what these boys are proposing—it's bigger than your vendetta."

"I cannot, and I will not, work with *him*."

Resentment settled, stale and stifling, between Agnes and Rosevelt.

Sully and Tobias looked at each other in that way that only two entirely innocent people could. Like they didn't know the depth of the betrayal that those around them had. But Agnes knew. He knew what he'd done. Had it been right? No. Letting Rosevelt take the fall to get the eyes away from him and his people hadn't been right. He knew that even as he was doing it. But he hadn't had very many options at the time. Someone needed to go down for everything that had happened. Someone needed to draw Gaston's ignorant eyes away from Agnes's inner circle. Rosevelt had been a sacrificial lamb. The pawn one gives up to protect the queen. It was a cold-hearted, bitch move. He knew that. But sometimes, you didn't have any good choices to make.

Agnes gripped Sully's hand tighter, closed his eyes for a moment, and steadied himself. Anger wouldn't solve this. Nor would shouting and insults. He couldn't goad Rosevelt into things as he'd once done Sully. All he could do was make a proposal. Ask a question. A reasonable one, at that.

"Who do you want revenge on more? Me? Or the people who threw your father into that asylum?" It would be an easy answer, Agnes knew it would be. Rosevelt's hatred for him could not be stronger than her hatred of those who had locked her father away in a rubber room with no windows. Where he had slowly succumbed to a madness he hadn't originally had and eventually killed himself. She would choose to work with him if it meant they would pay.

He saw it, the moment she came to the only reasonable conclusion, just as he'd known she would. Her lips pressed into a firm line, eyes taking on a cold glint that, if he were a lesser man, he might have tried to wiggle away from.

"All right," Rosevelt said through her teeth.

Agnes returned her cold look with a hard, sharp smile. "We're going to burn them to the ground, Rosevelt. All of them."

Rosevelt's answering grin mirrored his. "What do you need me to do?"

Agnes returned his gaze to Sully to hand off the rest. He'd done his job. He'd gotten her on board. Now it was up to Sully.

"How familiar are you with communications drives in droids?" Sully asked, voice low as he leaned in to whisper to Tobias and Rosevelt across the table.

Tobias smirked, leaning back in his chair to eat. He had decided—it would seem—that his part of the job was done too. Now all that was left was for Sully and Rosevelt to work out the details.

"I know enough." Rosevelt shrugged, swallowing a spoonful of their mushy dinner, seeming unfazed by the cold or the texture. Agnes blanched, pushing his mush around with a spoon. "Depends on what you want done."

"You think you can manage to get a message from a med droid to a ship?"

Agnes stabbed the spoon into the squirming bowl of

grayness, where it stood up like a flag. "If it helps, I know Manu's got a mangled old H1-CCUP unit on board."

"What's he got a hunk of junk like that on the ship for?" Rosevelt snorted, curling up her nose as she shoveled in another spoonful. Agnes swallowed down a gag that would have maybe upended everything he'd already managed to eat. That would defeat the purpose, wouldn't it?

"Hell if I know." Agnes shrugged. "I just know the thing was sitting there puffing away the entire time. It was a hideous patchwork thing but seemed in okay working order."

"Was the comm chip intact?"

Agnes leveled her with an unimpressed look. "Do I look like the type of person to sit there and check the comm chip on every robot I meet? I don't know."

"Well, what *do* you know, Agnes?" Rosevelt spat.

He tasted blood as he bit down on his tongue to keep from saying something that would probably make her decide she'd rather see him wither away in the camps then raze MOTHER to the ground. "Only one way to find out. Right?"

"You didn't happen to get a serial number for the thing, did you, *Agnes*?" She said his name like it was a dirty word, and honestly, he couldn't fault her for it. He'd be pissed too if someone had thrown him under the proverbial carriage, just as he'd done with her.

"Of course not."

"Of course not," she parroted, annoyance lacing every word she spoke. "Any idea what year it was manufactured at least?"

Agnes shrugged.

Rosevelt dropped her spoon into her bowl, where it was slowly sucked to the depths of despair by the gray mass inside of it, and scrubbed at her face. "What information on the bot *did* you get?"

Another shrug.

"I need to have some way of directing the message to it. We don't want every H1-CCUP all over Daiwynn to get it."

"There can't be that many of those damn things left," Agnes argued.

"We don't know that," Sully said. It seemed like he and Tobias were going to be the voice of reason in this, and Agnes had to hope they'd be able to keep he and Rosevelt from killing each other. Because honestly, he was on the verge already.

"Exactly. MOTHER could have a hoard of them just hanging around in a warehouse somewhere. We don't know." Rosevelt picked up her spoon again to point it at Sully, her expression relieved as if someone was finally talking sense.

"Would a direction spell help?" Tobias sat forward again, his arms bracketing his empty bowl. Agnes wasn't sure when he'd eaten. It was like one moment the bowl was full and the next it was empty. But that light in his eyes showed that he'd been paying attention, and he thought he'd come up with a solution.

"Well, yeah. But I'd need something to connect it to. Something personal about the person who owned it. A piece of hair. A nail clipping." She was eating again, talking around a mouthful of gray that made Agnes queasy.

"And then there's the matter of doing magic with this thing," Sully reminded, holding up his wrist, which still sported an iron shackle.

"That's an easy enough fix." Tobias shrugged. "You just need a siphoning spell, and you can use all the latent magic everyone here puts off. It'll only take a little from everyone. Not even enough to be noticed."

"What about the ship name?" Agnes asked, interrupting that thought process.

Rosevelt pursed her lips thoughtfully, tapping at her chin for a moment. "It's a pirate ship, I'm assuming?"

Sully nodded.

"And he's the . . ."

"Captain," Agnes supplied.

"I've never done it before." Rosevelt's delicate brow wrinkled in the center. She seemed to be working over the problem as if one plus one was somehow coming up three. "How personal is the name of a pirate captain's ship?" The question was muttered only just loud enough to hear. "Yes. Yes. I think that might work." She nodded, a little smile curling up one side of her lips. "I've never done it before, mind you," she said. "But it's worth a shot!"

When she said nothing more, Agnes relaxed.

"How long will it take you to figure this out?" Sully asked, the question that clung to the insides of Agnes's throat. He was afraid to ask. He didn't want to hear that it would take her months and months. He didn't think he could survive months and months. Agnes's grip tightened on Sully's hand, sure he was hurting Sully, but Sully didn't complain.

"Depends on the shape of the droid. Anywhere from a couple of hours to a couple of days."

Days. The word echoed through Agnes's mind, washing over him with relief. Days. They could leave the labor camp behind them by next week!

"She'll have it to you in enough time to send a message tomorrow night." Tobias's grin was that of a man who had complete faith in someone they cared for deeply. Agnes supposed out of any of them, Tobias would know Rosevelt's skills best. He just hoped Tobias wasn't giving her too much credit.

"I'll do my best." An embarrassed blush had stained Rosevelt's cheeks at the almost paternal praise, but she didn't deny it outright. That was a good sign. Or at least Agnes hoped it was.

"Great," Sully said. "Now we just need to get you to the medical shed. Agnes has been going during the day, but I'm sure they'll notice if you miss work." He had scrunched his nose up as he spoke. *His thinking face*, Agnes's memory supplied. *Cute.*

"Oh, that part is easy enough." Rosevelt smirked, and Agnes decided very quickly he didn't like that look on her face.

He liked it even less when Sully cocked his head at her and Rosevelt lurched to the side to vomit loudly onto the floor. The whole hall erupted in noise, either disgusted gasps, or pitying murmurs. Chairs scraped across the floor, inmates backing away from Rosevelt as if she were contagious. The guards moved too, backing toward the door.

"Get yourself down to the med-shed!" one of them shouted from where he had plastered himself against the wall and lifted his hand to cover his nose and mouth. As if that would keep the germs from infecting him. Then he pointed a shaking hand at Sully. "You. Take her."

Sully was still for a moment, and then he nodded. "Right. Yes, sir."

He took Rosevelt's arm, pulling her from her chair and supporting her weight with his shoulder. Rosevelt, for her part, played every bit the weakened, sick woman that she wanted them to see. Agnes tried to ignore the subtle twist of jealousy at seeing Sully care for someone else. Touch someone else. In the way Sully had always touched him.

Sully looked back at him, worry etched his face as if perhaps he were afraid of what would happen when Agnes was left alone.

"I've got him," Tobias volunteered. "You two go on."

Sully nodded with a grateful smile and bent to scoop Rosevelt up entirely. She looped one arm around his neck, letting her head lull a little as if she couldn't quite keep it up right.

"That was brilliant," Agnes heard Sully say with a laugh. And oh, how he hated it. Oh, how he hated that impressed laugh directed to anyone but him.

"Stick around. I'm full of good ideas." Rosevelt winked at Agnes. She knew exactly what she was doing. That bitch.

Sully didn't like the look he saw on Agnes's face when he'd turned back to check on him from the door. Agnes looked . . . conflicted? No. That wasn't the right word for it. It was an expression he'd never seen on Agnes's face before, and Sully decided immediately that he didn't like it.

"Stop gazing longingly at your boyfriend and let's get a move on," Rosevelt hissed from where her head still lulled backward.

Ripping his eyes away, Sully nodded and took them out into the falling darkness of the labor camp. With the sounds of the mess hall behind them, Sully and Rosevelt were left to their own company. Sully wasn't so sure he liked that either. After all, Rosevelt and Agnes apparently didn't get along for whatever reason.

"I know what you're thinking," she started, lifting her head to keep from straining her neck. "And no, it's better if you don't ask. What's between Agnes and I—well, you shouldn't stick your nose into it. It won't make anything better."

"If we're going to be on the same side—"

"We won't let it get in the way of working together.

Agnes and I have always been very good at compartmentalizing our anger. He'll swallow it down, and I'll just glare at him until I feel better."

Sully sighed, shaking his head. It didn't seem right. Nothing about this did. Least of all the bit where they were doing this without Eddi's backing. He'd never really liked them, but Eddi was the head of the Uprising, and it seemed like they should be in charge of something like this. But then, would they have had Rosevelt if they worked through Eddi? She didn't seem like she liked the Uprising, or maybe Sully had read it wrong.

"What's *your* deal with him anyway?" Rosevelt asked, breaking into his thoughts.

"He saved my life when I was a baby." Sully was thankful for the interruption. He didn't particularly want to go down the rabbit hole of if what they were doing was right or wrong. It didn't matter at that point which it was, because at that point it was their only option. Agnes was correct: if the Uprising had it their way more lives would be lost than necessary, and Sully didn't want the blood of Tobias, Delilah, Benji, and all the others on his hands.

"Agnes did? That stodgy old unicorn actually saved a baby?" Rosevelt said, disbelief layering every syllable. She laughed.

"It was a long time ago. I guess maybe he's gotten more . . . bitter since then." Was bitter even the right word? Sully wasn't sure.

"Yeah, guess so." She shook her head, and they fell into silence for a time.

The medical shed came into view, just as lopsided and unkempt as it had been a few days prior when Sully had been carrying Agnes. He was much more careful this time when he nudged the door open, not wanting to ruin what little privacy Agnes might have there while he was away.

With the door shut behind them, Rosevelt wriggled to be put down, and Sully dropped her to her feet.

"All right. Where is it?" Her eyes caught on the droid and she frowned, shoulders sagging. "Is that the droid?"

"Yeah, that's it. Is there a problem?"

A gusty breath left her as she stepped over to the rusting machine. One of its visual circuits, the things that looked like eyes, had rusted away entirely and it looked like a mouse had made their home inside. All Sully could pray was that wouldn't affect the internal mechanics, and that the mouse had left whatever wiring they needed intact. If Agnes had had a backup plan, Sully was sure he'd have shared it. That meant there was none. Everything hinged on this. They had closed the droid back up, and returned it to its spot along the wall lest anyone swing by the shed and realize what they were doing with it.

"I guess I won't know till I open him up and have a look. Get him up on the table." Rosevelt's expression had shifted. Her lips pursed, and she'd pushed her glasses up further on her nose so her lashes nearly brushed the lenses. This, he hoped, was the face of someone who knew what the hell she was doing.

Sully scooped up the robot, careful not to dislodge any of its rustier parts, and laid it onto the table. Something from within it squeaked and hissed, and for a minute Sully almost thought the robot was going to come to life. But in the end, a small family of mice scurried out of the hole where the robot's eye had been. They chittered angrily at him.

"Shoo!" Rosevelt hissed, swatting her hands at them until they made a neat line across the table and down the rickety leg before disappearing. "Tch. Vermin. You don't suppose there are any tools, do you?"

"I was able to find a stitching kit, but I think the best we can hope for is probably medical supplies. There might be a scalpel or two around here." He started digging through the drawers. Sully wasn't sure what she'd be able to do without proper tools, but Rose seemed the industrious sort, so they might be all right.

"Dull, I'm sure." Rosevelt snorted, her fingers flittering over the rough metal of the droid. "What shall we call you, my little friend?"

"I'm sure he's got a serial number somewhere." Gauze. Bandages. Antiseptic. There had to be something more useful in the drawers somewhere!

A loud screeching noise accompanied the opening of the next drawer, where Sully found another small family of mice that glared up at him indignantly.

"Sorry," he muttered, shutting it.

"A serial number does not a name make." He wasn't looking at her, but Sully knew that tone of voice. Rosevelt was rolling her eyes. "What about Hubert?"

"Hubert?"

"Yeah, looks like his serial number is H-U-1-3-3-R-T. Hubert."

"That doesn't spell Hubert." Sully shook his head, crouching down to dig through another cupboard. He didn't even want to think about what the thick layer of dust was laced with in there. He probably should have found some gloves to put on. But that was an issue for someone who had more time to deal with it.

"Sure, it does," Rosevelt insisted. "Look, if you don't like it, you can just name him yourself."

"How are you so sure it's a him?" Sully found a promising-looking wooden box and grinned. When he picked it up, it made a noise like metal clanking against metal. Maybe they were getting lucky.

Rosevelt didn't dignify that with an answer; she snorted.

"Besides, you don't want me to name it. We had a goat on my parents' farm, and they let me name it when I was five. His name was Mr. Goat. Agnes never let me live it down." Sully laughed.

Another snort. "Yeah, you just lost all of my respect. What'd you find?"

"A box," Sully drawled, setting it down on the table beside the droid.

"I think I hate you more than Agnes. And that's saying something." Rosevelt snatched the box and tried to pry it open with a fingernail. The lid held firm, probably locked to keep the inmates from reaching the sharp implements.

"Give me that." He took the box back. There was a bit of a lip where the bottom met the lid. Not much, but it would be enough. Pressing the very tips of his fingers against the lip, he pulled as hard as he could. The lid flew off, flinging the contents of the box everywhere.

Rosevelt yelped, jumping away from him and the flying set of scalpels he'd unearthed. "Watch it! You could have killed me!"

"You're as dramatic as Aggy," Sully muttered, bending down to grab one of the instruments from the floor. "You think this will work?"

"Anything is better than nothing." She snatched it from him and got to work. "Set the empty box there. I'll put the screws in it, so we don't lose them."

Silence reigned as minutes ticked by into hours. Rosevelt took her time disassembling Hubert's chest, carefully setting each piece beside him on the table so that she'd know where it had come from, and how it went back. Sully did his best to stay out of her way.

At some point, he moved to the door, pushing it open a crack to keep an eye on the alley beyond. The bedtime bell had rung some time ago, and he wasn't sure how long before the guards came looking for them. They'd need to be able to hide Hubert and their work if someone came. Rosevelt had yanked a curtain over for around the table just in case. It sat ready at her feet. But so far, they had been lucky.

"Ha!" Rosevelt crowed, breaking the silence, and making Sully jerk hard enough to hit his knee on the doorframe.

"Shit." He rubbed it and shut the door, locking it behind him, then moved back over to the table. "What? What is it? 'Ha' what?"

"You see this?" She tapped a strange copper square somewhere near the base of Hubert's throat. "This is his comm chip."

"So he has one." Sully's words were slow. He didn't see what was so great about finding it. They'd known the robot had to have a communication chip; otherwise, it wouldn't have been able to speak with its patients.

"It's intact!" Rosevelt giggled, bouncing on her toes. "It's intact, and look—look." She pulled the chip carefully from Hubert's innards with a pair of needle nose tweezers they'd found amongst the other instruments and turned it over. "You see this bit?"

She was pointing at something, but Sully couldn't for the life of him tell what. It just looked like a bunch of tiny, raised, silvery bits. "Ummm . . . sure?"

Rosevelt huffed a laugh, shaking her head. She was still bouncing, making his view of the chip blurred and all the more confusing. But he didn't think it would have made a difference. Besides, her excitement had to mean something good.

"This bit," she said, pointing again and speaking slowly as if she were talking to a small child, "is for long range communications."

It took an embarrassingly long time for those words to filter through Sully's mind but when they finally had, he shouted. He threw his arms around Rosevelt, hugging her tightly.

"Watch it! You'll make me drop it," she snarled, jerking away from the hug and curling her body protectively around the little chip. It wasn't any bigger than the two fingers she was using to pinch the tweezers. If it flew off somewhere, it'd probably be gone forever. Or worse, broken.

"Sorry. Sorry." He patted her shoulder awkwardly.

"But yes, that means we can definitely contact the *Duchess*. We just need Tobias and Agnes here to help us work the latent magic spell, and then we can get it out." She set the chip carefully back inside Hubert's chest, reconnecting it with a care and precision Sully was sure he'd never be able to mimic.

"What about Hubert? Will he work?"

She laughed, patting the robot's shoulder. "There isn't anything at all wrong with Hubert. He's in perfect working order apart from that one visual socket, and some rust. But we can fix that easy. The guards here probably just haven't bothered having anyone treated in a long time."

Rosevelt didn't wait for him to ask how she planned to fix that. She rooted around in a drawer under the table and pulled out an eyepatch, looking quite pleased with herself as she strapped it over Hubert's missing visual socket. Sully laughed, shaking his head. It was ridiculous. Silly. But it was good. Almost too good to be able to laugh and play when so much else could go wrong with this plan.

"I just need to put him back together and give him a jump start. I should be able to rewire that lamp easy enough to use." Rosevelt nodded to the light at the corner of the table that looked like had been placed there to aid in surgeries.

"Just don't electrocute yourself," Sully warned, heading back to the door to peer out into the darkness.

"Pft. Don't electrocute yourself, he says. What does he think we are, Hubert? Idiots?"

"How long will it take you to get him in working order for us to send a message?" Sully's leg shook as he looked out, nervous energy manifesting itself. It didn't matter. Soon. Soon they would be out of here.

Rosevelt glanced up at the clock on the wall. It was high up near the ceiling and caged in as if they were afraid someone would steal it.

"I should be done a couple hours before the breakfast bell rings. We can bring Tobias and Agnes in then and hopefully make it to the mess hall before anyone notices we've been missing." Rosevelt had already begun putting the robot back together, hands moving quickly and diligently, tone disinterested.

They fell into a companionable silence for a little while. Rosevelt didn't seem interested in making conversation, and Sully wasn't interested in throwing off her focus. The quicker she got that done, the better.

"And the comm chip's connected to the motherboard. The motherboard's connected to the power source. The power source is connected to the circuit board." Rosevelt had started to hum under her breath as the pieces of Hubert slowly disappeared back inside.

The sight of Sully and Rosevelt leaving together—two peas in a very annoying pod already—gnawed at him, ate away at his thoughts, the emotion threatening to color everything Agnes knew, even as he refused to identify the emotion for what it was. Because the fact was, Rosevelt was beautiful, even with the short-cropped puffy curls atop her head. Her bone structure was fine. Her eyes were bright. She was clever and she was good. But above all else, she was new. Agnes couldn't compete with new, nor could he help but notice the glint of amusement in Sully's eyes.

The whole scene played out over and over in Agnes's head as Tobias pulled him to his feet and led him back to the cabin. That glint was supposed to be his and his alone. It belonged to no one else.

As if he'd read Agnes's mind, Tobias moved up beside him, and patted his shoulder. "Don't you worry, m'boy. That young man is desperately in love with you."

Agnes wished he could say that Tobias was the first person who'd said as such. Each had been disregarded in their turn, just as Tobias was now. How could any of them know? How could any of them be sure when not even

Agnes himself was? He'd known Sully the longest. He should have known Sully the best. But Sully had never said the words, and without that, there was just no way to know. At least, not in Agnes's mind.

"He's never said as much," Agnes muttered petulantly.

Tobias's gray eyes blinked at Agnes, as if perhaps he couldn't believe the stupidity of such a statement.

"Yeah, well . . . have you ever said it to him?"

The question struck Agnes silent. He blinked hard, trying to think. His mind raced over moments and memories, fitting each of them together like a puzzle piece. There had been kisses and smiles. There had been love making, and tenderness. The brush of a hand on the small of his back. The smell of a meal half burned but made specifically for Sully with care. But had he ever actually said the words?

"No," he answered when each moment was discarded.

"Then I guess you had better get on that, yeah?"

"Yeah. I guess I had better," Agnes agreed, feeling like a complete moron and hating Tobias for having pointed it out. The old man didn't rub it in, though; he merely nodded, and they continued on toward the bunks.

They stopped just shy of Agnes's when the wind picked up around them, and the rushing sound of a zeppelin landing in the field roared through the camp.

"We shouldn't be getting any new arrivals right now." Tobias frowned, his head tilting.

"Let's to go see what's going on." Agnes turned from the door to his bunk and started through the narrow alleys of the camp before Tobias could stop him. They had to know if there was any change, no matter how minor, anything that could upset the careful balance they'd found.

The man's face was in shadow as a set of guards shoved him from the cargo hold. A grunt of pain left his lips, swallowed by the sound of the still-ticking engines of the zeppelin. And then he crossed beneath a light, and Agnes blinked hard, not sure he was seeing what the thought he was.

"Roy?"

"You know him?"

"Yeah . . . I left him in charge of my group inside MOTHER." Agnes's fingers itched at his sides, his toes scraping at the bottom of his boots as he struggled to keep himself in place. He needed answers, but he couldn't rush forward and get them right away.

"He must have gotten caught." Tobias had moved just enough to put his crooked shoulder in front of Agnes, subtly blocking him from moving closer.

"He's human."

"You think that matters to them? He's a traitor. He's lucky they didn't hang him just to prove a point." Tobias shook his head, letting out a breath. "We should get you to your bunk. I promised Sully."

"But—"

"Let me look into Roy. No one is going to pay attention to an old imp." Tobias took Agnes's wrist and tugged him toward the bunks again. "I'll get you some answers. Or I'll send him your way."

Agnes wanted to argue, to rip his wrist from Tobias's grasp and run to Roy. To shake Roy until he gave Agnes answers about how everyone was. About if he'd gotten everyone out. Gladys and Penny and Sabina and all the others. But Tobias's grip was like iron around his wrist, and the old imp was right. Agnes wouldn't be any good to anybody if Wilson got his hands on him.

They were in front of Agnes and Sully's bunk again, the door slightly ajar where it didn't shut quite right.

"See you tomorrow, Agnes. Have a good rest." Tobias

clapped Agnes on the shoulder. There was a smile on his face that had not a hard edge to it in sight. It was kind, caring. The kind of smile Agnes hadn't ever had directed toward him before. Not by anyone but Gladys, anyway, and suddenly he missed her horribly. What would she have said to Agnes about this situation? Probably the same thing Tobias had, in all honesty.

"Yes," Agnes said stiffly. "Thank you, Tobias." The words felt strange to his lips.

It wasn't until a while later, when he was tucked beneath the blanket that still smelled of Sully, that Agnes wondered when the last time was he'd said thank you. Years, maybe. Perhaps longer.

He shook the thought aside. Now was not the time. No, he needed to get rest. He needed to sleep, or he'd be no good to Sully when the droid was fixed, and it was time to cast the spell. He couldn't have that. He had to be ready.

And as he drifted between sleep and waking, he remembered something—a faded, distant memory, the first time he'd spoken Sully's name.

He remembered that moment very clearly, even now.

It had been months since Agnes had saved the child from his insane handler. After that debacle of a mission, MOTHER had kept him on a short leash. Meaning he hadn't been able to get away to check in on the babe. There was a strange nervousness in the pit of his stomach when Agnes lifted his hand to knock on Sloan and Dalton Hunter's door.

Almost as soon as the knock sounded, Dalton opened the door with a bright smile. His hair was in disarray, and dark smudges and rumpled clothes spoke of happy exhaustion. Far happier than he'd been the last time Agnes had seen him.

"Agnes! Come in! Come in!" Dalton didn't wait for

Agnes to accept or reject the invitation. He grabbed Agnes's wrist and pulled him inside.

There was a fire blazing in the hearth, Sloan sat in one of the large chairs beside it, rocking a bundle of blue blankets. Agnes blinked, looking between Dalton and Sloan's smiling faces. He had only known the couple for the last few months because of the baby, and by extension the Uprising, but he hadn't put much thought into what Eddi had said. When he'd reached out to find a safe place for the child, they'd suggested the Hunters, who had wanted a child of their own for so long, but had never been able to become pregnant. They'd taken to the little creature as parents would to their own child. It helped push aside the worry Agnes had been feeling.

"I'm sorry if I'm interrupting. Perhaps I should have sent word first." Agnes felt strangely out of place in their happy little bubble. They were a family, and he did not belong. He never would.

"Nonsense, Agnes," Sloan scolded in a hushed tone. Her eyes remained fixed on the little bundle of blankets with a content smile on her face despite the bags beneath her eyes. "Come, meet Sullivan."

It took an embarrassingly long time for the words to register in Agnes's mind. "Is that his name?"

"It was my father's name. Seemed fitting that he have it. Isn't that right, Sully?" she asked the baby, who let out a little gurgle.

"Come. Come. You have to hold him," Dalton said, pushing Agnes into the chair beside Sloan's.

Agnes shifted awkwardly. How did one sit when they were about to hold a baby? He didn't know. But Sloan didn't give him time to figure it out either, as a second later she'd risen and deposited the baby into his arms. Agnes hadn't forgotten what those dark eyes looked like, but they struck him all over again as Sullivan looked up at him wide-eyed and innocent.

What did one say to a baby whom they had saved? What did one say to a baby at all? Agnes had never so much as held a baby before rescuing Sullivan, much less been left with one to try to talk to it. Would the little thing even understand him? Probably not. Yet, as they stared at each other, and the seconds ticked by, he found words unnecessary. There seemed to be an understanding between them.

"Sullivan," he'd said the name then—trying it out, but it didn't seem quite right. "Sully," he tried instead.

The child giggled, lifting one chubby, dark-skinned hand to grab a lock of Agnes's rainbow hair, and tug it gently. Agnes's heart tugged right along with the lock of yellow hair.

IT WAS EARLY in the morning—too early, if you asked Agnes, long before first light—when Sully burst through the door. His eyes were wild, and he was panting. Agnes hadn't been asleep long, if he'd been asleep at all. The tread of Sully's shoes made quick thumps on the cold dirt floor, eating up the distance between the door and their shared bed.

"What is it?" Agnes asked, trying to get the sleep from his eyes.

"Rose has almost got him working." A broad smile split Sully's features. Agnes held back a groan of annoyance at the combination of the early hour, that wild happiness, and the knowledge that Rosevelt had become Rose overnight. "You've got to come."

"Why?" Agnes grumbled, grabbing the blanket and rolling over to face the wall. That way he didn't have to see that excited light in Sully's eyes. Even without seeing it, the memory was burned into the backs of Agnes's eyes, where it would likely never go away.

"I want you to be there with me when we send out the message," Sully whispered. His hand had reached to tug gently at Agnes's shoulder, not forcing him but asking for Agnes to roll back over and face him. Pleading for eye contact.

"Why?" Agnes repeated, petulant, a grumpy child who'd been woken much too early and didn't want to face the day.

"Because I want to do this with you, silly." Sully huffed a laugh. He didn't say 'because we need you for the spell'. He didn't say 'because you're the leader of this ragtag group of misfits'. He didn't say because 'this was your idea'. He just said 'I want you there, with me'. Agnes felt his heart clench. There was no fighting that. "Come on. Now's not the time for lying in bed."

He hadn't said it, Agnes realized, as he swallowed down the disappointment threatening to make his words sharper than they ought to be. Even when asked point blank, Sully still hadn't said it. Perhaps he never would. Perhaps Tobias had been wrong, and Sully didn't feel it. Or maybe . . . it was something worse? Maybe Agnes *would* have to say it first.

Agnes let Sully pull him from the bed and out into the gray morning light. They ducked between two buildings to wait for one of the evening guards to pass by. Most of them had already headed to bed, but it would seem there were stragglers. Or perhaps he was a daytime guard headed to the mines. It didn't matter. There was no difference to Agnes.

Once he'd passed, Sully made his way out of the alley again. Agnes reached out and grasped Sully's wrist just above the iron shackle, pulling him back to face him.

"Sully," Agnes said—tasted the name for the first time in what felt like years. It felt strange in Agnes's mouth. Too intimate. Too raw. He'd said Sully's name a million times since the moment Sloan had said it to him, and yet this felt like the very first time.

That first time was it. That had been the moment Agnes had been lost to Sully forever. No one else had ever held his heart the way Sully had, and that little kelpie had grown into the man before him who was looking at him with an expression of worry and concern.

"Sullivan."

"What is it? What's wrong, Aggy?" Sully asked.

"I just . . . I just—" Agnes had thought the words so many times over. He'd felt them right down to his very marrow, but he'd never once been able to push them past his lips.

Sully's expression grew more concerned, a wrinkle forming on his forehead. Agnes closed his eyes, took a deep breath in through his nose, pressed it out through his lips, and nodded to himself. With Manu and Persinette no doubt on their way, this place would become a battlefield very soon.

Now, he told himself. *It is now or never. For who knows what tomorrow might bring.*

"I just need you to know before . . . before this place is set ablaze." It was hard. Why was it so hard? The words were simple, and they were there. They lingered on his tongue, getting caught somewhere between his heart and his lips. "That I—I . . ."

The words hung there, in the back of this throat, refusing to come forward. Agnes coughed, trying to force them out, but they were lodged there, unmoving. Still, without saying them, Sully seemed to understand. A smile started at the corners of Sully's lips and grew until it was a wide, toothy affair.

"Oh, Aggy, I love you too." Sully laughed, shaking his head. He didn't hesitate. He didn't have to force them. The words seemed to spring from his tongue as if they'd been living there all along, waiting for the moment when they could finally be said.

Agnes moved up onto his toes, pressing his lips to Sully's without another thought. Sully's arms scooped him up closer, and Agnes melted in against Sully. His knees gave way beneath him with a gasp. There had been kisses before this one, of course. But this one was different some-how; it tasted of longing and understanding. Of forgiveness. Of rightness. As if pouring everything that hadn't been said for decades into it. Agnes's head spun from lack of air, but he refused to stop. He couldn't. Not if he wanted to, which he didn't.

Distantly, Agnes heard a cough, but he didn't care. And he wasn't going to let go, not ever. Not if all the air was gone and his heart stopped. He'd cling to this moment until there was nothing left of him. But damn it all if the cough would be ignored. Whoever it was followed the cough up by a nudge.

Sully pulled away first, eyes cutting toward the person who'd bumped them. Agnes couldn't quite choke down the giggle at the scathing look Sully gave the person.

"Well . . . hullo again, Sullivan, Agnes," Roy said with a knowing smile and an embarrassed flush in his cheeks.

"Roy?" Sully said, confusion replacing the narrowed look.

Roy nodded.

Agnes thought perhaps he and Sully ought to be

ashamed of being caught as they were in a place that wasn't exactly safe. They were trained agents, right? But he couldn't find it within himself to care. Not when Sully's eyes were half-lidded, lips swollen, and a faint blush painted his ears.

"Where did you come from?" Sully's brows knitted in the middle, but he seemed loathe to let Agnes go.

Then Agnes heard Rosevelt in the distance. That bitch. Complaining about something. "Have you found them?" she called.

"I'll explain later," Roy said to them, his voice wavering with laughter. "Yeah, I did. They were making out."

"Oi! Lovebirds," Rosevelt huffed, rounding the corner with a narrowed look of irritation. "Could you maybe stop trying to swallow each other's tongues long enough to get this done? Breakfast bell is in twenty minutes!"

It was Sully who pulled back first, though Agnes could see there was some regret in it, a stupid love-drunk smile still on his lips. "She's right. We should get this done."

Agnes nodded, clearing his throat.

"Then we can go shopping," Sully teased, winking.

"I like the way you think, darling," Agnes cooed, grabbing Sully's hand to tug him the rest of the way to the medic shed.

Rosevelt made a not-so-subtle gagging noise behind them, and Roy just laughed good-naturedly. Agnes didn't give a flying shit.

The droid was sitting up on the examination table, one eye covered with an eyepatch, the other glowing faintly. Agnes tilted his head at it.

"His name is Hubert," Rosevelt supplied, moving to the table and tapping the robot's shoulder affectionately.

"Why the eyepatch?" Roy asked.

"He was missing a visual circuit. It seemed appropriate."

Rosevelt grinned. "Now, we just use the spell, and we should be good to go."

"Should be?" Agnes said, still looking at Hubert with his head cocked. "How will we know if it's worked?"

"I mean, theoretically, they'll be able to send a message back, but only if it goes through, and only if Hubert's receiver is working properly."

"That's a lot of ifs."

"What other choice do we have?" Rosevelt said flatly.

"Fine, let's get this over with," Agnes huffed. He dragged Sully closer by the hand, and the small group formed a circle around Hubert. Latent magic hummed low between them, flowing from the air like the buzz of static, bits and pieces, scraps from every being in the camp. Not enough for any singular being to do something on their own, but enough when gathered together to send a message. It glowed, swelling as they spoke the words which Tobias had scratched onto a bit of an old medical chart, making Hubert's eye glow brighter.

"All right, that should do it." Rosevelt nodded, dropping Sully and Roy's hands. "Press that button and start talking."

Agnes eyed the button dubiously. It was dark red with age. Puce, really. "That's it?"

"We've been at this all night, Aggy. Isn't that enough?" Sully asked, sounding tired.

"Seems a little simple."

"Just push the damn button, Agnes!" Rosevelt snapped.

Agnes huffed and pressed it.

Hubert made an angry grinding sound, like a fork in a garbage disposal.

"Is it supposed to make that noise?" Agnes was pretty sure robots were *never* supposed to sound like that.

"Just talk, you idiot," Rosevelt hissed.

"Right." Agnes leaned in closer to Hubert, unsure of where the speaker was.

Sully nudge him a little, and then pointed to a small hole in the robot's shoulder. Agnes nodded his thanks.

"Manu. Persinette. This is Agnes." He cleared his throat, feeling awkward having a one-sided conversation that may or may not reach the person who he wanted to hear it. "Sully and I have discovered that the best time to attack will be just before midday. There are fewer guards on duty then. We'll need two days to get everyone in the camp ready for the attack. With or without a response, we'll be waiting for you . . . in forty-eight hours. I hope you're close enough for that. I hope this reaches you." He released the button, and then the four of them stood in silence.

Waiting.

"What's it doing?" Stella asked, alarmed, as they all stared at Hiccup.

Hiccup, who had been in the middle of making his way across the worn wooden floor with a tray of tea, had stopped dead halfway between one armchair and the couch. The little lightbulb atop his head dimmed and brightened in a strange pattern that Persinette didn't recognize. And he didn't appear to be looking at anyone. Persinette wasn't sure how she could tell, she just could.

"Maybe his bulb is about to go out?" Persinette frowned, cocking her head at Hiccup. She rose from her chair and moved to his side to inspect him. "Hiccup. Are you all right?"

The door swung open, and in came Benard holding a tray laden in sandwiches. "I didn't know his communication chip was still working."

"If he's receiving a message, shouldn't he be talking?" Manu asked, nose scrunched.

"Well . . . yes." Benard sat down the tray. "But if Felicity didn't fix his voice box, then he won't be able to vocalize anything. Has he ever talked before?"

"I don't think so."

Persinette shook her head. "He whistles sometimes, but he doesn't talk."

"Then she probably didn't fix it."

"What do we do?" Persinette's hands hovered over Hiccup's little brass head, wanting to reach out and touch, to help, but not knowing how. Her heart raced at not knowing what to do. "Do we know who's sending a message? Is it something important? Maybe it's Eddi. Maybe they can't reach us by their normal means of contacting us."

Panic. That's what that was. It gripped her insides, filling her up with nervous energy, making it hard to breathe around it.

She wasn't sure when Manu had stood, but he was beside her then, his hand reaching for her elbow, following the line of it down to her hands and taking it between his own to squeeze them gently. "Breathe. Just breathe, Pers."

Persinette nodded, taking a deep breath in through her lips, holding it for a beat, and then exhaling through her nose.

"That's it. Calm down." His words were a rumble as he pulled her in close, pressing her head to his chest. Persinette listened to his heartbeat, steady and slow. She focused on it, counting the beats. One. Two. Three. Four. "It's all right. Just relax."

Persinette forced herself to suck in another deep breath, inhaling the smell of pineapples that always seemed to cling to Manu. This was better. This was so much better. She could think. She could breathe. There was more to the world than just the pinprick of light that her panic had narrowed it down to. When her breathing returned to normal, she gave Manu a pat. "I'm okay now."

He nodded, pulling back but not letting go of her hand. "Who could it be?"

Benard shrugged.

While Manu had gotten Persinette settled, Benard had taken hold of Hiccup and forced him over to Manu's desk by the window. He pulled a typewriter from one of the shelves of Manu's antiques, setting it on the desk with a definitive *thunk*.

"I don't know. But when he gets done, he can transcribe it with this. Then we can decide what to do about it." Benard grabbed a sheet of paper from the drawer and loaded it into the typewriter.

Persinette was glad one of them was thinking. The room fell silent, every pair of eyes watching the little robot as his light continued to blink strangely.

After what seemed like too long, Hiccup regained control of his faculties and dropped the tray. The noise of shattering teacups seemed to upset him, and he let out a strained whistle, the light on top of his head blinking on and off quickly as it always did when he thought he was in trouble.

Benard patted Hiccup's shoulder gently. "It's all right, Hiccup. They can be replaced."

Hiccup twittered, his mix-matched metal hands shaking.

"We can deal with that in a little bit. Do you think you can type it out for us?" Benard's tone was gentle, like he was speaking to an injured animal or a frightened child. "Just try to go slow, so it doesn't get jumbled."

Hiccup nodded, his hands hovering over the typewriter. They had stopped shaking. The click-clack of metal digits against metal keys filled the air. When he finally stopped, Hiccup looked up at Benard, as if asking if he'd done well. Benard patted the robot's head and pulled the paper from the typewriter. He adjusted his glasses, pressing them up further along his long nose, and sighed.

"What's wrong?" Stella asked.

"The space bar is broken. I thought you were going to get that seen to, Cap'n," Benard scolded.

Manu laughed, rubbing at the back of his neck with his free hand. "I ran out of time?" His lips stretched into that charmingly beautiful smile, the one that Persinette always imagined got him into more trouble than it got him out of. "You know, what with planning two big prison breaks and all."

"Uh huh."

Manu didn't bother to look guilty. He never did, in Persinette's experience. He dropped Persinette's hand and felt his way across the room to a chair where he unceremoniously flopped into it. Dust motes flittered up from the cushion. "Well, what's it say, Benard? Can you decipher it?"

"In a moment, Cap'n," Benard said with an annoyed look softened only by fondness at his antics.

Persinette shook her head at Manu, biting back a laugh. She paced across the room, moving onto her toes to lean over Benard's shoulder and watch as he worked. He'd grabbed a pen from the desk and scratched neat lines into the places where a space should be. She reached around to tap one he missed.

"Thanks."

"Mhm." Persinette pursed her lips as she looked over the message. It wasn't Eddi. It was . . . Agnes? "How far are we from the location Roy gave us for the camp?"

"Two days, I think?" Manu's forehead creased in thought. "We've been sticking pretty close just in case. I wanted to be ready if Sully reached out."

"We're armed and ready?" Persinette's hands smoothed over the front of her corset as she stood.

"Why? What is it?"

"It's Agnes. He'll be ready for us in forty-eight hours. He wants us to strike midday. He's determined that's when the camp will be at its weakest."

In a room full of people, Persinette could have heard a gear drop. No one's eyes moved from her and Persinette saw her own feelings reflected in their faces, a combination of determination and concern she wasn't sure how to sort through. It wriggled and mixed inside of her in a sickening way that she thought might be best to ignore.

They had known this was coming. This was not the final battle with MOTHER, but it was a turning point. They had no inside man to send them a map of the buildings. The people they were rescuing would have no way to defend themselves. There was another ship to consider. The camp was out in the open, leaving both ships and her respective crew unprotected, vulnerable to attack. The *Duchess* would land, making her all the more vulnerable. The potential for fatalities was too high. Persinette didn't like it. But she didn't see any other choice in front of them.

"Then I suppose we had better set a course." Manu nodded, standing from his chair. "Benard, set the heading. When you're through, come back here. We have tactics to discuss."

Benard all but sprinted from the room.

"Should we send a message back?" Stella asked. Her hands had moved to grip the arms of her chair, turning white-knuckled as nails dug into the velveteen fabric.

"I don't think we can." Persinette shook her head with a frown.

"We don't know what droid it came from," Manu agreed.

A harsh exhale gusted out through Persinette's lips. She hunched forward, bracing herself against the desk, her eyes catching on the typed words again. Agnes. He wanted them to come for him. He was asking for their help, again. And she wouldn't let him down.

"What's the plan?" Stella asked, her voice breaking the quiet in a strangely giddy way. When Persinette looked up, she found Stella looking back at her with a manic smile upon her lips.

"Hiccup. Could you please clean up the tea mess?"

Hiccup chirped at her and bent to stack the shattered china onto the discarded tray. Persinette patted him lightly, and then moved back to the chairs where she took up residence in the one beside Manu. She felt Stella's eyes following her, but she didn't rush. One leg crossed over the other, she made herself comfortable.

Manu waited until he heard the chair stop creaking under her weight, and then he reached out for her hand. Persinette met him halfway, giving a firm squeeze.

"One of the ships will need to land, and the other will provide cover so we can go in and get as many people out as possible," he said, his thumb brushing across her knuckles. What he didn't say—didn't need to say—was that they may lose more than they'd save.

"Sounds messy." Stella's tone contradicted the words. There was a knot of excitement, of blood lust, in it. Persinette didn't like that either, nor did she like the light in Stella's eyes at the thought of bloodshed.

"It'd likely be best if you, and a portion of your crew were the ones to provide cover for us. Agnes and Sully know us, and our crew. They're expecting us." Measured. Thoughtful. Persinette didn't want to tip Stella off that she didn't entirely trust her, but she also didn't want to put the whole mission in jeopardy. Sully and Agnes were counting on them. Panic crept around the edges of her mind again, but she gripped Manu's hand tighter and focused on the rough brush of his skin on hers. "Meanwhile, you'll give us some men to help get everyone out and keep the guards at bay."

They'd talked about this, she and Manu. Over the last couple of weeks, they had discussed their best options, what would be the safest, and this had been the plan. It wasn't foolproof, but it was the best they had. Knowing that there was a plan and putting it to words helped calm Persinette more.

"Then what?"

"Then, we make the trip to the Waste," Manu said.

"I thought you were joking about that." Stella laughed. "You two really are crazy."

"We've discussed it with many of the crew. This is the best solution. Until MOTHER can be dispatched, there is no safer place for them. Some of those we saved from Headquarters even want to go." Persinette felt exhaustion settling in where the panic had been, replacing nervous energy with a pit that needed to be filled.

"There's nothing out there." Stella shook her head. The crazed light still hadn't left her eyes, but it had dimmed a little. "No cities. No towns. Nothing. Where will they go?"

"We have been in touch with some of the settlements." Manu passed a hand over his face, leaning over a little in the chair to press closer to Persinette. A subtle gesture to provide comfort to both of them. "They haven't developed into towns yet, but they have managed to make homes for themselves. At least these people will be safe there."

"They're marked." Persinette's throat felt scraped raw by the words, but they had to come out or they'd fester. She felt the number on her own arm burn like a brand. "Each one of them has a number tattooed into their skin. A target they can't scrub away. If MOTHER were to catch them again . . ."

"Do they know we're coming?" Stella's manic smile had morphed into something more thoughtful, and Persinette appreciated this. She appreciated that in spite of how daring and hungry for adventure Stella was, she also seemed to be worried for the people who would be in their care. Maybe they could make this work after all.

"Yes. Benard has made arrangements with their leader, Alys White. Once we're far enough from the camp, we'll take a count, and he'll let them know how many are coming."

Stella nodded. The conversation dissolved from there into talks of arms, and most-qualified crew, but Persinette tuned most of it out. She couldn't think past the idea of saying goodbye to some of her crew. Some of her little family. It wasn't fair to keep them on board when they were limited on space, but she'd miss them.

LATE THAT EVENING as Persinette and Manu retired to the Captain's quarters, they settled onto the large leather sofa in front of the fire. Persinette curled up at his side, his arm tucked around her to hold her close.

"You're awfully quiet tonight." She took the hand he'd pressed into her arm, rubbing her thumb over his palm, following the lines there. "What's wrong?"

Manu huffed, the breath ruffling the short lavender hairs on her head. But he didn't deny the accusation.

"I won't be able to lead the attack." The words seemed to cling to him, tugging down his features and making him look older than he'd ever looked before. He hadn't been sleeping. There were dark smudges beneath his eyes.

This. This had been what kept him awake.

"I know that." Persinette hadn't thought much about it herself. It only made sense that in Manu's condition, it wasn't safe for him to head up the attack, and she was perfectly capable. She thought she'd proven as much. "That's why we decided I'd lead them."

He didn't say anything. He didn't have to. She saw the worry play across his face, wrinkling his forehead and tightening his lips. Persinette thought if she tried hard enough, she might be able to read the words going through his mind as they ran across his face. She didn't try. He'd tell her when he was ready.

"I know that's the best solution," he said finally, voice low and vulnerable.

"It is. But?"

"But." His brows knit closer. "But I'm worried about you. I won't be there to have your back and I don't know what I'd do if something happened to you. It sounds senseless, even to my own ears. You've proven what you're capable of. You aren't some . . . some delicate flower that needs me to protect you. If anyone were able to lead them in my stead, it'd be you. I wouldn't trust anyone else with this. With their safety. And yet . . . and yet I'm utterly terrified of what could happen to you without me there."

He'd pressed the words out on a breath, and once they were gone, he seemed to deflate, shriveling up and wrinkling and folding in on himself like an old balloon. Persinette laughed, completely unbidden, a smile pulling at her lips of its own accord. She leaned in and quickly pressed a kiss to his lips.

"It's stupid, I know," he mumbled. But Persinette could

see the fear there. No doubt, he was remembering the Persinette from before, the Persinette she had been. The scared young woman hiding away in a tower. But somewhere along the way, she'd left that woman behind. She'd found her own grit and determination. "They owe you their lives."

"I didn't ask for that."

"No, but they pledged them to you anyway." He leaned in to press his forehead to hers, bumping it once. Twice. "It's stupid."

"No. It's sweet. You're sweet Manu. Like a pineapple!" She pressed her smile into his lips, half hoping it'd be contagious.

"Pineapple?" Manu's nose wrinkled up, on the verge of a laugh.

"Yes! Exactly!" She laughed, pressing a finger into his ribs to tickle lightly. "All rough on the outside, but sweet and a little bit sassy on the inside."

That was it. That was all it took. A low rumble started in his chest and swelled outward until it was a laugh. Persinette watched as the weeks of stress melted away. He'd needed this. She'd known he did. He'd lost everything. Been plunged into darkness. He felt useless, and more a hindrance than anything else. If she could do anything to take some of that weight from him, she would. If she could act as his guiding light, she would. He'd saved her, she'd do the same.

"Is sassy even a flavor?"

"Don't argue with me." She poked his rib harder, making him yelp.

"No, ma'am. Wouldn't dream of it, Captain." He leaned in to steal another kiss. A mumble of contentment added a sweetness to it, letting her know, at least for the moment, she'd succeeded.

Hiccup whistled his disapproval from where he'd been standing beside the couch.

Persinette pulled back, pressing her cheek to Manu's so she could look at Hiccup. "I don't know what kind of fruit you are, Hiccup. Maybe you're a vegetable?"

"He's a parsnip," Manu declared.

Hiccup whistled again, the light atop his head flashing.

"He doesn't like that." Persinette wrinkled her nose. "What about a Brussels sprout?"

The metal pieces overtop Hiccups eyes jerked in what could only be described as a scowl.

"No? Well . . . hmm." Persinette hummed in thought, tapping her chin. "What if you're a carrot?"

"Carrots aren't sour," Manu muttered.

"Neither are Hiccups! They're sweet!"

Manu laughed, shaking his head a little, his temple bumping into hers in their closeness.

"What about a sweet potato?" Persinette asked.

The bulb on Hiccup's head swelled, and he twittered his approval, steam puffing from his ears.

"So, you're a potato," Manu said, unimpressed.

"A sweet potato," Persinette corrected, laughter making her voice quiver. But Hiccup seemed pleased enough with this assessment. "Well . . . at least he's happy."

"We should head to bed. We have an exciting couple of days ahead of us," Manu mumbled against her temple, closing his eyes as he took a deep breath of whatever smell lingered in her hair. Probably just shampoo.

"Then, I bid you good night, my dear captain." She rose from her place against him. Manu whined at the loss, but didn't try to stop her. "Hiccup, it's your job to make sure he actually makes it to bed this time. You think you can handle that?"

Hiccup nodded with a faint squeak.

"Good." Persinette bent down to give Manu another quick peck to the lips, and then backed away before he could grab her and pull her into him again. She walked backward until she reached the door, grinning, before she spun around to head to her own quarters.

They waited. And waited. Until the sun had well and truly risen. Until the breakfast bell rang, and the work bell rang after that.

No return message came.

"Now what?" Rose asked, looking up from Hubert to Agnes, her gaze expectant.

Agnes let out a long sigh, his expression deflating with it, the bags under his eyes becoming more pronounced. Sully hated seeing him this way. The stress of all of this was bringing Agnes so much pain, and if there was one thing Sully hated, it was to see Agnes hurting.

Soon, he reminded himself. Soon Manu and Persi would be there. Soon they would be free. But for now, they needed Agnes to be their leader. He had the mind to plan this all out, and they needed him to keep it together, for just a little bit longer. Sully needed to make sure he offered Agnes whatever support necessary to make it through this.

Reaching down, he took Agnes's hand in his own, giving it a firm squeeze. Reminding Agnes that he was there. That he would continue to be there for however long Agnes needed him. That Agnes was not in this alone. It was all

Sully could give him right now, but he wished he could give him so much more.

"Now," Agnes said, "you all get down the mines. We need everyone ready for when they come. Every inmate needs to know they're coming by the end of tomorrow." In spite of the tiredness making Agnes's shoulders sag, he found the strength to keep his words steady and sure.

"All right then." Rose rubbed her hands together. "How would you propose we do that?"

"Sully." Agnes lifted his chin to meet Sully's hopeful gaze. "I'm assuming you have a plan for this?"

Sully nodded, pushing his shoulders back a little. This was it. This was the best way he could help and support Agnes. He had to do it right, or Agnes would never ask him for another favor. He'd never been the one who planned—that had always been Agnes's job—but Agnes didn't know the camp the way Sully did. He'd been too caught up in his wallowing. Sully would have to do this bit. He *could* do this bit.

"One person at a time," he said with more certainty than he really felt. "I'll tell someone, you'll tell someone, and then they'll each tell another person, and we'll tell two more."

Rose tilted her head to the side, looking a little annoyed at the simplicity of it.

"That it?" she asked, her nose wrinkling.

Sully nodded.

"Well . . ." She tilted her head the other direction. He could see her mind working lightning fast. "Gossip does spread pretty quick in this place. Everyone should know by supper."

"Right then," Agnes said, dropping Sully's hand so he could clap his own together. "You lot better get to work. I'm going to head back to the cabin and get some sleep."

He headed for the door without a backward glance, and

Sully felt the loss of those thin fingers, cast adrift in a sea of unknowing. He didn't like it. He didn't even remember telling his hand to reach out, but it did, grabbing at Agnes's fingers again.

"Not so fast." Sully gave his hand a firm tug, buying himself a moment to think what he needed to say. There had been no plan. Just the need to keep Agnes close. "I'll walk you back, to make sure that guard doesn't bother you anymore."

Once the words were said, Sully felt satisfied with them. That's what he'd needed to say, even if he hadn't known it at first. And it wasn't open for discussion, even as Agnes's face twisted into something that looked like disagreement.

"No. I'm all right. Really." Agnes shook his head. "You all need to get started. And I don't want you in trouble for being late to work."

"It wasn't really a suggestion."

Agnes's eyes narrowed, and he stared at Sully, sizing him up, likely trying to sort out if Sully were serious or not. Whatever he saw in Sully's face forced him to nod.

"All right."

Sully smiled, pulling Agnes in closer before he turned back to Rose and Roy. "You got this covered?"

Rose snorted, rolling her eyes. She opened her mouth to say something, but Roy nudged her lightly.

"Don't worry about us. You two lovebirds do your thing. We'll get started." Roy smiled with an understanding in his eyes that Sully would be grateful for the rest of his life.

"We'll get Tobias up to speed, and he'll help out," Rose said with a nod.

"Thank you." Sully let out a laugh as Agnes half dragged him to the door.

"Yeah. Yeah. Yeah." Rose waved him off, ducking her head back to look over Hubert one last time.

The early morning air outside held a bit of a chill, but Sully sucked it in, letting it calm the heat threatening to overtake his cheeks. He pulled Agnes into him, wrapping his arms tightly around Agnes's lithe frame.

"Soon," Sully whispered like a promise against Agnes's neck. "Soon we'll be breathing free air again."

"They aren't charging us for the air, Sully," Agnes teased.

Sully barked a laugh, letting his head fall forward to rest against Agnes's shoulder, squeezing his eyes shut. The laughter ebbed and swelled for a long time, and he just let it. Let himself drift away on it. Forget everything else, and just laugh. It lightened the load. When it was done, he pulled back to look at Agnes with a broad smile.

"You're ridiculous. Do you know that?"

"I most certainly am not," Agnes huffed, tilting his chin up.

"You are," Sully insisted, pulling himself up to his full height so he looked down on Agnes. He tilted Agnes's chin back further so he could meet his eyes. Then he dipped down to press a chaste kiss to Agnes's lips, craning his neck awkwardly so Agnes didn't have to. "And I love you for it."

A contented, little murmur left Agnes before he pulled away from Sully's hold on him.

"Nope. None of that. There is too much to do!"

"No more kisses?" Sully's voice shook with a chuckle.

Agnes nodded.

"That's insanity!"

"Not until we're safe." Agnes dropped Sully's hand and started back toward the cabins, his mind seemingly made up. "Now, come on. You have work to do."

"Yes, sir." Sully followed him, shaking his head.

SULLY TOOK his time tucking Agnes into their small bunk, pressing the blankets down around him, and brushing his hand over Agnes's back until he was sure Agnes would be warm enough. With that worry assuaged, Sully headed to the mines with a whistle on his lips. Now that he'd said the words and knew how Agnes felt, Sully couldn't help the warmth that swelled up in his chest, threatening to turn the world around him a glowing shade of pink.

He ignored the angry look he received from the guard on duty as he collected his equipment and made it down to his respective sector. Tobias and Delilah were already working, and Roy had joined them.

"You're late. Again." Delilah glared at him, her eyes trying to bore a hole into the side of his head. "He's late again!" she shouted to a guard at the opening to their tunnel.

"Shut up," the guard snapped back, banging his baton against the wall of the cave hard enough to make dust flutter dangerously down from above. "Back to work."

He waddled off to yell at someone else. Delilah coughed pointedly, her sharp eyes slicing into Sully as best she could. "I hate people who aren't punctual."

"I noticed," Sully said, unable to keep the bite of a chuckle out of his voice. This only seemed to infuriate Delilah more. She turned back to the cart, slamming the rocks in her hands down into it.

"So, it looks like you two had a nice chat." Tobias slinked over to Sully's side, keeping his voice low so as not to disturb Delilah any further.

"Oh, they did," Roy said, a grin on his face.

Sully cleared his throat, ignoring the burn of a blush he

felt creeping up his neck. It didn't matter, there was no denying it. And he didn't want to. He'd never want to.

"Let's just say"—he grinned—"it has been a victorious morning, in more ways than one."

"How victorious exactly?" Tobias's gray brows rose.

"I think we'll know exactly how victorious in about two days." Sully shot him a meaningful wink.

"Two days, huh?"

Sully nodded.

"Well . . . isn't that something? Mind if I tell my friend, Janet?" The smile that spread Tobias's face was a slow thing, as if it were afraid of seeming too hopeful, too joyous, this early on. Still, there seemed no stopping it and it shone in his eyes, wrinkling the skin about them in a way that seemed ever so natural. Sully wondered if perhaps this was the first smile he'd seen on the old man's face since coming here.

"Please do," Sully said with a matching grin. He looked down at Roy, who smiled back at him. They were doing this. They would be free soon. So soon.

It went a little like that from Tobias to Janet. From Janet to Michael. From Michael to Alfonse. From Alfonse to Sarah. And so on and so forth until, by the time supper rolled around, it seemed the entire camp buzzed with it, just as Rose had predicted.

"Someone is planning an escape," a fairy whispered near Sully in the line as he and Agnes waited for their turn. "That's right. Two days."

Agnes peeked up at Sully with a conspiratorial smile tugging at the corners of his lips. The look brought an answering smile to Sully's face. In all of the years they'd known each other, Sully had never once seen Agnes look truly hopeful before. It made Sully's heart flutter in his chest, and all he wanted was to pull Agnes from the mess hall, out into the darkness where they could be alone for a while.

"Next," the serving droid called in a tone that could easily be mistaken as annoyed.

"That's us," Sully muttered, moving forward. He wondered how many times the droid had called them, then quickly discarded the thought a moment later because he didn't care. Tonight's dinner—which looked a lot like last night's dinner—slapped onto his plate, bubbling angrily at him. "Thanks."

The droid stared at him blankly, all programming and ticking clockwork. Then it seemed to make up its mind about something. "Next!"

Rose, Tobias, and Roy waited for them at the table.

"So, does the whole camp know already?" Rose asked. Sully had already decided he rather liked Rose but the 'I told you so' smirk sealed it. It reminded him a lot of Agnes.

"It would seem so," Agnes said, scooping up a spoonful of their dinner, holding it a foot off his plate, and letting it drop back down with harsh plopping sounds. "I can't wait to eat real food again."

"Not long now," Tobias offered jovially. "Nope. Not long now." He looked for all the world like Christmas had come early, and twice.

"How long have you been here?" It hadn't been the first time Sully had thought about it, but it was the first time he put words to the question. He knew Tobias had been in Camp 9C for a while, but he didn't know exactly how long. It had been at least a hundred years. But Tobias always seemed too spirited for him to have been imprisoned there long.

The expression of happiness that had been on Tobias's face melted almost as quickly as it'd come.

Rose frowned, kicking Sully beneath the table, the rubber of her shoe digging into his shin.

"Ouch! Hell. What was that for, Rose?" Sully frowned at her, rubbing his shin.

She glared back but didn't say anything.

It was Agnes who answered. "You don't ask people that, Sully."

"Why not?"

"You just don't." Agnes shook his head. Rose had leaned in to give Tobias a tight hug, kissing his cheek as one would a grandparent.

"I'm sorry," Sully muttered, ducking his head in shame. For as old as he was, Agnes still had the ability to make Sully feel as if he knew nothing of the world.

"But hey, you'll be out soon, right? And you won't have to eat"—he picked up his spoon to examine the gray mush closely, but gave up trying to figure what it was a short second later—"whatever this is, anymore."

"Hear, hear!" Rose agreed, holding up her cup of water.

"Hear, hear!" The group clinked their cups together with a hollow tap of brass on brass, only quieting down when a passing guard cut them a dirty look.

They parted ways when supper was finished. Sully's hand tight around Agnes's as they headed back to their bunk.

"You get some rest, Aggy." Sully's voice was low in the din of people readying for bed. "I'm going to go check on Hubert. It won't take but a half hour." He pulled the blanket up to Agnes's chin, pressing a kiss to the wrinkle on his forehead, hoping to smooth it. "I won't be long."

"You shouldn't. There are more guards out than normal. It's not safe." Agnes reached from under the blanket, awkward in the motion, to grab Sully's hand and hold him firmly.

"I'll be all right."

"Then I'll come with you." Agnes was already pushing the blanket down, making to sit up.

"No. You won't. You'll stay right here and get some rest. You didn't sleep at all last night, and we need our leader coherent when they get here. Do you understand me?" Sully let his easygoing tone drop into something more serious. An order.

"I understand," Agnes whispered, cheeks flushing a little at the command.

"Good." Sully nodded, leaning in to steal another kiss, then he was off and away into the night of the camp again. The iron cuff on his wrist jiggled—a weight dragging him down. Without his magic, it was harder to see in the dark, but he'd make do.

He ducked into the shadow of one of the bunks, holding his breath as a guard passed him. Too close. It was too close to get caught now. If he got thrown in solitary now, he wouldn't be where he needed to be when Manu and Persinette arrived. Agnes had been right: he should have stayed in the bunk, but it was too late.

The door to the medical shed creaked open, revealing Rose with a wrench in her hand and a smudge of grease on her cheek. He wasn't sure where the wrench had come from and decided he probably didn't want to know. With a mind like hers, there were any number of ways she could have gotten a hold of it.

"What are you doing here?" she asked, brows tightening behind the wire frames of her glasses.

"I came to see if we'd gotten a message back." He

crossed the small space and looked down at Hubert on the table. Rose had opened him up again. "What are you doing?"

"I figured it can't hurt to have a med droid on hand. Even if your friends have a medic, we might need the extra help." She shrugged, setting the wrench down so she could reach inside and flick a switch in Hubert's chest. His gears turned and ticked quicker than before. Then he sat up, his one visual circuit glowing brightly. "We haven't gotten a message back yet."

"Okay." Sully made his way over to the cupboards along the one wall, retrieving some fresh bandages and antiseptic for Agnes. "You should get to bed too. We'll need everyone at their peak, not just Aggy."

"I'll go soon." Rose's head ducked over Hubert again, her hands working to bolt his front panel back into place. Sully knew that tone; she was only half paying attention to what she was saying. Her primary focus was the machine in front of her, and there was likely nothing he could do to change that.

"All right." He nodded, deciding not to argue with her. He wanted to get back to Agnes and taking the time to force Rose to bed would only hold him up.

"Oh. I had a question for you." Rose's voice stopped him right before he opened the door, her tone like someone who'd only just remembered something. "That guard you and Agnes were talking about before . . ."

"What about him?" Sully's grip tightened on the supplies in his hand. It was bad. Whatever this was. It was bad.

"Keep him away from Agnes, if you can." Her words were muted, but something about the pleading look in her eyes made Sully's heart pick up into a panicked beat.

"Why?" It took everything he had to keep him there,

feet planted, facing Rose. All Sully wanted was to race back to Agnes. To hold him close and protect him from whatever Rose was about to tell him.

Rose looked down at the droid again, frowning as she seemed to think over her words. Her mouth opened, then closed a few times. Shaking her head, she tilted it from side to side in thought and then nodded.

"The last man Wilson took a liking to didn't survive the, uh . . . the infatuation."

"You don't think he'd try anything . . ." The words were half-choked, disbelieving. They scraped his throat raw as the panic gripped his lungs, making it had to breathe. Two days. Wilson had two days to get his hands on Agnes. Two days would be more than enough to do some damage if they weren't careful.

"Sully"—Rose frowned, her eyes turning sad, and sympathetic—"he already has."

Panic disappeared, replaced with rage. How dare anyone touch his Aggy. Sully must have lost himself to that anger, the control on the kelpie slipping so far even the iron couldn't completely stave it off—because the next thing he knew, Rose was at his side, pressing her hand to his shoulder, and he heard water dripping from his fingertips to the floor. Soft splashes, unlike the torrent they would be without the iron.

"I didn't tell you this to upset you," Rose said calmly. "I told you this so you can protect Agnes. Don't let your anger make you do something stupid. We don't have time for it. But you needed all of the facts."

Sully didn't want logic. He didn't want rationality. He wanted to rush from the med shed and hunt Wilson down in the night. He wanted to drag Wilson to the nearest river and pull him beneath the surface. He wanted to hold Wilson there as he thrashed and clawed and tried to get back to the light. Wanted to watch the life leave those eyes.

Instead, he let his feet carry him back to their bunk. The others were already asleep, but Agnes had sat up in their bed, his back against the wall and their blanket pulled over his shoulders. He looked so small. So very small. Wilson could have hurt him, so easily. Could have ruined what little chance they had, so easily.

"What's wrong?" Agnes whispered, his voice carrying in the silence. There was a worried wrinkle creasing his cheek. "Did you get caught? Was there a message? What happened?"

"I need to ask you something." Sully breathed the words because if he did more than that, he was sure he'd scream. "Did that guard . . . Wilson . . . did he try to—to take advantage of you?"

Agnes, who had been reaching for him, pulled his hands away as if burned. His knees curled into his chest, and Sully watched as Agnes pulled in on himself, a look of shame crossing that beautiful face before it was hidden behind his arms and knees.

"Oh, Aggy." Sully sighed, pulling Agnes's hands to his so he could kiss his knuckles. "You don't have to worry. I won't let him near you again. I promise. You're safe with me."

"I was weak," Agnes whispered brokenly.

Sully stilled, frowning deeply at the words. He wasn't sure he'd even heard correctly.

"I couldn't fight him off. I was weak."

"What? Aggy, no. No. This isn't your fault. None of this is your fault." Sully climbed up onto the bed beside him, his hands reaching for Agnes's face to try to get Agnes to look at him. But Agnes remained stubbornly curled around himself.

"I should have been able to fight him."

Sully's hands shook, but he forced them still. Then he took Agnes's face gently in his hands, tilting it up to look at him. "You listen here, Agnes. This was not your fault. This will never be your fault. What happened to you, or almost happened to you, that was not your fault. It was his fault. That coward did this to you because he needed to feel big and strong and powerful. Don't you let him make you feel weak just because he is."

Agnes shrugged, making to duck his head away again, but Sully held his chin firmly.

"Do you understand me?" he asked, earnest, heart hammering against his chest. He needed Agnes to understand this. He needed to make this clear to him. "Do you understand me?"

"The words make sense," Agnes said slowly. "But they don't seem to register anywhere but my brain."

"They will. In time. Just keep telling yourself that over and over. And I will too. I'll remind you every day. Every time it makes you feel small, I'll be right here. You are not small. You are Agnes the ornery unicorn. You are mighty."

Agnes nodded. He let Sully pull him into a tight hug. He let Sully kiss him tenderly on his temple and hold him for a long while. When their breathing had settled, he let Sully redress his wound. And then Sully held Agnes to his chest, not bothering to lie down. He waited until he heard Agnes's breathing slow and settle. And only then did he let himself go to sleep.

Four days!

It had been four days since they had sent the message. Agnes had told them they'd have the camp ready in two, and they had. But now, here they were, four days out and Agnes wasn't sure how much longer he could sit around and wait for a rescue envoy that may never come.

Sully, of course, was no help.

He was the picture of calm and patience, and that made Agnes itchier.

"They'll get here when they get here," Sully had said that morning at breakfast.

Small mercies. It wasn't just Agnes who was restless. Everyone in the camp seemed to be on edge. It was like the entire camp held its breath, waiting on tiptoes at the edge of a cliff. There had been a fight just that morning over whose turn it was in line, which had to be broken up by two half-awake guards.

"What if they didn't find enough help? What if Eddi stopped them? What if they got caught by MOTHER? What if they decided not to come at all?" All these questions and more raced through Agnes's mind too fast for them all to filter out to his tongue.

"They'll come, whether they have help or not," Sully assured. "Whether Eddi approved the mission or not. Whether MOTHER caught them or not. They made a promise." Sully sighed, and patted Agnes's knee under the table. "I've got to go to work—are you all right to make it back to the cabin on your own?"

Sully had asked this every morning since the night he'd found out about Wilson. Agnes didn't like being put on the spot like this. He liked it even less how every set of eyes at their table swept the room for Wilson, or how they all relaxed when he was nowhere in sight.

"Looks like the coast is clear," Tobias muttered. "I'll see you at work, Sully."

Tobias stood to dump his tray. Sully rose behind him, giving Agnes a gentle smile.

"Try not to work yourself into a tizzy today, Aggy. They'll be here soon." He brushed his hand down Agnes's bare neck, and across to his shoulder, ending the comforting motion in a little squeeze.

"I do not tizzy." Agnes huffed, his breakfast gurgling back at him in protest as he pushed it across the plate with a spoon.

Rosevelt snorted loudly from where she sat across from him. Agnes cut her a cold glare that would have made even penguins shiver. He got no such response from Rosevelt, which was deeply unsatisfying.

"You're tizzy-ing right now." She looked unimpressed, meeting his glare head on.

"I am not! Sully, tell her I'm not tizzy-ing."

"Of course not, dear." Agnes could hear the laugh in Sully's voice, but he seemed to be holding it back. In its place was a grin. "See you later."

"Yeah. Later." Agnes dropped his spoon onto his tray with a clatter. There was no swallowing what was left of it. Anything more just wouldn't go down. It settled into the bottom of the bin with a squelch, joining everyone else's leftovers.

Agnes had promised Sully that he wouldn't wander the camp alone; it was too dangerous. He saw the sense in it. And he'd kept that promise . . . for *four days*. Today was different. Today he needed air and movement. He needed to stretch his muscles and get ready for battle.

His legs burned a little as he forced them to trace a path through the winding streets of the camp. It felt good. For the first time in too long, he felt that he had freedom. He could walk wherever he wanted just because he wanted, and the guards didn't bother with him. Maybe because of his attitude. Or maybe they had just decided it wasn't worth the hassle. He couldn't leave the camp, no. The iron manacle was a constant reminder of that. But the illusion of freedom within his fenced in prison was not something Agnes would take for granted.

He'd just passed a building that looked like it might have once been some kind of recreation center—from a time when MOTHER had actually cared about providing quality of life for their Enchanted prisoners—when the first explosion shook the earth. Agnes's eyes jerked up to the sky —fluffy white clouds, an ocean of blue, and the shimmering shape of two large airships hidden by cloaking spells as they descended upon the camp.

Smoke clouded his view, filtering up from the guard tower on the west corner.

It took time for Agnes to fully comprehend what he saw, his mind tripping over itself to put the pieces together.

"They're here," he whispered. "They're here!"

He had to sound the alarm! He had to let everyone

know they had finally arrived! Agnes's breath came in hard pants, a little whoop of victory crawling up his throat and out of his mouth. Free at last! They would finally be free!

Another explosion shook the ground, nearly toppling Agnes from his feet. He looked up just in time to shield himself from the debris of the southern guard tower. He pressed his hands over his ears to try to stop the ringing, but there was no time. From where he stood amongst the buildings, he could see the *Duchess* landing, kicking up dirt as she did, her cargo hold opening to begin the ground assault.

Agnes took off, running through the winding path, back toward where he'd come. He needed to alert someone. He needed to help them get out of the mines. He needed to—

"Shit!" he yelped as the ground was ripped from beneath his feet when someone grabbed onto the back of his uniform. There was a crack—a sickening sound the likes of which no one wanted to hear their own skull make—as his head banged against the building closest to him. The world became a soft-focused blur. Just shapes and colors. A lumbering form grabbed at the front of Agnes's uniform.

"Didn't think I'd let you get away that easy, did you, little unicorn?"

Agnes didn't have to make out the face through his blurry vision—he knew that voice. He knew those words.

Wilson.

The restless energy in the camp was palpable, and Sully would have to have been dead not to feel it. He felt it down to his toes, the subtle itch under his skin. The need to do something, to prepare.

Perhaps his reasons were different than Agnes's. For Sully, it was not his own need for freedom, but his need for Agnes to be free. He was worried what would happen if Agnes stayed in the camp much longer. Worried about the permanent damage such a gray and lifeless place would have on a unicorn. Would his hair grow back rainbow as it had been? Or would it come back in shades of gray?

Agnes had regained much of his strength and his fighting spirit. It seemed like he was on the mend both physically and mentally. But there was still the matter of Wilson. The guard's presence hung over Sully like a cloud, always somewhere in the corner watching and waiting for him to slip up. Sully hadn't said as much to Agnes. He knew if he had, Agnes would just brush it off, but Sully could see it. He could see the way Wilson lingered on the periphery for the perfect time to get Agnes alone.

Sully refused to baby Agnes, even if that's all he wanted to do, because he knew how Agnes would react to it. He swallowed down the feeling wriggling in his gut telling him to escort Agnes everywhere. Tried to forget the images that Agnes's story had conjured up. Now was not the time. There was too much else to do. Too much else at stake.

Forcing his feet down to the mines was a struggle, but he managed. He congratulated himself that it was only with one backward glance toward Agnes.

"When do you think they'll come?" Tobias asked, just loud enough to be heard over the clank of pickaxes on stone. He hadn't even bothered to look away from the wall he and Roy were working on. That was probably for the best.

"Soon. I hope." Sully sucked in a shallow breath, pulling the collar of his uniform up so he wouldn't breathe in the dust directly. Tobias had asked the same question for four days, and Sully had given the same response. Soon. He hoped very soon. But he had no way of knowing. Just like he had no way of knowing how much longer he could keep Wilson at bay.

Tobias fell silent, continuing his work. His eyes turned to track a guard that passed the mouth of their cave. Once the man was gone, Roy gave Sully's shoulder a comforting squeeze.

"Agnes will be all right, you know that. We won't let anything happen to him."

"It won't stop him from trying." The words made Sully's stomach turn. He knew they were true, even if he'd tried to deny them. The truth was, so long as Agnes was there, so long as he remained in 9C, he was in danger. There was no amount of guarding they could do, no amount of watching, nothing. None of it would protect Agnes if Wilson truly wanted to cause him harm.

Roy sighed, shaking his head, Tobias did too. They both knew it was true: everyone did. But none of them wanted to say as much. Nor did they want to say that it was just a matter of time, and they might not have much longer before Wilson got tired of this game of cat and mouse. Their only hope was that Agnes's strength had returned enough to fend Wilson off when the inevitable did happen. Or that Manu and Persinette showed up first.

Sully did his best to push those dark thoughts away. He tried not to imagine all of the things that Wilson would do if given the chance. He forced himself to focus on the clank of metal on stone. On the repetitive motion of lifting his pickaxe and chipping away at the wall a little at a time.

It lulled him into a stupor, the burn of his muscles enough to distract him from the whirring of his thoughts. That, combined with how deep underground they were, meant they didn't hear so much as feel the first explosion. It broke chunks of dirt off from above them, raining down enough dust to send them all coughing. But all sounds of work stopped. Everyone waited. Unsure of what exactly was going on. Even the guards had stopped patrolling. The one outside of Sully's little cave stood there, eyes wide, looking up at the ceiling of dirt as if it held all the answers.

Then there was another explosion, and a deafening alarm rang through the caves.

"What's that?" Delilah screamed, folding the tips of her big, pointed ears into themselves to block the sound.

"I think," Tobias shouted, a manic smile overtaking his face, "that might be the calvary."

"We better make a break for it!" Roy shouted.

Tobias laughed, and when Sully looked at him, his eyes were crinkled near closed. Sully shook himself. *Move.* They needed to *move.* The guard outside their cave had walked off, and when Sully peeked around the edge into the main tunnel, he saw others staring back at him, waiting for him to tell them what to do and where to go. His throat clenched, brain whirring in panic. They needed a leader. They wanted *him* to be their leader.

Standing up straight, he forced his mind to clear. He took a step, deliberate and slow, from his cave. And then another. Others joined him, more slowly and carefully, ducking behind him in a way that he didn't have time to think about.

The big guard—who up until that exact moment had been standing at one end of the tunnel, gaping like a fish— rounded on Sully with a glare.

"What are you doing? Back to work! Back to work, all of you! Get back to your sector!" He brandished his baton like a bat, taking purposeful strides toward Sully. Sully heard someone behind him pick up one of the spare pick-axes from the floor, then another, the sound of them dragging against stone like nails on a chalk board. "I said back to your sectors! It's just a malfunction of the alarm system! It's nothing!"

Another explosion rocked the earth. The guard staggered, his expression turning fearful as he backed up the slight incline toward the mouth of the mines. He was outnumbered, Sully realized. For all the power the guards seemed to wield, they were outnumbered by the sheer mass of Enchanted inmates. If they had wanted to take the camp long ago, they could have. They just needed a reason. Something to fight for. A place to go when the fight was done. Sully and Agnes had given them that. It would be up to them to do the rest.

The guard turned and ran back toward the entrance, shouting and babbling as he went. "B-block—block the doors! They'll get out! Keep them from escaping. Block the doors!"

Sully looked back at those who had crowded behind him. Everyone had picked up some weapon or another.

Tobias stood the closest, and when Sully looked at him, the old man nodded.

"Right," Sully said on a breath. Then he turned and led them up the incline into the main cavern of the mines. The guards had blockaded the entrance—moving carts and tools and whatever else they could find—to keep the Enchanted from escaping. A group of five guards had their hands on their weapons, expressions cut into something grave and determined. A small force meant to frighten.

But they wouldn't scare Sully. Not now. Not ever. "Move."

"And unblock the door," Roy added.

A shout went up through the group. Sully frowned. Mob mentality was setting in quick, he needed to keep that under control. It wouldn't help them if they descended into chaos. There would be madness and not enough of them would get out. He wouldn't have that. They had to keep the bloodshed to a minimum and get to the ship with as little fuss as possible. That was their best chance at survival.

"Back to your sectors!" one of the guards ordered. He stood up taller, puffing out his chest. *To look bigger.* This was an intimidation tactic, for as he lifted his arm, pistol aimed at Sully's chest, his hand shook.

Sully cocked his head, meeting the young man's eyes, and waited. It didn't take long for whatever bravery he had to fade, the gun seeming to grow heavier and heavier in his hand, lowering slowly.

"Move," Sully repeated.

There was a growl, and someone shoved Sully forward, making him stumble toward the terrified guard. Panicked, he fired his pistol. The shot echoed off the walls, making Sully's ears ring so loudly that it took him far longer than it should have to realize that, even though the gun had fired, he felt no pain. There was no biting, ripping feeling of a bullet through flesh.

Tobias stumbled, grabbing for Sully's hand, before his body hit the ground in a dull *thud* that sounded far louder than the gunshot ever could.

Silence.

A collective breath.

And then chaos. Screams and cries of war. The Enchanted swarmed the small group of guards, pushing past Sully. It took every ounce of strength he had to keep them from trampling Tobias in their rush.

"You old fool," Sully muttered, scooping Tobias up and off the floor.

Tobias smiled up at him, a wrinkled hand moving to cover the slowly growing crimson stain on his side. "Somebody's got to lead them."

Another crack of a pistol. The bullet lodged in a guard, dragging him to the floor where he sputtered and choked on blood before falling still in the puddle left behind. The gun was still smoking where it rested in the steady hands of Delilah. Her eyes gleamed. She turned the weapon on the crowd, and then the guards.

"I'm going out first! Everyone, get out of my way!"

The four remaining guards backed away, lifting their hands slowly. They'd moved to press themselves into the harsh rock of the mine walls. With another hard look from Delilah, each pulled their pistol out and set it on the ground carefully, trying to keep as much distance as possible between themselves and the wild-eyed goblin.

"You better get that before she kills someone else," Tobias wheezed.

"I'm going to come back and get you. I'm not leaving you behind," Sully promised. Then he set the man on the ground again, careful not to jostle him too much.

"You do that." Tobias nodded with a smile that settled too easily across his lips.

Sully stepped away from him to Delilah. She was still holding the gun, pointing it now at two trolls.

"Unblock the door," Delilah ordered, leveling the gun at the troll's stomach.

With her looking the other way, Sully closed the distance between them in a couple quick strides, then swung back and punched her as hard as he could. He felt something in her jaw crack. Delilah hit the floor, sprawling. The pistol skittered across the stone out of reach. He scooped it up quickly.

"Elderly and children first. Someone help me move all this junk." Sully looked down at Delilah, eyes hard, begging her to argue with him. When no words came, and she just held her ruined jaw tenderly, he nodded and moved on.

The trolls, and a few other more muscular Enchanted, helped Sully remove everything from their path. With them working together, it was the work of less than a minute before the doors were pushed open and daylight streamed into the cavern.

No one moved.

Everyone turned to look to Sully again. He looked down at the pistol in his hand, fidgeting with the grip, with the hem of his uniform, with anything to buy him a minute to just think. He wasn't meant for this. Agnes was supposed to be here. Agnes was supposed to lead the troops. That had been Agnes's role, not Sully's.

A wheezing laugh from Tobias ripped him from his stupor finally.

"You," Sully pointed to one of the trolls. "I need you to carry Tobias."

The man nodded and went to lift Tobias carefully.

"Does anyone, other than our goblin friend, know how to fire a gun?"

Two ginger leprechauns with identical bright green eyes and matching freckles raised their hands. "We do."

"Our father taught us," one said.

"Good—take those two pistols. I need you to bring up the rear." Two identical nods, and the twins melted into the crowd again. "The rest of you, follow me. We should be pretty well-covered so long as we're amongst the buildings. Once we reach the open field, we'll have to hope reinforcements are there to cover us. But no one, and I repeat *no one*"—his eyes cut to Delilah in warning—"leaves the group. Am I clear?"

More nods of understanding.

"Right then. Let's go." Sully led them out into the alley in front of the mines. All he could hope was that Agnes would meet them at the ship. That had been the plan they'd agreed on. The rest of the camp was their first priority. But Sully knew . . .

If Agnes didn't meet up with them, he'd go back for him.

THIRTY-ONE

PERSINETTE

"**A**ren't you nervous?" Felicity asked, the pistol in her hand clicking as she loaded it. Her blue head was bent over the gun, eyes narrowed in focus on the task.

"I am. Of course I am." Persinette's fingers fidgeted, fluttering sparks of lavender magic into the air. "But I can't let that stop me."

Felicity nodded, then clicked the cartridge back into the pistol and held it out for Persinette. "I guess I better wish you luck then."

"It's going to be okay, Felicity." Persinette sighed, pulling Felicity into a tight hug, and laughing lightly when Felicity patted her back awkwardly. "We're going to save them."

"I know you are," Felicity muttered into Persinette's shoulder. She pulled back, pressing a kiss to Persinette's cheek, embarrassment coloring her young face. "You're going to bring them home. Just like you did for me and Drea."

"Exactly." Persinette pulled a confident smile onto her lips, pushing down whatever nerves she might have had. She needed to be brave now. She needed to show Felicity and the others that she could protect them. She was a captain. She took the pistol and tucked it into the holster at her hip. "Now, you and Drea are in charge of getting everyone we board someplace safe. I don't want to come back here to find this cargo hold full of people. Are we clear?"

"Yes, Captain." Drea gave a lazy salute, even as her face settled into a look of determination.

"Good. Benard should have given you a chart of what rooms are available on the *Duchess* and the *Sultana*?"

"Got it." Felicity held up the clunky tablet. It steamed angrily at her for the sudden motion.

"And Hiccup is with Manu, helping him lead the attack," Persinette said it like she was ticking items off a list, making sure all her ducks were in a row before she left. It was easier to check boxes than to think about what they all meant.

Drea gave Persinette's shoulders a squeeze. "You've got this. Just calm down and get them on board, we'll take care of the rest."

"And for gods' sake, give me a kiss before you go off on daring do!" Manu called from the top of the stairs that led into the cargo hold. "We don't have all day."

Persinette laughed, letting a burble of amusement push the nervousness away. Then she climbed the steps, moved onto her toes, and kissed Manu. It was easy. It had always been easy with him, the affection that simmered low and warm between them. She didn't have to question his feelings, or her own. And she let that warmth swell up inside her enough to push away every other thought. She would be all right. Everyone would be all right. Because they were ready for this. And because Manu and his crew had their backs.

"No time for romance, darling. Off to save the world!" She giggled, running back down the stairs to the group waiting for her command. Manu huffed indignantly. Shaking her head, she turned her attention back to the small group of fighters Benard had helped her choose. "Our primary goal is to provide them with cover while they get to the ship. Sully and Agnes will get them as close as they can without weapons, but we need to get them the rest of the way. Especially across the open field. Your job is to get them here, minimal incident, minimal bloodshed."

A murmur of understanding went through the group. Persinette looked around them, a smile settling onto her face. They could do this.

WHEN THE *DUCHESS* set down minutes later, Persinette and her crew were ready. The shots that took out the two nearest guard towers were their signal. With a bang, the cargo hold door opened and they rushed out. A small group formed a perimeter around the door, while the others followed Persinette toward the crop of defunct buildings.

By the time Agnes had fully come to, his hands were bound behind his back, and Wilson was dragging him through the alleys, deeper into the camp. Agnes's ears rang, but he could hear the battle being waged above the sound.

"Let them set the whole damn place on fire. They'll never find you," Wilson muttered. He yanked Agnes closer, breath hot in his face. "You hear me? They'll never find you!"

"What will your superiors think?" Agnes managed enough breath to snark, even as the wound on his shoulder pulled, threatening to steal what little he had left.

He'd pass out again if he wasn't careful. He could feel all of Sully's careful stitches tugging to near breaking. Just a little more and he'd be in serious danger. He didn't know if he could keep conscious through the pain. He breathed through clenched teeth.

"Abandoning your post while the whole camp is going to hell in a hand basket? Can't imagine they'd be pleased."

A hollow laugh left Wilson. He pulled Agnes in closer, pressing their bodies together in a way that made Agnes's skin crawl. "Who cares? They'll be dead soon anyway! They all will. Even your little friends."

Wilson's hard chuckle echoed off the walls of the building. This one sounded absolutely manic. A shiver ran down the length of Agnes's spine. This could be it. This could be the end of Agnes the ornery unicorn. He might never get to kiss Sully again. He might never get to make another snarky comment. He might never get to wear another beautiful cravat!

He took a deep breath, squeezed his eyes shut, and called upon his training. He'd only spent the last several decades preparing for this. He could do this. He just needed to think. "Think Agnes. Think."

Between the fuzziness of his mind and the racing panic gripping his heart, Agnes couldn't get a thought past the memory of his last kiss with Sully. What if that had been the last one?

"What? No snappy retort? Got nothing to say?" Wilson's voice shook on a laugh. He reached down to grab Agnes by the collar of his uniform, pulling him up by it and pressing Agnes's back into the cold stone of the alley. "Kelpie got your tongue?"

Wilson's breath was hot on Agnes's face, making Agnes gag as his stomach churned. Then he did the only thing he could. He reared back and kicked Wilson as hard as he could in the shin. Wilson jerked a little, a moment of mild annoyance passing over his face before he barked another hard laugh.

"You're still too weak, you idiot. Do you think we feed you anything to keep you creatures strong and healthy?"

Terror tightened around his heart, and Agnes thrashed. Wilson was right: he felt the energy he'd had right after breakfast waning quickly the more he struggled. That didn't stop him. He had to get free. He had to get to the ship.

Sully would be waiting for him. Sully wouldn't let them leave without him. Not now. Not after all that had happened. He had to fight. Agnes thrashed more, using every ounce of the strength he had to throw himself out of Wilson's hands.

Wilson gripped him harder, fingers biting bruises into Agnes's skin, his uniform shirt ripping. When the fabric gave way, Agnes tumbled to the ground. A groan ripped from his throat at the way the fall jarred his injured shoulder. He rolled, scrambling to get to his feet, but Wilson caught him first, sending a sharp kick to Agnes's ribs that ripped another strangled noise from his lips. A second kick followed, making Agnes whimper when he felt something snap.

"Shit." Agnes gulped air to force into his lungs and found it hurt more than it ought.

Another kick. Another broken rib.

Then as quickly as they had started, the kicks stopped. Their cessation was followed by a loud thump. Agnes opened his eyes to see a wide-eyed Wilson lying unconscious in front of them.

"Get up, you idiot. We don't have all day," Rosevelt grumbled, bending to help him to his feet, and then undo the bindings keeping his arms behind his back.

"Did you just . . . save me?" Agnes breathed.

With his arms unbound, Rosevelt grabbed him by the wrist to drag him back the way he'd come, not bothering to wait for him to comprehend what had just happened.

"Don't let it go to your head," she said. "I just did it because, otherwise, Sully would have us searching this whole damn place for you. Come on."

The words filtered in through his ears, but it was another second or two before Agnes fully understood them.

"We aren't going to be friends after this," he said with a sniff.

"Nope."

"Good."

Sully's small army of Enchanted had managed to escape the mine and made slow progress through the buildings of camp 9C. They were getting close to where the space between buildings gave way to the wide-open field. Sully could just see the balloon of the *Duchess* above the rooftops. The sound of gunfire reverberated through the alleys, and the sharp, metal smell of magic lingered in the air.

One more turn and the end was in sight. Two long buildings created a narrow alley, and at the end of it was the dusty old rec field. It was so close. So very close! In his excitement, Sully picked up his pace, and the others behind him moved faster.

In their rush to reach the light, they missed the guard standing in the doorway of one of the buildings. No one noticed him as he raised his pistol and opened fire on the crowd.

Someone screamed. A thud echoed after—their body hitting the ground. Then it was chaos. Everyone forgot what they were supposed to be doing and made a mad dash for the opening, stumbling over one another in their hurry to get away from the guard—who had reloaded and fired more rounds into the crowd. Screams. So many screams. How had Sully miscalculated? How had he lost sight of what mattered?

He stopped, letting the others run past him. He turned to the guard, eyes narrowed into slits, and lifted the pistol at his side. Even with the jostling screams around him, silence fell. Sully took aim and fired. One shot: that's all it took to fell the guard. The man stumbled back, giving the others enough time to get away.

With everyone else further ahead, Sully went to check on those who had been wounded. He moved each in turn, mindful of their injuries. Fifteen shot, seven alive. Those that he could help, he pulled to their feet and leaned against the wall.

"Go on," he urged, watching as a young woman stumbled on a gushing leg.

By the time he reached Delilah, she was gone, but she'd used herself to shield a small pixie child. The little girl shook, her eyes glassy as she looked up at Sully in fear. He swallowed, sucked in a breath, and cleared his face so as not to scare her further.

"Come along, little one. We're almost there." Sully kept his voice low, his tone gentle. Then he scooped her up, letting her curl into his chest. He sent up a silent prayer that Persinette and Manu would provide them enough cover to pass from the safety of the buildings to the *Duchess* unscathed. Sully slowed his pace, staying with the injured, offering an arm to the ones who needed it.

A short, freckled girl waited for them at the end of the alley. Her brilliant green eyes lit up, crinkling at the edges when she smiled. "Sully! It's good to see you again!"

Sully frowned, eyes flicking over her face. She looked familiar. He was sure he'd seen her somewhere before —*Persinette*. That's who this was. Persinette. Minus the long lavender hair that had marked her clearly as an Enchanted.

"Miss Persinette, you look . . . different." He chuckled, shaking his head. It wasn't the loss of hair, not really. It was the way she held herself now. Her shoulders back, a pistol in one hand, and pale purple magic glittering around the other. She held her chin high as she looked for all the world like she belonged in a battlefield. She had come a long way.

"No time to catch up, I'm afraid. We've got to go." She winked, waving the magic-wielding hand through the air. It twisted and turned, morphing into a beautiful glittering parasol large enough to protect them all from the bullets raining from the remaining guard towers. "Come along. I've got you."

The young woman with the leg wound rushed forward, stumbling in her hurry and nearly falling to her knees. Persinette moved faster, a deft hand gripping the woman's arm to steady her.

"Easy. We can take our time. Manu and Stella have us covered."

"But—" the woman argued, gripping Persinette's arm tightly.

"They'll wait," Sully said.

She nodded, and the small group began their slow progress toward the ship. They couldn't move very quickly, and there was some shifting that had to be done to remain under the protection of Persinette's parasol. With two guard towers still in perfect working order, Sully could hear the bullets pinging off the magic like rain on a tin roof.

Bodies littered the field. Some Enchanted. Some guards. But with everything going on, it was hard to tell who was who, and Sully supposed it didn't matter. Not right then. The magic sizzled, faded a little, and then grew stronger again.

"Will it hold?" Sully frowned, wondering if he could provide some energy to it. But he knew there was little he could do with the iron shackle still around his wrist.

"It'll have to." Persinette didn't look at him, her lips pursed in concentration. The magic was taking its toll; her face was paler, and a sheen of sweat had settled onto her neck. But she didn't seem in any hurry to let go of it or shrink it.

By the time they made it to the cargo hold, Persinette's breaths were ragged. She stumbled to sit against a crate.

A blue-haired girl ran across the room and grabbed Persinette's hand. "You've overextended yourself, Captain."

"Find the medic." Persinette shoved her hands away, reaching behind herself to grip the crate so she could stand again. "We'll worry about that later."

"But, Captain, you should—"

"Felicity, I gave you an order."

Felicity nodded, her eyes lingering for a moment longer before she moved to check on the others. Once she was on her feet again, and not relying on the crate to keep her upright, Persinette faced him with an arched brow.

"I'm impressed." Sully chuckled.

Persinette blushed brightly, shaking her head.

"No. Really. I remember you. You were scared of them, of your power, of everything. Now look at you!"

"Where's Agnes?" Persinette asked, changing the subject handily.

A bucket of cold water blanketed Sully, ripping the smile from his lips. "He's not here?"

Why had he just assumed that Agnes had gotten out? How could he have left without him? He should have been there. He should have gone back for Agnes first. Gone to the cabins to pull Agnes out after him.

"No. We've only boarded those who were in the mines

and the laundry." Felicity reached for the pixie, helping her carefully from Sully's arms. "If there are others, they haven't made it here yet."

He had to go. He had to go before anyone could stop him. Sully lunged through the opening in the cargo hold, out into the open again. A bullet whizzed by his ear, reminding him that without Persinette there to shield him, he'd be shot before he could make it back to Agnes.

Persinette grabbed his wrist and yanked him back inside. "Don't be an idiot."

"He's still out there!" Sully panted. He wasn't sure when all the breath had been sucked from his lungs, but it had been. And now he found it impossible to get it back. "We can't leave without him. That was the whole point! I have to go get him."

"Well, if you're going to be stupid about it," a raven-haired werewolf huffed. She grabbed a pair of bolt cutters from a row of tools along the wall, and the shackle gave way with a crunch before falling to the floor. "Least we can do is give you a fighting chance."

The broken shackle landed with a dull thud, and that's all it took. The rage took over, leaving nothing of Sully left. Only kelpie. His pupils swallowed his irises and then the whites of his eyes, making them black. His tightly curled hair grew steadily, dragged to shoulder length by the constant pull and drip of water. Someone gasped behind him.

He turned to look at the woman who he and Persinette had helped through the field. Felicity was wrapping a bandage around her leg. He winked.

"I'll be right back, girls. I've just got to go catch a unicorn." The words vibrated through the air, echoing off of nothing and everything, as if he hadn't really spoken them at all, but they'd simply appeared in the minds of everyone around him.

Then he was off, racing back through the field, bullets raining around him, going unnoticed. Just minor annoyances. He had better things to worry about.

"We are not," Agnes panted, voice cold as he glared at the rusted med droid, "I repeat—are *not*, bringing that hunk of junk with us. This is stupid."

"His name is Hubert," Rosevelt said matter-of-factly, her lips pressed into a thin line. "And we most certainly are."

She helped Hubert to the floor, and the little thing let out a squealing sound that didn't sound right.

"We don't have time for this."

"They won't leave without us. Calm down. Besides, we'll need him."

Hubert rolled forward a little bit, making an angry grinding noise as it wobbled on one lopsided wheel. It looked like it was going to fall over or fall apart at any given moment. But by some small miracle, or maybe through sheer stubbornness, it made it to the door without doing either.

"And why will we need it?" Agnes felt his lip curl in disgust. He couldn't see where the rundown droid would be good for anything outside of scrap metal.

Rosevelt didn't dignify that with an answer and

followed Hubert to the door. "You coming or not, Hagnes? I don't have all day."

"My name is Agnes." He turned his glare on Rosevelt, eyes burning into the back of her head as they made their way into the alley beyond. Agnes swallowed down a groan when walking jerked his body, rubbing a rib against something it likely shouldn't be rubbing against.

"Maybe it is. Maybe it's not. But I like Hagnes. Because you're a hag, get it?" Rosevelt grinned, satisfied with this little pun.

Agnes wasn't sure if she was saying it just to aggravate him or if she was trying to distract him so he couldn't argue anymore about the piece-of-shit med droid. It didn't matter. Either way, he was annoyed. Not enough to ignore the pain of his shoulder, but enough to keep moving.

"I get it." He rolled his eyes, stumbling suddenly when his vision swam and the world blurred into wet blobs.

Rosevelt moved to his side, looping his arm over her shoulder, and helped him down the alley.

Hubert let out a grinding noise that Agnes could only assume was an attempt at communication, for a moment later Rosevelt responded.

"Yes, I know. He should have let you look at him, Hubert. But unfortunately, Hagnes is a stubborn ass."

"I'm going to kill both of you," Agnes growled through clenched teeth.

"Maybe later. Right now, you *need* me," Rosevelt chirped.

Their group continued the slow progress through the camp, Rosevelt supporting at least half of Agnes's weight, and Agnes pretending not to notice. The only sound was the battle in the distance and Hubert's grinding wheel.

A loud crack echoed off the buildings around them and

something ripped through the tender skin around his bruised ribs and sent him stumbling, nearly taking Rosevelt to the ground with him. A warm gush of blood followed, soaking the uniform around where the bullet had entered Agnes's torso.

"Didn't think I'd go down so easy . . . did you?" Wilson slurred, taking a lumbering step toward them. Red dribbled from his temple where Rosevelt had hit him, and his steps were unsteady, but that didn't negate the pistol in his hand. "Well, I got you now. Both o' you."

"Sir, you have a concussion." Hubert's voice sounded more like an engine that wouldn't start, but the words were clear enough. "You should be resting."

Hubert rolled to Wilson, reaching out to help him. Wilson growled, shoving the robot away.

"Gerroff o' me."

An opening. Rosevelt and Agnes took it. Their feet scuffed, hobbling down the alley together, looking for an outlet to get them out of easy firing range of Wilson. Or, at the very least, somewhere that Rosevelt could rest Agnes and run for the ship on her own. At least then she stood a fighting chance. Agnes wouldn't begrudge her leaving him behind. It didn't make sense for them to both die there.

Another crack. Agnes heard the guard stumbled forward again.

"If I can't have you, neither can he." Wilson took aim.

Agnes squeezed his eyes shut, sure this time that'd be it. This bullet would lodge somewhere that even an immortal couldn't survive. He wasn't ready to die. He didn't think he ever would be. But then, that was the nature of dying, wasn't it? The people who died often weren't ready for it.

A terrible crunching sound took over where the ringing of the pistol had fallen silent. It was wet and squelching. He didn't notice the bullet whizz past them. Rosevelt and Agnes turned, and there was Sully, his arm forearm deep in Wilson's chest, blood running down to his elbow to drip into the dry dust below. There was a moment, hardly even the intake of a breath, where Wilson shuddered, trembling as if he could escape. And then another wet sound of something inside the man being squeezed until it popped in Sully's big hands.

His heart, Agnes thought.

In the next breath, the light faded from Wilson's eyes and his body went limp, held up only by the arm still dug deep into his chest.

"Sully," Agnes breathed. He pulled away from Rosevelt, taking shuffling, careful steps toward the black-eyed kelpie. Sully turned on him, eyes squinting dangerously. He pulled his arm from Wilson and the man crumpled like a marionette without the strings. But there wasn't time to deal with the horror of that, not now. "Sully, we need to go."

An inhuman growl rumbled low in Sully's throat. His lips curled back to bare his teeth in warning at the slowly approaching Agnes. Water dripped from every inch of him, joining the blood and dust on the ground.

"Agnes, I don't think you should do that," Rosevelt whispered. She made an aborted motion to reach for him, to stop him, but didn't see it through when Sully's eyes flicked to her.

Agnes didn't take his eyes off of Sully and took deliberate steps, one at a time, ignoring how they jarred his injuries. He swallowed down a wince, kept his eyes clear of any emotion aside from the calm he knew Sully needed. Then he stretched out a hand to Sully, steady, grounding.

"Sully, it's me. It's Aggy." Agnes kept his voice low, kept his hand where it was and didn't allow it to shake. He was within arm's reach of Sully soon enough. Close enough that if the kelpie decided its thirst for blood hadn't been quenched with Wilson, he'd go for Agnes next. And Agnes wouldn't have any time to escape from him. Not that he'd ever want to. "It's me. It's Aggy."

Agnes pressed his palm to the tensed muscles of Sully's heaving chest, willed himself not to shake. He wasn't afraid. He never would be afraid of Sully. But he knew that the kelpie—that monster that always bubbled just under the surface of Sully's smile—wouldn't stop until it was satiated. And it would have no trouble turning its rage on Agnes.

He waited, watching Sully glare down at him, holding Sully's gaze in a way that most wouldn't dare try with a raging kelpie. It took a minute, a minute that felt like an hour, before Agnes's words broke through the haze of Sully's anger. He could see it when they finally did. The hair at Sully's shoulders dried, the briny water dripping away, and like a fruit left in the sun too long, it shriveled. Next came the eyes, the black pits of what some might call a demon, but Agnes had taken to know as something else. They cleared, the black giving way to whites and deep brown irises.

"Aggy?" Sully asked, his voice unsure, far away. Like he was just waking up from a dream, or a nightmare.

Agnes opened his mouth to respond, but couldn't get the words past his lips before he sagged forward into Sully's arms, injuries and adrenaline leaving him weak. Sully scooped him up, pressing Agnes to the warmth of his chest, and holding him securely even as an explosion rocked the ground beneath them.

Smoke filled the sky, pouring from the airship that had been providing cover for the *Duchess* and her charges.

"That's probably a good indication that we need to get moving," Rosevelt said. She grabbed Hubert and spun him in the direction of the rec field again. "Come on."

Sully nodded, tucking Agnes in more closely against himself, and followed. Agnes pressed his face into Sully's chest, letting the warmth and the steady drum of Sully's heartbeat make him feel safe and lull him into a dark, comfortable sleep where there was no pain.

THIRTY-FIVE
SULLY

"Is that everyone?" Felicity asked as Sully and Rose climbed aboard the ship. Her eyes swept to the unconscious Agnes in Sully's arms, but she didn't comment on it.

"Everyone that's alive." Rose stepped away from the cargo bay door. "Let's get out of here before they call for reinforcements!"

There were some shouts, and the rest of the crew climbed aboard. A whistle preceded the scraping and screaming of gears as the door lifted, and then fell into place with a jolt. Another series of shouts and orders, all of them drowned out by the slow ebbing of adrenaline in Sully's ears—then he felt them leave the ground with a shudder.

"What happened to Agnes?" Persinette came from somewhere deeper within the hold, probably where she'd been giving orders. She looked a little better than she had, the blood returning to her face now that she'd rested.

"What *didn't* happen to Agnes would be the better question." Rose snorted from where she'd crouched to tighten some of the bolts on Hubert's torso. They must have come loose when Wilson had knocked him aside.

Sully frowned at her, shaking his head, but Rose paid him little mind.

"Where's the medic?" he asked, turning back to Persinette, and holding Agnes more gently now that they were out of harm's way.

"This way. Your friend Tobias and some of the others are there too." Persinette jerked her head for him to follow her, and then started up the stairs.

"How is Tobias?"

Persinette's shoulders lifted with a breath and sagged on the exhale.

"He's not doing well, Sully," she said, tone gentle. "The doctor says there is nothing we can do for him. It's just . . . it's a matter of time."

"Oh." Sully wasn't sure why that news stunned him so much. Or why it nearly knocked him from his feet. He'd known when he'd seen Tobias last that the old man wouldn't survive the wound. And still, he felt frozen at the confirmation that there was nothing they could do for him. No trick they could pull. No magic spell they could cast. Tobias would die. That was that.

"I'm sorry."

Sully shook his head. He didn't want her apologies, not really. They wouldn't change anything. And this was the price of war. Lives were lost. More than just Tobias would die before this was all over. Many of them, Sully realized with some bitterness, whose names he'd never know. At least Tobias would be remembered.

He followed her through the halls of the ship, toward the med bay. She held the door for him and then shut it behind them. The med bay had only a handful of beds, and many of them were full already.

"What's this? What's this?" A thin little goblin wearing a pair of too-large goggles came from behind a curtain to see who had come into his domain. "Oh. Another patient. Sit him over here."

Sully nodded and set Agnes gently onto one of the last open beds in the room. The medic came over with a pair of scissors to cut away the soiled shirt clinging to Agnes's torso, his boney fingers flying too fast, but so gentle, over the wounds on Agnes's chest and sides. The medic *tsked*, shaking his head.

"Will he be all right?" Sully was almost afraid to ask. But he had to know if Agnes was beyond repair. He had to be ready for it. Now, while the grief for Tobias was still fresh.

The medic looked up at Sully as if he'd forgotten that he was there at all. "This cut looks infected. He's sustained a gunshot wound. And it looks like he's broken"—Agnes groaned in his sleep from the medic's gentle prodding— "three ribs. If everything missed internal organs . . ." The medic gave way to muttering to himself too fast and too quiet for Sully to understand.

"Doctor Crugbort, you're doing it again," Persinette said gently from where she had taken up residence at the foot of Agnes's bed.

Doctor Crugbort blinked at her, then he seemed to shake himself and realize what she'd meant. With a nod, he continued. "Right. Yes. He should be fine. But he'll need rest. Lots of it. So, you should go and let me work."

The doctor waved boney hands at Sully, shooing him off. But Sully didn't move.

"I'm not leaving him." Sully planted his feet. Doctor Crugbort frowned at him, confused eyes magnified a hundredfold behind the too-large goggles that seemed to take up his whole face. "I'm staying right here."

"That wasn't really a suggestion," Persinette said. "Agnes is in good hands, and you can see him after the doctor is done working his magic. For now, it's best if we're out of his way." She took hold of his wrist, giving it a gentle tug. A question, not an order. "Let's go see Tobias."

"What if he wakes up and I'm not here?" Sully's heart stuttered at the thought. He'd hate to think of Agnes waking up in a strange place, surrounded by strange people, without him. Not after everything. Not this time.

"We're not leaving the room. We'll just be right over here." She tugged at his bloody arm again, seeming not to mind the quickly drying sludge under his nails and in the crevices of his skin. This time, he let her drag him over to a bed with the curtains drawn around it. Before opening the curtains, she called inside, "Tobias, it's Persi. I have someone to see you. Is it all right if we come in?"

"Please do. I'm bored out of my wits in here." Tobias's voice was weak, but Sully could hear the smile. Persinette pulled back the curtains, and Tobias offered Sully a wide grin. "Sully! My boy!"

The excitement must have irritated his injuries, because he coughed uncomfortably a moment later into a handkerchief, tucking the cloth away before Sully could get a good look at it. Sully frowned. If he had gotten Tobias here sooner, would things have been different? Would they have been able to save him?

"How are you feeling, Tobias?" Sully asked, taking the seat Tobias gestured to beside his bed.

"I could be better. But . . . hey." Tobias's eyes wrinkled. "I'm breathing free air! And ain't that something!" He wheezed again, another coughing fit started, and this time Sully didn't miss the crimson staining the handkerchief.

"The doctor said to take it easy, Tobias," Persinette scolded, moving to adjust the old man's pillows.

Tobias snorted, rolling his eyes at her. "I've not got much more life left in me. Let me use it how I want, Cap'n."

"All right." She sighed, shaking her head and pulling away from the bed. "I'm going to check on the others, and Felicity should be reporting in soon. I'll leave you two to it."

She left them, and Sully waited in the breath that stood between her reassuring presence, and the finality of this conversation. It felt like a goodbye. Sully hated goodbyes.

"Now, Sully," Tobias said, "tell me: how is your Agnes? I heard you had to go back for him. Word gets around quick here, even faster than in the camp." Tobias tapped the side of his nose and winked in a gesture so familiar and heartwarming, Sully couldn't help the smile that lit his face.

"The doctor says he'll be all right. But Tobias . . . how are you?" he insisted, reaching out to take Tobias's hand and squeezing it.

"War is a young man's game, I'm afraid." Tobias shrugged, returning the squeeze with a weaker one of his own. "But I got to breathe free air before I go. So, don't you worry about me. Just take care of that unicorn of yours."

"I will. We'll take care of each other. Don't worry about that." Certainty. That's what Sully felt. And it was good to have a firm grasp on something when it felt like everything else in his life was slipping away. But he and Agnes? They were a certainty. A fixed point.

"I know you will. Just don't forget. I forgot once . . ." Tobias let his words fade off. He shook his head, clearing his throat, and looked away from Sully at something in the distance. Something Sully couldn't see nor guess at. "That's neither here nor there. That'll all be over soon," he whispered to himself. Then he focused on Sully again, suddenly serious. "Just promise me, will you? Promise you'll all look after each other. You and Agnes. The captains. Rose. Roy. All of you. You'll look after each other?"

"Tobias . . . what—what are you talking about?" There

was something strange in Tobias's tone, something urgent. Sully didn't understand it.

Tobias reached out, taking a hold of Sully's other hand with surprising strength for a man so weak.

"You have to promise me, Sullivan. You all will need each other. Before this is all over, you'll need each other so, so much. Don't let go." Tobias sounded almost delirious now, the monitors beside him beeping frantically. "You can't make it through this thing without people."

"We will, Tobias," Sully promised, more afraid of what would happen if Tobias didn't calm down than of what he was saying. It didn't make sense. "We will. We're friends."

"No," Tobias argued, shaking his head, and leaving no room for Sully to say anything against it. "You're family. Thicker'n blood. Promise me."

"I promise," Sully said. He didn't want to think about the strangeness in Tobias's eyes, or the way he held Sully's hands like they were a lifeline. He didn't want to remember Tobias this way, crazed and needing Sully to promise something he didn't wholly understand. "I promise."

Tobias nodded, relief washing over him. The monitors beeped louder.

Doctor Crugbort was suddenly at his side, pushing Sully away. "Away. Away. Let him rest. He needs rest. Go to your unicorn and let this one rest."

Sully frowned, but with a nod from Tobias, he let himself be shooed out of the curtained stall. For a moment, he watched the shadow of the doctor flit around Tobias's bed, listened to the murmurs as he tried to calm Tobias down.

Sully shook his head and went to find Agnes. He would worry about that later.

Agnes was sitting up in his bed, glaring around the

room, looking for all the world like a pissed-off Pomeranian.

"Well, don't you look like you got run down by a horse-less carriage?" Sully's voice shook with laughter. He crossed his arms over his chest and gave Agnes an unimpressed look as the unicorn turned his glare on Sully.

"Everything hurts. And I'm dying." Agnes's eyes narrowed in annoyance, his tone petulant.

"You're not dying." Sully laughed, walking to the bed to sit on the chair beside it. "I just spoke to the doctor. You're fine. Don't be a baby."

"I'm not being a baby. That bastard *shot* me." Agnes had the audacity to pout at Sully. And were Sully a weaker man, it might have worked. All right . . . it kind of *did* work.

"I remember. I was there."

"Right here." Agnes pointed to the spot where the doctor had stitched him up.

"I remember. I was there." Sully repeated, smiling more at the obvious ploy for sympathy from Agnes. Who knew he'd be adorable when injured?

"It hurts," Agnes whined. He reached for Sully's hand and tugged Sully up from his chair to sit on the bed beside him. Then he leaned heavily onto his shoulder.

"I'm sorry it hurts." Sully sighed. He wrapped his arm around Agnes, adjusting himself so they both sat against the headboard more comfortably. "Did Doctor Crugbort give you anything for the pain?"

"He said I also have a concussion. And I can't take pain medicine with a concussion." Agnes tugged Sully's bloody hand up to examine it. The gore had dried and begun to flake, but beneath it, Sully could see where it had stained some of his skin darker. The crimson stains looked strange in comparison to Agnes's pale fingers as he dragged the tips of them over the lines in Sully's palm.

"I'm sorry I scared you back there." He hadn't thought much of it until he was really looking at what was left of Wilson on his hands. The memories were hazy. They always were when he came back from a trip down kelpie lane, but he remembered Agnes's face swimming in his vision.

Agnes shrugged.

"I was shot," Agnes repeated, seeming disinterested in talking about the rage that had overtaken Sully.

"Yes." Sully laughed slightly, shaking his head. "I remember. I was there."

"Right here." Agnes lifted Sully's hand to press it to the bandage taped just under his chest muscle.

"Yup," Sully agreed with a chuckle. "Right there."

Then Sully dipped his head to silence Agnes's pouting with a kiss. He let himself linger there, kissing Agnes and holding him close. He let himself remember that, for the first time in decades, they were both free. Free to be here, to pout, and tease, to kiss and hold, free.

EPILOGUE

wo months later, the crew of both ships stood on a small hill out in the country. It reminded Agnes of the one where he'd first asked Sully to join the Uprising. But it wasn't. They had chosen this particular hill because it was far enough away from any of the labor camps that Sully considered it to be 'free' land, even if it was still under the queen's rule.

The morning after the battle, Tobias had passed peacefully in his sleep. The doctor said it was better than they could have hoped for, considering his injuries. Agnes mostly healed—stood beside Sully, holding his hand tightly. It felt strange but good to do that. To be able to stand out in the open and hold hands when, for decades, they had loved one another in secret, too entrenched in the battle between MOTHER and the Uprising to allow themselves something so small. They took a moment, closing their eyes, savoring the warmth that spread from one palm to the other.

"He's free," Agnes whispered to Sully as the body was lowered into the ground.

"He is." Sully nodded.

"Finally." Rose sniffled loudly and took the handkerchief Agnes extended to her. She wiped her eyes.

"Don't get it all snotty," Agnes said snidely, which only earned him a glare as Rose lifted the cloth to her nose and blew loudly into it.

"How long had he been there?" Persinette asked from where she stood, tightly wrapped up in Manu's arms.

"He told me once he'd been there over a hundred years." Rose balled up the handkerchief, fist tightening around it.

"He told me he'd been brought there as a child," Roy added, pressing his face into Penny's hair.

"He'd never known a life outside of those fences." Manu grimaced, holding Persinette tighter to himself, shielding her from the breeze that rustled the grass around them.

"He's free now." Sully's hand tightened in Agnes's, needing the gentle pressure of his fingers to ground him.

"And he's the last person we'll let this happen to." Agnes's voice held an air of finality, a decision made, a choice he wouldn't change. Everyone turned to him, but he didn't meet their eyes. Instead, he focused on where the two droids were filling the hole again, creating a mound of freshly churned earth, a hard expression thinning his lips. Sully thought Agnes looked every inch the vengeful unicorn.

"What?" Rose sniffled again.

"We aren't letting this happen again." Agnes's voice was hard, cut from steel and forged in fire. "No one else will grow up in those places and die there without ever breathing free air. Tobias was the last."

Sully's heartbeat raced a little as he watched the resolution settle into Agnes's eyes. It was never really a choice to begin with. Sully smiled, pride swelling low in his gut and warming him against the cool wind. It had been so long since he'd seen Agnes like this: steadfast, determined. But this . . . this was the Agnes that Sully loved. The avenging angel. The righteous man. The one who had an ideal of the world and would stop at nothing to see it to fruition.

"How will we do that?" Persinette's voice didn't sound afraid. It was cut from the same metal, forged in the same fire. A wild, defiant smile crept onto her lips. Sully's eyes flicked around, drinking in the expressions of the others. Their faces mirrored Agnes's determination.

"We're going to put an end to all of this." Agnes's words were quiet, the wind threatening to take them away with it, but they carried. "No more MOTHER. No more queen. No more Uprising."

Those words settled into the group around them. Into the young ones like Felicity and Drea. The old ones like Benard. The leaders like Persinette and Manu and Stella. The followers like Owen, Roy, and Penny. They settled warm and sure. A blanket of understanding and certainty. This was what was right. This is how it always should have been. They would see this thing to the end.

No. More.

Acknowledgments

First off, thank you—the reader—for reading Agnes and Sully's story. The Girl in the Clockwork Quest has been two years in the making, and I'm so grateful to you for having read it. I hope you enjoyed your first glimpse into the world of Daiwynn, and are thirsty for more.

Although this book is over, Agnes and Sully's story is far from finished. The world of Daiwynn is large, and holds many more tales. Rest assured, this isn't the last you've seen of our favorite unicorn and kelpie.

Next, I'd like the thank my small hoard of beta-readers. You guys gave some excellent insight, and I really appreciate all of your hard work!

And last but certainly not least, thank you to my small writing support group. Tiss, Elle, and Jasmine—without you there would be no Lou.

About the Author

Born and raised in a small town near the Chesapeake Bay, Lou Wilham grew up on a steady diet of fiction, arts and crafts, and Old Bay. After years of absorbing everything, there was to absorb of fiction, fantasy, and sci-fi she's left with a serious writing/drawing habit that just won't quit. These days, she spends much of her time writing, drawing, and chasing a very short Basset Hound named Sherlock.

When not, daydreaming up new characters to write and draw she can be found crocheting, making cute bookmarks, and binge-watching whatever happens to catch her eye.

Learn more about Lou and her future projects on her website: http://louinprogress.com/ or join her mailing list at: http://subscribepage.com/mailermailer

facebook.com/LouWilham

instagram.com/lou.wilham

Also By Lou Wilham

The Curse Collection
    The Curse of The Black Cat
    The Curse of Ash and Blood
    The Curse of Flour and Feeling

The Clockwork Chronicles
    The Girl in the Clockwork Tower
    The Unicorn and the Clockwork Quest
    The Rose in the Clockwork Library

The Heir To Moondust
    The Prince of Starlight
    The Prince of Daybreak

The Witches of Moondale
    The Hex Next Door

Sanctuary of the Lost
    Of Loyalties and Wreckage

Completed Series
The Tales of the Sea Trilogy
Villainous Heroics

Sneak Peek!

continue reading for a sneak peek of Lou's

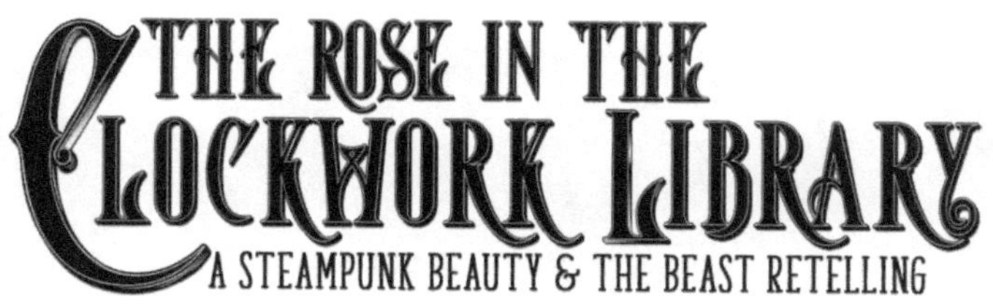

LOU WILHAM

ONE
ROSE

"I don't know why I agreed to this," Rose said, her fingers brushing down over the borrowed dress. It didn't fit quite right, too short where it had been adjusted to Persinette's smaller stature, but it would do in a pinch, she supposed. And in a pinch, they were, because Agnes had woken up two mornings ago with the inexplicable urge to get married, and Sully wasn't going to let that opportunity pass without seizing it. So, the crew of the *Duchess* had thrown together a wedding in haste. Rose wondered if it was more Tobias's funeral or the Wastes' steady approach on the horizon that had Agnes so anxious, but she wasn't going to ask him.

"Because you and Agnes are secretly best friends?" Persinette teased, a hopeful smile splitting her freckled face. The young co-captain had been trying to become Rose's friend since the moment Rose had stepped foot on the *Duchess*, and honestly, Rose was sick of it. She wanted to scream at the girl that not everyone had to like each other, but it felt too much like kicking a puppy, and Agnes did enough of that for all of them.

"That's not it." Rose pushed the short tight curls back from her forehead where they had begun to tickle. Persinette held out a headband, and Rose took it with a grunted, "Thank you."

"Because you're a closet softy?"

Rose's expression could have curdled milk, she didn't have to see it to know that, because Persinette's smile fell for a fraction of a second. Plus, her glasses were starting to cut into the wrinkle on the bridge of her nose. She'd had to adjust them, again, after they'd been knocked from her face in the engine room last week, and they weren't quite right.

"Okay, maybe that's not it either." Persinette lifted a hand to fiddle with her short lavender hair. It looked like she'd borrowed some pomade from Manu and was trying to wrangle it into something resembling neat, but there was a cowlick where a curl would normally have been that wasn't cooperating.

Rose sighed, taking the comb from the vanity, and murmured, "Let me."

. . . Maybe she *was* a closet softy after all.

They worked in silence for a few moments, Rose wrangling Persinette's hair into something more orderly, and Persinette fiddling with the long necklace around her neck.

"It's a shame Tobias isn't here," Rose said when the silence got to be too much for her. After years in the labor camp, she craved constant noise, to the point that Benard, the *Duchess's* first mate, had gifted her one of Manu's old gramophones from storage—not that she'd asked him to, mind you, she didn't ask for things from people. Why bother when she could get it herself? She didn't know what it was about the crew of the *Duchess*, but they did things like that for each other. They cared in a way that Rose had never experienced before. . . Well, not since losing her father, anyway. She didn't think she liked it. It was too much of an uncomfortable weight around her neck, a responsibility. That's why she said, "He'd have been the better choice."

Persinette reached back to still the comb, her fingers tight around Rose's wrist until Rose met her gaze in the mirror.

"It *is* a shame," she agreed softly. Persinette hadn't known Tobias long before he'd passed, but Rose had seen the way the two of them had connected. It was like they had each found a kindred spirit after all these years. Rose had been a little jealous of it, if she were being honest with herself. Which she made a habit of doing when she could be bothered. Tobias had been a second father to her, he'd raised her, but that didn't matter when she saw how happy he was chatting with the lavender-haired captain. Persinette squeezed her wrist again, pulling her back to the moment before saying, "but there isn't a better choice."

She wanted to argue. She opened her mouth to do just that, but Persinette shook her head, and Rose's jaw clicked shut. With a nod that was more for herself than for Persinette, Rose turned back to Persinette's hair.

"Are you two ready yet?" Sully asked, poking his head in through the door. He'd missed a button on his shirt, and the cravat Benard had picked for him was hanging askew around his throat, but for all the world he looked like the happiest man Rose had ever seen in her life. His dark eyes danced with joy, and the smile on his brown face could have lit the whole of Daiwynn with its brightness. If only she could bottle that joy, maybe then she'd be able to break it down into molecules and matter and understand it better.

"Almost." Persinette hummed, rising from the vanity,

and brushing her hands down over her gown to check for wrinkles. "I feel like I'm missing something. Oh, my—"

Rose snatched the hat from the bed, and tucked it behind her back. "You're not wearing this feathered monstrosity to Sully and Hagnes's wedding, I don't care what Manu says."

"I wish you'd stop calling him that," Sully mumbled, though it sounded like he was laughing, at the same time Persinette asked, "But then how will they know I'm a captain?"

"Trust me, they'll know." Rose scoffed, keeping herself bodily between Persinette's searching hands and the hat. It had a wide, floppy brim, and the plume dangling from it was so long that it brushed the floor, gathering dust, even when it was atop someone's head. It was unsightly. Agnes hadn't said he hated it, but Rose had seen the look on his face when Manu had given it to Persinette. If she wanted to get any peace at all for the foreseeable future, she had to keep Persinette from wearing it. "Now go on. Sully's waiting for you to walk with him. And for gods' sake, fix his shirt. Agnes will never forgive us if we let him go to his own wedding looking like that."

Persinette huffed, her hands on her hips, but when she turned to look at Sully she deflated. "Oh, all right. It is your day after all."

"It is," Sully agreed, that smile still in place though it strained at the edges now, not quite reaching his eyes. "And Agnes's. And if he sees that hat, he's told me he'll call the whole thing off."

"Manu will be disappointed." Persinette wilted further, her shoulders drooping.

"Manu will live, it's not his wedding." Rose tossed the hat into a corner. Hopefully it would be carted off by bilge rats, but if not, she could always light it on fire. She was sure if anyone would enjoy a bonfire at their wedding, it would be Agnes. "Now go on, before Agnes gets cold feet and takes the first dingy out of here."

Sully mouthed a quick 'thank you' as he ushered Persinette out into the hall, and Rose dipped her head. "Agnes is in our room, if you could. . ."

"I'll talk to him." *Yeah, I'm was definitely a closet softy*, she realized with a disdainful snort. That was the only way to explain how she'd been wrangled into being Agnes's best woman, walking him down the aisle, and now apparently dealing with his pre-wedding jitters. Tobias was probably laughing in his grave.

"*Look at you, my little girl,*" she could practically hear him saying, a smile making his voice lilting and pleased. "*All grown up, with her own family. I'm so proud.*"

"He's not my family," she muttered.

"*Isn't he?*" She imagined Tobias would ask.

He'd be right, of course. She didn't like Agnes, but she'd realized rather quickly, that you didn't have to like someone to love them. That didn't mean she was going to agree to such a thing out loud for the all world to hear. Nor that she was going to let Agnes or any of the others wiggle under her skin any deeper than they already had. No. Better to keep them at arm's length.

Shaking her head to dispel Tobias and his nonsense, she knocked on the door to Agnes and Sully's room. "Are you decent?"

"That's one word for it." Agnes grunted, and Rose assumed that meant she was allowed to enter. She found the unicorn sitting on the bed, facing the long mirror on the back of the closet door, his pale, nimble fingers fiddling with his cravat. It was blue, to match his eyes, and it looked hopelessly wrinkled like he'd retied it at least five times. The rest of him was immaculate, from the tips of his well-polished boots to his neatly trimmed pastel rainbow hair. "Did Sully send you to make sure I haven't gotten cold feet?"

"I think you know the answer to that." Rose moved to swat his hands away from his cravat, giving it a sharp tug.

"I suppose I do," he said his shoulders hunching forward a little, making him seem much smaller than Rose had ever seen him. Agnes was tall, annoyingly so. A head shorter than Sully, but that wasn't saying much when the kelpie towered over everyone else. "Tell me whose bright idea this was again?"

"Yours. Hubert, could we get a little steam?"

The robot tilted his head at her expectantly from where he stood near her hip, blinking his one working visual sensor at her. He'd gotten rather sassy since coming to the *Duchess*. Rose wondered if Felicity had mucked about with his programming, or if he was just learning it from Hiccup. There was only one way to tell. Rose sometimes wished people were as easy as robots. Able to be taken apart and put back together so that she could see how they ticked. Maybe then the crew of the *Duchess* would make more sense to her.

"Please," Rose amended, and Hubert's visual circuit brightened in approval before he let out a little puff of steam through the opening that some might call a mouth. Rose used it to smooth the wrinkles from the fabric. "There, that's better."

"He should be here." Agnes's voice was quiet, the words seeming mostly for himself, and Rose didn't have to guess at who he was talking about. It was strange how quickly Tobias had become important to all of them. Well, not strange, not really. Tobias was special that way, Rose had always known it. With the ability to burrow under people's skin and take root there, dandelion fluff on the wind just looking for a good place to go to ground.

"I like to think he's here in spirit."

Agnes huffed a laugh. "You believe in that kind of thing? I thought you were a woman of science."

"First rule of Thermodynamics," Rose said, retying the cravat into something less extravagant but definitely tidier, "no matter nor energy can be created or destroyed." She tilted her head to one side, then the other, looking at the knot from different angles until she was pleased with it. Then she gave a short *hm* before continuing. "Kind of hard not to believe in that sort of thing when you think about it that way."

Her words made Agnes unclench his jaw, his shoulders relaxing, and his chin lifting. It wasn't quite a smile, but Rose knew better than to expect one from him. "Thanks for that. I . . . I think I needed it."

"I think that's the first time you've ever said, 'thank you' to me." Rose teased, giving the cravat another sharp tug before she pulled away to admire her handiwork.

"You better burn it into your memory, it'll never happen again." Agnes grumbled, standing up, and heading over to the mirror to look at himself again.

"Felicity did a good job with the alterations." Rose tilted her head, surveying the way the lines of one of Owen's old suits had been pulled in to fit Agnes. It was amazing what one girl could do when motivated, and given free rein to pilfer through someone else's closet.

"Is that a compliment?" Agnes asked, a smile quirking up one side of his face.

"For Felicity."

"Of course." Agnes chuckled, shaking his head. "All right. This is as good as it's going to get, I think."

Pulling her watch from a pocket, Rose checked the time.

"We've got about five more minutes for you to panic, if you're feeling like you need to breathe into a bag or something."

"You're the worst." Agnes huffed an annoyed laugh, but Rose would swear she heard some fondness in it—maybe they were *all* going soft. It was strange to have a friend like him in her life. It was strange to have friends at all. She'd spent the last twenty years avoiding everyone but Tobias, sure that at any moment they'd be ripped from her fingers, and she'd be alone again. Now she had all these. . . *people* who seemed to want her around whether she was grumpy or not, whether they legitimately seemed to like her or not.

"So I'm told." She took a breath, rubbing at the bridge of her nose under her glasses, feeling where the nose pads had left indentations behind in her skin. She moved behind Agnes to look at him over his shoulder in the mirror. She had to move onto her toes to accomplish it. "If you repeat this to anyone, it'll be the last thing you do," she warned, and Agnes lifted one dark, arrogant brow in question, tilting his head to look down his long aristocratic nose at her, even in the mirror. Bastard. "You look handsome. You know, if you're into pompous unicorns. Which Sully clearly is so. . ." She shrugged.

Agnes wrinkled his nose at her, but she could see the corners of his lips twitch upward into something that might have resembled a smile. "Well then, let's go get me married, shall we?"

"We shall." Rose stepped back, and held an arm out to him which he looped his own through casually, before they headed into the hall.

"I'm telling everyone you said that, by the way," Agnes said just as they reached the double doors into the galley.

"No one will believe you."

"Sure, they will. Hubert will back me up. Won't you

Hubert?" Agnes nudged the little robot in front of them with his foot.

"I do not know what that means," Hubert said, voice grinding with gears. Rose wasn't sure if he was being sarcastic, or bluntly honest, but she had to choke back a chuckle either way when Agnes scoffed.

Agnes had just enough time to mutter the word 'brat' under his breath before the music started, the doors swung open, and it was time for Rose to escort her maybe-sort-of friend down the aisle.

Funny how the world can change in just a few months, she thought as she watched the beaming faces of the *Duchess* and *Sultana*'s crews pass by them.

If you loved the first chapter of *The Rose in the Clockwork Library*, you can grab your copy at https://books2read.com/u/3GWAxn

More Books You'll Love

If you enjoyed this story, please consider leaving a review.

Then check out more books from Midnight Tide
Publishing!

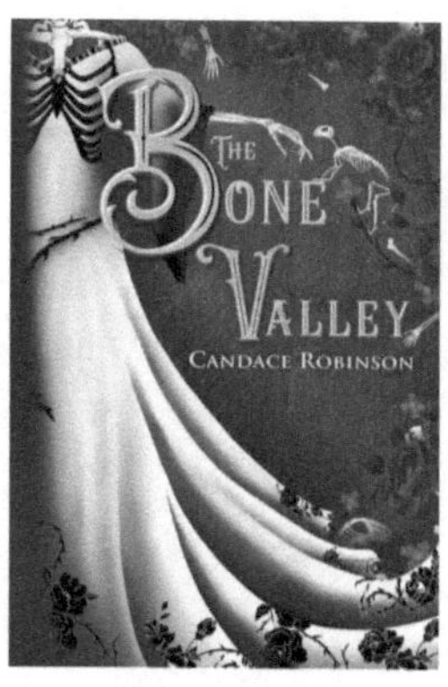

Bone Valley by Candace Robinson

He's a lover. She's a thief. A magic bond like no other will tie them together.

After the death of his parents, Anton Bereza works hard to provide for his younger siblings. Love has never been in the cards for him, especially after desperation forces Anton to sell himself for coin. And he has no idea that, beneath the city of Kedaf, lies a place called the Bone Valley.

When Anton's jealous client plots against him, he is cursed to spend eternity in a world where all that remains are broken bones. There, Anton meets Nahli Yan—a woman who once tried to steal from him—and his cards begin to change. But as the spark between them ignites, so does their desire to escape. All that stands in their way is the deceitful Queen of the Afterlife, who is determined to wield her deadly magic to break Anton and Nahli apart. Forever.

Available on
October 13th, 2021

The Castle of Thorns by Elle Beaumont

To end the murders, she must live with the beast of the forest.

After surviving years with a debilitating illness that leaves her weak, Princess Gisela must prove that she is more than her ailment. She discovers her father, King Werner, has been growing desperate for the herbs that have been her survival. So much so, that he's willing to cross paths with a deadly legend of Todesfall Forest to retrieve her remedy.

Knorren is the demon of the forest, one who slaughters anyone who trespasses into his land. When King Werner steps into his territory, desperately pleading for the herbs that control his beloved daughter's illness, Knorren toys with the idea. However, not without a cost. King Werner must deliver his beloved Gisela to Knorren or suffer dire consequences.

With unrest spreading through the kingdom, and its people growing tired of a king who won't put an end to the demon of Todesfall Forest, Gisela must make a choice. To become Knorren's prisoner forever, or risk the lives of her beloved people.

For fans of Sarah J. Maas, Jennifer Armentrout, A.G. Howard, Casey L. Bond, and Naomi Novik.

Available On
November 3rd, 2021

Ephesus by Christis Christie

As a soul lost before it could live, Ephesus was gifted a special role—he must collect the dead.

Ephesus has known no other existence than reaping souls, experiencing life only from the shadows. Remaining separate was easy, until the day he meets a unique little girl with an ability she should not possess.

But can friendships be nurtured when life and death aren't meant to mingle beyond the point of passing? Ephesus must navigate the world fulfilling his purpose while also balancing his newfound curiosity of the girl's life. However, when a threat arises, will it mean their ruin?

Available October 20

www.ingramcontent.com/pod-product-compliance
Lightning Source LLC
Chambersburg PA
CBHW061345190726
48288CB00005B/1599